Death on
Demand

Design for
Murder

BY CAROLYN G. HART

Death on Demand
Design for Murder
Something Wicked
Honeymoon with Murder
A Little Class on Murder
Deadly Valentine
The Christie Caper
Mint Julep Murder
Southern Ghost
Dead Man's Island
Scandal in Fair Haven

Available from Bantam Books

Death on Demand

Design for Murder

Carolyn G. Hart

BANTAM BOOKS

DEATH ON DEMAND/DESIGN FOR MURDER
A Bantam Book / October 2008

Published by
Bantam Dell
A Division of Random House, Inc.
New York, New York

These are works of fiction. Names, characters, places, and incidents either are
the product of the author's imagination or are used fictitiously. Any
resemblance to actual persons, living or dead, events, or locales is entirely
coincidental.

All rights reserved
DEATH ON DEMAND copyright © 1987 by Carolyn G. Hart
DESIGN FOR MURDER copyright © 2008 by Carolyn G. Hart
Cover art copyright © 1987 by Bantam Books

Bantam Books and the rooster colophon are registered trademarks
of Random House, Inc.

ISBN 978-0-553-38617-2

Printed in the United States of America
Published simultaneously in Canada

www.bantamdell.com

OPM   10 9 8 7 6 5 4 3 2 1

Death on Demand

To Kate Miciak, an imaginative, creative, exciting editor.

One

Alone, each item was insignificant. Some were easily found. A few were stolen from friends or acquaintances, but their value was so slight that the losses occasioned mild puzzlement and nothing more.

A pair of doctor's rubber gloves.

A spool of black extra-strong button-and-carpet thread.

A handful of assorted keys.

Clear fingernail polish.

Polish removor.

One dart.

There was just one more item, the most important one of all.

Two

The big collie barked first, then the cockers chimed in shrilly, shifting nervously in their pens. The deep-throated *woof* of the German shepherd boomed against the plastered walls.

In the hallway, the figure bending near the keyhole of the third door stiffened.

Goddam those goddam dogs.

Sweat slid between skin and the tight sheath of the rubber gloves, making it hard to work the keys.

All the dogs barked now, even the sleepy, ancient dachshund.

The fourth key worked. The lock clicked and the door swung open. Once inside, the figure shut the door, then switched on the flashlight. The bright beam danced over the immaculate linoleum floor, bounced up to the work-table, then to the rows of wooden cabinets. These, too, were locked.

It took patience. The dogs continued to bark, and the frantic yelps rebounded from the walls and tore at the senses. When the fifth cabinet door was open, a gloved hand reached up to pull out the third drawer. There were two small plastic vials in that drawer. The labels read *Succostrin*.

Jill Kearney always drove too fast, with the windows down. She loved the feel of the cool October night air against her face. She'd always liked nighttime. Nothing looked quite the same after dark, not even this road, a road she knew so well she could drive it automatically. She hummed softly. What a wonderful job she had, even if everyone thought she was crazy to love it. Usually, she didn't have to go back to the hospital after her ten o'clock check, but that big Doberman had to be turned every three hours after his surgery to prevent pneumonia.

The road dipped just before her turnoff. The lights from the Honda skimmed across an automobile parked deep in the shadow of a live oak. Odd place to park. Must have had car trouble. The Honda picked up speed, and she leaned into the curve. Because the road curved so sharply, the Honda's lights flashed up into the sky, and the moving beam of light in the third window on the east side of the clinic was sharply distinct.

As the Honda squealed to a stop, Jill flicked off the motor and the headlights, staring at the now dark row of windows.

Something had disturbed the dogs. Even out here in

the parking lot, the sound of their frantic barking rose and fell.

A light had moved behind one of the windows. She was sure of it.

She looked around the graveled parking lot. It was empty, of course. No one had any business at the Island Hills Veterinary Clinic at one o'clock in the morning. No one but she.

Perhaps she had imagined the light, but she wasn't imagining the barking. She'd better check the rooms on the east side. Just to be sure. She picked up her ring of keys and slipped out of the car.

Opening the back door, she flipped on the hall lights. Except for the almost deafening rumble of barks, accented by the high-pitched yapping of the cockers, everything seemed just as usual: the hall floors glistened from their final swab of the day, the air smelled of disinfectant and dogs.

Jill hesitated, then pivoted and walked up the hallway, unlocking doors as she went.

She unlocked the third door, the door that led into the dispensary, pushed it open, and reached out to turn on the light.

Her hand never touched the switch. The side of her head exploded in an agony of pain.

Three

Annie Laurance stared first at the telephone, then at the list she held in her hand.

Should she call all of them? Tell them it was canceled? What could she say? That she had smallpox?

She took a deep breath and glared at the telephone. It

was *her* shop, *her* Sunday evenings. If she wanted to call it off she . . .

Beneath her hand the phone rang. Annie and her black cat, Agatha, both jumped.

"Agatha, love, it's all right," she called, but Agatha was already streaking toward her usual hiding place.

The phone shrilled again.

Annie yanked it up, remembering at the last moment to insert a modicum of cheer in her voice.

"Death On Demand."

There was an instant's pause, then a familiar voice, an upsettingly familiar voice, inquired mildly, "Do you provide a choice? Defenestration, evisceration, assassination?"

"Max!"

She winced at the enthusiasm of her greeting. Determined to put that right, she repeated crisply, "Max," the inflection pleasingly even.

"I liked the first Max better," he said in that lazy, good-humored, oh-so-Max-satisfied voice.

"Where are you?"

"Dear Annie. Always straight to the point."

"Look, Max, I'm busy, and I've—"

"No time for old friends? Dear friends?"

She could picture him, leaning casually against something, a newel post perhaps, as if it were a play. Or he might have a cellular phone in his Porsche. Max always liked to have the latest in everything. His blond hair would be rumpled, his mouth quirked in an expressive grin, and his blue eyes, those damnably vivid blue eyes, alight with laughter.

"I've had the devil's own time finding you, love. You could at least ask me how I did it."

She waited. Max never needed encouragement to display his cleverness.

"They were very friendly to me at your old alma mater, via long distance, of course. I spent enough to keep Sprint solvent for another quarter."

"You called SMU?" She heard the bleat in her voice and winced again.

"Did you think I didn't listen to your tales of college days?"

"You have a brain like a sponge."

"I will take that as a compliment. When I explained to the drama secretary that I was casting director of a new off-Broadway play, and that we'd lost your number... Well, it worked like magic."

Annie objected, "They don't know where I am."

"But they knew the name of your best chum, one Miss Margaret Melinda Howard, who now lives in Lubbock, which sounds like a cross between a hillock and a sick sailor. I chatted long enough with Ms. Howard to finance a major promotional campaign by Sprint. She was thrilled to tell me that you, her most favorite orphan friend, had inherited the not-quite-beneficent estate of your crusty uncle Ambrose and were now living on an island off the coast of South Carolina, which I brilliantly located on a large-scale map."

Annie almost corrected him. She wasn't really an orphan. Her parents had divorced when she was three, so she didn't remember her father, and the fact that he was apparently alive and well in California wasn't important. Margaret knew of her mother's death, of course. Annie realized she was twiddling her mind with every extraneous detail possible to avoid responding to Max's magnetism. It was to no avail. She felt the same old weak-kneed dizziness that swept over her every time he used to come around her tiny Greenwich Village apartment. But she had settled with that, done with it once and for all, and she wasn't going to stand here and let it all start up again. Besides—she glanced at the antique clock above the mantel—she was running out of time.

"Look, Max, it's great to hear from you. But I've got to make some phone calls, something I have to attend to."

Unintentionally, the worry throbbing deep inside spilled over into her voice. She knew he heard it just as clearly as she did.

"What's wrong, Annie?" The light tone was gone.

"Nothing big," she said lightly. "Just some stuff with the shop."

"You're upset."

She took a deep breath. Upset was putting it mildly, and if she didn't get busy on the phone right this minute...

"Max, it isn't your problem."

"Come on, my love. What's upset you?"

She forced a laugh. "Nothing. I just need to cancel a party for tonight."

"Where's the party?"

She was so obsessed with her problem that she'd forgotten everybody didn't know. "It's here at the bookstore."

"Bookstore? Oh, hey, I like that—Death On Demand."

She glanced at the clock. "Look, Max, it's swell to talk to you." It wasn't swell. She steadied her voice—good, straight, crisp inflection. Good girl, Annie. Always knew there was a superb actress in you. "But I've got to get off the phone and cancel that party."

"Don't cancel it, Annie. You know I love a good party."

She stiffened. "Look, Max, you *are* in New York, aren't you?"

He chuckled. "Not by a long damn shot. See you at the party."

The line went dead. Annie glared at the humming receiver.

He couldn't be in South Carolina.

Max here. She looked out the front windows of the shop at the green water surging against the rock wall of the harbor. He couldn't actually be here.

Before she could assimilate the thought and order her emotions, her heart—that untrustworthy, undisciplined, irritating member—gave a happy leap.

Annie banged down the receiver. All right. Let him come. If he'd ferreted out her new home, followed her down here, just let him come. She'd never change her mind, no matter how much he piled on his careless charm.

They were poles apart, and apart they should stay.

She was poor.

Max was rich.

She'd grown up in a shabby frame house in a Texas prairie town.

Max had lived in lots of houses: a white stone mansion high above a Connecticut river, a rambling, weathered summer home with its own tennis court on Long Island, a penthouse high above Fifth Avenue, a medieval castle near a Scottish loch.

She'd scrimped through school on a drama scholarship.

Max lounged languidly through Princeton.

She liked life to be foursquare, aboveboard, and predictable.

He delighted in ambiguities, disdained certainties, and loved above anything to puncture pretensions.

But oh how happiness bubbled inside her. Max in South Carolina.

Footsteps sounded on the wooden porch. The shop was closed on Sundays, so it couldn't be a customer.

But it was. Annie felt a spurt of irritation and wished she had a flag just like Dell Shannon's, complete with a striking snake and the legend DONT TREAD ON ME, to hoist outside the main door when she wished to be undisturbed. Of course, Shannon raised her flag when she was hard at work on a new Luis Mendoza. And Annie doubted whether any flag would ward off Mrs. Brawley, who now stood with her fox-sharp nose squashed against the north window. Her snapping black eyes quite clearly saw Annie standing beside the cash desk next to the phone. Trust Mrs. Brawley. She must have followed Annie here from the early service at St. Mary's-By-The-Sea.

Mrs. Brawley tapped on the window.

Mrs. Brawley bought books by the *carload*

Resignedly, Annie moved through the foyer. She opened the door and stepped out onto the slatted wooden planks of the verandah which fronted all the shops. The smile she managed wasn't exactly hospitable, but it would do for a Sunday morning.

"I'm sorry, Mrs. Brawley, Death On Demand isn't open now. I'm just here to catch up on—"

Mrs. Brawley had learned early on in life that persistence might outrage, but it was effective. She ignored Annie's opening salvo.

"Miss Laurance, you *promised* you would get the latest Mrs. Pollifax for me. I came by the store Friday, and here it is Sunday, and I thought it might have come in on the late ferry yesterday. Couldn't you just check your shipments and see?"

But Annie, standing with the shop door open, wasn't listening. Her eyes were on the tall figure striding negligently across the plaza, obviously en route to Death On Demand. A wolfish smile exposed strong white teeth as Elliot Morgan looked up and saw her discomfiture.

Elliot Morgan. The last person in the world she wanted to see right now.

Four

Max pressed the switch on the dash and a softly humming electric motor opened the Porsche's sunroof. The marsh-scented air swirled gently around him. Damn, he liked this country! Enormous pines hugged the narrow blacktop. The dense woodland was broken by watery stretches where golden-stalked grasses rimmed dark green pools. He began to whistle, a slightly off-key but cheerful rendering of an almost forgotten tune about a happy wanderer. And that's what he was, a happy wanderer. His goal was almost at hand.

Annie.

He frowned slightly. Annie with her sunny smile and serious gray eyes. Flyaway hair that couldn't quite decide between spun gold and chipmunk brown. His happy... Max's frown deepened. Not so happy at the moment, from the sound of her voice when they talked that morning. Well, whatever it was, he would soon put it right.

Coolness suddenly tingled beneath the warm sweep of air as a cloud briefly obscured the sun. He looked up, then squinted against the brightness as the cloud sped on. A road sign flashed by. Broward's Rock Ferry, 5 Miles. He grinned and again sounded the song's refrain. Nice place, all right. But he would be happy slogging up a rutted trail in the Mojave Desert if Annie waited at journey's end. Still, South Carolina charmed him, although this narrow road left a little to be desired. Finally the Texaco truck straddling the center line pulled off into a two-pump country station. For the moment, the road lay straight and empty before him.

Leaning forward, he pressed the accelerator. The Porsche leaped ahead, and the handful of varicolored speeding tickets jammed behind the visor fluttered hard.

Intent on her mission, Mrs. Brawley ignored Elliot Morgan. "I don't want to be a bother," she prodded, clearly not meaning a word of it, "but if you will just *check* your storeroom." Her ingratiating smile had all the charm of the shark in *Jaws*.

"Mrs. Brawley, I phoned the publisher on Friday to place a special order, but even special orders take a few days."

The sharp eyes flickered past Annie to the open bookstore door. "I talked to Mr. Parotti and asked him if you received any packages this weekend. He said you did."

Annie accepted defeat.

Both Mrs. Brawley and Elliot followed her down the central aisle, and they all turned left to troop into the storeroom at the back, where Annie slit open the shipping carton and displayed forty copies of the latest Dick Francis— and nothing else, despite Mrs. Brawley's energetically skeptical probes into the packing material.

"Well," she sighed. "I do so *want* that latest Mrs. Pollifax."

Annie took her firmly by the elbow, without a great deal of subtlety, and tugged her away from the storeroom.

When they were even with the watercolors displayed along the back wall, Mrs. Brawley jerked to a stop.

"Miss Laurance, I've just got one question about that second one—"

"No hints," Annie replied firmly, and gave a little shove toward the central corridor.

Deigning to move, Mrs. Brawley twisted her head to stare back at the paintings.

"These are just *too* hard," she complained peevishly. She hugged a worn brown purse to her skinny chest and wriggled her bony shoulders in irritation. Then her face brightened. "I'm ahead of everyone else. This time I'm going to win. Just you wait and see." She shook free of

Annie's restraining fingers. "If I figure out that one, then I'm going to be the winner this month—and I'll get my Mrs. Pollifax *free*." She peered anxiously at Annie. "Have you heard anything about it? Is it supposed to be as good as the others?"

"I'm sure it will be wonderful, and I'll call you as soon as it arrives." One last push, and Mrs. Brawley was out the door and onto the porch.

Annie closed the door, took a deep breath, and turned to face Elliot Morgan.

"One of the joys of running a bookstore—dealing with booklovers," he observed.

"Don't enjoy it so much," she said sourly. "I was just going to phone you."

He grinned. Again she was reminded of a wolf, dark eyes deep set, pugnacious jaw. He stood at ease beside the enormous stuffed raven which perched on a pedestal just inside the door. The raven's feathers shone a glossy black, uncannily like Elliot's hair.

"Two minds that work as one?" he inquired lightly. "I dropped by to see if you wanted to lunch at Smuggler's Inn."

Annie was nonplussed, then infuriated. How could he possibly think she would lunch with him—ever—after his performance last week at the meeting of the Sunday Night Regulars? She stared at him, feeling wordless rage begin to boil.

He looked down at her, his darkly handsome face tilted. When she'd first met him, she'd been mildly impressed. Physically, Elliot was an imposing man—tall, lean, and well-built, with a bold, uncompromising Roman face. She realized now that he always turned a little to the left to present his best profile. He had the same pose on his most recent book jacket. That book sat right now in a ten-deep pile on a table behind her that held local authors' latest efforts.

Annie had never before felt the urge to engage in book burning.

Still, maybe it wasn't too late. Maybe she could keep disaster from happening.

She made a muscle-hard effort to sound pleasant. "I need to talk to you."

"Oh?" Another wolfish smile. "Now what could you want to talk to me about?"

A dull flush spread over her face. *Oh, Lord, don't let me lose my temper.* He was obviously going to be difficult.

Quirking an inquiring eyebrow, he lit one of his ever-present, abominable Turkish cigarettes.

"Those are going to make you very sick someday," Annie commented through clenched teeth. A wisp of acrid smoke spiraled past the No Smoking sign prominently posted over the raven's head.

He shrugged. "If I need a nursemaid, I'll pick a nubile Swedish import. Besides, living too long is folly."

"If you keep on the way you're going, you may not live past tonight."

That amused him.

"Are some of the pigs squealing?"

"Elliot, these are your friends. Why are you doing this?"

"So who needs friends?"

"Who do you think you are, Sam Spade?"

"I was a private investigator once and a damn good one. Everybody will see that tonight." He blew several perfect smoke rings, enjoying himself enormously.

How could she ever have thought him attractive?

He picked up on that, too.

Elliot reached out and his fingers brushed her cheek. "Now, Annie, don't be so damn soft-hearted. It will stir them up. They'll probably all write best-sellers in revenge."

She jerked away from his hand. "It isn't funny," she snapped. "You know, Elliot, you're a louse."

"Really?"

"For the last time, will you change your topic tonight?"

He drew deeply on the cigarette and pondered the smoke.

"No."

Her hands clenched. His face was very unpleasant now, the heavy bones bunched up in a tight, hard frown.

"Then the party's off."

Lazily, he shook his head.

Annie exploded. "Look, this is my bookstore—I set up these sessions—I can cancel them."

"Sure. But you won't."

She dug her nails into her palms. "You didn't listen. *The party is off.*"

Taking one last puff on his cigarette, he moved casually around her to snuff it out in a small skull-and-crossbones tray on the cash desk, scattering paper clips. "I guess I never told you that I invested my money from *Blood Tales* in island real estate."

Annie looked at him blankly. *Blood Tales,* his most successful book, was a current Edgar nominee.

He tossed his head toward the dim interior of the shop. "Check your lease, Ms. Laurance. This belongs to Pleasanton Realty, lock, stock, and John D. MacDonalds." He paused, then said coolly, "And yours truly is Pleasanton Realty."

Elliot shook loose another cigarette. "Screw with me, baby, and you'd better be ready for a little increase in rent. Like another thou a month."

Annie took two quick steps and yanked open the door. "Get out of here, Elliot."

He didn't hurry. He sauntered out onto the wooden porch, then looked back over his shoulder at Annie, a small, furious figure in the doorway.

"I thought we might go eat clams, but something tells me you aren't hungry. Oh well, I'll live. See you tonight, Annie."

"Go to hell!"

A weathered board proclaimed in faded letters: Broward's Rock Ferry.

Braking the Porsche in a swirl of gray dust, Max leaned out the window to peer at the sign. He could barely decipher days and times, but it did seem to indicate the ferry ran at 10:30 A.M. and 3:30 P.M. on Sundays. He looked around. Not a creature stirred in any direction. At least, not a creature in a New Yorker's vocabulary. No people. No cars. But the waterside teemed with life, and in the quiet after he turned off the throaty Porsche, he heard the rustle of the grasses in the on-shore breeze and the slap of water against the pilings of the ferry dock. Gulls skimmed just above the water and a V of brown pelicans expertly searched the water for mullet.

10:30. He had a little while. Max smiled ruefully at his

pell-mell dash down the Eastern seaboard. Patience had
never been one of his virtues. He picked up the *Mobil
Travel Guide,* flipped open to South Carolina, then searched
for Broward's Rock.

BROWARD'S ROCK ISLAND
Pop: 890   Area Code: 803   Zip: 29929

An all-year resort island, Broward's Rock was first
settled four thousand years ago by hunter-gatherers.
Traces can still be seen today of their descendants in
the famous Indian Shell Mound, which contains oyster shells, animal bones, and clay pottery dating to
1450 B.C. White settlement began in 1724 with the
arrival of Capt. Josiah Broward, who established the
first plantation. Its ruins are visible today in the
Island Forest Preserve. The island contains the remnants of Civil War fortifications. The sea-cotton econ-
omy of Broward's Rock was devastated by the War,
and did not recover until the late 1960s, when con-
struction began of a resort community patterned after
its more famous neighbor, Hilton Head island. Two-
thirds of Broward's Rock is a controlled access community with several hundred villas and condominiums. There are two golf courses, forty-five tennis
courts, and eighteen miles of bicycle paths. The
island is skillet shaped, seven miles long and five
miles at its widest. It is home to deer, raccoons,
alligators, and the endangered Atlantic loggerhead
sea turtles, which can reach 400 pounds in weight.
Climate is subtropical with more than 280 growing
days a year. The island can be reached only by ferry, a
20-minute trip across Port Royal Sound.

Max slapped the guide shut and opened the car door.
He stretched, welcoming the sea-scented breeze, then
walked to the end of the dock and looked out across the
Sound, shadowing his eyes against the bright morning sun.
That must be it, that dark green, dimly seen hump low in
the water to the southeast.

It sounded like Eden.

*   *   *

Annie thumped the door with her fist and contemplated disaster. Every penny Uncle Ambrose left her was invested in renovating this store. Her uncle would have approved. Under his stewardship, Death On Demand had been a wonderful place, a pipe-smoky, dim, comfortable, welcoming center for writers, but she had taken the shabby, down-at-heels interior and fashioned it into a bookstore that even Carol Brener and Otto Penzler might envy, discarding Uncle Ambrose's functional steel shelving for the softer orange-brown gleam of gum, reflooring with heart pine, and creating, on the right, between the diagonal shelves slanting off the central corridor and the south wall, an enclave of American Cozy, a cheerful space scattered with rattan chairs with soft yellow and red chintz cushions and cane-topped tables. Tangly green Whitmani ferns sprouted from raffia baskets. Onyx-based brass floorlamps spread golden pools of light, augmenting the high oval windows above the shelves along the south wall. In her heart, Annie knew this was what it would have been like in the sunroom of Mary Roberts Rinehart's three-story house on Massachusetts Avenue.

She smoothed the silky black feathers of Edgar on his pedestal just inside the door. Just past the raven, hanging beads marked the arched doorway that led to the children's corner, and its stock of all of the Nancy Drews and Hardy Boys, plus lots of nail-biters by two-time Edgar winner Joan Lowery Nixon. Annie had pined for just such a corner full of treasures when she was a kid.

She rattled the hanging beads, then started down the central corridor. The shelves that slanted diagonally on either side contained categories of mysteries. She didn't believe in lumping all the books together alphabetically. Cozy readers would never dream of picking up a horror story. Hardboiled enthusiasts would prefer the Yellow Pages to romantic suspense. The first case held all the Agatha Christies because, quite simply, these were and always would be Annie's personal favorites. She never tired of Dame Agatha's perceptive eye and clever plots. On the left side, the shelves held true crime books. These had been Uncle Ambrose's specialty. Everything from Lizzie Borden and Jack the Ripper to the Boston Strangler and Capt. Jeff MacDonald was represented here. Annie passed the spy novels and thrillers on the right and the caper and comedy mysteries to her left. From habit, she stopped to alphabetize the Craig Rice titles. Then came romantic suspense (all the Mary Stewarts) on one side of the aisle and psychological suspense and horror/science fiction on the other. The south wall held classic mystery books, John Dickson Carr through Edgar Wallace. Used books filled the shelving on the north wall. She must remember later to pull a copy of *A Judgement in Stone* off the shelf for Capt. Mac.

She paused at the end of the aisle and frowned unhappily at the coffee bar. This was where the Sunday Night Regulars always met. Not too much expense there. Five tables with straight-back chairs. Annie looked up at the east wall. This was her pièce de résistance, absolutely guaranteed to engender loud and sometimes acrimonious disputes. But it certainly brought in the customers, not only the mystery writers and readers, but the artists, too. Every month she huddled with an island artist, Annie providing the information, the artist creating the watercolors. The collaborations pictured scenes from famous mystery novels; the viewer's challenge was to recognize and identify book and author. This month, there were five paintings. In the first, a rosy-cheeked, white-haired old lady tumbled in front of a speeding car on a crowded London street. In that instant before oblivion, her pink face mirrored horror, fear, an awful knowledge—and a curious lack of surprise. The second painting featured a delightfully antiquated butler, who raised an arthritic arm to open the blinds in an ornate drawing room. The artist beautifully captured the rheumy fuzziness in the butler's pale blue eyes. The third watercolor was a still life, revealing the contents of a jumbled closet: two pairs of skis, a pair of oars, ten or twelve hippopotamus tusks, fishing gear, a bag of golf clubs, a stuffed elephant's foot, a tiger skin. In the fourth painting, a young man supported himself with a cane. His face twisted in disgust as he handed a letter to a slim, pale-haired young woman. In the final watercolor, a group of guests in formal evening clothes sat around a supper-club table, looking up expectantly at a middle-aged man who stood, a fluted champagne glass in his upraised hand, obviously ready to make a toast.

The first person every month to figure out which books the scenes represented received a month's free coffee and a new book. It wasn't quite in the same category as Edgar Wallace's £500 reward for the solution to *Four Just Men* in 1905. Still, it was unclear who enjoyed the contest more: Annie, or her customers.

And Elliot Morgan wanted to take all of this away from her. For a week, she'd known this coming evening held peril, but it had never occurred to her that she was personally vulnerable.

Annie paced slowly into the fern and rattan enclave, kicked at the rug, then sprawled in a cane chair. She wished she'd never come to the store today. On Sundays after early church, she usually jogged or swam. Now, she fervently regretted that she hadn't kept to her regular schedule. Normally, she loved Sundays, especially now that it was October and the island once again belonged to its own. She smiled at her calm assumption of belonging after three months in permanent residence. (Since it had taken Max three months to find her, he couldn't be too distraught at her leaving New York.) But she almost qualified as an old islander. As a girl, especially when her mother was so sick, she'd visited Uncle Ambrose every summer. That was when he'd introduced her to the delights of mysteries. Everything ultimately comes right in a mystery, and that made those uncertain teenage years easier for Annie. So she had a former summer visitor's approval for summer people, and now she had an islander's appreciation for their spending clout. But now that it was October, the summer people were gone. Their generous spending would be missed. Their penchant for dripping mustard from hot dogs or Coke from leaky cups would not. She had a sign at the front of the store, of course, that said No Food, No Drinks, Except for Coffee in the Rear. It was fascinating that people who seemed to be shopping for books were apparently selective in their reading skills. Her part-time helper, Ingrid Jones, never minded scolding, "No food, please, no food," but Annie found it difficult. After all, these were *customers*. And money was so tight.

She twisted in the chair. Time was running out. The

Regulars would arrive on schedule at 7:30 P.M. unless she canceled.

Damn Elliot.

She was so proud of the Regulars. They had been her invention, too, although under Uncle Ambrose the store had long been the community center for area mystery writers. At first, Annie was astounded at their number, but Emma Clyde, doyenne of the mystery world, had explained.

"This is the only mystery bookstore this side of Atlanta, Annie. Of course we all come here."

Annie had looked at her in bemusement. "How can one little island have all these writers?"

"This isn't just any island, my dear."

Emma's point was well made. Broward's Rock wasn't just another low-slung swamp off the South Carolina coast. It was rapidly gaining in fame on Hilton Head and Kiawah Island.

As Emma said, most writers valued exclusivity almost as much as fame—but not quite. Annie's uncle had been quick to see the possibilities, and his beloved Death On Demand became *the* place for writers to meet, drink choice coffee, tout their latest novels, gossip, argue, and talk shop.

Uncle Ambrose. She was so very glad she'd come for her regular summer visit this year, since it was to be their last. When he was gone, and her visit drawn out because of the funeral and the need to settle his business affairs, every passing day had made New York seem farther away and less of a home. She had thought about her apartment, a one-room closet, actually, and her valiant but unrewarded efforts as an actress (seventeen tryouts without one callback). Then she had thought about Max and the future. The decision to stay on Broward's Rock was astonishingly easy to make, and she threw herself headlong into renovating her favorite bookstore in all the world. That was three months ago.

Until now, she hadn't regretted it once. That wasn't to say that some moonlit nights didn't cause a twinge when she thought of Max, but she was nobody's fool, and she especially wasn't going to be Max Darling's fool.

Max Darling.

She'd accused him once of making up the name. He'd

answered rather stiffly that the Darlings were a long-established family with illustrious antecedents, that it was his mother's maiden name, and that he used it in preference to his father's because he got damn tired of people either resenting him or fawning when they recognized his father's surname as that of one of the great financial clans of America.

Annie had answered sharply. "You don't need to change your name. You need to change your habits."

"You sound like my prep school counselors," he retorted equably. "And you're much too pretty for that."

"Don't be condescending. Look, you're smart and capable. Why don't you—"

He interrupted primly, "Live up to your potential?" He shook his head. "I've heard it all, Annie, chapter and verse. 'Maxwell, it's such a waste. Why don't you become a lawyer/journalist/doctor/foreign service attaché/stockbroker?' "

"Why don't you?"

"Lovey, my great-great-grandfather made enough money to buy anything the world has to offer." The laughter fell away. "The funny thing is, there isn't anything I want to buy. The world isn't clamoring for my services. I'm a fair writer, a competent actor, a damn fool at figures. I'm bored by business, I hate quarrels, and my interest in science stopped with a sixth-grade film about a turtle giving birth in the sand."

"What do you like?"

The grin was back. "People. People in all their wonder. I hawked sausages at the World's Fair in New Orleans. I've dived for pearls off Japan. Now I'm massaging talent as an off-Broadway producer. What the hell, Annie. Why can't you go with the flow?"

But she couldn't. She bunched a pillow more comfortably behind her. Damn him. Why did he have to reappear in her life?

Irritably, she slapped her hand against the chair arm. She had to decide what to do about Elliot and the Regulars tonight.

Tonight.

The Regulars.

There was no way she could afford another thousand a

month in rent. Could Elliot really do that? Her lease
expired in two months. She groaned. He probably could.
The only shop presently vacant on the harbor front was
much too small. He probably owned that one, too.

She couldn't lose her bookstore. It was the first thing in
all her life that had been her own, and it was her only link
with the happiest portion of her past, those idyllic summer
days, curled up in a hammock behind Uncle Ambrose's
tiny house, poring over the adventures of mousey Miss
Silver, elegant Lord Wimsey, and gimlet-eyed Miss Marple.

Annie relished running Death On Demand. She'd loved
mysteries since her first Nancy Drew. She loved mystery
readers, who ran the gamut of society, with a small s. She
enjoyed tipping readers to new, good writers, such as Jane
Dentinger, Dorothy Cannell, and Charlaine Harris. She
liked the way readers could surprise you: the wispy-haired
spinster who never missed a McBain, the island plumber
whose favorite author was Amanda Cross. Now, there was
an accomplishment: to become a best-selling mystery writer and also win tenure at Columbia—the twin achieve-
ment of Carolyn Heilbrun, who writes as Amanda Cross.

She'd enjoyed meeting writers during her summer vis-
its, but she'd never until now had a chance to know any of
them well. She had to admit she didn't exactly love all
these mystery writers. Still, she liked some of them a lot.
Elliot was a stinker.

The phone at the cash desk rang.

Blast Max. He probably needed directions.

Steeling herself, she stayed put.

Would everybody come tonight?

Her Sunday Night Specials, when the store was open
only to writers, were popular. At least, they had been until
now. Every Sunday evening, one of the Regulars provided
an informal program. One Sunday, the Farleys, who wrote
children's mysteries, told the Regulars about Harriet
Stratemeyer Adams, who built a mansion high above the
Hudson with her profits from the Nancy Drew and Hardy
Boys books and several other series which first her father,
then she, authored. The Stratemeyer syndicate had worked
under nearly fifty pseudonyms and sold over one hundred million books. During one session, Harriet Edelman,
whose own hero was infamously clever, traced the history

of the comedy mystery from Mary Roberts Rinehart's first injection of mild humor in *The Circular Staircase* through Constance and Gwenyth Little, Craig Rice, Donald Westlake, Stuart M. Kaminsky, and Joyce Porter to Gregory Mcdonald's triumphantly cocky and irreverent Fletch books. Another Sunday, Captain McElroy, or Capt. Mac as they called him, drew on his experiences as a former police chief to explain with stolid thoroughness how to avoid leaving fingerprints on almost any kind of surface. He was an unpublished author, but warmly welcomed by the group because of his expertise—he'd spent several years early in his career in the Miami Police Department. One thing he'd learned: In searching for a killer, try nearby cafes for descriptions of customers shortly after the murder. Killing makes people hungry.

Until now, the Sunday evenings had been special and a lot of fun. Until last week, when Annie realized something odd and ugly was happening to her Sunday evenings. That night, Harriet Edelman had arrived early and made straight for the coffee bar at the back.

"Give me some of that good Kona stuff."

Annie poured the dark, aromatic coffee into two white mugs and handed one to Harriet, whose battery of bracelets jangled musically as she took it. She stared down into the black coffee, then said savagely, "I swear to God, if you won't screw an editor, you can't get anywhere!"

"Surely it's not that bad. Besides, aren't most editors women?"

Harriet's mouth twisted. "Maybe, but I still say you can't get anywhere if you don't have pull—and you've got a lot better chance if you live in Manhattan and know the bastards." Her faded blond hair drooped across a high, domed forehead. Thick horn-rimmed glasses increased her owlishness. Oddly enough, Harriet wrote frothy mysteries which featured wryly funny heroes. Annie chalked it up as one of nature's jokes.

"Dropping sales, half-assed reviews, and if everything weren't lousy enough," Harriet continued bitterly, "some low-life wrote my editor and told her my last book had a stolen plot. Can you believe that?" Harriet's voice rasped up into shrill outrage.

"Oh, ignore it," Annie soothed. "Didn't someone once say there were only ten plots, and they've all been used?"

Harriet wasn't listening. Her sallow face glistened with anger. "Don't think I don't know who did it."

Annie looked at her with concern. The hatred in her voice was shocking, and horribly inappropriate against the snatches of conversation as the writers milled toward the tables in the coffee area.

"*Stick*'s his best. No doubt about that."

"No, no. *Switch* is tighter, tenser."

"I'll tell you who has the most original mind in crime fiction today—Tom Perry, bar none."

"Don't tell me you still read Dorothy Sayers?"

Bullish voices, didactic, perhaps, but none with the frightening edge of desperation in Harriet's.

Harriet's fingers dug into Annie's arm. "If it really is him—if he did it, I'll kill him."

Was it fate or irony or black humor that Elliot chose that moment to clap his hands for attention?

Annie looked up sharply and broke free of Harriet's grasp. What was Elliot up to? Emma was scheduled to speak tonight.

The writers settled swiftly around the tables at the back of Death on Demand. Elliot stood near the coffee bar, the customary spot for the speaker. He clapped his hands again. "I know everyone's eager to hear Emma tonight."

The Regulars looked obediently and expectantly toward Emma Clyde, whose fictional detective Marigold Rembrandt was second only to Miss Marple in readers' affections and earned Emma an astounding seven figures a year. Plump, motherly, and utterly down-home, Emma always seemed slightly bewildered by her fame, but Annie noticed that her mind worked with the precision of an IBM PC*jr.*

"No doubt Emma will be happy to share the secret of her enormous success," Elliot continued unctuously. "You know, I really felt pretty uncomfortable when I realized I would be following her next week. However, I've given a lot of thought to the program I plan to present."

Ego, ego, Annie thought. Elliot can't bear to spend a whole evening listening to another writer, so he's going to horn in on Emma. She got ready to move forward and cut him off before he did any more damage.

"I've been doing some investigating, some *real* investigating. You know, digging out those delicious little secrets people try so hard to hide."

"More true crime? Some shoplifter's memoirs?" Fritz Hemphill's thin voice was sardonic.

Elliot's head swiveled toward Fritz.

Annie was reminded unpleasantly of a snake.

Fritz wrote male adventure with blood, guts, and enough macho for a battalion of Green Berets.

"Not a shoplifter. No, I have something much more special in mind. My publisher and I are convinced this will be a best-seller."

"Like *Kiss a Stranger*?" Fritz asked sarcastically.

Oh, wow. Only Fritz would be courageous or crazy enough to say that aloud. Everyone knew Elliot's last book was a bomb and had been remaindered six months after it came out. It was a true-crime book, a horrific description of a Hollywood starlet's foolish and deadly passion for a hitchhiker.

Someone snickered, probably Harriet.

Elliot's face darkened, but his voice remained pleasant. "No, this little volume will knock their socks off. You know how the public has this enormous appetite to know all about their idols? Dirty laundry and all? Well, I've decided to tell everybody the truth about a very special group. Don't you agree it will make a hell of a book to tell all about some well-known writers? Mystery writers, that is."

The silence was absolute.

"The real truth—all the gritty, nasty little secrets." Elliot's eyes glistened with malicious pleasure as he scanned the frozen faces of his listeners.

"Sounds boring to me," Emma said lightly, but her light blue eyes sparkled angrily. "Not enough sex appeal, Elliot."

"I can assure you, my dear, there will be plenty of sex."

That was last week. Everyone had stayed for Emma's presentation, but they all scurried out afterward without the usual good-natured bickering and jousting. All week long Annie had procrastinated on deciding what—if anything—she could do to prevent tonight's explosion.

It was her shop. It was up to her.

But, after all, these people were adults. They certainly

didn't need her to play Big Momma. They might even resent it.

It was her store—and she resented Elliot using her evening to poke and gouge at her friends. Moreover, she wasn't about to let him believe he'd cowed her with his threats to raise her rent.

Okay. She would . . .

Annie sat bolt upright in the cane chair and looked toward the central aisle. She couldn't see it, of course, not from her comfortable lounging spot on this side of the diagonal bookshelves. She didn't have to see the central aisle or into the coffee area to recognize that sound. When the back door to Death On Demand was pulled shut, a loose cupboard in the receiving room always snapped to with a sharp crack, like a .22 rifle.

She reminded herself that it was Sunday morning, she was alone in her store, and the back door was locked. But she'd heard that sharp, unmistakable crack.

Annie slipped to her feet, skirted the table, another cane chair, a floor lamp, and the clinging fronds of a fern. The central aisle was shadowy. Afraid she might attract another Mrs. Brawley, she hadn't turned on the lights. She'd wanted peace and quiet to ponder her problems. So it was quite dim here in the center of the store. She could see a portion of the coffee area. It was utterly quiet, utterly still.

She opened her mouth to call out, but there was something so heavy and ominous in the waiting silence that her throat closed.

This is silly.

But that cupboard *had* slammed shut. She'd *heard* it.

Stealthily, feeling vaguely foolish, she edged down the central aisle, her eyes seeking out the shadowy corners, that dark splotch near the doorway to the delivery room.

A sudden wave of panic swept over her. She remembered something Capt. Mac had said in his talk. "Listen to your instinct. If you ever feel, even for an instant, that something is wrong, dead wrong, run. Run and scream."

Terrific advice. Except she couldn't scream. Her breath was bunched like a pineapple in her throat, and her legs wobbled.

Annie turned toward the front of the store and crouched,

like a track athlete waiting for the starter's gun. Okay. As soon as she could force a deep breath, she was going to break and run for the front door and . . .

Annie blew out the bulge of air in a whoosh and felt like a fool.

She stood and walked a little unsteadily up the aisle and stopped to look into Agatha's languorous green eyes.

"You'd think I wrote mysteries, wouldn't you, Agatha? What an imagination!" She scooped up the sleek black cat from her basket, which rested on top of the Christie section, and stroked her gleaming fur, knowing Agatha would tolerate the effrontery for only a moment. A predictably independent feline, Agatha never stayed in the same room with a stranger. In fact, with few exceptions, she fled to hide beneath her favorite fern the instant anyone entered the shop. Obviously no stranger had come into the storeroom. She'd probably imagined that noise. Perhaps it was the crack of a broken branch outside. In any event, it was time to stop behaving like a Barbara Michaels' heroine.

Agatha growled politely.

Laughing partly from relief and partly from embarrassment, Annie put Agatha gently back on the shelf. Agatha, of course, jumped down. Everything was okay; it was just another Sunday morning. How absurd to imagine anyone would break into the shop. After all, there was absolutely no reason for anyone to break and enter. It wasn't as though there would be cash in hand. She'd almost have to borrow money to buy lunch. The whole episode was just a product of her overly vivid imagination. Like reading *My Cousin Rachel* when she was fourteen and, for a doom-laden week, suspecting that Uncle Ambrose intended to do away with her.

Nevertheless, she checked the back door. It was locked.

There was nothing to worry about. As for the evening, she would fix Elliot's wagon. She would take the floor first and point out that the Sunday Night Specials were supposed to have programs beneficial to the writers, and she felt there was a lack of interest in Elliot's program, and why didn't they take a vote on it? That would put Elliot in his place, all right.

Five

The whistle was frankly admiring and subtly erotic.

Annie didn't open her eyes. She didn't need to.

"How did you find me?"

"Dear Ms. Laurance, always so direct. I arrived on the ten-thirty ferry. Since there is only one ferry on Sunday morning, I was forced to count fiddler crabs while waiting. Fascinating creatures. When I reached your snug little island, I immediately rented a condo near the harbor and began my quest. I will confess I was surprised to find that the proprietress of Death On Demand is so slothful that she doesn't open on Sundays, but I recalled that said proprietress is tiringly vigorous and deduced that she would probably be found on the beach, either jogging or swimming. How disappointed I am to find her stretched out on a beach towel with her face covered by the latest issue of *Vogue*."

Annie yanked the magazine aside, opened one eye, and squinted. "I just ran three miles on the beach. How did you know it was me?"

"As has been said in perhaps another context, I would know that body anywhere."

She opened both eyes and laughed. He looked wonderful, of course. All six foot two inches of him. And she would know *his* body anywhere, every lean, muscular inch of it. To distract herself, she waved him down beside her.

Max flipped out a blue-and-white striped Ralph Lauren towel and dropped down, spattering sand.

"What took you three months?"

He shoved a hand through his thick, tangly blond hair, and rolled over on his elbow to stare down with ink-blue eyes. "Didn't your mother ever tell you it was rude to ask direct questions?"

She struggled to a sitting position and fished a sand-filmed bottle of Hawaiian Tropic from her beach bag. Studiously ignoring both Max's body and his eyes, she began slapping the coconut-scented oil on her legs, overlooking his appreciative "m-mm."

"Why three months?" she repeated brusquely.

"You didn't call to tell me where you were."

"No."

"Why?"

Annie looked up at him, and it was suddenly hard to breathe. "Dammit, Max, I was afraid you'd persuade me to come back to New York."

"Would that be so bad?"

This side of Broward's Rock faced out into the Atlantic. A clear, softly blue sky arched overhead. The air carried the pungent scents of salt water, tar, seaweed, and Annie's coconut-scented suntan oil. The water stretched endlessly to the east, as richly green as pea soup; a gentle surf strummed a seven-mile length of oyster-gray sand. There was a sprinkling of sunbathers and swimmers scattered up and down the beach, enjoying the eighty-degree day, but no one was near them. This stretch of beach was all their own.

"Max, it won't work. *You* don't work. Life is just a joke to you—a compendium of one-liners."

"So you'd like me better if I were earnest." He frowned, then the corners of his mouth twitched. "Let's see. What sufficiently important career could I pursue?" He leaned back on his elbows, staring pensively at the horizon.

Annie fought down a disquieting desire to touch the mat of hair on his chest, glistening a light gold in the sunlight.

Sitting bolt upright, he slapped his palm down and sand sprayed against her oiled legs. "I know. Annie, would you love me if I were a priest?"

"Max!"

He grinned. "Anglican, of course."

"Max." She used both hands to shove him backward, but he caught her as he fell, and they rolled together in the sand.

*   *   *

Max, who had helped brew the coffee, sniffed with theatrical appreciation when Annie poured him a mug. Lifting it to drink, he paused to look at the inscription in red cursive letters against the white background. "The Listening House. Do houses listen?"

"That's a title. If you looked on the bottom, you'd find the author's name."

Obediently, he raised the mug high enough to see the bottom. "Mabel Seeley."

Annie waved her hand abstractedly toward the rows of mugs shelved behind the coffee bar as she filled the cream pitcher. "Each mug has the title of a book which is considered important in the history of mystery novels." She put the cream pitcher beside the sugar bowl and reached for the corkscrew to open the bottles of sauvignon blanc.

Max moved behind the coffee bar and called out an occasional name that attracted him. "*The Mystery of Dr. Fu-Manchu, The Thirty-Nine Steps, The Rasp, The Tragedy of Y, The Cape Cod Mystery, Rebecca, Home Sweet Homicide*." He turned to look at her. "Where did you find these?"

"Oh, I did them."

"In your little home kiln?"

She laughed. "No, silly. I didn't *make* them. I painted the titles."

"Annie, I learn something new about you all the time. It never occurred to me that you could paint as well as act."

"I'm not exactly a threat to Van Gogh," she pointed out crisply.

He started to count the mugs stacked on the shelves behind the coffee bar but his attention soon strayed. "You haven't read all those books, have you?"

"Nope. But lots of them."

"A misspent youth, obviously."

"I suppose you were busy with Saint Augustine's *Confessions*?"

"Oh, in a manner of speaking. I suspect old Auggie would have been a *Playboy* man himself."

"The point is, he changed his ways."

"But not altogether for the better."

Since she wasn't winning this exchange, she concentrated on completing the ham, salami, and cheese tray. Agatha twined expectantly around her ankle. Annie held down a piece of cheddar for her. "Cats aren't supposed to eat cheese, silly."

Agatha demanded more, and, like a well-trained owner, Annie obliged.

"How many do you expect?" Max asked.

Among their other activities that afternoon, she'd told Max all about the Sunday evening sessions and Elliot Morgan. After all, it was something else to talk about besides Max's disinclination to toil and her determination to treat life in the serious manner it deserved.

She added them up, one finger after another.

"Elliot himself, of course. Then there's Emma Clyde. You know who *she* is. And the Farleys, Janis and Jeff. They write children's mysteries. Their latest is *The Secret of the Red Dragon*. Harriet Edelman does those clever Harrison Macintosh books. Fritz Hemphill wrote *Death in an Alley*. His heroes are always sleazy and very, very tough. You know, the guy busts open the villain's head with a tire tool, then gets beaned himself, slugs down some scotch, runs up a fire escape, and has sex on the tenth landing with a blonde he just met."

"That's six." Max paused teasingly. "Hey, maybe I could be an accountant."

Annie was dreading the coming session, but, somehow, that awareness couldn't dampen the bubbly sense of fun she'd felt ever since Max dropped down onto the sand beside her. Now he stood looking at her ingenuously, his thick blond hair carefully combed and dampened, his face fresh from a shower, his white broadcloth shirt crisp, and she thought he looked wonderful standing by the coffee bar at Death On Demand.

Sternly, she forced her mind back to her guest list.

"Okay, six. Oh yes, there's Hal Douglas. He writes caper novels like S. S. Van Dine but not as good. And Kelly Rizzoli. She goes in for psychological fiction à la Ruth Rendell. And Ingrid Jones, the woman who helps me out part-time, usually comes. That's every...oh no, I'm forgetting Capt. Mac. I told you about him."

"The somber sleuth."

Annie considered it. "No, not somber. I mean, he's extremely serious about everything, but he's really a nice man. He was wonderful when Uncle Ambrose died. Oh, Max, that night was so *awful*—"

"Annie, don't dwell on it. You can't undo the past."

"He must have taken ill, felt faint. Why, he spent more time in that boat than he did on land. He couldn't just have *fallen* off. If only I'd gone with him—" She stared down into her mug, face strained. "We found him floating only a few feet from the boat, right here in the harbor."

"You and Capt. Mac?"

"Yes, I phoned him when Uncle Ambrose didn't come home that night. I think I knew right from the start that something awful had happened, though Capt. Mac tried to persuade me I was being silly. He couldn't have been more wonderful when we found—Uncle Ambrose. He called the police and stayed with me the whole night."

"That was helpful." Max sounded faintly strangled.

She looked at him in surprise.

"How old is this noble Galahad?"

"Mmm. Fiftyish, I guess."

"The James Garner type?"

Max was jealous.

"Oh, I'd say more the James Bond type." Her voice fell seductively. "Absolutely irresistible to women of all ages."

Max's chin jutted out alarmingly.

"Actually, Max, he's built like a sumo wrestler, and his eyes look positively glacial, gritty and gray. But he *is* a very nice man, and he's invited me out for lunch a couple . . ."

The front door bell jangled. Agatha streaked past, en route to her special hiding place deep in the shadow of the largest fern.

The Sunday Night Special was about to begin.

The first arrival was Capt. Mac. He was, in a sumo way, attractive, his short black hair nicely frosted with white, his blunt, intelligent face softening as he looked down at his hostess. She glanced at Max and enjoyed his struggle between manners and immediate hostility.

"Max Darling," he said crisply as he thrust out his hand.

"John McElroy, but call me Capt. Mac. All these kids do."

Max's smile looked a little strained.

Emma Clyde and the Farleys came in next. Emma was carrying a covered bowl and two large bags of chips.

"I remember how these wolves devoured your food last time, Annie, and I thought I would pitch in. Shall I just put these things on the table?"

Emma wore a Hawaiian print caftan and looked like a wildly painted tugboat. Her hair sprouted in stiff bronze curls, and Annie was positive she'd paid a long visit to Island Beauty Inc. on Saturday. Emma neither looked nor sounded like a millionaire author, but Annie noticed her intensely blue eyes sweep the room. Was she looking for Elliot? But it was Max she fastened onto.

"A friend of Annie's! That's so nice. I'm delighted to meet you."

The Farleys stood at the edge of the coffee area. As usual, they gave Annie the creeps, which immediately made her inject extra warmth into her greeting.

"Jeff. Janis. I'm *so* glad you could come."

They looked at her unsmilingly. Jeff wore light blue slacks and a white crewneck sweater. He looked like an overage cheerleader despite his sleek blond beard and horn-rimmed glasses. Janis, slim and pale, stayed a pace behind him. Her large green eyes flickered nervously from Annie to Jeff and back to Annie. Janis had a quality of seeming more her husband's appendage than a person in her own right, a posture Annie found exceedingly irritating.

"Some coffee?" Annie urged. "Or would you prefer wine?"

Janis looked to her husband for guidance.

Even as the door bell jangled again, Annie had time to notice Max gravitating to Janis, who certainly did have a soft magnolia appearance. Trust Max. Jeff watched them, too.

Fritz Hemphill nodded a brusque hello. Ingrid Jones slipped in behind him, and in her self-effacing way began to help serve the wine and coffee. Her thin face flushed with pleasure at Max's friendliness. Ingrid was one of life's nicer surprises, a retired librarian who knew everything about books and genuinely liked to help. Moreover, she was content with part-time work at the minimum wage, which was all Annie could eke out of a slender budget. If

the store ever made enough money to pay off the money
she owed for improvements, an increase in Ingrid's salary
was first on Annie's list.

Hal Douglas and Kelly Rizzoli came next, heads close
together, which didn't surprise Annie. Instinct told her a
romance was in the offing, if not yet in full bloom. Hal and
Kelly were really the most normal of all the writers. They
made an attractive young couple, Hal cheerfully chubby,
Kelly slight, with dark red hair and an appealing air of
vulnerability. There was almost always a genial smile on
Hal's open, honest face. Annie liked Kelly but wondered a
little at the force of her imagination. Her books focused on
the dark and torturous impulses that drive decent people
to evil. They were not good late-night solitary reading.
Her most recent book uncomfortably reminded Annie of
Margaret Millar's powerful *Beast in View*.

The room hummed with sound, the quick, insightful
chatter of people who knew each other well. As she made
sure everyone met Max, Annie felt grateful to him. His
presence was helping. Maybe she had exaggerated the
possibilities of disaster. Everyone seemed quite cheerful
and animated, except, of course, for the Farleys, but Max's
good-humored teasing was bringing a flush of excitement
to even Janis's pallid cheeks. Jeff looked on darkly. It
would be good for him, Annie decided virtuously, refusing
to acknowledge any murky stirrings in her own psyche.

She began to enjoy her own party. Maybe Elliot wouldn't
even show up.

"I told you there would be a good turnout."

He had come up behind her. At the sound of his voice,
she managed not to jump. She turned slowly.

"Oh, Elliot, I'd like for you to meet Max Darling."

"Sure. I'd like to meet him. I know a lot about him."
The ever-present cigarette dangled from Elliot's mouth.
"Think I'd left you out of my research, darlin'?"

He might as well have thrown a red flag into a bull's face
or dropped a match in gunpowder. Knowing her own proclivity for explosions, Annie normally kept a scrupulous
rein on her temper, but too much had happened: Elliot's
threats that morning, Max's unexpected arrival and all it
might imply, the frightening, long moments when she'd
thought someone was in the empty store.

Her control shattered like glass hitting concrete.

"That's the last straw. I've had enough of you and your insulting, obnoxious behavior, Elliot, and I'm warning you, I'm not going to let you ruin my Sunday Night Specials."

The room fell abruptly quiet. Heads swivelled, and Max started weaving his way across the room. The expression on his face, even in the midst of her fury, made Annie step forward to stop him. Dear Max. He looked *murderous*— and everyone else looked shocked.

Her face flushed. How could she have been so stupid? Elliot was an ass, a blowhard, a bully—and she was playing right into his hands by overreacting like this.

Everyone started talking at once, and Max was trying to push past her to Elliot when the string of bells at the door jangled, and a high-pitched voice shrieked: "My God, everyone, have you heard? Isn't it the most awful? What can we do?"

Harriet Edelman's wispy blond hair quivered, her light green eyes bulged. Leaning forward, she paused, savoring her moment in the spotlight. One hand was outstretched dramatically, and the large ruby on her hand winked like a cat's eye at night.

"She's dead, her head all bashed in. It's murder. Murder here on Broward's Rock."

A vocal melee broke out. It was Capt. Mac's stentorian bellow which finally brought quiet.

"The facts, Harriet," he instructed, with a former cop's authority.

With dreadful curiosity, everyone subsided and listened. In just such a fashion, Annie thought with a shiver, a Wentworth mystery began. She scanned the faces in the room.

Harriet's information was meager but grim.

"It's Jill Kearney."

There was a gasp from one of the circle, and Annie felt a pang of horror. She knew Jill. She *liked* her. Murdered?

". . . at the Island Hills Clinic. Her body was found this morning in the dispensary. Bludgeoned to death. Police are seeking information from anyone who saw her last night."

"Are any drugs missing?" Emma was crisp.

Harriet repeated blankly, "Drugs?"

"From the dispensary," Emma said, giving her tinted head an impatient shake. "Morphine, codeine, what have you."

Harriet's self-importance collapsed. "I don't know. I just heard about it a few minutes ago. I had on KM103, and they broke in with a news flash."

Capt. Mac moved toward the counter. "Annie, may I use the phone?" But he was already dialing.

They waited respectfully, avoiding each other's eyes. Capt. Mac got through immediately to Frank Saulter, Broward's Rock's aloof police chief. His questions were brisk and concise. But, when he hung up, he stared down for a long moment, and Annie could see the hard ridges in his face. Finally, he turned to face them.

"The body was discovered at 9:05 this morning by a boy who comes in on weekends to feed the animals. Everything seemed normal when he arrived, back door locked, no sign of forced entry. He unlocked the outer door, went in, and started to go directly to the kennels, when he noticed the dispensary door ajar down the hall. Shouldn't have been open. Walked in, saw Jill lying facedown on the floor. Said he knew she was dead, but he touched her anyway, and she was cold. Ran like hell to the phone, called Frank at home."

He paused and now not only his eyes looked glacial. His face might have been carved out of ice. Dirty ice.

"Was the dispensary rifled?"

Capt. Mac looked at Emma with respect. "No signs of it. They called in Dr. Foster."

Foster was Jill Kearney's partner.

"Damn funny place for a drug heist," Fritz Hemphill objected. "How about strangers? Jimmy Moon clock anybody in?"

The island residents understood the significance of that question. When the skillet-shaped end of the island was developed, the Halcyon Development Company set up a checkpoint past the old main street near Heron's Point. To reach any of the new condos, the golf courses, the tennis courts, the luxurious homes, the harbor shops, and, of course, the Island Hills Veterinary Clinic, cars traveled the single blacktop road that passed a checkpoint manned by a Broward's Rock resort employee. Jimmy Moon, an ex-

Marine sergeant, had Saturday night duty. He knew everybody on the island. Strangers were admitted only with a pass from the Realty Company.

Capt. Mac's voice was uninflected. "Jimmy didn't admit any strangers Saturday night or Sunday morning." He didn't have to underscore it. "Looks like it happened early Sunday. M.E. sets the time of death after ten P.M. Saturday and before two A.M. Sunday. Her boyfriend, Si Whitney, took her home from the Island movies at shortly before ten. On their way, they stopped by the clinic for Jill's last check, but he said she intended to come back about one A.M., something about a dog that needed to be turned after surgery."

"Last ferry off the island leaves at ten," Fritz said, twisting a paper napkin.

They considered this in silence. Of course, someone could have come or left by boat, but it was a good twenty-minute boat ride to the mainland. Broward's Rock was a self-contained community. Casual marauders were unlikely. No, it had to be a resident or a visitor familiar with the clinic. Moreover, unless Jimmy Moon was mistaken, Jill's murderer had to be a member of the resort community because no stranger had passed the checkpoint.

"Why would anybody murder Jill?"

Capt. Mac shook his head. "It doesn't look drug-related. Foster checked the cabinets. All the morphine and codeine are accounted for."

"Was anything disturbed?" Emma Clyde's almost square face creased in thought.

"Nothing. Nothing at all."

"Was she assaulted?" Emma asked immediately, and Annie could almost see her mind tearing along, throwing up one scenario, then another.

"No. Nothing like that. Just the one blow to the head." He jerked out the next words. "Damn shame. M.E. said the girl had an unusually thin skull. Anybody else might have been knocked out and suffered nothing worse than a headache. Jill hemorrhaged. Damn shame."

"Some kind of maniac is loose on the island," Harriet hissed. "Nothing else makes sense."

"Something will make sense," Emma Clyde mused. "This doesn't have the hallmark of a senseless killing. Mark my words, when we know everything, there will be a motive."

"Any fingerprints?" Fritz inquired.

Kelly spoke at the same time. "What is known about Jill Kearney? What kind of person was she?"

Like sharks at feeding time, their intellects fed on Jill's death. Annie held up her hand.

"Hey, everybody, this is awful. I didn't know Jill well, but she was kind and—" Annie thought about Boots and what Jill had done. Oh, God. "Let's not talk about her like she's a lab report." With a pang, she realized that Jill was now just that. "Anyway, let's call it off for tonight. We can get together next week."

Harriet squealed. "Oh, I can't possibly go home now. I'll dream about it all night. Besides, maybe we can pool all of our brains." Her bony face was alight with greedy curiosity. "Don't you think we can solve it, if we try? Why, there can't be a better set of criminal minds—"

"For once Harriet's put her finger on it," Elliot interrupted.

He stood and moved toward the coffee bar. "*Criminal Minds*, that will be a wonderful title for my new book. Perfect." He bowed mockingly toward Harriet, who flushed an ugly crimson. "I have to thank you, Harriet. I wasn't pleased with any of the titles I'd come up with. *Criminal Minds*. Perfect."

He was leaning against the coffee bar, at ease, cigarette in his mouth, the noxious odor hanging heavily in the air.

"Come on, everyone, let's respect our little Annie's sensibilities. She doesn't want to talk about Jill's murder. Besides, I imagine we've exhausted all the information our police friend has, so why not take your seats? I promise to entertain you. In fact, I think each and every one of you will find my talk absolutely riveting, as they say in cover copy."

"Shall I boot him out on his ass?" Max hissed in Annie's ear.

She hesitated, but, with the harsh reality of Jill's murder, Elliot's swaggering suddenly seemed terribly unimportant—and so was her scheme to call for a vote on whether to hear him. Anything had to be better than sitting around talking about Jill.

"Oh, let him go on. It will fill up the time, then we can

send them all home—and I don't ever want to see them
again. This is my last Sunday Night Special."

Comfortably propped against the coffee bar, a half-
smoked cigarette in his mouth, Elliot filled his *Puzzle of
the Silver Persian* mug with steaming coffee.

Reluctantly, with muted murmurs, the Regulars took
their places.

Thoroughly enjoying himself, Elliot smiled maliciously.
"I can't provide a real-life crime—except, you know,
maybe I can. No body, of course. That would be too
difficult. But I can rattle a skeleton or two. My agent
thinks I'm onto something hot, really hot. We writers
spend a lot of time talking about motivation. Wouldn't it
be fun to know what kind of crimes a few well-known
mystery writers have been personally involved in?" He lit
a fresh cigarette from the stub of the first, dumping the
discarded butt in the tepid coffee in the *Unexpected Night*
mug someone had left on the coffee bar. "We're talking big
sales, maybe a fifty thousand first printing and six figures
for paperback rights. This book has it all, blood and guts
and some particularly nasty—"

The lights went out.

Dusk comes early in October. It was already dark when
the first arrivals came. Now it was solidly black outside,
and heavy clouds masked the moon. No light penetrated
the stygian darkness in the back of the shop.

There was a squeal. Harriet. Then a flurry of movement. Someone bumped against Annie in the dark.

Capt. Mac called out reassuringly. "Annie, must be the
power station. Where do you keep a flashlight?"

She was already resolutely groping her way toward the
storeroom. A flashlight hung from a nail in the east corner.
It was absolutely black, the only pinpoint of light the red
dot of Elliot's Turkish cigarette.

Suddenly, there came a succession of sounds, a fluttering,
a solid thump, a grunt, the noise of something heavy
crashing to the floor.

A woman screamed.

Six

Capt. Mac yelled for quiet.

"Sit down! Shut up! Stay where you are."

"What's wrong?" Harriet shrilled. "What was that noise? Somebody turn on—"

"Shut up, Harriet."

Hurrying, Annie smacked into a chair and yelped in pain.

"Who's that?" Emma asked sharply.

"Just me. I'm trying to get a flashlight."

"Annie's going to find a light." Capt. Mac's voice was reassuring, though Annie thought she could detect a faint undercurrent of stress. "Check the circuit breakers first," he instructed.

"Yes. Hold on, everybody. It will just take a second."

She moved as fast as she dared through the inky darkness. Reaching the door to the storeroom, she was surprised to find it ajar. Pushing it, she stepped inside the storeroom, and saw a pale oblong of deep blue light. The back door was open. She stared at it in surprise, then moved diagonally, sure of her course now, and reached up. Her fingers brushed against the rough cedar of the unfinished wall. The flashlight was hanging from a nail just about *here* . . .

She touched the wall, the nail.

The flashlight wasn't there.

It had to be there. She hadn't moved it. She'd seen it there, noticed it, at least peripherally, that morning when Mrs. Brawley was there.

At least she knew where she was now. The circuit box was just a couple of feet to her left. Unless it was an island-wide brownout, she should be able to turn the power back on. She couldn't imagine why the breakers should have flipped. Maybe the fault was in her wiring. She groaned. The cost of an electrician . . .

Her fingers found the circuit box—and its open door.

For the first time Annie felt cold.

She pulled the panel all the way open. The breakers were flipped to the right, all four of them, which would indicate some kind of massive overload.

One by one, she clicked them back to the left.

As the second breaker moved, the lights in the coffee area came on, and light spilled through the storeroom door.

Someone screamed again, but this time the scream began high and held and held.

Annie jerked around and ran across the storeroom to the doorway, then stopped short and clung to the frame.

There wasn't much blood, just a trickle. It was almost obscured by the dark, spreading pool of coffee.

Then Capt. Mac's stocky bulk came between her and Elliot Morgan's body, but she would always remember just the way Elliot looked as he lay lifeless, crumpled at the foot of the coffee bar. A smear of unbelievably crimson blood oozed around the shaft of the dart that protruded from the fleshy softness of his throat. *The Puzzle of the Silver Persian* mug lay empty beside him.

Annie started to shake. How many bodies had she viewed in her mind over the years, from Ruby Keene in Colonel Bantry's library to the blackened, unidentifiable lumps in *Ice Station Zebra*? But none of her reading had prepared her for this. She hadn't liked Elliot Morgan. She had even feared what he could do to the shop that she loved, but none of this mattered now. Elliot was dead. It was clearly, unmistakably murder. Not illness as with her mother. Not accident as with Uncle Ambrose.

But how could a dart kill someone? This was madness. First, they hear of the murder of a pretty young veterinarian. Then the lights go out, and a man falls dead from a dart in his throat.

Darts can't *kill* anybody.

Annie said it out loud.

"Darts can't *kill* anybody." She looked up to find Max at her side. His face was pale beneath its tan.

"I know, my love. But we just saw it happen."

"We didn't *see* it."

"Don't be so literal."

Capt. Mac, his face grimmer than ever, brusquely ordered everyone into a line at the far side of the coffee area.

"Don't touch anything."

"Why not?" Kelly Rizzoli asked politely. There were dark stains on her white linen skirt. She must have spilled her coffee when the lights went out, Annie thought automatically.

"This is the scene of a crime," the former policeman replied curtly. "Do as you're told, Ms. Rizzoli."

Fritz Hemphill grudgingly took his place in the line. "Look, McElroy, remember you're retired."

Capt. Mac ignored him and was already on the phone.

"I don't care where Saulter is. Find him, and tell him to get over to Death On Demand pronto. We've got another murder."

It was a tense wait.

Once Annie almost suggested they move away from the coffee area to the cane chairs grouped near the north wall, but there wouldn't be enough seats. Then she dismissed the thought. Clearly, she was no longer a hostess with guests. She was a hostess with murder suspects.

Annie looked at them in turn.

Emma Clyde stood a little to one side, as if disassociating herself. Her intelligent blue eyes moved from face to face, and Annie would have loved to know her thoughts. Then those vivid eyes locked with Annie's, and she was no longer certain she cared to know. Emma looked shrewd, tough, and frighteningly self-possessed.

Ingrid Jones's narrow little body seemed to have shrunk. She clutched her notebook, which she brought every Sunday evening, and stared determinedly at the horror section. The better, Annie guessed, to pretend she wasn't there at all.

Fritz Hemphill looked as comfortable as if he were waiting to tee off. He flicked an occasional impassive glance at the corpse, then picked up *The Bourne Supremacy* and began to read.

Capt. Mac made occasional forays around the coffee area; once he poked his head into the storeroom, then returned to the coffee bar and made notations on a napkin, his face creased in concentration.

An old firehorse, that's what Capt. Mac was. Annie felt reassured. Like Inspector Maigret or Steve Carella, he represented order.

Janis Farley clung to Jeff's arm. Her ivory complexion was tinged with green. Jeff stood stiffly, as if he were alone. For heaven's sake, his wife looked like she was about to faint. Why didn't the bloody idiot do something?

"Capt. Mac. Please. Let's get a chair for Janis."

He looked up, then nodded.

There was a little flurry: Ingrid Jones poured a glass of water, then brought some wine while Max dragged over one of the cane chairs and Annie helped Janis into it. She was shocked when she touched Janis's arm and found it bony and sharp like an underfed cat's spine.

Harriet's face was splotchy with excitement and terror, and her eyes shifted nervously between Elliot's motionless body and the others.

Hal spoke up suddenly. "My God. *Murders in the Rue Morgue. The Mystery of the Yellow Room. He Wouldn't Kill Patience. Death in a Top Hat.*"

Harriet enthusiastically moved from the general to the particular. "A classic locked-room situation. He's standing in front of a room facing—" she counted "—eleven people, the lights go out, presto, he's dead. The murderer has to be one of the eleven."

Emma Clyde's forehead puckered. "*Death in the Air.*"

Jeff Farley swung toward Harriet, high spots of anger burning in the gaunt cheeks above his beard. "Be careful what you say. Nobody's going to call me a murderer."

"I'm not calling you a murd—"

"She's just saying you have to look at the obvious," Hal explained earnestly.

Kelly Rizzoli's dark red hair swung in gentle negation. "Nothing is ever obvious. Certainly, this will not be."

"The back door was open."

Annie's quiet declaration created immense interest, and Hal was starting for the storeroom to investigate when Capt. Mac summoned him back.

Emma Clyde spoke authoritatively. "That answers the

question, then. There's no question of a locked-room murder—if the back door is open."

The murder maven was looking at Annie with approbation. Then, as clearly as though she'd actually said it, Annie realized Emma believed she'd opened the door herself!

A siren sounded in the distance.

"Nutty," Frank Saulter muttered in disgust.

Capt. Mac rubbed his jaw. "It would take a damn writer, wouldn't it?"

Saulter ignored him. "Wonder if he had a weak heart? We'll have to call on the county for help. The boat picked up the Kearney corpse two hours ago. Now they'll have to come get this one." He took a deep breath. "I guess we'd better get started."

He turned to study the assembled writers.

Dislike was instantaneous on both sides.

Saulter was humorless, dogmatic, religiously read *Sports Illustrated* in the barber shop, and liked Broward's Rock better before all *those* people came and moved into the elegant beach houses. The summer tourists were the worst, but he didn't much hold with the year-rounders either if they talked funny and drove those expensive cars. He especially didn't like ex-cops who'd made money and thought they were too goddam good for plain people anymore, like Hemphill with his fancy-dan golf clothes and McElroy with a saltwater swimming pool. When had they ever dropped by the station to visit? Now McElroy was acting like he was the only cop in the room. Saulter's ulcer burned like melting tar in August. It hadn't helped when he got the call on that vet, though the way she drove her car, he'd always expected to find her dead someday anyway. But not with her head bashed in. By God, he could handle it. And he didn't appreciate any off-island cops—or former cops—telling him how to run things.

Saulter pursed his mouth into a miserly line. "It's pretty clear what happened."

They'd all been standing on one foot then another for almost an hour. This pronouncement got everyone's attention.

"One of you people killed him."

Emma Clyde drew herself up and managed to look

imposing, despite her five-foot-three stature and the flow-ing, outrageously colored caftan.

"My dear man, that is an unwarranted assumption."

"You people were sitting in this room. Eleven of you. The lights go out, and somebody tosses a dart. So who else could have done it?"

Annie stepped forward. "When I went to check the circuit box, the back door was open." All eyes scrutinized her, some avidly, others skeptically. "Someone must have come in that way because no one left the tables, so none of us could have turned off the lights."

"How do you know nobody left the tables?" Saulter demanded. "You left—and nobody saw you, did they?"

"I went to see about the breakers."

"So *you* moved," Saulter said icily.

Max stepped closer. "Somebody else could have moved, too."

Saulter took one look at Max and decided to ignore him. He concentrated on Annie. "You went to put the lights on. How did you know you could do it by flipping the breakers?"

"I didn't know it," Annie said reasonably.

Saulter's eyes were accusing.

She straightened and met his gaze directly. "I knew that was the first thing to try. I figured there'd been a power failure, so I was going to get the flashlight. But it was gone."

"Where did you keep the flashlight?"

"On a nail in the storeroom."

"So when the lights went out, you were the only person here who knew where the circuit box was and where to find a flashlight. Right?"

"I suppose so—"

Capt. Mac interjected, "I found the flashlight, Chief. It was on the floor by the storeroom table."

The back of Saulter's neck reddened. "Did you touch it?" he snapped.

"Of course not."

Saulter didn't pursue it. Instead, he swung again at Annie. "Pretty convenient that the flashlight was in the wrong place. It had to be if you were to have some extra time—"

Max interrupted sharply, "That's an unwarranted as-sumption, Chief. If the murderer rigged the lights to go out, he could easily have moved the flashlight, and anybody here could have gone back to the storeroom earlier in the evening when everyone was talking and milling around here."

"But what made the lights go off?" Saulter's narrowed eyes were still on Annie.

For Pete's sake, did he think she had a device rigged to cause the blackout?

"Let's go look . . ." Max began, but Saulter and Capt. Mac waved him back and moved toward the circuit box.

Everyone waited tensely, leaning toward the storeroom in order to unabashedly eavesdrop.

"Look, Chief, there's thread tied to the breakers," they heard Capt. Mac say.

"Don't touch it," Saulter growled.

"Wouldn't matter. You can't lift prints from a surface that narrow. At least you can print the box. Somebody tied that thread to the breakers."

"I don't need you to tell me what to fingerprint." Saulter's voice bristled.

The two men moved back into the coffee area, eyes scanning the floor. "Probably ran the thread in here somewhere and left it on the floor," Capt. Mac theorized. "To cut the lights, the murderer gave a yank. That pulled the breakers, and it was absolutely dark."

Saulter looked skeptical. "Totally black?"

There was an enthusiastic chorus of assent.

"Then how the hell did the killer get Morgan with the dart?"

"That was easy, Chief," Emma offered, her cornflower-blue eyes disdainful of official slow-wittedness. "Elliot was a chain smoker. All your killer had to do was grab the dart and throw it at the lighted tip of his cigarette."

"Jesus," Saulter snorted. "That's the craziest goddam thing I ever heard of."

"It worked," Capt. Mac said drily.

"Yeah." Saulter sourly surveyed the survivors standing around the coffee area, as if he wished them all dead, too. "Okay. I want to know where everyone was. Exactly. Take the places you had when the lights went out."

Harriet shuddered and pointed a skinny, beringed finger toward the lifeless bundle that had once been Elliot Morgan.

"Are you just going to leave that there? This seems exceedingly distasteful to me."

"It won't hurt him," Saulter answered laconically.

Reluctantly, they drifted back toward the tables where they had been sitting when the lights went out. Ingrid Jones came along with Annie and Max to the farthest of the tables. Max spoke softly to Ingrid and Annie watched her hand him her tablet. He remained standing, his pencil flying over the page. Peering around his shoulder, she saw the bookstore take form on the tablet page.

As Annie watched, Billy Cameron, one of Saulter's assistants, began taking photographs of the murder scene. The second assistant, Bud Jurgens, dusted the circuit box and, Annie was glad to see, the back door, with fingerprint powder. Cameron and Jurgens constituted Chief Saulter's entire force. Annie thought of the well-trained men of the 87th Precinct and felt distinctly unimpressed.

Kelly Rizzoli and Hal Douglas sat at the far right table. Kelly's delicate face looked surprisingly untroubled, and her eyes were bright with curiosity. Hal picked up his coffee mug and swished the liquid around as if hoping it would still be hot.

Fritz Hemphill and Emma Clyde had the center table. Fritz looked frankly bored. Annie wondered if that were not perhaps the ugliest response of all. Emma, as usual, appeared confident and capable. Her stubby hands lay open and relaxed on the table in front of her.

Janis and Jeff Farley were at the next table. She huddled miserably in her chair. Jeff continued to be oblivious to his wife's discomfort. Angry patches of red stained his cheeks.

Capt. Mac and Harriet silently took their places at the table nearest the back wall. The retired policeman surveyed the coffee area thoughtfully. Harriet, of course, was enjoying herself, however much she might protest their proximity to the corpse.

Saulter shuffled from one table to the next, sighting toward Morgan's body, obviously figuring a possible trajectory for the dart. It looked to Annie as though the dart had caught Elliot almost dead center.

"The murderer could have moved the minute the lights went out," she pointed out. "In fact, there was a sound of movement."

MAX'S SKETCH OF DEATH ON DEMAND

Capt. Mac nodded. "She's right. There was definitely a feeling of movement. I sensed it, too."

Saulter scowled, but walked over to stand beside Annie's chair. It was, she realized with a sinking feeling, almost directly in line with the body.

His artistic assistant trained his Polaroid on all of them in turn, then Saulter ordered fingerprints taken, a messy and subtly dispiriting chore. No one objected, not even Emma Clyde. Somehow, Annie didn't think Emma Clyde relished ink on her fingers, but even she kept her mouth shut.

When the fingerprints were made, Saulter brusquely gave everyone permission to leave as soon as Billy Cameron wrote down their names and addresses. They stood in line by the coffee bar, uncomfortably close to the now sheet-shrouded form.

"Hey, Chief!" It was Capt. Mac, and his voice vibrated with intensity. Annie thought of the high, keen baying of a bloodhound.

"By God." The stocky policeman crouched beside the wicker wastebasket by the far end of the coffee bar. "This answers some questions, all right."

Everyone surged toward him, but Saulter barred the way. "Stand back." Then he hurried to McElroy.

Once again, they all bent forward to listen.

"I don't see—" Saulter began.

"Smell it, man."

Saulter, too, hunkered down beside the wastebasket.

Capt. Mac pulled a couple of quarters from his trouser pocket and used them as pincers to lift out a sodden ball of white cotton.

Saulter sniffed. "Fingernail polish remover." He stared blankly at Capt. Mac.

"I've only run across it once before," the former police-man explained, "but I'll bet my pension on it. The mur-derer covered the tips of his fingers with clear fingernail polish to keep from putting prints on the dart. I can see it now." He pointed toward the coffee area and the tables. "The lights go out, the murderer has the dart hidden nearby. Probably on the floor by the wall. The murderer grabs the dart and throws it. While Annie's going to see about the lights, there's time to use the cotton drenched in polish remover to wipe off the polish, then drop the cotton into the wastebasket. Saulter, there won't be a damn print on that dart. By God, that's clever."

The two men stared at each other, then slowly rose to face the watching suspects.

"Fingernail polish remover," Saulter repeated. He looked at the women in the room one by one, then his gaze locked on Annie.

Perhaps she should have kept quiet, but she was getting tired of his not so subtle suspicion.

"We all paint our fingernails, Chief."

"But nobody knows this room as well as you do," he retorted.

"We've all spent a lot of time here," Capt. Mac said quickly. He cleared his throat. "Chief, I'd be glad to lend a hand with your investigation."

"Thanks. We can take care of *our* job. For now, you're all free to leave. We'll be in touch with everyone tomorrow."

Everyone started up the central aisle toward the front, but McElroy hung back. "I'd hate to see anybody get off on the wrong foot," the retired policeman said. "Why, Annie couldn't possibly have killed anybody."

Harriet Edelman stopped and slapped her hands on her hips, and her bracelets clanged gratingly. "So you think little Miss Pretty Face shouldn't be considered a suspect? I happen to know she and Morgan had a hell of a spat this morning."

Saulter wanted to hear all about that, of course.

"I was going by on my bicycle when she slammed the door on him. I saw it with my own eyes."

Annie hadn't seen Harriet, which wasn't too surprising. At that point, she had been so furious with Elliot she wouldn't have noticed an audience of dancing tarantulas.

Saulter gestured impatiently for them to keep moving toward the door. "Don't worry. I don't give a damn about pretty faces, and I'll be interviewing everybody tomorrow, including Miss Laurance, about their relationships with the deceased."

"That's reassuring." Emma looked sardonic.

"Or pots of money, either."

Agatha chose that moment to leap up on the Christie section and hiss.

Janis clutched at her husband.

Fritz Hemphill laughed.

"She wants out." Annie opened the front door, and Agatha shot out into the night. Annie was right behind her. When she looked back, she met Saulter's eyes. Now she knew how a fox felt when sighted by the hounds.

For once Max drove at a reasonable speed.

"I don't understand why he sent us all home," Annie mused.

"What else is he going to do?" Max peered through the night. "The Black Hole of Calcutta can't hold a candle to a country lane on Broward's Rock. No pun intended."

"No street lights," she replied absently. The tourists always complained, too.

"No lights of any kind. Not even moonlight." The beams from the headlights scarcely pierced the gloom beneath the spreading live oak trees whose branches met over the roadway. The pleasantly cool night air, drifting through the open windows, smelled of marsh water. "Are you sure Hansel and Gretel don't live down this way?"

"I guess it's a little daunting at night."

"I'd take Central Park after dark anytime." He abruptly slammed on the brake, and she jolted forward, restrained by the seat belt.

"Good God, what's that?"

The thick, low-slung creature darted swiftly across the dusty dirt road, clearly illuminated by the headlights. "That, city slicker, is a raccoon."

Max eased the car forward.

"He didn't even ask any questions."

"Like, 'Miss Laurance, did you do it?'"

"All right, smartass. Turn to the right, down that lane."

Max slowed and swung the Porsche to the right, scowling. "This isn't a lane. This is a bloody footpath."

"Actually, it's pretty rustic. Now, slow down. I live in that second tree."

"The second tree. You did say *tree*?"

"It's a bargain. Some developer got the notion everybody would want to live like Robinson Crusoe, and he built a half dozen houses that are really platforms up in oak trees. Unfortunately for him, they didn't go over very well."

The Porsche's lights illuminated the tree house now. Wooden steps curved gracefully up from the ground to a circular house built around the main trunk.

"That is really homey," Max commented drily. "Just you and the earwigs."

"The realty company sprays every month," she said severely. "I am bug-free."

Max braked and clicked off the lights, but Annie was already opening her door. "That's okay. You don't have to get out."

"I know I don't, but behavior patterns are ingrained. I do not drop a girl off at her front door, especially when it is up in a tree in the middle of a swamp."

"The South Carolina Tourist Association would frown on the term swamp."

But he came around to take her arm and gallantly insisted on coming inside and checking every room.

Annie stood quietly in the center of her circular living room, waiting for Max, who was on his knees at the base of her bed, peering beneath it, to return. "Now, why did you do that, Max?"

"Because I've got the wild suspicion the island air isn't too healthy right now." He glanced around at the hexagonal living room. The walls were eleven-foot-tall sheets of glass, which, in daylight, bathed the room in light and warmth. Now, with the blinds up, the night pressed against the glass, threatening, disturbingly inimical.

Annie quickly lowered the slatted, tropical blinds, and leaned down to turn on a Tiffany lamp. With the night closed out, she felt a good deal more secure. The room was familiar again, the comfortable rattan furniture, fortunately so appropriate for a seaside dwelling, and so affordable. Here, too, as at Death On Demand, bright cushions provided splotches of orange, burnt sienna, and Texas red clay. Her latest photographs were pinned haphazardly to a square bulletin board in the center of the bookcases that filled the wall between the living room and bedroom. She was especially proud of the shot she'd taken at dawn near Moccasin Creek of a Little Blue Heron, his feathers slate blue on his body and purplish red on his neck. Her Nikon lay on an end table, next to her trophy for being the winning pitcher for the Island Dolphins. The colorful paperbacks stuffed into every inch of the bookcases added another note of cheer. Her favorite books: all the Agathas, the wonderfully funny Leonidas Witherall books written by Phoebe Atwood Taylor as Alice Tilton, the Constance and Gwenyth Little books. Her room, safe and friendly.

"Nobody would want to hurt me."

"How do we know that?"

Annie dropped down on the largest wicker couch, and Max settled right beside her. There would have been room left over for several others to sit. She scooted over a few inches. He followed.

"Look, Elliot was begging for trouble. He was threatening to talk about—well, you heard him—he was going to rattle skeletons. Somebody didn't want his or her bones disturbed."

"What about the lady vet?"

Annie sighed. "I can't imagine. Oh, Max, she was such a lovely person. Right after I came here to visit Uncle Ambrose this summer, Boots was hit by a car."

She would never forget how Boots had dragged himself to her uncle's house, his back legs useless, his fur matted and streaked with dirt and blood. The memory still hurt.

"Anyway, I took Boots to the Island Hills Clinic. I didn't know Jill then, and Dr. Foster took a look at poor Boots. He was nice enough but disinterested. He told me the only thing to do was to put Boots down, there was no hope. I asked what they would do, and he said they'd give him a shot of succinyl-choline, and he would be out like a light. A girl came in while Foster was talking, but I didn't pay any attention to her. Foster left, and I was saying goodbye to Boots when a boy came to get him. She spoke up and said, 'Don't give him succinyl-choline. Use 5 cc.'s concentrated sodium pentabarbitol.' Of course, I wanted to know what the heck, and then she told me. Foster was old-fashioned and a lot of vets might use succinyl-choline, but she didn't advise it. She said the animal suffocated. She said it was cruel." Tears filled Annie's eyes. "So you see, it couldn't be a *personal* murder with Jill. Maybe it will turn out to be something like a drug robbery, after all."

Somehow, Max's arm was now tightly around her shoulders.

"I don't have a glimmer why anybody coshed her, but two murders on an island within twenty-four hours! They're connected, or I'll eat that raccoon."

"It isn't our problem," she objected. She was unbelievably tired. "It's that unpleasant man's problem. But I still don't understand why he sent us all home. He did say nobody was allowed to leave the island, but there isn't a ferry until morning anyway. He didn't even *try* to find out anything."

"I imagine he's busy doing that right now, my dear. And they have to examine the crime scene. Your old chum was still hanging around as we left."

Her old chum. Max meant Capt. Mac. Suddenly, Annie wished fervently that Capt. Mac were in charge of this investigation.

"Max, did you see the way Saulter looked at me?"

The floor creaked.

Annie swam up from the depths of sleep, rolled over, and stifled a scream. She bolted upright, her hair tousled, realized her nightgown was more than drooping low, and hastily yanked a sheet up to her chin.

"What the hell are you doing here?"

"You are at risk," Max intoned sternly.

Annie yawned and started to rub her eyes, then grabbed again at the sheet. "Let's start over," she said patiently. "*I* am in bed. *I* am asleep. Perhaps *you* could tell me what *you* are doing in my bedroom at the crack of dawn?"

"Anybody could get in this house. I spent the night in my car—and I've got a stiff neck." He milked a pause for sympathy and tried to rotate his head. "Ouch."

"You rented a condo. Why don't you stay in it?"

"Because there is a double killer somewhere on this island . . ."

"Not in my bedroom," Annie objected.

"He could be."

"Or she."

"Annie, listen to me. This house is as full of holes as Swiss cheese. Do you know how I got in?"

Annie was stubbornly silent.

"I picked up a stick at the foot of the steps, tiptoed up, and pried open a window in the kitchen."

"I didn't hear you."

"You sleep like an elephant, my lovely. The point is, this place isn't secure. So I'm going to get my stuff—"

"No."

"There's plenty of room. I can curl up on the couch."

"You won't have a stiff neck, you'll have a rigid spine. No, Max. I appreciate it, but I'm a big girl, and I am perfectly capable of taking care of myself."

They squabbled about it all the way through breakfast.

Annie poured each of them a second cup of coffee and watched with fascination as Max wolfed down his fifth sugar-covered doughnut. They sat on the airy porch outside the kitchen. The soft air was fragrant with pine, marsh, and tar; sunlight slanted through the tall sea pines. A blacktopped path disappeared into a dense clump of palmettos, southern red cedars, yuccas, and bayberry shrubs. The beach was only a ten-minute bicycle ride away. For a fleeting moment Annie wished that today could be a holiday for her and Max, that they could go walk down a dune with an October splash of flowering herbs, violet, magenta, yellow and cream, to the long spread of gray sand with nothing more to think of than sun and water and play.

"I guess I'll open the store as usual."

Max nodded, his mouth full, then said indistinctly, "That's the best thing to do. Act completely normal." He swallowed and said clearly, "Besides, I bet a buck they'll all come by, one by one, to see if you know anything."

"Who'll come by?"

"Our suspects."

"God, I hope not."

"Hey, Annie, don't be silly. This will be our chance to pump them."

"I don't want to pump them. Why should I?"

"Saulter is a dummy. Anybody can see that. We can solve it."

"Oh, no. Count me out. I don't want any part of it."

Max licked a trickle of sugar from the corner of his mouth, and rattled the empty doughnut bag. "We need to do some grocery shopping. Don't you ever eat at home?"

Uncertain which argument to pursue first, Annie opted for anti-detection.

"Max, listen carefully, because I am only going to say this once. I am not a detective. I am not even a mystery writer. I just happen to run a bookstore where a man got murdered. I intend to scrub that floor and rearrange the coffee area and forget it ever happened. Mysteries are a business for me, not a vacation. This is not a game. There is no way I am going to get involved in this investigation—and I mean it, absolutely, positively, and without any shadow of doubt. Period."

Max grinned.

Seven

The argument continued on the stairs of the tree house. "I'm going to work just as usual. I do not want to talk about murder."

"Murders."

"It has to be a coincidence," she said mulishly. "Jill and Elliot didn't even know each other. He didn't have any pets."

"How do you know?" Max barred her way down the steps.

Since she didn't want to go into that, she ducked under his arm. "Look, I've got to hurry, or I'm going to be late." She'd already informed him in no uncertain terms that he was not coming to the store with her. To divert him, she offered, "I'll have lunch with you. Come to the shop about one, and we'll go have a mango sundae."

Max took a childish delight in new tastes, and Annie was pleased at her skill in deflecting him. This was not the time to admit that she'd dated Elliot a couple of times and had once been invited to dinner at his house. That evening was enough to frost any interest on her part. Elliot collected West Indian art and artifacts, including voodoo dolls from Haiti. Her appetite had been seriously damaged by his long-winded and ghoulish description of the walking dead.

Ugh.

Annie ran on down the steps, then realized her car was still in the crushed oyster-shell lot near the plaza, the closest parking place to her store. Of course, Max had brought her home last night.

Since he drove this morning in the old mode, fast and hard, there was no time for conversation.

Annie's home was on the fringes of the developed part of the resort area. The tree houses had been a builder's short-lived fancy. She loved living in a remote area, and delighted in the daily surprises of marsh life. Her tree house overlooked the high marsh, and from her sun porch she could watch the never-ending play of light and wind on the thick cordgrass. Salt myrtle, marsh elder, and southern bayberry flourished. A single narrow road snaked inland through palmetto palms and sea pines toward the populated area. Spanish moss shrouded the glossily green live oak trees. Alligators sunned on the banks of shallow green ponds, and turtles, frogs, and snakes slipped silently through the water. The soft air shimmered a paler shade of green beneath the tree limbs.

When Max's red Porsche plunged out onto the blacktop that circled the island and ran past the luxuriant green of a sleekly mowed golf course, he commented, "From the boondocks to the country club."

"Part of the charm."

The blacktop served the access roads to the islands' mansions, which overlooked the fairways of the Island Hills Golf Club. The three-story Tudor-style Club House glistened in the morning sunlight. Ornate, twelve-foot-tall bronze gates were already open to admit early morning foursomes.

She pointed toward an imposing home on a gentle rise near the fourteenth green. "That's Emma's house."

Max grinned. "Her little place in the country."

Annie nodded. "Right. I saw a feature on it in *American Country Homes*. That little cottage is valued at just under two million."

"Crime does pay."

"For her."

Max squinted against the sunlight and upped his speed to sixty.

They flashed by more magnificent homes, some barely glimpsed through the spreading live oak trees.

Max decreased his speed almost immediately because they were already upon the harbor area. Red-tiled roofs marked the beginning of the condos, Swallows' Retreat. The stores and cafés bordering the basin gleamed a soft gray, the natural wood exteriors weathered by the sun. Max pulled into the crushed-shell parking area.

"She could have done it."

Looking ahead to Death On Demand, Annie didn't make the connection.

"Who could have done what?"

"Emma could have murdered Elliot. She's smart enough."

"Max."

"Somebody did it," he said virtuously.

"Somebody did," she agreed. "And that charming Chief Saulter can figure it out."

To Annie's surprise, Max didn't even attempt to come into the shop with her. In fact, he dropped her off at the edge of the plaza, promised to meet her for lunch, and waved goodbye with an annoyingly cherubic smile.

Curving around the natural harbor that served as the marina, the plaza was the social hub of Broward's Rock. Since it was well past the summer season, some of the sailboats were battened down for winter, but most were moored by the wooden docks, ready for island owners to enjoy on idyllic October days. On the far side of the harbor were yacht slips. There were only three big yachts left now, and one of these was Emma Clyde's, *Marigold's Pleasure*.

Annie loved the little harbor. It was as elegant as a Fabergé egg. From her front windows, she could watch sailboats scud into the sound and sea gulls swoop and hover near pier's end in hopes of free fish. All of the shops built on the curve of the plaza were open, but now that the tourist season was over, the atmosphere relaxed perceptibly. The occasional shoppers were more likely to be year-rounders. It was a good time of the year to inventory, to decide on new stocks for next summer, to savor the relaxed hush.

As she crossed the plaza, she was thoughtful. Why was Max so easily dissuaded from accompanying her? And what was happening in the investigation into Elliot's death? A *dart*? That still seemed impossible—and contrived. The more she thought about it, the crazier it seemed.

She walked up on the verandah that fronted the shops and stopped at her own storefront. *Death On Demand* marched in square gilt letters in the center of the south window. The north window carried the information painted in bold scarlet: Mysteries, Suspense, Horror, Adventure, New and Old.

She looked appraisingly at the display behind the north window. The *Murder Ink* mystery companions took pride of place. Hard to imagine a true mystery aficionado without them. Her latest and most prized old books, first editions all, lay enticingly in front of the trade paperbacks: *Dog in the Manger* by Ursula Curtiss, the eight volumes of complete Sherlock Holmes published by Collier, and a rare $110 copy of Elizabeth Lemarchand's first book, *Death of an Old Girl*. New hardcovers, with splashily bright covers, filled the south window. Annie nodded approvingly. It was always a plus when she could offer a new Martha Grimes or Ken Follett. Readers flocked. All right. She couldn't stand there forever and put off going inside. No matter what had happened last night, she was determined to erase the memory of Elliot's murder. She had work to do.

Annie was fishing her key ring from her purse when woodpecker-quick steps tapped up behind her. Ingrid Jones, her springy gray head bobbing, swooped up, waggling the key. "Decided it would be a good morning to shelve those books from that Texas estate."

Ingrid usually worked only on Saturdays and during lunch hours in the off-season. Annie wasn't sure what prompted her early arrival, but she knew darn well it signaled support, and she felt a rush of affection. How nice it was to have friends! Then, insidiously, she wondered what made Ingrid decide it was time to rally round the flag.

Ingrid unlocked the door, and led the way inside, flicking on the lights and chattering nonstop about the snowy egret she'd spotted that morning over near McAlister's Point. Annie followed slowly, not really listening, but very grateful for human—and animal—sound. Agatha streaked inside, meowing imperiously. Annie stopped by the cash desk and looked down the main corridor toward the dark coffee area.

No one was there.

She had almost expected to find that corner cordoned off and a policeman in residence. But that was ridiculous. With a police force of three, and two murders taking place in less than twenty-four hours, Chief Saulter could hardly spare the manpower.

She tucked her purse in its accustomed place beneath the cash register, then walked down the central corridor, flicking on lights. Agatha loped silently ahead. At the coffee bar, Annie stopped.

A wobbly chalked outline marked the long oblong where Elliot had fallen. She looked quickly away and went around the bar to open the refrigerator and get out Agatha's milk. When it was poured, she shook some cat food into the blue ceramic bowl that was inscribed in white script, *The Grande Dame*.

The bell jingled. Annie jumped up to peer down the central aisle, then struggled to look normal as Ingrid welcomed Sam Mickle, the postman.

"Good morning, Sam."

"Morning, Ingrid. Miss Laurance."

Annie murmured for a moment to Agatha, who expected salutations along with provender, then moved unhurriedly up the aisle to glance through the pile of mail Ingrid had stacked on the cash desk. Despite everything that had happened, Annie was beginning to relax. It was a marvelously normal Monday. She thumbed through the material, dropping junk into the wastebasket, bills into a pile to her left, *Publishers Weekly* to the right. She would read *PW*, then... She held a small square package between thumb and forefinger and stared at the bold, slanted writing of the address.

There was no doubt in her mind who had written her name in thick, dark strokes.

But why would Elliot Morgan have mailed a small, square package to her? Shades of *The List of Adrian Messenger*, she thought miserably.

It didn't take Max long to figure the layout of Broward's Rock. Of course, it wasn't very big, seven miles long and five miles at its widest. One blacktop road circled the island, beginning and ending at Heron Point where the ferry landed, and funneling into the resort area through the checkpoint. The guard on duty nodded respectfully at the Porsche as it scooted by. The ferry office was part of a tin-roofed beer joint and bait shop owned by Ben Parotti, who could chew tobacco and guzzle Schlitz concurrently. When Halcyon Development Company decided to create a rich man's refuge, it bought the skillet end of the island, intending to leave the narrow handle with its old, weathered homes, some of them shacks, for "support personnel," as the developers delicately phrased it. However, Halcyon Development found the smelly bait shop and dank beer joint by the ferry landing unappetizing. Since rich prospective residents would arrive by ferry, Halcyon decided to buy the ferry service and its accompanying office/baitshop/beer joint, planning to build a tasteful cottage by the terminal. Square, stumpy Ben Parotti, who also captained the ferry, intended to continue his life as it had always been, and no sum could budge him. It was a singular experience for the young Halcyon lawyer from Atlanta, whose credo until that moment had been that enough money could buy anyone.

Max took the three wooden steps in one stride and pushed open a creaky door. Inside, he paused, his eyes adjusting to the rank dimness, his nose crinkling at the mixture of smells, chunks of bait, stale beer, sawdust. A bottle-scarred wooden bar ran along the wall to his left. The mirror behind it might last have been polished just before Pearl Harbor. Two round wooden tables with kegs for seats completed the hospitality area. Straight to the back were the cash register and coolers holding chunks of black bass, grouper, snapper, squid, and chicken necks. To Max's right, a worn, golden oak desk that might once have stood in a country school provided office space for the Parotti Ferry Service.

Max tried to look genial while not inhaling too deeply. "Bud Light."

Parotti squinted at him with interest.

"Summer folk don't drink beer this early. And you ain't no boozer." He frowned at Max's crisp blue-and-white seersucker suit. "You another damn lawyer?"

"God forbid," Max said piously.

Parotti chuckled. "That's good. But you want somethin' besides beer."

"Information."

Parotti fastidiously pulled the tab off a can of Schlitz. "Funny. You're the first rich dude to ever pay me the time of day."

Max looked at the bent but still recognizable sign of a Flying Red Horse, which hung crookedly on the wall back of the cash register. "You've been here a long time. I figure you probably see everything that happens on this island."

"Maybe."

"The cops ask you how many people came on the ferry yesterday—and Saturday?"

"Sure. Told 'em four. You're one of them. You were the only stranger."

Max drank the cold Bud Light with relish. "That's what I figured." He nodded companionably at Parotti. "That means I need to know about some people who live here."

"Why should I tell you?"

"The hell of it." Max drank more of the beer, then smiled his most winning smile.

Parotti chuckled, looking like an amused but slightly sinister and very tatty leprechaun. "I like you, young fella. Who do you want to know about?"

"You know a fellow named McElroy? They call him Capt. Mac."

Parotti nodded and tilted his can of Schlitz. "Keeps to himself pretty much. Comes by here for beer, bait. He was a police chief some place in Florida. Gets a lot of packages on the ferry, picks 'em up here."

"What kind of packages?"

Parotti shrugged. "Electronic stuff, I think. Maybe he has one of those computers. Most of them do."

"Most of them?"

"The writers. The ones you want to know about." The shrewd blue eyes were amused.

"So you already know all about me?"

"You're friends with the new girl, the one who took over Ambrose's shop."

"What do you know about the rest of them?"

Parotti took a paint-stained rag from his back pocket and noisily blew his nose. "I'm not in the business of talkin' about people."

"You know Saulter?"

The old man's face twisted. "Always tryin' to pick trouble with me, he is. I won't tell him nothin'."

"He's trying to pitch the murders on Ambrose's niece."

"Yeah?" Parotti rubbed his nose. "He's a dumb bastard, all right." He hitched closer to Max along the dingy bar. "Listen, what did happen last night?"

Max described it all. Then concluded, "So, you see, I've got to find out about all the writers who were there. One of them did it." He ticked their names off, one by one, starting with Emma Clyde.

Parotti muttered under his breath a couple more times about Saulter, took a large gulp of beer, and made up his mind. "Yeah, I can tell you lots. Now, that Emma Clyde, she's a tough lady."

"How do you mean?"

"Had a husband, younger than she was. Everybody said he was slipping around with a Cuban girl. Now, he's not around anymore."

"What happened to him?"

"Fell off her big boat. Late one night. Accident, they say."

"You think it was an accident?"

Parotti pursed his mouth. "Most rich folks are smart enough not to fall off their boats when they're anchored." He drowned a snigger in his Schlitz.

"What about Fritz Hemphill?"

"Keeps to himself. Plays a lot of golf. I did some work for him once, digging for a sea wall. He tried to cheat me. I told him what happened to the last man tried that."

"What happened?" Max asked dutifully.

"Funny thing. His car blew up one morning when he started it." Parotti's rheumy blue eyes were as cold as an early frost.

"Hemphill pay what was due?"

"Yep."

"Know anything about the Farleys?"

Parotti jerked his head eastward. "They live a couple miles from here. One time I ran out of gas near their place. Heard somebody screaming."

"Screaming?"

"A woman. I went up to the house, called out, and in a minute he came to the door. I asked if there was anything wrong, told him I heard screams. He said his wife had burned herself, spilled hot grease on her hand."

Max remembered Janis's air of tension and the way she looked constantly to her husband for support. Hot grease.

"Do you know the middle-aged blonde, Harriet Edelman?"

Parotti grimaced. "I stay away from women like that. Reminds me of my first wife." He shuddered in loving reminiscence and gulped down the rest of his beer.

"How about Hal Douglas?"

For a moment, Parotti looked blank. "You mean the fat one that lives on Blue Magnolia, grins a lot? He seems all right. Another newcomer. Just been here about a year."

"There's one more, a pretty redhead, Kelly Rizzoli."

Parotti opened the refrigerator door and surveyed the contents before taking out another can of Schlitz.

"That's a funny one. Saw her one night, streaking down the beach like a crazy woman. Turns out she was chasing another female. Caught her on a dune not far from my cabin. They were kickin' and rollin' around in the sand, and I almost went out to see what the hell, then the first woman kind of gave up and started bawling, and the redhead led her away down the beach."

*   *   *

Annie hadn't been in the store fifteen minutes before she understood why Ingrid had shown up. It was a deluge. Twenty-seven customers before lunch. She didn't even have time to do more than open Elliot's package, see that it was a floppy disk with a folded note, and slip it behind a package on the storeroom table.

It took only a few more minutes for her to realize that half the curiosity seekers believed this was their big chance to rub elbows with a Lizzie Borden—her. Typical was Mrs. Porter Fredericks, who bought six hardcovers while watching Annie with walleyed fascination. The woman didn't even know the books she'd grabbed up, which included one first edition Mike Hammer and two James Bond titles. Annie was tempted to offer to cut off a sprig of hair and price it at fifteen dollars. Ingrid worked grimly and fast, saying once out of the corner of her mouth, "By God, if they come in, they're going to buy something!" Annie would have been delighted at the constant ring of the register, but the price was pretty high. More than one customer jumped back perceptibly when she approached. Ingrid finally shooed her off to the storeroom. "I can handle this." She resembled a militant sparrow, darting up and down the aisles coercing the sightseers into purchases. Annie was absurdly grateful for her support.

Mrs. Brawley squeezed down the central aisle at one point and poked her head into the storeroom. "Miss Laurance, I hate to bother you—"

"The Pollifax is not in."

"Oh, I know that, but I wondered if you could just give me a *little* hint on that picture with the butler in it." She fluttered her bejewelled hand toward the watercolors pinned to the back wall. "I think I have all the rest of them."

Annie was impressed at this evidence of singleminded devotion to the hunt, but she shook her head chidingly. "Now, now, Mrs. Brawley. That would be cheating, wouldn't it?"

Grudgingly, Mrs. Brawley turned away. She was still posted in front of the watercolors twenty minutes later, and Annie heard her muttering to herself, "Just one more, and I can get my Mrs. Pollifax free!"

The only fellow suspect to come in was Harriet Edelman, whose arrival almost caused a traffic jam on the verandah when people realized they could see *two* of the people who were *there*.

Max drove fast. He had time for just one more stop before he met Annie for lunch.

He tossed the names up in his mind like confetti, then glanced down at the crude map he had drawn with Parotti's help.

Max squealed onto Sandpiper Terrace. Number Eleven was the third house on the left, a yellow two-story stucco with a long clear pane of glass in the front foyer. The largest hanging fern he'd ever seen glistened in the sunlight on the front porch. He parked and strode up the manicured gravel path past crisply trimmed monkey grass. Summer marigolds and zinnias still bloomed. Mauve and gold chrysanthemums flooded a square plot by the front steps with autumn colors.

He stepped up on the recently painted porch and rang the bell.

A voice boomed, "Come on around here. I'm out in the garden."

Turning, Max saw Capt. Mac. He wore khaki slacks and a tattered pale blue polo. Max's mouth turned down. James Bond. Then he managed a smile.

"Glad I caught you."

McElroy led the way down a flagstone path past the house to a tiled patio beside a swimming pool. He waved Max to a white, webbed patio chair. The air carried the scent of honeysuckle and crape myrtle from the back stockade fence.

"You wanted to see me?" McElroy's voice was friendly, but his gray eyes were wary.

Max tried butter. "Annie tells me you were a super cop."

"Really? I don't remember ever talking about my work with Annie, Mr. Darling."

Strike one.

"I guess someone else must have told her. You were a police chief in Florida?"

"Chief and assistant chief. On the Gold Coast. Before

MAX'S MAP OF THE ISLAND

that, I was a cop in Miami. The Gold Coast is a good deal more pleasant."

Max glanced up at the house. It wasn't large, but it was nice. Very nice. And the figure-eight pool was a beauty.

"You retired to the same kind of place."

"Right. The only difference is, I don't know all about everybody here."

"You didn't like that?"

"A police chief in a high-class resort gets to know more than he wants to sometimes." Capt. Mac's face was no longer genial, and Max suddenly had a glimpse of a tougher, harder persona than the retired man usually revealed.

"Is that true of Saulter?"

"Ask him." Not unpleasant, but not exactly forthcoming. Capt. Mac sat solidly in his deck chair, his posture almost military.

"I'm surprised you aren't lending a hand."

"Lending a hand?"

"Helping out. I don't suppose Saulter's ever handled two murders in one weekend. Or maybe even one."

"He knows the drill." But was there in that dry comment just a hint of disbelief in Saulter's ability to properly run such an investigation?

"You keep on top of it last night?"

McElroy leaned forward in his chair. The polo shirt fitted him snugly, revealing the strength of his upper torso. "Saulter didn't quite want to throw me out, so I hung around. He did okay. He secured the area, made a list of all the physical evidence. Photos. Dusted for fingerprints."

"What did he come up with?"

Capt. Mac squinted. "What's your interest, Mr. Darling?"

"Call me Max."

McElroy waited.

Finally, Max said baldly, "My interest can be summed up in one word: Annie."

The deeply tanned face softened. "That I can understand." He scowled. "I'm a little worried there, too."

Max had an uncomfortably empty feeling in the middle of his chest. If this ex-cop were a little worried, Max was a lot worried.

"Why?" he asked sharply.

McElroy picked up a cigar from a humidor on the glass-topped patio table and offered one to Max, who declined. He rolled the cigar in his fingers. "I don't want anybody to think I'm critical of another cop."

"Of course not."

He took his time putting the cigar in his mouth, lighting it. He didn't look at Max.

"Thing about it is, Saulter thinks the simple answer is the best." He blew a thin stream of smoke that hung in the soft, pine-scented air. "Of course, that's how cops are trained to think. The simple answer usually is the right answer."

"So what's the connection between the simple answer and Annie?"

McElroy tapped the ash from the cigar. "Let me tell you how a cop thinks. One, who had the best opportunity to set up the kill? Two, does that person have a motive? Saulter's worked it out.

"Who could rig the lights to go out?

"Whose fingerprints are all over the circuit box?

"Who could hide a dart at her leisure?

"Who had an argument with Elliot Sunday morning and was obviously furious with him on Sunday night?

"Who faced financial disaster if Elliot raised the rent on her shop?

"Who was the champion pitcher and batter on the Island softball team in August?"

Capt. Mac took a deep breath and frowned significantly.

"There's one name that fits—and that's Annie."

"What about the writers?" Max demanded hotly. "Didn't you tell him what was going on? That Elliot was about to dump everybody's inmost secrets out on the floor? Did you tell Saulter about that?"

"Sure, but that's too fancy for Saulter. Besides, how much dirt could Elliot possibly have on these people? If they'd done something criminal, how could Elliot know about it and not the authorities? No, I'm telling you, Max, Saulter sees this as an open-and-shut equation: Annie fought with Elliot, Annie was mad, it's Annie's store. Who did it? Annie. All he's doing now is looking for proof."

Max felt like someone had kicked him in the stomach.

But Capt. Mac wasn't through. He gripped the cigar so hard it dented. "And there's something you don't know, son. Something bad. Saulter's got another damn fool idea—"

Eight

One of Annie's first purchases for Death On Demand was an Apple computer to keep track of inventory and sales. It was a wonderful, almost miraculous timesaver which could balance her books, churn out a mailing list, keep an appointment book, and check her spelling.

What it couldn't do was read the disk Elliot Morgan had mailed to her.

Okay. She understood that. Elliot used a different computer. She remembered one evening when the writers had discussed their machines. Elliot had an Epson. Some of the machines were compatible if you had the right software, but she didn't have the right software or the right machine.

Elliot knew that. So he mailed this disk to her with a snide note:

Dear Annie—I figure you are the only one of the Sunday Night Regulars who can be trusted not to destroy this on receipt, so be a good scout and keep this for me for a few days. Your wearisome honesty must be a result of your provincial upbringing. Don't you see how the wages of sin are infinitely more rewarding? I have the goods on everyone on this disk. I'll share it Sunday evening. Yours in sleuthing, E.M.

Of course, he'd been far too arrogant to expect that he was going to be murdered. Obviously, however, he was uneasy. Why else would he send her a copy of the disk? Had he intended to safeguard himself by telling someone that another copy of the information existed? What was on that disk?

She set to work unloading the used books she'd bought
from the Texas estate sale and tried to ignore the sounds of
shuffling feet and whispers outside the storeroom. She
briefly considered going out to help Ingrid, then furiously
decided to deny those sensation-seeking eyes their afternoon treat. She lifted out the seventh Phoebe Atwood
Taylor novel, a first edition. What should she do with the
damn disk?

This would drive Max crazy. He had pestered her for
information on the Sunday Night Regulars. With any luck,
the disk contained whatever dirt Elliot had managed to
scrape up on all of them.

But someone had killed Elliot to prevent him from
revealing what he knew. That information absolutely had
to go to the police.

Still, she argued, she didn't know for a fact that one of
the writers had murdered Elliot. Sure, it was a reasonable
assumption, but the back door to Death On Demand *was*
open last night. It would be unspeakably cruel to throw
everybody on that disk to Saulter. At least, not until she
knew what was on it. Max wouldn't hesitate: he was dying
to investigate the whole mess anyway. Personally, she
didn't want to have anything to do with it. But she did
have that damn disk.

Did anyone else on the island have an Epson?

She ran through them in her mind. Writers are inordinately
proud of their word processors, each convinced his own is
best. No, the only Epson belonged to Elliot.

The only way to read the disk, then, was to use Elliot's
machine. Which brought up an interesting question: Was
Elliot's house being watched?

She frowned. Probably not. After all, Saulter only had
two men on his force. The house would be locked up, but
Elliot lived in a tree house, too, and Max had already
demonstrated how easy they were to enter. On the island,
no one worried about security. At least, no one had until now.

The storeroom door began to open. Annie's heart lifted.
It was almost lunchtime. Lunch with Max. Despite everything, she began to smile. Max. Why did he have to be
such a bum at heart? If only...

"Miss Laurance."

Annie's smile vanished. Not Max.

There wasn't a vestige of warmth on Chief Saulter's face.
He stood only a foot or so from her worktable, a bigger man
than she'd realized. Last night she'd wondered about the
look in Saulter's eyes. Now there was no question about it:
he was clearly hostile. He had a bony, worn face with faded
brown eyes, sallow skin, and a tight, thin mouth. She was
excruciatingly aware of the revolver that rode in a shiny
black leather holster high on his hip, emphasizing the power
behind the tan uniform shirt and pants.

She felt her hackles rise, but she managed a pleasant
"Good morning, Chief Saulter."

He didn't bother with pleasantries, but pulled a small
spiral notebook from his pocket, flipped it open, then
looked at Annie, his eyes as lifeless as agates.

"I'm interviewing the people who were present last
night." He looked around. "Could we bring a couple of
chairs in here?"

He did help move the chairs from the coffee area to the
storeroom. The customers ostensibly in search of horror
reading shifted their attention from the chalked outline on
the floor and watched them with avaricious delight. As
Saulter closed the storeroom door, Annie heard a woman
say, "I've heard there's going to be an early arrest. Do—"

Those cold eyes bored into hers, but he spoke in a
monotone. "I'm advising you, Ms. Laurance, that you are
a murder suspect. I am also advising you of your rights.
You have the right to remain silent. You have a right to
have counsel present when you are questioned. You may
waive these rights. Do you wish to remain silent or will
you consent to be interviewed?"

The Miranda warning. For her.

"I don't have anything to hide," she said hotly.

"I'm advising you further that at any time you may
refuse to answer my questions or you may request counsel."

"Yes, I understand." Her tone was combative. Did that
surprise him a little? Well, he wasn't going to find her easy
to push around.

"All right, Miss Laurance. Tell me about yourself."

The apparently innocuous question surprised Annie. It
seemed irrelevant, but Saulter's tone of voice was deadly
earnest—and cold.

"What do you mean?"

"Where you're from. Your parents. Where you went to school. Why you came here last summer."

Once started, it was fairly easy. After all, she'd put together so many resumés these last few years.

"I was born in Amarillo. My mother was Claudia Bailey Laurance. She divorced my father when I was three. I don't remember him. She died of cancer when I was a freshman in college. I went to SMU, received a bachelor of fine arts degree in acting."

Saulter stolidly took notes.

"After college, I went to New York and tried to get work as an actress."

"You didn't succeed." It wasn't a question.

"I did all right."

"You came here because you were down on your luck." Saulter's bony face jutted forward.

"No. I came to visit my uncle, just as I had every summer since he retired and moved here twelve years ago from Fort Worth."

"You didn't have any money."

Okay, her bank balance was $35.21 when she arrived on Broward's Rock. "I had enough."

"You could stay for free at your uncle's."

"He didn't charge rent," she agreed sarcastically.

"He was your mother's only brother."

"You seem to know all about my family. Why are you asking me?"

Saulter studied her as if she were a particularly repugnant piece of flotsam.

"Suppose you tell me how you killed your uncle, Ms. Laurance."

Annie felt her shoulders press back against the hard ridges of the straight chair. There was a funny roaring in her ears, but she heard distinctly every word Saulter said.

"Ambrose Bailey was a good man." Saulter's voice changed. The chief had truly liked her uncle. But then who hadn't? Ambrose Bailey *was* a good man, a devoted friend, an implacable enemy, determined always to see justice done. That had been his reputation as a man and as a prosecuting attorney in Fort Worth. "A fine man. And you came down here and shoved him into the harbor so you could inherit his store. That's what happened, didn't it? Elliot

Morgan found out and threatened you—and we see what happens when anyone threatens your security. Morgan died. And you cleverly did it in a way to throw suspicion on all the people who came to your bookstore. But no one else there had a quarrel with Elliot Morgan. Only you."

"Uncle Ambrose—it was an accident."

"Is that what you claim? Is that what you're going to tell the jury? Did you see him fall, Ms. Laurance?"

"How dare you!" she exploded. She was on her feet, glaring furiously at Saulter. "He went out about nine. He was by himself. I guess he went to check on his boat since he was leaving town the next day." Poor Uncle Ambrose. He'd been looking forward to his trip, a combination of research and fun. He'd been so pleased that she'd come to visit and could look after the store. She'd watched the Johnny Carson show. It was almost midnight before she began to worry. "When he didn't come in—"

"You dialed McElroy. I guess you thought that would be a good way to have the body discovered."

"Nobody *killed* my uncle."

Saulter's thin face flushed, and he rose to loom over her. "Oh, yes, Miss Laurance, somebody killed Ambrose Bailey. I should have known it at the time. Last night, I rechecked that autopsy report. There was a small contusion behind his right ear. Maybe it happened in a fall, but now that two other people are dead, I don't believe it."

Annie watched him with sheer fury in her eyes and in her heart—but the words rang terrifyingly true. Uncle Ambrose knew boats, and he had been well that night, that last night.

"My God."

Saulter's mouth twisted. "A big surprise to you. Is that how you're going to play it? Maybe you should have stayed an actress, Miss Laurance. Well, you damn well can't do that over Doc Kearney. It's pretty clear why you had to get rid of her."

It was like standing in the shadow of an erupting volcano and watching tons of burning debris and roiling mud sweep down toward you.

"You didn't play that one too good. You told too many people how swell the doc was, how she didn't use succinylcholine to kill your cat. Too damn cruel. Wasn't it pretty cruel to watch Elliot Morgan suffocate?"

"A dart killed him," Annie said stubbornly.

"Sure thing. A dart with a wad of cotton that'd been dipped in Succostrin. That, little lady, is the trade name for succinyl-choline. And who on this goddamn island ever heard of the stuff until you went around blabbing about it?"

Annie felt a surge of adrenaline. Her body recognized danger. In a flash, she remembered the boarder in *Mrs. McGinty's Dead*. If it hadn't been for Poirot, the boarder would have been hanged for a murder he didn't commit. Circumstantial evidence could kill you. But she wasn't like that boarder. Saulter had a fighter on his hands this time.

"Maybe if you told me all about it, you would feel better. Why don't we start with your uncle's murder? Tell me how you did it, Miss Laurance."

Anybody with sense would keep her mouth shut. She knew it. But she absolutely throbbed with anger. This big-mouthed galoot wasn't going to sit there accusing her of murdering her uncle. By God, she was going to tell him in no uncertain terms exactly what—

"My client has nothing further to say."

Both she and the chief jerked around. Max stood in the open door of the storeroom.

Annie's mouth closed.

"Your client?" Saulter demanded.

Max nodded, and his eyes warned Annie to keep on keeping quiet. "She is entitled to the advice of counsel, and my advice is to say nothing more."

"She can talk, Mr. Darling, or she can come to the station."

Max didn't yield. "Ms. Laurance isn't going anywhere. Do you have a warrant for her arrest?"

Max loved Annie's eyes. Usually. He could get lost in her eyes, dark gray eyes with golden flecks. Sometimes they were as sensuous as a Rubens painting, and sometimes as laughter-filled as a picnic afternoon. But, right now, they glinted with fury and reminded him of bright flashes from target pistols.

"Cool it, sweetie. Never lose your temper. That's always an advantage to your opponent."

"I'm too mad to be careful."

"Honey, when you are dangling from a hair-thin lifeline over the side of a precipice, it's time to be careful." It worried him to see Annie so visibly angry. At all costs, she had to avoid provoking Saulter. He pushed down his own impulse to pound something hard with his fists, preferably the doltish face of a certain police chief. Dear Annie, his stubborn golden girl, with her sun-streaked hair, freckle-spattered cheeks, and prickly, independent, explosive nature.

"He's not going to get away with it." Then she jammed her hand through her hair. "My God, Max, somebody *did* kill Uncle Ambrose." Her face compressed into a stern frown. "And Saulter's pitched on me. That means we have to find out what really happened."

"Sure. We'll do it. But, Annie, don't hassle with Saulter."

"That man is not going to bully me."

"Of course not, but you keep your lips buttoned, Laurance. Okay?"

Diverted for a moment from the object of her ire, she said briskly, "Listen, it was great of you to try and help me. But I wouldn't suggest pretending to be a lawyer. You'll end up in jail."

"It would take Saulter a hell of a long time to do a fifty-state check to see whether I've passed the bar."

"But one phone call to the American Bar Association would take five minutes. Max, this isn't a laughing matter. Although, I'd bet he's a lot more interested in putting me in jail than in running checks on you."

"Right."

Anger glinted in her eyes.

Max could have kicked himself. If she got mad again—

"Look, our job now is to figure out what the hell's been going on before either of us ends up in jail. We need to check up on your uncle. Why would anybody murder him?"

The catamaran tilted a little, and Max adjusted the tiller.

Annie steadied herself. There was something nice about the delicately cut white swimsuit that emphasized the tawny richness of her skin.

Mmm. Mmm. Mmm. Max wanted to . . .

"Uncle Ambrose murdered— It's absurd!"

The catamaran lifted on the port hull. Spume rose over them like a gauzy curtain. They hung between sea and air, skimming the water like a hungry pelican, until Max moved the tiller, and the sail eased down.

Beads of water clung to Annie like seed pearls. Max knew just how it would feel to slide his hand gently over her soft skin.

"If somebody killed Uncle Ambrose, that same person killed Jill and Elliot—and Saulter's convinced I did all of it. So we've got to solve it ourselves." In her excitement, she scrambled up on her knees.

He shoved the tiller out of the way. The cat jerked, whipped, then started to tip.

Max reached out for Annie as they began to fall, and he felt her long, warm length against him. It was, he discovered, quite possible to choke on salt water and smile at the same time.

Nine

"**H**ow old were you here?" His finger rested on the black-and-white picture of a scrawny, pigtailed girl standing in front of a palmetto.

"Eleven. That was my first summer on Broward's Rock. See, here's Uncle Ambrose."

Oh, and she remembered that magical summer so well, the way the hot sand felt on her bare feet, how it smelled sitting on the end of a dock with her first pole in her hands, not expecting a thing to happen, the excitement when something yanked on her line, and her delight when Uncle Ambrose helped her haul out a toadfish.

The photograph of Annie and her toadfish was on the

next page. It had curled a little with time, but it clearly
showed the slimy brown, large-mouthed fish and Annie,
grinning through a filigree of braces.

"Mouthwise, you and that fish were neck and neck."

But she was looking at the pictures of Uncle Ambrose.
His hair was still a chestnut brown then, only lightly
touched with white. Uncle Ambrose, who taught her so
much more than how to cast a line or dig for clams.
Because she never knew her father, she felt shy and
uncomfortable around men until this gruff old curmudgeon
given to long silences took the time to spend his summer
days tramping the beaches with his niece and summer
evenings pointing out the constellations that glittered in
the southern sky like diamonds against black velvet.

"He made all the difference in my life," she said simply.
"When mother died, he helped me with school, and he
always made it clear I had a home with him."

She flipped to the last page of the album, then reached
out and gently touched the photograph of a distinguished-
looking elderly man standing on the deck of a sailboat, the
Sleuth. The aquiline face looked amused, skeptical, fiercely intelligent.

"A hell of a guy, huh? So why would anybody kill him?"

"He was a hell of a guy—to me, to his friends. But there
were people who would have feared him at one time.
Remember, he was a prosecuting attorney for years in Fort
Worth, and he hated crooks. He had a passion to catch
lawbreakers. He called them renegades, and he had no
pity for them. He said pity should be for victims, not
abusers."

"So somebody out of his past, somebody with a grudge,
comes to Broward's Rock twelve years after the guy retires
here and shoves him off of his sailboat?"

"I know, I know." Annie thumped a pillow in frustration.
"It doesn't make a lot of sense. But people can hold
grudges. Think about *The Count of Monte Cristo*."

"But he was the guy who'd been screwed. You're talking
about a crook wanting revenge for going to jail."

"*High Noon*."

"That wasn't twelve years later. No, it has to be something immediate, something urgent."

"Something here on Broward's Rock," she said thoughtfully.

Max closed the scrapbook. "You said he had a passion for justice. Right?"

Annie nodded emphatically.

"If he spent his life putting the baddies in jail, he'd find it hard to ignore it if he ran into something criminal on Broward's Rock." Max's shoulders hunched forward. He looked like an All-American tackle ready to spring.

She was concentrating on her uncle's life, trying to think, but she did take pleasure, purely aesthetic, of course, in the animal grace so close to her.

"Don't you see," he continued earnestly, "if Elliot could come up with stuff serious enough to get himself murdered, what're the odds your uncle had picked up on the same information?"

Annie clapped her hands to her head. "My God, true crime. That's it. That has to be it! Uncle Ambrose's book."

"He wrote books, too?"

"Not like the others. He'd been collecting material for years for a different kind of true-crime book. He was fascinated by the ones who got away, always on the look-out for accidents or suicides that might really have been murders."

"A shove down those attic stairs for dear old Grannie Whipple? Or over the cliff with Cousin Alice?"

"Or the side of a boat. Like Emma's husband—and, oh, Max, Uncle Ambrose himself!"

"Better wait until after dark," Max urged.

Annie disagreed. "I can't see in the dark. Besides, there are snakes and things. No, I'll pretend I'm out getting some exercise. I can see if anyone's lurking around. I'm going to go now."

"I'll come with you." He did look wonderfully like an anxious Mountie, stalwart and true.

"We don't have time. You do as we've planned. I can take care of this by myself."

"Dammit, I don't like it."

He continued to frown reprovingly as she rolled her bike out of the shed. She dropped the neatly folded towel in the white vinyl basket, then turned to beam at Max. She maintained the smile until she was out of sight, a

matter of riding six feet, then dipping down into an
aquamarine world. The late afternoon sunlight filtered
through the trees in a green and gold haze. The three-foot-
wide bicycle path wound through luxuriant swamp growth.
Live oak trees, pines, palmetto palms, and flowering shrubs
vied for life in the spongy, wet ground. Thick vines hung
from trees, wrapped around trunks, snaked along the
ground. As she pumped the old-fashioned bike, twigs
skittered from beneath the wheels, and her approach
disturbed the seen and unseen inhabitants of this peculiarly
private domain. A flock of blue-green tree swallows circled
noisily, looking for their last insect snacks before dusk.
Three sunning turtles slipped into dark green water. An
alligator raised his head.

Annie pedalled harder. It was eerily silent on the bicycle path. In the summer, families wobbled through the
damp heat, and daredevil ten-year-olds rode fast enough
to imperil anything in their way. But now, late on an
October afternoon, the sunlight already waning, it was
pleasantly warm but isolated.

She was pleased she had decided not to turn the disk
over to Saulter. There was no reason on earth to put the
innocent writers at risk. But Capt. Mac had made it clear
to Max that Saulter wasn't impressed by Elliot's threat to
reveal some nasty truths about his fellow writers. For the
chief, that was entirely too fancy a motive for Elliot's
murder. Instead, Saulter saw her as a killer driven by
purely financial fear. That was an understandable motive.
Money mattered. Saulter knew it, and Annie knew it.
Still, she thought, reputations mattered, too, especially to
the Sunday Night Regulars.

The disk. Annie's only hope was to load it, read the
information it contained, and, armed with this knowledge, face down each suspect. If she were lucky, it
might shed some light on what had happened to Uncle
Ambrose.

She and Max would discover the murderer before Chief
Saulter came to arrest her. Max was on the phone right
now, seeking information about the Sunday Night Regulars, seeking some lever to help them break through a
false face of innocence. Emma Clyde, Janis and Jeff Farley,
Harriet Edelman, Capt. Mac, Fritz Hemphill, Hal Douglas,

Kelly Rizzoli. One of them had a secret that must be kept— whatever the cost.

Annie braked and let the bike coast to a stop. Here the path curved, crossed over a short wooden span, then melded into the dusty gray road that led to Elliot's tree house. She dragged the bike down the short incline, keeping an eye out for snakes, and put the bike beneath the wooden bridge. Carrying the folded white towel, she climbed back to the path, and peered over the railing. Good. The bike wasn't visible.

She stopped in the shadows of a towering pine and stood there for at least five minutes, listening to the occasional honk of a frog, the slither of a woodland animal, the sibilant rustle as leaves slipped down through the green and gold air to land on the road and among the underbrush. It was so beautiful and peaceful on the island. It seemed impossible to believe two people had been murdered there. Three, if the chief were right about her uncle.

Even though Elliot hadn't been dead twenty-four hours, his tree house had already acquired a deserted air. The blinds were closed. There was a dusting of sand on the steps. Leaves bunched along the walk, already carpeted with pine needles. On Broward's Rock, the swamp didn't take long to reclaim its own.

Satisfied that she had his tree house to herself, she stepped briskly onto the road and walked swiftly, the gray dirt scuffing up beneath her tennis shoes. She stopped once and looked sharply around, nagged by an uneasy sense of being watched, but no one moved on the rutted, uneven road, so she hurried the last few yards to the steps and ran lightly up them, the towel in her hand. She tried the front door. Locked. She moved around the porch. She stopped at the kitchen window and pushed. It moved grudgingly, caught, then, after a hearty shove, screeched sharply and rocketed up.

Annie's heart thumped. She looked frantically around, but nothing disturbed the silence.

Knowing Tessa Crichton had never hesitated in search of clues, she balanced awkwardly on the sill, stepped into the sink, then jumped to the floor.

*   *   *

In Elliot Morgan's living room, a microphone taped to the underside of a chair picked up the sound of the opening window and Annie's arrival, recorded them, magnified them, and carried them to a receiver in another living room on Broward's Rock.

The occupant of that room was lifting a glass to drink, but the sounds halted the movement of the hand. So someone had come. That bastard Morgan must have been telling the truth: he had given a copy of that damned disk to someone.

Too much curiosity killed cats—and people.

Harriet Edelman wore baby blue jogging pants and a yellow t-shirt. She hadn't been jogging, but she was comfortably dressed for a long vigil on her widow's walk. She'd waited most of the day, eating her lunch here, carefully staying in the shadows, but always keeping her field glasses trained on Elliot's tree house. She'd been certain someone would come. It was too much of a coincidence for Elliot to be killed on the night he was going to reveal all the garbage he'd gathered about all of them. Somebody was bound to come searching for what Elliot knew.

Her thin mouth twisted. Served him right. Such a know-it-all, such a busybody. She smiled grimly. Not a busybody now. The smile turned to a grimace. To claim she'd stolen the plot to *Deadly Diamonds*. She hadn't even read the manuscript that idiot woman had sent her to critique. She'd mailed it back without looking at a single page. It was coincidence, that was all. Coincidence.

And let anybody try to prove differently.

But it could have been awkward, Elliot having an affidavit from that woman and threatening to send it to her publisher. Publishers were so antsy, scared of their shadows.

Shadows...My God, look who was here, creeping around the side of Elliot's porch, breaking in. If that wasn't the damnedest thing. She'd never expected it to be Annie. Not pretty-faced Annie Laurance, of all people. Why, she wasn't even a writer. What could Elliot possibly have known about her?

Harriet picked up her Minolta, removed the lens cover, and focused it. She snapped two pictures as Annie climbed in the kitchen window. That ought to be enough proof the girl was up to no good.

She could just envision the newspaper headlines: *Mystery Writer Solves Crime*. That ought to jack up her sales. Grimly, she trained the camera again on Elliot's tree house, took two more pictures, then lowered the camera and snatched up her binoculars to watch another familiar figure walk up the steps.

A dull flush suffused her face.

She was the one who had watched all day. By God, she was going to get the credit. Dropping the binoculars and the Minolta on the wooden seat, she hurried to the ladder. It would only take her a minute by bike path to get to Elliot's house.

The phone rang. Annie jumped three feet, her heart thudding. The phone rang and rang and rang.

Frozen in the doorway to the living room, Annie thought, *Lord, this room gives me the creeps!* The last shafts of sunlight glittered on Elliot's collection of steel drums. One entire pane of glass in the hexagonal room was covered by carnival masks—several shaped like bats, one of the Devil with horns, a tail and spear, another of a red-haired Viking. A massive painting of an old black man, his face fierce and threatening, rested against an easel. Papa Bois, the spirit of the forest. He protected animals, Elliot had told her. Any animal in his right mind would take one look at Papa Bois and head for the city. The furniture, blood-red leather chairs and ebony black tables, contributed to the aura of unhealthy darkness.

She steadied her heartbeat and tiptoed across the uncarpeted living room floor. From the evening she had dinner with Elliot, she remembered that his office was in the second bedroom. She was, obviously, alone. That phone call would have roused anyone. Moving with more confidence, she opened the door into the second bedroom. She didn't turn on the lights, though. No point in advertising her presence.

Elliot had worked on a table in front of the window. Again, the blinds were closed. Annie left them closed. The CPU, monitor and keyboard were neatly covered with a clear plastic hood. Annie removed the hood and sat down. She studied the set-up and found the on-off switch on the right side of the CPU toward the back. She turned it on. Red lights flashed on the keyboard, then green letters centered against the black screen: *Insert Disk-ette*.

Her hands were sweaty. "What do you expect," she scolded herself wryly, "for a first-time housebreaker?" She unfolded the towel and lifted out the disk. Slipping it out of its white jacket, she put it into the right-hand disk drive and pushed it in. The operating software was already in place in the left-hand drive.

The cursor flashed in the upper left corner, then green letters centered on the black screen: *Initial system checks satisfactory. Please wait for system to load*.

A clock ticked somewhere across the room. Outside, a sea gull shrilled. A dripping noise obtruded. Just a slow leak in the bathroom.

An odd, uneven creaking sounded behind her.

Annie jerked around.

A faint bar of sunlight edged into the bedroom.

Must be from the kitchen. Those window curtains were open. Dust motes swirled.

God, she was jumpy. There was no one here. She had an oppressive feeling of danger. But that was easy enough to understand. After all, she had broken into a dead man's house. If Saulter found her here, he'd carry her off to jail for sure. The sooner she looked at the disk and got out, the better.

The terminal hummed with on-screen commands: *Fonts loaded. Loading Valdocs system. Loading interrupt and background support modules*.

It was taking forever.

Finally, the message flashed: *Press any typing key to enter editor*.

Almost there. Only seconds away now.

As the document window appeared, Annie studied the keyboard. She pressed the index key.

The index listed all the files stored on the disk. This was pay dirt, all right.

There were eight files.

1. EMMA CLYDE	10/8:03
2. J/J FARLEY	10/8:01
3. HARRIET EDELMAN	10/9:02
4. FRITZ HEMPHILL	10/9:01
5. HAL DOUGLAS	10/9:02
6. CAPT. JOHN MCELROY	10/10:03
7. ANNIE LAURANCE	10/10:02
8. KELLY RIZZOLI	10/10:01

She studied the dates. Elliot was killed on Sunday the thirteenth, so he'd finished working on the files on Thursday. That figured. He must have dropped the disk into the mail to her on Friday for arrival Monday.

Should she take the files in order, beginning with Emma Clyde?

She pushed back a curl from her forehead. The tiny house was incredibly stuffy. She looked longingly at the air conditioner in the rear window. It wouldn't do any harm to turn it on. She reached over, switched it on, then turned back to the screen and punched the command to retrieve a file. The cursor blinked by Emma Clyde's name. Annie almost pushed return, then, remembering Elliot's taunt about all the information he had on Max, tapped the down arrow until the cursor blinked by her name. It would only take a second to see what Elliot had put in her file. She punched return.

Within seconds, the sentences began to form, fluorescent green against black.

Good grief, how did he know about that week in Santa Fe? He must have talked to Richard.

He had the goods, all right. When Elliot claimed that he could ferret out information, he wasn't kidding. Yes, here was the stuff on Max.

Her eyes widened. Well, for God's sake. Max had never told her . . .

The blow caught her completely unaware. A streak of fire flared on the side of her head, then nothing more.

Max groaned and massaged the back of his neck. He'd never before appreciated the fatigue associated with constant phoning. Somewhere in all of this jumble there had to be the one fact they needed. Figuring out which fact mattered, that was the rub.

Absently, he picked up his glass, finished the last of the Bud Light, and ignored its faint warmth. Time to organize.

He rolled paper expertly into Annie's portable Olivetti. He'd mastered a fast hunt-and-peck when he worked as a reporter one year. He typed quickly, and, when he was finished, he reread the compact bios, ignoring typos.

EMMA CLYDE—Doyenne of American mystery writers, author of 76 classic mysteries. Born Jan. 18, 1922, Billings, Mont. Graduated from Cincinnati · Heights School of Nursing, 1942, U.S. Army Nurses Corps, 1942–45, discharged as 1st lieutenant 1945. First mystery, *Murder in Casablanca* (1946). Married same year to Harold Caston, owner of several Memphis boat stores. They met on a troop transport returning to the U.S. from N. Africa. Surgical nurse, St. Jude's Hospital, Memphis, Tenn., 1945–1950. Five more mysteries published. Divorced from Caston, Aug. 13, 1950. No children. Moved to NYC as full-time writer. Active in Mystery Writers of America, serving three times as Chairman of Book Awards, recipient of two Edgars for Best Mystery of the Year, winner of Grand Master Award. Married June 8, 1982, to Enrique Morales, prop. Horizon Villas in Boca Raton, Fla. Purchased resort home on Broward's Rock, July 15, 1982. Morales drowned in boating accident fifteen months later. Morales and Emma returned after midnight that evening by motorboat to her yacht, *Marigold's Pleasure*. Morales decided to smoke a cigar by the stern. Emma went to bed. She discovered him missing the next morning, alerted authorities, and search began. Body was found floating 50 yards from the yacht. Coast Guard theory is that Morales became dizzy, lost his balance, fell overboard, and drowned because his heavy sweater became waterlogged and he was a poor swimmer. *Marigold's Pleasure* was anchored far out in the bay to avoid public notice, as Emma was often besieged by fans.

*   *   *

Emma Clyde. It might be fascinating to take a peek at the police report on Morales's death. Max rubbed his nose. Funny. She was apparently never known as Mrs. Morales. The bare bones suggested that Morales stopped running his resort (motel? vacation apartments?) as soon as he married and took up a cushy residence on Broward's Rock. Of course, his drowning might have nothing to do with the murders now. Emma's secret could go back as far as her days as a surgical nurse.

HAL DOUGLAS. Harold Clifton Douglas, born March 18, 1955, in Wiesbaden, W. Germany, son of career Army officer. Grew up on Army posts in Europe and the United States. BA from Washington University at St. Louis. Married to Lenora Harris 1978; writer with Hallmark Cards, Kansas City, 1976–79; publicist, Sierra Leone Films, Hollywood, Ca., 1980–82. First novel, *The San Bernardino Heist*, a 1983 best-seller. Bought home, Robber's Nest, on Broward's Rock, March 12, 1983.

Max frowned and reread the paragraph on Douglas. Annie had mentioned Douglas and Kelly Rizzoli as a twosome. So where was Lenora Harris Douglas?

HARRIET EDELMAN. Born July 5, 1948, Carlisle, Pa. BA from Penn State, 1969. Lived in Nice, France, 1969–75. Immediate success with Macintosh series, the first two, *Ride a Wave* and *Gentleman's Smile*, set in Nice. *Ride a Wave* Edgar winner for Best First Mystery. Contributor to *Armchair Detective*. Purchased a home on Broward's Rock in 1976.

Zero on weaselly-faced Harriet. The net hadn't fished up anything useful. But Annie'd mentioned that Harriet'd been mad as hell at Elliot, because he was hinting she'd cribbed somebody else's book.

JEFF and JANIS FARLEY—Jefferson Allen Farley, born Feb. 3, 1953, St. Louis, Mo. Foster child. Married Janis Corey 1970, BA in journalism University of Missouri, 1974. Collaborated on their first book, *Danny's*

Delight, in 1975, Jeff plotting and writing, Janis drawing the pen-and-ink illustrations. Jeff employed as a crime reporter on the *St. Louis Post-Dispatch*, 1974–1984. Purchased island home Sept. 22, 1984.

Janis Corey Farley, born April 11, 1955. Foster child. Married Jeff Farley 1970. Illustrator.

Jeff and Janis Farley. Could be volumes there. Both of them foster children and marriage at a sadly young age for Janis. It helped explain her utter dependence on that stiff. No schooling for her, but lots of talent with pen and paper.

FRITZ HEMPHILL—Born April 16, 1945, in Long Beach, Ca. Graduated from Long Beach City (Jr.) College, 1964; U.S. Army, pfc., 1964–66, Ft. Ord, Saigon, V.N.; BA, Loma Linda University, Loma Linda, Ca., 1968; LAPD, 1968–80, patrolman, sergeant, detective; married Doreen Norris 1968, divorced 1980. One child, Alice, now sixteen. First police procedural, *The Agony Chain*, published 1972. Third novel, *Kerrigan's Heart*, runaway best-seller, sixteen weeks on *The New York Times* best-seller list. Purchased Broward's Rock harbor condo Sept. 1, 1980.

Max wiggled his shoulders and stretched. Without losing his place, he rose and used peripheral vision to cross the living room to the kitchen, open the refrigerator, and pick out another Bud Light. This time he settled on the couch, feet propped on the rattan coffee table, took a double gulp, and continued to read.

JOHN MCELROY, police captain (ret.). Born April 24, 1930, in Ft. Walton, Fla. Attended Jacksonville University, 1948–50; OCS U.S. Marine Corps, 2nd. Lt., 1950–52, Camp LeJeune, La., Korea; Miami PD, 1952–60; Asst. chief, Silver City, Fla., 1960–80; capt., Silver City police, 1980–84. Married Thelma Farris 1954. Three children: John, age 30; Theodore, 28; and Michael, 26. Divorced 1962. Purchased home on Broward's Rock, July 20, 1984.

KELLY RIZZOLI. Born Aug. 26, 1959, Ft. Smith, Ark. Attended College of the Ozarks, 1977–78. BA in psychology, University of Arkansas, 1983. First novel, *The Shuttered Mind*, a paperback best-seller in 1983. *Sad Song* sold 55,000 in hardcover two months after 1984 publication. Bought Magpie Plantation on Broward's Rock in July 1984.

Max pulled a legal pad closer, sighed, and rubbed his face, then downed the rest of the tepid beer. Damn, he was getting hungry.

He looked up. For a moment, his tired eyes refused to focus, then they noted the open living room windows, the slatted, tropical blinds not yet closed for the night.

For the night...

Darkness had fallen. He looked at his watch, and an empty, sick feeling moved inside him. 7:15. Annie had left for the five-minute bike ride to Elliot's house a few minutes before six.

Where the hell was Annie?

Ten

Annie moaned. The sound came from her, but it seemed separate and far away. She tried to lift her head, and pain seared down into her shoulder. She moaned again and rolled her head. The pain caused her to cry out. She opened her eyes. And saw nothing. An instant of panic flared. Her heart thudded erratically, and she fought down the nausea.

Elliot's house. The disk.

She was lying on her back, her hands outstretched. Something heavy lay in one hand, her left hand. Something heavy and nastily sticky.

Unsteadily, Annie rolled on her side. She let go of the horrid thing, whatever it was, and propped herself up, then attempted to get up.

She stood and swayed as if the floor moved beneath her feet.

She was going to be sick.

Moving heavily, one hand clasped to her mouth, she reached the doorway. Elliot's tree house was built to the same pattern as hers, the only difference was his second bedroom. She turned left toward the bathroom, flicked on the light and made it just in time to heave violently into the toilet. Sick. Sick. Sick. Finally, clinging to the edge of the lavatory for support, she knew the sickness was past.

Breathing unevenly, she stared down into the basin.

Then she saw the reddish stickiness on her left hand. Slowly, she turned her hand, looked down at the palm, at the blood smeared across it. Blood streaked the whiteness of the lavatory where she had gripped it.

Blood.

Her head.

Annie looked up and saw her face in the mirror. A smeary face. Blurred vision. Clumsily, she moved her right hand up to her head, gingerly touching her scalp behind her right ear. The swelling felt spongy. But her fingers located no cut or fresh wet blood. She turned the spigots and thrust her hands under the cold rushing water, ridding them of the unpleasant stickiness, then patted water on her face. She used a pale yellow towel to dry her hands. It was pink where she had touched it.

Her head. Somebody hit her. That's what had happened to Jill Kearney. But Jill had a skull like an eggshell. Annie's head felt like hell, but it must be as thick as Max had always maintained it was. No blood. Where had the blood on her hand come from? Must have been a little cut, already dried.

Dried. God, how long had she been here? She'd better get—

The disk. She was reading the disk.

Annie moved like a drunken june bug, misjudging distance. Swaying unsteadily, she reached the hall, started up it toward Elliot's office.

She saw the blood first, spatters of it dark and ugly against the ridged bamboo wall. As if blood had sprayed upward, clots of it, then finer particles...

The head was shattered, unrecognizable. Blood and tissue were smeared across the back of the pale yellow t-shirt. One hand was outflung. Even in the dim light, Annie recognized the large red ruby ring that Harriet always wore.

Bludgeoned. That's what Harriet had said had happened to Jill Kearney. Harriet was wrong. Jill had been struck once. Harriet had been bludgeoned, the entire side of her skull was a pulpy mass—bone, tissue, blood, and hair indistinguishable.

Annie jolted around and again made it to the bathroom just in time.

Harriet dead. Why? Crazy, crazy... Saulter called it nutty when Elliot was killed. Elliot was dead, and Saulter suspected her of his death and of Uncle Ambrose's. Now here she was at the scene of another crime. Good luck, Annie Laurance. Who would believe she hadn't done it? Just like Pam Frye in *Octagon House*. But she didn't have Asey Mayo to save her. Then the fiery pain in her head gave a measure of relief. Her own head. That was it. Someone had struck both her and Harriet down.

Resolutely, Annie once again faced the hall. This had gone too far. This time she had to call Saulter. She moved sideways down the hall, like a reluctant crab. God, she couldn't get past Harriet, get past all that blood. Elliot's office. There would be an extension in there.

She stepped into the office and turned on the light. She was stumbling across the room, her hand outstretched to pick up the telephone when she saw the blackjack. Her shoulders hunched.

A blackjack. And then she knew. Someone had killed Harriet with that blackjack. There was blood on it and hair. The blackjack lay where she had been. Heavy. Blackjacks were heavy. The blood on her hand. She had awakened with the blackjack in her hand. Her fingerprints would be on it. She remembered what Capt. Mac told them, that Sunday evening. Leather holds fingerprints very well. Very well indeed.

Moving in a thick gray fog, the only reality the pounding

ache in her head and the thick crimson spatters on the bamboo wall, Annie returned to the bathroom. Her movements were slow and clumsy. She used the towel hanging on the rack and carefully scrubbed the toilet, the lavatory, and the light switch, pausing occasionally to retch.

What else had she touched there? Nothing.

She rubbed the walls in the hall, then went to the kitchen. She leaned out to wipe the window, the sill, and the area around the sink.

In Elliot's office, she took time to turn on the monitor. At first she was hopeful. There was a disk in the right-hand drive. It took only a moment to discover it was blank. It must have taken her attacker forty seconds to erase the files forever. Annie wiped the disk, the disk jacket, the side of the CPU, the keyboard, the chair.

Her head throbbed and furious tears burned in her eyes.

What else had she touched?

The doorframe, the floor where she had lain, the light switch.

Although nausea threatened again, she used one end of the towel to pick up the bloodied blackjack, and the other to wipe it clean. She bent down to pick up the towel she'd brought to cover the disk.

A thunderous knocking erupted at the front door.

Beneath the low-flung skirt of a pine, Max crouched. The whirling red light atop the police car threw scarlet flashes around the clearing and against the dark masses of foliage.

Max strained to see. Saulter thumped again on Elliot's door, then waved a hand behind him. Max lifted his head. Another man waited on the other side of the clearing, and Max understood. Saulter thought someone was in Elliot's tree house, and he intended to flush out the intruder for his deputy to grab.

From his vantage point, Max could see the deputy waiting near the police car, Chief Saulter at the top of the steps, and a slender form outlined against a window on the side of the tree house.

Saulter couldn't see Annie. But if the deputy turned his head, he would.

Max reached down, scooped up a large pine cone, and heaved it as hard as he could. It splatted against the back of the police car.

The deputy immediately dropped out of sight on the ground.

"Halt, or I'll shoot!"

Max smiled. That shout would forewarn Annie nicely. He scooped up five cones, nice solid ones, and, wriggling backwards, began to move toward the bike path he knew she would take.

The second and third cones landed on top of the tree house.

"Come out with your hands up," the deputy yelled frantically, and ran, crouching, toward the back of the house.

Max moved to intercept Annie, a slight silhouette momentarily limned by the flashing police light.

He hissed urgently, "Annie—this way."

She was moving oddly, a kind of drooping shamble. He caught her as she stumbled and fell.

A shower and a clean cotton nightgown helped. But best of all was the double whisky Max thrust in her numb hands.

"What if I have a concussion?"

"Best thing in the world for it."

It did ease the throbbing pain. But not even telling Max eased the horror of that evening.

Max looked as grim as she had ever seen him—and that was scary.

Annie rested against the bright cushions of the wicker divan, a patchwork quilt across her knees. She shivered, though her blue terrycloth beach robe was warm and soft. "He'll arrest me, won't he?"

"Hell, no."

It had a hollow ring. Max managed a smile. "Look, Annie, this is the truth. We were here all evening. We never left the place." His dark blue eyes narrowed in thought. "The phone rang once, maybe about six-thirty, but we didn't answer. We didn't give a damn about the phone. Come on, Annie, stop brooding about it. We've got to figure out how to solve this."

He handed her the notes he'd made from his calls while she was at Elliot's, then rolled up his sleeves and fixed ham sandwiches and brewed fresh coffee, black and strong. He brought her a tray, then plunked down in the easy chair next to her and fussily insisted she eat every bite as she read the bios. This wasn't her old, familiar, cavalier Max. There were dark shadows under his eyes, a stubble of beard on his chin. He stayed very close and occasionally reached out to touch her, but his voice remained crisp.

"All right. Let's go at it from the first—from the murderer's side."

"The murderer's side?"

"Sure. Let's figure out what the killer did when and why and fit that against the suspects. We know Elliot's murder was premeditated, of course."

"Because of Jill and the poison?"

"Right. The murderer needed to do several things. Get a dart, steal the poison, and set it up so the lights would go out at precisely the right time Sunday night."

Annie shot up straight, then winced. "Max, the murderer is a woman."

"Why?"

"Because the dart had to be carried into the store Sunday night. A woman could bring it in a purse, but there's no way for a man to get a four-inch dart in the store."

"No. I don't see it that way. That would be too risky. The dart would already have the wad of cotton soaked in succinyl-choline on the end. That would leave traces. No, I see it this way. The murderer got into the store sometime Saturday night or Sunday morning..."

"Sunday morning," Annie interrupted.

"What time?"

Annie figured for a moment. "About nine forty-five. I heard the cabinet slam, and that meant someone had closed the back door. I was all set to beat it out the front door, then I saw that Agatha wasn't upset, so I thought it was some other noise. That means that Agatha knows and likes the murderer."

"If Agatha could only talk."

Max grabbed a sheet of paper and scribbled out a timetable:

SUNDAY:

1 A.M.—Jill killed, poison stolen.

9:45 A.M.—Death On Demand entered, string tied to switches, dart hidden.

7:45 P.M.—During cocktail chatter, back door opened, storeroom door left ajar.

8:10—Lights out.

8:12—Dart thrown.

MONDAY:

6:10 P.M.—Annie knocked unconscious.

6:15 P.M.—Harriet murdered.

Annie took the sheet. It didn't help a hell of a lot, though Archie Goodwin would probably have deemed it a creditable effort. But Archie was awfully good-humored.

"How did the murderer get in?"

"How?"

"How? I had the place locked."

His face crinkled in thought. "Okay. Keys. Presumably the Island Hills Clinic doesn't leave its doors open for the world to enter, so the killer had keys there. It isn't hard to come up with keys, and there's nothing special about the locks at either place."

The idea that a killer could come and go in her shop at will wasn't exactly a cheering one.

"The killer came into my place about nine forty-five. The phone rang about ten minutes earlier, but I ignored it. Whoever called figured the place was empty."

"You wouldn't normally be there Sunday morning?"

"No. I was trying to decide what to do about the Sunday evening session."

"It would only take a couple of minutes," Max reconstructed. "Nip into the store, hide the dart on the floor by the wall, then tie thread to the breaker switches, and run that along the floor into the café area. Presto, the stage is set for a murder."

Annie couldn't help admiring the plan. "Whoever did it was damn smart. It was beautifully plotted. You know, I told Elliot those cigarettes would make him sick someday. And they really did, because the murderer counted on the red tip of his cigarette to serve as the target for the dart. Hell of a throw."

"Avoid talking about good throws," Max cautioned. "Let's hope Saulter doesn't dwell on your softball prowess."

"I skunked his pitiful team, eleven-zip."

"Poor planning." Max absently rubbed his bristly jaw. "Unlike our murderer. It all went like clockwork. During the confusion of the blackout, all he had to do was yank on the thread until it broke and reel it in. When the lights came on, he could drop it unobtrusively into the wastebasket, along with the cotton soaked in polish remover. Voilà: one corpse and nothing to link the murderer to the crime."

Annie pulled the quilt up to her shoulders. "I'll bet Dr. Thorndyke could have found some traces if he'd been there with his small green box."

"He didn't have to trifle with search warrants, *et al*."

"Lacking the good doctor's expertise, let's try to ratiocinate, like Sherlock Holmes. Okay, Dr. Watson, why was the back door open when I came to check the circuits?"

"Just a little bit of insurance. It would have been easy for the murderer to slip into the storeroom and open that door while everyone was squabbling over the coffee and snacks. That open door was to make sure Saulter considered the possibility of an outsider."

"But Saulter didn't look past me," Annie said bitterly, "much less outside."

"Well, you have to admit it was brilliantly thought out." He sighed and got up to pour himself a drink. "And we don't have an iota of proof to show Saulter."

Annie gingerly massaged her temples. If only her head didn't ache quite so much. Words jiggled in her mind: scraps, proof, papers . . .

"My God, Uncle Ambrose's book. Max, his *book*!"

"You told me about it," he said soothingly. "He was working on a book about accidents that just might have been murder."

Annie threw back the quilt, pulled herself to her feet, and wobbled, but her words came fast as shotgun pellets. "Don't you see? We said Elliot might have picked up on what Uncle Ambrose suspected. Well, somebody beat us

to the disk at Elliot's, but we can go through Uncle
Ambrose's papers!"

When Annie unlocked the front door and turned on the
lights at Death On Demand, Agatha rose, stretched leisurely, and focused two luminous, quizzical eyes on them.
Annie scooped up the cat from atop the bookcase and
rubbed her cheek against the ebony fur. "Who came in
Sunday morning, Agatha?"

But Agatha wriggled free and stalked down the center
aisle. It wasn't the proper time for Annie to be in the shop,
and her tail indicated her disdain for Annie's unprofession-
al hours.

Her nagging headache was forgotten. They were nearing
the end of their hunt. She felt almost lightheaded as she
led the way to the storeroom. The chalked outline was no
longer in front of the coffee bar. Dear Ingrid. She was
holding down the fort in every way.

"I gathered up most of his stuff and put it in the two
back cupboards," she chattered to Max. "There were
folders and photographs and news clippings, along with his
manuscript pages. I never had a chance to go through any
of it, I've been so busy with the store."

Max hauled out two huge cardboard boxes.

It took almost an hour to wade through it all.

When they were done, Annie stared soberly at the
heaps of materials. "Oh, Max, he *was* murdered. There
isn't a single page of his manuscript here. Not a page."

"Are you sure he had actually written any of it?"

"Of course I am. He never talked much about it, but he
worked on it at home in his den. He typed on an old
Smith Corona and used yellow second sheets for copy
paper."

"Are you sure the manuscript was in this stuff when you
packed it all away?" He waved his hand at the materials
spilled across the worktable.

"I'm sure." She looked grim-faced at the empty cartons.
"Some bloody thief took it out."

It could have happened at any time in the three months
since Uncle Ambrose died.

Without a great deal of hope, Annie went to the front desk and dialed Capt. Mac.

"The cases Ambrose was interested in?" Capt. Mac paused. "Let's see. There was the explosion in the Armbruster plant in Montana, killed Old Man Armbruster. Supposed to have been a labor dispute, but he had a worthless son who inherited six million. And Ambrose was suspicious of the Vinson suicide in Hawaii. You remember that one? And, of course, the Winningham case. That happened when I was at Silver City, but I was only assistant chief, and the chief played investigations pretty close to his chest, so I didn't know much that was helpful to Ambrose. That's all I remember. You know how close-mouthed your uncle was. A great one for letting the other fellow talk."

"Did he ever mention a case that involved anyone here on Broward's Rock?"

"Oh. I see where you're going. No, he didn't, and frankly I don't see any connection with the three cases I mentioned. That Armbruster heir lives in New York, and Mrs. Vinson's husband stayed in Hawaii. As for the Winningham case, everybody involved is dead. Cale Winningham went down in a plane crash not long after he 'accidentally' shot his wife. If Ambrose was onto something close to home, he never let on to me. Sorry, Annie. I wish to hell he had."

She walked down the central aisle back to the coffee bar, scuffing her feet in mounting disappointment. Max was making a diligent foot-by-foot survey of the entire store.

She called after him, "Capt. Mac doesn't know whether Uncle Ambrose was onto a lead here, but, dammit, I know it in my bones—it all goes back to him. I'll bet the store he found out something, and somebody pushed him off his boat to keep him from making his research trip."

Max was moving from table to table, then turning to sight where Elliot had stood. Annie looked at each table in turn, mentally placing the Sunday Night Regulars on the fateful evening. Elliot had been standing just there. Sure-ly, it should be possible to figure where the dart had come from its angle of entry. Dr. Thorndyke would have been able to do it. But not, apparently, Chief Saulter. Annie wasn't geometrically talented, but she gave it a try. She and Max and Ingrid were at the table nearest the storeroom, and the Farleys at the table opposite theirs. Capt. Mac and Fritz Hemphill had the table nearest to the watercolors on the west wall. Emma Clyde and Harriet sat next to the central corridor, and Kelly Rizzoli and Hal Douglas nearest to Elliot and the coffee bar. Of course, Elliot could have turned just the moment the dart was thrown. She gave up, and turned back to Uncle Ambrose. Had any of these people ever been involved in a case of accident or suicide that could have been murder? Annie recalled Max's typewritten notes, and Emma Clyde's name flashed in her mind like a six-foot neon sign.

She whooped and told Max.

"Yeah, that's a real possibility. Of course, there's the question of Hal Douglas's wife. Where is she? It's really too bad you didn't have a chance to read Elliot's disk."

"The killer's too smart for us. He must have destroyed my uncle's manuscript months ago, slick as a whistle. Now he's wiped out Elliot's disk. How the heck did he know I was at Elliot's house?"

"I don't know. If we knew that . . . Think back, Annie. Did you hear anything? Was there a noise or a smell, anything that might give some hint to the murderer's identity?"

"Nothing. I was sitting there, reading . . ."

Max looked at her sharply. "You actually started reading the disk? Did you find out anything?"

"I certainly did. Max, why didn't you ever tell me you had a law degree?"

For an instant, he looked absolutely blank, then he began to shake with laughter.

"Annie Laurance, for shame. There you are, inches from discovering a murderer's identity, and do you call up one of the suspect's files? No, you call up Annie Laurance's file."

She tried to brazen it out. "I thought it would take only a minute."

"It merely proves you are human, my love, succumbing to that feminine weakness for gossip before duty."

"I may be weak, but you are deceitful. And chauvinistic."

"Did I ever tell you I *didn't* have a law degree?"

"Max, be serious. Why didn't you say you did?"

"Oh, that was filed under miscellaneous information. You already know all the important things about me: I'm wondrously handsome and charming, sinfully rich, exquisitely perceptive, staunchly devoted to the intellect. I have three sisters and an enormous summer house on Long Island. I'm—"

"You are evading the issue. You are perfectly well qualified to practice law. You can have a *serious* career."

"I'll tell you what, Annie. After we find the maniacal killer who is rampaging across wee Broward's Rock, I will give every consideration to pursuing what you term a *serious* career."

"Do you mean it?"

"Of course. Now look, you called up the index, and decided to check out your own file. You didn't perchance look at anyone else's?"

"No. And when I came to, the disk had been erased."

"Rats." He scowled darkly. "You are looking at the screen, somebody comes up from behind and biffs you." Max paused. "Why did he—or she—just *biff* you?"

"That was the only Epson on the island, and anybody looking at the index would know I had only looked at my own file."

"How?"

"Every time a file is stored, the machine records the date."

A green expression flitted across his face. "Thank God for your curiosity."

Annie pondered it for a moment, then felt a little sick, too. "If I'd looked at the wrong file, read the killer's, then... It would have been like Harriet."

"Harriet must have walked in on the killer."

Thank God, indeed, for her curiosity. Then, as her head twinged, she felt a flash of her old temper. "By God, I don't like being slammed. Okay, so I didn't get to read the files. We'll still figure it out."

"You bet we will." Max pulled the typewritten bios out of his pocket. "Come on, let's get to work."

"What are we going to do?"

"Prep you."

"Prep me to do what?"

Max bent forward to tell her.

Eleven

Annie felt the arm on her shoulder, shaking, shaking. She blinked and struggled to turn her face away from the piercing light.

"Come on, Annie. Open your eyes. I have to check your pupils. My God, I think you do have a concussion. This is like trying to wake a South American tree sloth."

"Go away," she mumbled, thrashing out blindly. "You've checked every bloody hour on the hour all night long. Go away."

"One eye open. Just one."

Finally, miserably, she opened one eye, glared, closed it, and sank back on her pillow.

Annie breathed in deeply of the hot, swirling air in her shower.

"Need any help?" Max caroled just outside the shower door.

"I'll call if I do," she sang back sweetly.

"Always ready to help out my fellow man."

When she'd dried off with the thick, fluffy blue towel Max had thoughtfully draped over the wicker clothes hamper, Annie slipped into a yellow-and-blue patterned skirt and a soft yellow cotton pullover. She brushed her hair very carefully to avoid the swelling behind her right ear, wiped the steamed mirror and peered at her head. Well, she looked normal. No visible bumps or bruises. She probed the skin behind her ear and winced. It still smarted, but she couldn't help smiling as she listened to Max bustling cheerfully around the kitchen. When she came in, he waved her to a seat.

"Chef Darling at work. Observe and enjoy, Madame."

Potatoes and onions sizzled invitingly in the skillet, and Max whipped the eggs to a froth.

"One exquisite frittata coming up."

They carried their plates to the wooden-planked table on the balcony outside the kitchen.

As Max poured the coffee, he stooped to kiss the top of her head. "Just a preview of *one* of the myriad pleasures of connubial life."

"Oh, Max, why aren't you willing to invest this kind of effort and energy into a job?"

His coffee cup paused midway to his mouth. His eyes widened. "What an obscene thought."

"I'll have you know I'm serious."

"I know. That is both your great charm and your great failing, my sweet. You are very serious." He sighed. "Annie, don't you believe in fairy godmothers?"

"Not really. I believe in hard work and devotion to duty."

He sighed lugubriously and tried again. "Annie, what if I—or your fairy godmother—slipped a freighter ticket to Singapore under that four-leaf clover? Couldn't you take it and run away with me?"

"No."

"Why not?"

"I wouldn't have earned it."

"Look. Think about it this way. You know the guy who won thirty million dollars in the New York raffle?"

"What about him?"

"Is it immoral for him to accept his winnings from a raffle?"

"Well, no, I guess not."

"Annie, look on me as a great, big, loving raffle ticket!"

She was fashioning a withering retort when the police car pulled up in front of the tree house. She slowly put down her coffee cup.

"Remember, we were here all night," Max said calmly.

Chief Saulter walked heavily up the steps. He looked tired, and Annie wondered if he had been up most of the night. She rose to meet him.

The police chief looked at her intently, then past her at Max.

"We're having breakfast," she offered.

"I want an account of your movements last night."

"My client has nothing to say, Chief Saulter."

"Innocent people don't need that kind of advice."

"Innocent people need the protection of angels, Chief Saulter."

Annie and the chief both looked at Max in amazement.

He smiled fatuously. "Did I understand you to ask for Miss Laurance's movements last night?"

"That is correct."

"Then I can tell you very simply. She was here. I was here. We were here all evening." He couldn't have been more insouciant ice skating at Rockefeller Plaza.

"All night?"

"Most of it. We went to the bookstore for a few minutes about eight. Why?"

"Any phone calls? Anybody come by to visit?"

"One phone call. We didn't answer it. Nobody came by. Why the questions about last night, Chief?"

The chief's chilly eyes turned to Annie, who was pretending to nibble on her toast. "You know Harriet Edelman well?"

"Moderately," Annie answered pleasantly. She repressed an image of the bloodied mess she'd last seen in Elliot's living room. "I had an autograph party for her a couple of weeks ago."

"She was murdered last night."

"Oh my God . . ."

"Where? What happened? Do you know who did it?"

"She was found in the living room."

Annie saw the trap, and skirted it. "She lived alone. Who found her?"

"It didn't happen at her house." The chief spoke grudgingly, his suspicious eyes intent on Annie's face.

"Where?" Max asked dutifully.

"At Elliot Morgan's house."

"Good grief," Annie exclaimed, "what in the world was she doing there?"

The Porsche jolted up a sandy track. "At least he didn't arrest me. Max, did you get rid of that towel?"

"That towel is well-wrapped around a heavy rock and resting at the bottom of a lagoon on the opposite side of the island. Even if it floated up, there's nothing to connect it to you."

"Right. But I wonder if my bike tires left a track under the bridge."

"Anybody could have used your bike. The shed is never locked."

She glanced at him grimly. "Is that counsel's argument for the accused?"

"We are going to make sure somebody else stands in the dock."

That sounded like a swell idea to her. This morning she intended to ask a hell of a lot of uncomfortable questions in her search for the real killer. Philip Marlowe, look out.

The red Porsche curved through the twelve-foot-tall bronze gates of the Island Hills Golf Course. The crack of a cleanly hit ball carried through the fresh morning air. Annie thought regretfully of her own clubs and wished she and Max could be walking down the broad wooden steps at the Club to the first tee. Max, of course, was a scratch golfer. A club tournament tennis player. An expert scuba diver. A fixed-wing pilot. Talk about a misspent youth!

"Nice," he commented laconically as they drove past one imaginative home after another: a modernistic two-story gray house built on four levels, the highest flat-roofed and topped by a deck; a modern version of an antebellum mansion, with slender Doric columns supporting two verandahs; a California Mission stucco in the palest of pinks. "My God—"

Annie laughed. "This is the one that drives the local homeowners crazy, but it's the natural outgrowth of not being able to have your cake and eat it, too. The zoning laws here are very particular about how many square feet, maximum height, things like that. But the local board very proudly fixed it so that there could be 'imaginative variety with artistic integrity.' They said they didn't want everything to look alike like Hilton Head, where all homes are built of wood and weathered to a natural gray."

The Porsche crept to a halt as Max craned for a better view. It was a two, no, three, could it be four stories? The building materials alternated between chrome, bronze, and quartz. Rooms thrust out at eccentric angles, and the whole was topped with a thirty-foot round tower of gleaming aluminum.

"I'd like to meet that owner," Max breathed.

"So would everybody else. It was built by Marguerite Dumaney."

He whistled softly. The aging Hollywood star's name was legendary. Checkout counter tabloids had whispered in recent years that she was a female Howard Hughes.

The Porsche moved ahead, curved around a bend, and arrived at the entrance to 603 Cormorant Road.

This home was, quite simply, lovely. Perfectly suited to the landscape, it was constructed of the unassuming native pine, softly weathered to a dusky gray. But it still had an unmistakable aura of elegance. The three-story entryway had a glass panel running from ground level to the roof beside the nine-foot front door. Beautifully tended beds of white-topped asters, tall goldenrod, and camphorweed fronted the path.

As she got out, Max gave her a thumbs-up. Then he called after her, "Remember—keep at least two feet from each subject, don't hesitate to use the mace, and make sure they know I'm waiting."

Emma Clyde wore a pink-and-white seersucker skirt and blouse and looked like summer candy. She was surprised to see Annie but gracious. Her lips, carefully painted a bright coral, parted in a smile, but the smile didn't reach her cornflower blue eyes.

"How nice of you to drop by, dear." A pause. "You know, I do write in the mornings."

They stood in the main entryway. The green and gilt terrazzo floor glinted in the flood of morning sunshine through the roof-high glass pane. Water fell musically from a corner fountain, artfully constructed to look like a miniature Hawaiian waterfall. Sprays of orchids filled crimson-and-gold Chinese vases. Annie remembered reading about Emma's prize collection of orchids. Shades of Nero Wolfe.

"I'm sorry to intrude, but I had to see you."

It was like being a kid and going up to the top of a slide that rivaled the Empire State Building. She felt that same mixture of utter exhilaration laced with fear. Was this how The Saint felt when he began an exploit?

"You *had* to see me?"

"You see, I really don't know what to do," Annie began.

Emma waited, blue eyes alert and calculating.

"Elliot sent me the material he was going to use Sunday night."

Emma continued to wait. She might look like summer candy, but she emanated an unyielding, icy solidity. The entryway had seemed warm and sunny when Annie first began. Now she felt as if she'd stepped into a deep freezer.

"I don't know what to do about it."

"Why ask me?"

"Some of the information concerns you." Did she intend to stand there like a sphinx all morning? Damn the woman, why didn't she react?

Emma's face looked like a mud mask in a beauty salon.

One more try. "Look, Emma, I don't want to go to the police with this. I thought if you could explain it to me, I wouldn't reveal the information about you. After all, surely what Elliot wrote can't be true."

"Of course, it isn't true," Emma responded. "The Coast Guard ruled it was an accidental drowning."

So that was it, the death of her second husband. What was it Max had picked up from the man who ran the bait shop? Rumor had it that Enrique Morales was secretly meeting a Cuban girl.

"Did the Coast Guard know about the Cuban girl?"

If it seemed chilly before, the atmosphere dropped to glacial in the elegant foyer. The soft splash of the waterfall was the only sound for a long moment.

Emma asked harshly, "How much do you want?"

"Want? Oh no, Emma, I don't want money. I'm just trying to understand what happened."

"It's all in the Coast Guard report." Emma's voice was clipped. "Ricky and I had a few drinks after dinner at the Sans Souci Club. When we came back to the boat, he said he wanted to stay on deck for some fresh air. I went below to bed."

"You didn't hear anything? A splash? A cry for help?"

"As I said, we'd had a few drinks, and I'd worked hard that day. I was tired. I fell asleep immediately, and I didn't realize anything was wrong until the steward brought my breakfast. I asked him to call Ricky for me, and he came back and said his cabin hadn't been slept in."

So they didn't share a cabin.

Emma had asked the steward to call her husband. Why didn't she call him? Was it because the very rich avoid all possible exertion? Or was it that she knew his cabin would be empty and wanted to get the search under way?

"Why did you want to talk to him so early in the morning?"

For just an instant, that smooth mask shifted. No one had ever asked her that question.

Annie knew then, just as surely as if she'd seen it happen, that Emma Clyde came up behind her non-swimmer husband on the early morning of Sunday, October 16, and pushed him over the low railing to drown.

"I wanted to talk to him about some investments."

On Sunday morning?

Her immediate assumption that Annie had blackmail in mind seemed to indicate she was accustomed to blackmail. But Elliot must have had more than suspicion if he were blackmailing Emma: Blackmail had to be based on more than speculation. There had to be a threat, something concrete Elliot had learned that could cause the investigation to be reopened, perhaps lead to a murder charge against Emma.

"The steward must not have been aboard that night."

"That's right."

"Did he normally have Saturday evenings off? What about the rest of the crew?"

"Only the steward and the cook remain aboard when we are anchored. I'd given them the evening off because Ricky and I had plans on shore."

"But the steward didn't go ashore, did he?" Here was

Elliot's source, the steward or the cook. Someone heard cries or saw Ricky and Emma on deck together. Elliot had found a witness to the murder of Enrique Morales.

Emma didn't change expression, but there was a sudden relaxation of tension. Annie's question must have revealed that she didn't possess the critical piece of information.

"It's always heartbreaking when such a dreadful accident occurs. Isn't it, dear?"

Those shrewd blue eyes dissected Annie now, probing, weighing.

The silence between them was ugly, freighted with unspoken meanings.

"I'm sure you know exactly how I feel. And how upsetting it is to be the subject of vicious gossip. You, of all people, should understand that."

It couldn't have been plainer if she'd shouted it. Emma saw a special kinship between them. Emma believed that she had pushed Ambrose Bailey to his death.

Annie clenched her hands. "Does everybody think I killed my uncle?"

"Hell, no. That's just her guilty conscience in action."

"She meant that everyone was talking about me." Annie felt as if something slimy had touched her. She had been so happy on Broward's Rock, confident of her place in her own version of St. Mary Mead. Instead, smiling faces hid ugly suspicions. The reality was a Ruth Rendell world.

As the Porsche ran beneath the interlocking branches of the yellow pines, Max reached over and squeezed her hands. "Don't let an old battle-axe upset you."

"I thought I had a lot of friends on Broward's Rock."

"You do. Lots."

Annie recalled the sensation seekers at the shop yesterday, and Chief Saulter. "Who?"

Max scrambled. "Ingrid Jones. And Ben Parotti. And Capt. Mac. Me. Look at it. Your very own four musketeers."

She knew who pictured himself as D'Artagnan. She managed a bleak smile.

"That's a girl. Don't let the bastards get you down. Come on, you're one up, not Emma Clyde. You got a lot out of her, and what you got is damn interesting."

She twisted in the seat. "Max, this changes everything. Elliot must have been a blackmailer."

The Porsche slowed for a stop sign, and Max turned back onto the main road. He glanced at his map and drove past the harbor shops off to the right, then followed the curve of the island to a sign pointing to beach houses. He turned right on Blue Magnolia. As he braked, he said abruptly, "No, that can't be right."

"Why not? I'd bet my first edition of *The Murder of Roger Ackroyd* that Emma's been blackmailed."

"What's the point of blackmail?"

"You pay to keep someone quiet."

"Right. But Elliot was going to stand up and reveal all to the world—or at least to the Regulars."

Annie got out of the car slowly. Then she poked her head back inside. "Maybe this was Elliot's fancy way of putting on the pressure for a bigger payoff."

She mulled that over as she walked up the oyster-shell path, then she brought herself in hand. She'd better play this next interview better than the last.

A battered station wagon stood in the drive. The zinnias in the front bed were choked with weeds and the weeping willow beside the porch desperately needed a trim. Yesterday's newspaper rested unopened next to an empty bait bucket, which still smelled like chopped squid.

Her reception this time was warm if puzzled. Chunky Hal Douglas, unshaven, wearing a soiled t-shirt and torn tennis shorts, offered coffee, beer, or a drink. Unlike Emma's elegant home, Hal's was furnished with happenstance furniture, a shabby maple sofa, mismatched easy chairs, and a card table in one corner stacked with old magazines, *Geo*, *Esquire*, *Playboy*, and *Omni*. He tried frantically to straighten the litter as he led her to the den, sweeping a pile of newspapers onto the floor and grabbing up a damp beach towel, tennis shoes, and a racquet.

He was boyishly friendly, and she hated going into her spiel. What a way to kill a friendship. How do investigative reporters manage? The thrill of power had to outweigh the human need for approbation. A trade-off.

Annie took a deep breath. She'd be as forthright as Dagliesh. "No, Hal, thanks. Nothing for me. Actually, I hate to be here."

That was true.

His round face compressed into a worried frown. "What's wrong? Can I help you? Is that cop bothering you?"

"That's the problem. And the thing is, I've got some information that could get him off my back, but I *hate* to give it to him."

"Don't hesitate, Annie. You can't protect anyone in a murder investigation."

Every kind word he uttered made her feel more like a louse. Another word and she would turn tail and run, but if she didn't see it through, she'd find herself in the island jail with the centipedes and roaches.

Annie blurted, "Elliot mailed a copy of his talk to me."

Hal's open face abruptly looked a good deal less pleasant.

"I don't want to tell Saulter the stuff about you. I thought maybe you could explain it away and then I won't have to."

For the first time, she realized how big a man he was—tall, powerfully put together, with bearlike shoulders and arms. He was maybe twenty pounds overweight, which gave his face disarming roundness. He might be soft, but he was clearly strong. She slipped a hand into the pocket of her skirt and gripped the oblong, two-inch container of mace.

"I don't want Kelly to know." He lifted those massive hands and rubbed his bristly jowls.

"I can understand that," she murmured.

Hal lifted his head, his eyes intent. "Does anyone else know?"

Careful, Annie.

"Just Max."

He whirled around, stepped toward the mantel. One hand swept out, knocking off a half dozen books. When he turned back to face her, he was breathing heavily.

She braced herself. If he took one step toward her, she'd pull out the mace. Surreptitiously, she flicked off the safety guard.

"Goddammit." Hal spoke jerkily. "She left town. That's all there was to it. Lenora left town."

"People said you'd been fighting."

His head wobbled on its thick neck. He no longer looked like everybody's nice guy. He looked like a fighter who'd taken one punch too many. "Elliot got that wrong, the sorry bastard. There wasn't anybody to see. We were at the cabin in the mountains. No neighbors for miles, but she'd been into town a lot, picked up guys, like she always did. I went fishing, and, when I came back, she was gone. No note. Nothing. Some bastard came by and got her."

There was nothing good-humored about that pudgy face now. It was twisted with remembered pain and hatred.

"You say Lenora went away. Surely you've heard from her since then?"

Hal smoothed out his face, evened his breathing. "No reason for her to get in touch. I'd told her, one more man and we were through. One more and that was it."

"Where was the cabin?"

"Near Tahoe." He moved restlessly, rubbed his hands against his thighs.

"Have you ever told Kelly any of this?"

"I don't want Kelly to know." There was a plea in his eyes. "And it doesn't matter, not for the two of us. I got a divorce in Tijuana. I'm all finished with Lenora."

"Where did you meet Lenora, Hal?"

"What the hell difference does it make?" Hearing the edge in his voice, he said, "In St. Louis. At school. But what difference does it make? It's all over with her." He forced an ineffective smile. "Annie, this was all no big deal. And it's been over for ages."

"Sure, Hal. I just wanted to hear it from you, not the way Elliot had written it."

Hal's eyes bored into hers. "What did he say about Lenora?"

"That nobody's seen her in years."

It was quiet for a long moment. Annie could hear his breathing, see the pulse pounding in his throat.

"Hell, Lenora's having a ball somewhere. Like she always did." But his eyes were so empty.

"Sure," Annie said again. "Sure."

As she walked down the path toward the Porsche, Annie wondered how hard it had been to dig a grave miles from that lonely cabin.

*   *   *

They took the container of Kentucky Fried Chicken to the beach. Max looked suspiciously at each piece as Annie emptied the barrel onto a paper plate.

"Perhaps we aren't compatible," he mourned, setting up camp chairs from the Porsche's trunk. Trickling sand through her fingers, Annie thought of Mary Roberts Rinehart and a trip she had made in 1925 into the desert near Cairo. At night her party rested in tents decorated with scenes from tombs. Oriental rugs covered the sand in their dining and bedroom tents. Dinner included soup, appetizer, roast with vegetables, salad with quail and dessert. Then fruit, Turkish coffee and candy. Gourmet picnicking. Max would have fit right in.

"I love Quarterpounders, too."

He winced.

Annie bit into the lushly crusted half-thigh, half-breast while Max turned an oddly shaped piece around uncertainly.

"Was this chicken double-jointed?"

"It provides variety—and surprise," Annie retorted, mouth full.

With an air of incalculable bravery, Max began to eat.

By meal's end, they had admitted to irreconcilable culinary tastes.

Max liked sushi.

Annie adored fried pies. Peach, not cherry.

Max admired nouvelle cuisine.

Annie was passionate about Texas chili.

Max detested pretzels.

Annie loathed quiche.

Then they walked, hand in hand, up the beach, stopping to look at sandpipers' tracks, turning over a shell-encrusted piece of driftwood and skirting the tendrils of a Portuguese man-of-war.

It was great fun, but it couldn't last.

Already Annie was looking ahead. "Time to get back to the fray," she said brightly. "Sherlock Annie continues in relentless pursuit of wrongdoers." Her voice was lighter than her mood. It was a good deal more fun to read about bearding suspects in their lairs than to track them down.

"That's a girl. And, remember, I'll be there, if you need me."

Just like Tommy and Tuppence.
Sort of.

Twelve

Jeff Farley stood unsmiling on the porch. The two-story, weathered wooden house on pilings overlooked a dune bright with October color, the pale violet of butterfly peas and the shimmering gold of camphorweed. Beyond the dune, the beach stretched two hundred peaceful yards to the ocean. No other dwelling was within view. Annie stood halfway up the wooden steps, clinging to the railing, and the wind off the ocean touched her with the light fresh scent of salt. This was a choice beachfront exposure on a perfect autumn day, yet there was a sense of darkness and isolation here. Did it come from the almost feral gleam in Jeff Farley's light brown eyes? He didn't look much like an overage cheerleader now, though he wore white duck pants and a white knit V-neck pullover with navy trim. He stood rigidly, his arms tight against his sides.

"I need to talk to you, Jeff." Annie raised her voice against the rumble of the surf.

"We're busy." His voice was flat and hostile. He was turning away to close the door on her.

"Then you want me to give Elliot's information to Chief Saulter?"

Jeff stiffened, then jerked around to face her. He lunged toward the ladder.

"What the hell are you talking about?"

"Look, Jeff, I've come out here to give you and Janis a chance to explain. If you can't or won't, I don't have any choice but to go to Saulter. You must see that."

The screen door behind Jeff burst open, and Janis rushed to the railing.

Annie's eyes widened. The right side of the girl's face was painfully swollen. A reddish-purple bruise spread from cheekbone to jawline, hideously distinct against her pallid skin.

Jeff glanced distractedly toward his wife. "Get back inside."

Janis looked at him fearfully, but she took one step, another, then ran to the edge of the stairs. "Oh, Annie, please don't tell. He can't help it. He doesn't mean it, it just happens sometimes. He gets so mad, and that's what they did to him when he was a little boy. That and worse. They burned him—"

Jeff caught her from behind and whirled her around. The back of his hand hit her face with a stinging slap.

Janis screamed as the blow struck that inflamed skin.

Annie yelled, "Stop that! Stop it!" Pulling the mace out of her pocket, she charged up the porch steps.

He was using his fists now, raining blows on Janis's bent back as she huddled against the wall of the beach house.

A stream of spray from the mace container caught the side of Jeff's face. He staggered back, his hands clawing at his face. A spasm of coughing and choking convulsed his body.

Janis, blood trickling from her mouth, turned toward Annie, arms flailing, and lunged vengefully at her, screaming incoherent curses as she rained blows on her astonished protectress. Max shot up the steps and caught Janis by the arms, imprisoning her.

"It's just mace. He'll be all right. My God, Janis, I had to stop him. He was hurting you!"

"He didn't mean it. You've got to understand. He doesn't mean to hurt me. He loves me," she whimpered brokenly. "You can't know what he's endured—"

"Did Jeff threaten Elliot when he knew Elliot was going to tell everyone?"

"That wouldn't matter," Janis said desperately. "It doesn't matter what he said—or what he does to me. Jeff wouldn't kill anyone. That's crazy. He wouldn't kill Elliot—or Jill or Harriet. Never."

"But he beats you," Annie said wearily.

"He doesn't mean it." Janis held out trembling hands. "Please, please don't tell anyone. If you do—"

"Shut up, Janis. Don't be a bloody fool." Jeff's face was mottled with rage and pain.

"Janis, don't stay here with him. Come with us. You can stay with me," Annie offered.

Janis wiped the blood away from her chin. Her eyes filled with tears, but she shook her head. She wouldn't come with them no matter how they protested.

"You'll have to get him to a doctor," Annie said urgently, "or one of these days, he will kill you."

But Janis wouldn't leave him.

"We'll have to tell Saulter," Max said grimly as they drove back to the main part of the island.

"If it gets in the papers, they'll be finished."

"Finished? What do you mean?"

"As writers."

"What does wife beating have to do with writing?"

"Probably not much—except in their case. They write for children. Do you think a children's publisher is going to keep an author who regularly bloodies his wife? Think again, Mr. Darling."

"Oh. So they have a hell of a motive. Both of them."

"Not her. She can't do anything without him."

"May I remind you that she was ready to tear your eyes out when she thought he was threatened. What do you think she would do to somebody like Elliot who was going to spread all this out for the enlightenment of the Sunday Night Regulars?"

"Punch him. At the least. Still, I can't believe Janis would have the gumption to figure out such a clever plan. But Jeff could—and she'd never give him away."

As the Porsche zoomed away from the beach house, Annie said tightly, "You know, I'd almost give Elliot's murderer a gold star—if it weren't for Jill and Harriet and Uncle Ambrose."

They were soon arguing over their next stop, Max plumping for Kelly Rizzoli, Annie preferring Capt. Mac, when a siren shrilled behind them.

Max pulled over. "Thirty miles an hour. I swear, I was going thirty miles an hour."

But Broward's Rock's only motorcycle cop was having a Mannix day. He wasn't thinking speed limits.

He dismounted and leaned down to look past Max. "Chief Saulter wants to see you, Miss."

Chief Saulter didn't want Max there, but Max wouldn't budge.

"You can talk to my client only if I am present, Chief." Max folded his hands across his chest and looked immovable.

"I can put your client in jail, Counselor."

"What charge?"

"How about first-degree murder?"

"I'll have her out on bail in two hours. You don't have a scrap of evidence."

The police chief clenched his jaws and built a teepee with his fingers. With a wrenching effort, he tried conciliation.

"Ms. Laurance, I just want some cooperation out of you. If you didn't kill the vet and Morgan and Edelman and your uncle, you should want to help the authorities."

"Four people. You honestly think I killed four people!"

"Somebody did, and you profit, young lady. You profit."

"Actually, Chief, Ms. Laurance doesn't have a financial motive." Miraculously, Max sounded casual and good-humored.

"Sure she does." Saulter ticked it off on his fingers. "She's broke. She inherits her uncle's estate, including the bookshop—and you know how she feels about that bookshop. Goodbye, Uncle. The rest of them are protection. Somehow Morgan figures out she shoved Ambrose into the drink and that spelled finish for him. Plus Morgan is threatening to run her out of business with a rent she couldn't pay. The vet is knocked off to get the medicine, and that damn Edelman busybody poked her nose into a buzz saw."

Max ran a hand through his hair and shook his head placidly. "Nope. You're off base. See, if Annie wants money—or needs money—all she has to do is marry me." His dark eyes glinted. "And, after all, Chief, that's a lot easier than going around slugging, darting, and bludgeoning —and guaranteed to be more fun."

Saulter opened his mouth, and Annie knew he intended to ask tartly just how much money Max had. As his eyes moved from Max to the window with the red Porsche in view, he abruptly closed his mouth.

"I intend neither to kill for money—nor marry for

money," Annie said acidly. Her counselor was finding this altogether too amusing for her taste.

"You never told anybody here on Broward's Rock about this fellow?"

"No, but—"

"Annie, tell the man truly. Could you marry me anytime you want to?"

"Yes, but—"

"So no motive." Resting his case, Max lifted his hands, palms upward. Annie glared.

"If you two can direct your minds back to the murders, and away from me, we might get somewhere. Chief, we believe the same person who killed Elliot murdered my uncle. Somebody has stolen his manuscript."

Saulter stiffened like a dog on point. "His book about the murderers who got away with it?"

For the first time since the lights went out in Death On Demand, Annie felt a glimmer of hope. Saulter knew about Uncle Ambrose's book. Surely he would understand the implications of a missing manuscript. She longed irrationally to present him with a copy of *The Bay Psalm Murder*.

"Exactly. Max and I figure that he found out about a crime involving somebody here on the island and—"

"Naw. I'd talked to Ambrose about his murders. He was interested in the Armbruster case." Saulter's forehead wrinkled. "And the Vinson suicide, so-called. And he mentioned the Winningham thing." The sudden flash of interest in those agate eyes faded. "None of that has a thing to do with anybody here. That's a false trail."

"The manuscript is missing."

"Sure." He might as well have said, "Good try."

"Look, Chief, you aren't going to pin this on me. If you won't help, I guess Max and I will have to find the murderer by ourselves. But you can at least listen to what we've discovered—"

Max was semaphoring messages with his eyebrows, but she was too angry to pay any attention.

"To begin with, Emma Clyde, Hal Douglas, and Jeff and Janis Farley all had terrific motives to get rid of Elliot."

"Is that so?" Saulter's tone wasn't encouraging, and Annie knew he was thinking in particular of Emma Clyde's considerable wealth and power. A leading citizen like

Emma could do a lot to influence next year's elections.

"That *is* so. Emma Clyde killed her second husband. She pushed him off her boat and let him drown. And Hal Douglas killed hs wife and buried her in the mountains in California, and—"

"Young lady!" Saulter boomed.

"Annie, my God!" Max cried.

She raised her voice resolutely: "And Jeff Farley beats his wife."

Saulter's palm thumped on his desk and the in-box slewed sideways. In the silence that followed, he scrutinized Annie with chilly contempt.

"Just how do you know all this, Ms. Laurance?"

Abruptly, Annie understood Max's semaphore. Oh, what an incredibly appropriate word "dumbstruck" is. She stared at Saulter. She wished she'd been born a deaf-mute. No, look what happened in *The Spiral Staircase*.

"Come now, Ms. Laurance, you're helping us quite a lot. But how do you know this?"

Annie picked words as carefully as footfalls on a canyon ledge.

"I keep telling you. Elliot Morgan had his big scene all planned, and everyone knew it was coming. Sunday night he was going to tell about a lot of very unpleasant things that people didn't want known." She described Elliot's planned book. "You see, the things he was going to talk about were criminal activities."

For the first time, she had Saulter's attention. "Criminal activities by all these people?" Saulter leaned forward. If he had been a dog, his nose would have twitched.

"The people who were at your bookstore—Mr. and Mrs. Farley, Emma Clyde, Hal Douglas, Kelly Rizzoli, Capt. McElroy, Harriet Edelman, Fritz Hemphill—and you, Ms. Laurance."

The last, her name, had a full, rolling sound like a tumbril on a cobbled Paris street.

That night in Santa Fe. Emily had been wrong—as the law sees right and wrong—but Annie had never regretted helping her. And she'd do it again without hesitation.

"No, sir. Not me. Or Capt. McElroy. We were the only people there, besides Ingrid, who aren't writers. And Max, of course. But Max doesn't count because he only happened to be there by accident that night. Elliot made it painfully clear to all of us that his book was going to expose the criminal minds of some well-known mystery writers."

"So you expect me to believe these accusations you've made are part of what Elliot intended to say?"

"Exactly."

"So what did Elliot have on the rest of them?"

Wham.

Annie opened her mouth, closed it, and remembered the last fish she'd hauled gasping out of the Atlantic. Brother, talk about empathy.

Max cleared his throat. "My client isn't at liberty to disclose that information at the present moment, Chief."

Saulter's head swung irritably toward Max. "Why the hell not? She couldn't wait to unload on the others." He swivelled back to Annie. "Come on, what's the dope on the rest of them—Edelman, Hemphill, Rizzoli?"

Annie shook her head decisively. "No, Max understands. I can't give you any further information until I have verified it."

They both looked at her blankly.

"It's a matter of principle." Hildegarde Withers could not have been more priggish. "Elliot was not trustworthy. Therefore, I can't possibly reveal the information he gave me until I have the opportunity to interview the accused person and confirm or deny Elliot's accusations. In our system of government, in our world view, all are innocent until proven guilty. Well, that's the way it is with me." A ringing speech, worthy of Perry Mason. Annie stood up. "So Max and I will get back to work. That's what we were doing, Chief, when your motorcycle cop so rudely stopped us."

Alas, Saulter wasn't quite that easy or that dumb.

"Ms. Laurance, just one more thing."

She paused at the doorway.

"You said Elliot gave you this material."

The sinking feeling swept Annie again. One peril past and on to the next. It was like surviving a ten-foot wave and looking up to see a fifteen-footer.

"When did he give it to you, and where is it?"

"When?"

Saulter didn't pong. He waited.

If she admitted the disk came in the mail on Monday, the chief could attack her for hiding evidence. Hiding it?

He could accuse her of losing it, because that's precisely what she had done. And she couldn't claim to have a typewritten copy, or she would have to account for that. She had *nada* to show Saulter. If she told him about the disk, he'd want to know what happened to it—and if he ever had any hint that she'd been in Elliot's house when Harriet was killed, Annie was one plucked goose.

She took a deep breath. "He didn't exactly give it to me."

"No?" The question was chillingly genial.

"My client has nothing further to say," Max interposed.

Saulter shook his head. "Oh, no, Mr. Darling. She's going to answer this one. Or I'm going to arrest her as a material witness."

Desperately, Annie glanced around the chief's office. A battered old Remington sat on a typing table. She remembered the outer office. Two secondhand desks for his two policemen, one desk for his secretary. Not a VDT in sight.

When in doubt, tell some of the truth.

"Elliot mailed me a floppy disk. You know, he was used to working on computers." She carefully did not suggest the disk had been produced on his own computer, and maybe, God willing, even in this electronic age, Chief Saulter might not realize that the material recorded on a floppy disk using one particular program and machine could not be read by any incompatible program and different machine. "Anyway, I read the disk—and I was so outraged by what he'd put down that I erased it."

"You what?"

"Erased it." She looked at him inquiringly. "Do you have a computer, Chief Saulter?"

When he shook his head, she felt Max's sigh. She leaned forward. "This is how it works..."

Max came out of Parotti's store bearing two Bud Lights.

"Parotti says no strangers came across yesterday."

Annie took the beer and looked puzzled.

"Just making sure," Max explained. "Whoever killed Harriet was already on the island by Sunday or came by private boat."

"Whoever killed Harriet was here Saturday night because the person who killed Harriet also killed Jill—and Elliot, of course."

"I believe it, but a defense lawyer could make some argument if some strangers arrived Monday."

Annie choked on her beer.

"Pretty weak defense."

Max shook his head. "Annie, did anybody ever tell you that you have mouthitis?"

"It sounds scaly."

"It can be terminal," he said bitterly. "And what the hell are we going to do when Saulter finds out that any disk Elliot produced could be read only on his machine?"

"I read it on my machine," she said stubbornly. "So Elliot must have had access to an Apple."

This time Max choked on his beer.

Annie sipped hers daintily.

"All right, Miss Clever Tongue. What are you going to tell the chief when he discovers that package arrived in the mail on *Monday* morning *after* Elliot's unfortunate demise? I mean, while he's busy charging you with destroying evidence."

Would Saulter check with her mailman? Would he begin to wonder about the accuracy of everything she'd said? Would he talk to somebody like Capt. Mac, who liked to repair computers for fun?

"How much time do you think we have?" she asked grimly.

"The rest of today. Maybe tomorrow."

"Then I suggest we get started."

Thirteen

A green lizard clung to the side of the house. The drapes were closed against the sliding glass doors that opened onto the deck. Afternoon sunlight flooded the deck with light and deepened the shadows beneath the eighty-foot sea pines. The only sounds were the occasional rustle as squirrels scampered from limb to limb, the soft thud of falling cones, and the tap of fragrant pine needles against the pitched roof of the house.

Sweat beaded Annie's face, slid down her back and thighs. Actually, it wasn't terribly hot, a pleasant seventy-eight degrees and not humid. The last time she broke into someone's house, the results—for her—were catastrophic. Think of what nearly happened to Grace Kelly in *Rear Window*. But this time she wasn't alone.

She turned her head slightly and whispered, "It looks okay."

Max put out a restraining hand. "I'll scout in front. If I don't see anybody, then I'll knock. You stick tight here and wait for me."

They'd agreed that Harriet's house deserved a once-over. After all, something must have prompted Harriet to show up at Elliot's house at—for her—just the wrong moment.

Had Harriet been suspicious of a particular person? If so, would there be anything in her desk or diary to reflect it? Annie knew she kept a diary. Harriet bought the blank-page books from Death On Demand, never failing to mention each time she did so that all *real* writers had the compulsion to record their thoughts and feelings for posterity.

Ho hum.

But now it might matter.

Annie crept forward and touched the low limb of a live oak. The warm air lapping against her was as soothing as a hot tub.

Today and maybe tomorrow. They had so little time. They still needed to talk to Fritz Hemphill, Capt. Mac, and Kelly Rizzoli. But what good would any of it do? What if they came up with a motive for everyone, but not a single shred of evidence linking a particular person to the murders?

Somewhere there had to be evidence. Real, physical, concrete evidence. How could anyone move unseen and commit three murders? Had Saulter checked to see if anyone out late had seen a car near the Island Hills Veterinary Clinic? But, of course, he would have. He was probably asking all and sundry if they had seen her 1982 blue Volvo.

There wouldn't be any fingerprints at the Clinic, not after that evening when Capt. Mac had so thoroughly demonstrated just what did and did not hold prints.

Would there be fingerprints at Death On Demand? Of course there would be, and everyone could shrug them away. After all, they'd been there many times. All Saulter cared about was her prints on the fuse box.

As for Elliot's house . . . She had that empty feeling that precedes awful knowledge. Had she left prints on the window sill or the floor? She'd scrubbed everything she thought she'd touched. She could always say she'd been at Elliot's for dinner a few weeks earlier. Still, her prints in a hard-to-explain site would be all that Saulter needed to clap her in leg irons. Once again, she felt a terrible impatience to be active. Surely if they looked long enough, hard enough, there would be a clue to reveal the murderer. Where the heck was Max? As if in answer, she heard his rattling knock on Harriet's front door. There was a pause, followed by another loud round of knocking.

In a moment more, he rounded the corner of the house. Annie gestured at him impatiently. He responded with a thumbs-up. Obviously, he was enjoying himself. She could see it in the glint in his dark blue eyes. He probably read *The Saint* as a boy. She'd have to ask him later.

"All clear," he whispered.

They crept across the flagstoned patio, Max in the lead. Annie was irresistibly reminded of playing Cowboys and Indians as a child.

Max tugged on the patio door.

Annie touched his elbow, pointed at the broomstick wedged inside in the door track.

"Was the front door locked?" she asked softly.

"I didn't try. There's a house across the street. It didn't look as though anyone was home, but I thought we'd better try back here."

The McGuires, Annie knew, lived across from Harriet. Mildred McGuire was a Sara Paretsky freak who had given copies of *Deadlock* to all her friends and had named her parrot Boom Boom.

Annie nodded, then motioned to him to follow. Feeling extremely conspicuous, she moved around the side of the house and tried the first door they reached. It opened, and they stepped into a laundry room. Light from the opened door illuminated a windowless, square utility room. Two concrete steps beside the washer and dryer led up to a door into the house.

"I'll bet the kitchen door is open. Hardly anybody locks up."

"Broward's Rock—robber's delight," Max commented drily.

"Until now, we've never had to worry about robbers—or murderers."

The kitchen door was unlocked.

Yesterday afternoon Harriet had left her home with no idea that she would never return. Ivy glistened in the kitchen window in a ceramic gingerbread house. The drainboards were immaculate. Harriet didn't litter. Annie thought regretfully about her own kitchen and the haphazard piling of bags of Fritos, pound cake, and cookies when the breadbox was full.

A recently vaccumed peach-and-cream oriental runner ran the length of the main hall. The living room, shadowy because the periwinkle drapes were drawn, reflected a warmth and taste that seemed oddly at variance with Harriet's abrasive personality. Obviously, she had treasured loveliness: Oil paintings of the Riviera coast hung above an unstained pine mantel holding matching cut glass vases. An ornately carved rosewood grand piano took pride of place before the closed French windows. October issues of *Antiques* and *Architectural Digest* lay on the square rose marble coffee table. The pale blue-and-gray oriental rug repeated the colors in the patterned wallpaper.

Harriet's housekeeping skills were evident throughout the house. No dust marred the butler's table in the entry hall or the mahogany desk in the library. Annie paused before the extensive collection of books on France, Impressionist painting, French cooking, wildflowers, and, of course, mysteries, and admired what appeared to be a complete collection of Rex Stouts. One even looked like a first edition—maybe even autographed—but she resisted the impulse to check.

In Harriet's office, her ITT was neatly hooded, her desk top clear.

Max eagerly pulled open the drawers. Check stubs and bill receipts in the first drawer, insurance policies in the second, publishing records in neat folders in the third.

Annie promptly located a row of cloth-backed books on the bottom shelf of the office bookshelves. Harriet's diaries, neatly numbered on the spine and dated.

She reached down confidently, then paused. The last diary in the row was dated June 23–October 1 of that year.

Obviously Harriet had begun a new diary October 2– but it wasn't on the shelf.

They looked in all the bookshelves. They checked the closets. They peered beneath the furniture and scanned the kitchen.

"Let's try upstairs," Annie suggested. "She probably wrote in it every night when she was ready for bed. That's where it will be."

She started up the stairs. Oyster-gray carpet on the treads. Harriet must not have expected much traffic. Annie, now excruciatingly aware of fingerprints, was careful not to touch the railing, which still glistened from its last polish with lemon oil. Her feeling of intrusion mounted. It seemed obscene for them to be here, poking their noses into Harriet's private domain. They bypassed the two guest bedrooms. Harriet's bedroom was dominated by a white, four-poster French provincial bed with a pink silk spread. A bisque-faced doll with delicate features and painted blue eyes—remarkably like Emma Clyde's—sat atop the matching white chest. Who had given the doll to Harriet? Was it all that remained of her childhood? The doll's delicate white lace dress looked freshly laundered.

Harriet's bedroom was as scrupulously tidy as the rest of the house. Only the warm-up jacket carelessly dropped on the pink silk bedspread indicated anything out of the ordinary. Harriet must have been in a hurry, tossing down the jacket, thinking she would fold it and put it away later.

It didn't take long to search that well-ordered room or the closet with clothes hung so precisely for a wearer who would not return.

Finally, Max shook his head. "It's not here. The diary's not in the damned house."

He was right. Someone had beaten them to it. Once again, a quick, clever, determined figure moved ahead of them, blocking them. Someone else had known Harriet kept a diary—and been determined no one should read it.

They were at the head of the stairs when Max stopped and looked up.

"That's funny. Why should that trapdoor be open—if that's what it is."

"It must lead up to Harriet's widow's walk."

Careful, house-proud Harriet would never have gone off leaving the roof door open. The sunshine pouring in would quickly mark and fade the expensive oriental runner that lay below.

At least, she wouldn't leave it open unless she were in a great hurry.

Annie and Max were neck and neck as they reached the ladder, but Max paused to let Annie swarm up the rungs first.

The widow's walk commanded a magnificent panorama of the marsh, the mudflats, the open sound, and the maritime forest. Annie's first reaction was surprise at the extent of the view. Her second, a sense of shock.

"Max, she could see both the front and back approaches to Elliot's tree house."

He tugged his crumpled map of the island from his back pocket and traced the curve of the salt marsh. As a crow flew, Harriet's house was on a direct line with Elliot's. Crows and Harriet standing in her widow's walk would not have their vision obscured by the sea pines and live oaks.

"I thought no one was around. Why, Harriet could see everything. She must have seen me come—and climb in that window."

Max reached down and picked up the pearl-inlaid binoculars and held them out to her.

Raising them to her eyes, she focused on the tree house. The kitchen window leapt to her eyes, every detail distinct.

"And look at this."

Annie whirled around.

Max held a Minolta camera.

Binoculars. Camera.

They both spoke at once.

"Max, do you suppose..."

"Annie, I'll bet..."

They turned and looked toward Elliot's tree house.

Annie felt like the Porsche had a big red X painted on it. She wasn't cut out for a life of crime—or even one of concealing evidence. She was uncomfortably aware of her purse, which held Harriet's film. Any way you cut it, that film was material evidence.

"Look, Max, we *have* to take that camera to Saulter."

"Perhaps you'd like me to present him your head on a platter, too? That camera's staying in the trunk until we can get to the mainland and get those photographs developed. We'll take the ferry over as soon as we finish talking to the suspects." On that point, he was immovable.

On one thing they did agree. Harriet didn't have the Minolta in the widow's walk as decorative art. She was prepared to take pictures. Presumably, she had seen Annie's arrival and photographed it.

"But the killer came, too."

"We don't know when," Max explained patiently. "She dropped the camera, scrambled downstairs so fast she just threw her jacket on the bed. She left the binoculars and camera in the widow's walk, and the trapdoor open. She was in a hurry, Annie. She was ready to confront you and haul you off to Saulter. Did she get the killer's picture, too? We've got to be sure before we let Saulter have that film."

The evening ferry didn't cross until six. Plenty of time to do their other interviews.

She finally tracked Fritz Hemphill to the tenth hole of the Island Hills Golf Course. She waited in the shade of a yellow pine just short of the green until he sank a thirteen-foot putt. He was playing alone.

It was a gorgeous day for golf, and Fritz looked perfectly at home on the exquisitely manicured course. In his pale yellow slacks, white ribbed pullover, and white golf shoes, he looked every inch the country club golfer, except for his short, crisp crew cut.

As he bent to retrieve his ball, Annie called out, "May I walk to the next tee with you?"

He pocketed the ball and waved her to the cart.

"No walking permitted, but I'd be glad to have you along for the ride." Despite the pleasantness of his voice, there was no mistaking the wariness in his eyes.

"Fritz, I might as well come right to the point."

The cart whirred onto the golf path.

"Elliot sent me a copy of what he intended to say Sunday night."

"So?"

"You know what he was going to say about you."

Fritz pulled a cigarette from his pocket, put it in his mouth, lit it, then blew out a stream of smoke.

"No. What was he going to say?"

It was like taking a step in the dark and missing a tread.

Annie spun through the brief number of facts she knew about Fritz. The very brief number.

Number one. He was an ex-cop.

That gave him his credibility and was a good part of the reason for his success. A cop telling it the way it is for cops. His hero cop, Dan Lundy, always fought against urban corruption and won. Fritz chiseled his prose with the gritty reality of a Joseph Wambaugh.

"If what you did came out, you might end up in jail."

The cart jolted to a stop. Fritz ignored her as he slid out and reached back to pick up his bag. As he slung the bag over his shoulder, he looked directly at her.

With a feeling of surprise, she realized she'd never looked into his eyes before. They were almost black and flat, like the eyes of a squid.

"Nobody ever proved a thing." His thin mouth stretched in an empty smile. "Funny thing is, Annie, dead men don't talk."

*   *   *

"He did it." Annie was adamant.

Max held up both hands. "No favorites yet," he protested. "We still haven't talked to Capt. Mac or Kelly. Besides, my money's on Emma Clyde. That is one tough broad."

"Max, you don't know how sinister it was. He snarled out of the side of his mouth, just like Al Capone." She paused portentously. "Besides, he was the only one who wasn't upset. And he said he didn't *know* what Elliot was going to say. He just waited for me to tell him—and the murderer is the only one who knows I didn't have a chance to look at those files."

"Right. But then again Hemphill may have learned a long time ago that the less you ante, the less you can lose."

"Maybe," Annie murmured doubtfully. "But we need to check into it. We've got to see if we can link Fritz to some dead men."

Max pounded the steering wheel once, hard. "By God, maybe it's just that simple. He was a cop. Maybe it was some kind of shootout, and maybe there are some cops or somebody who suspect Fritz didn't have to shoot. Something of that kind."

"Because why else would he stop being a cop? Fritz isn't old enough to retire like Capt. Mac. I wonder if he's really made all of his money from books?"

"Write all of that down," Max urged. "When we finish talking to everybody, we'll get onto these things. Like who might have seen Emma Clyde give the big push."

"We're getting some place, Max. We really are." She glanced down at her purse. "We need to get that film developed. Why don't we hire a boat?"

"Saulter'd be sure you were escaping and he'd haul you off to jail. Just be patient, Annie. Six o'clock."

She glanced at her watch. Two. Four hours to go.

The Porsche curved around Hook Point and turned onto the main road.

As they eased forward to a stop sign, their argument began again. Who should they see first, Capt. Mac or Kelly Rizzoli?

Fourteen

Capt. Mac beamed. "Annie, this is an unexpected pleasure."

He was the first person that day to evidence any pleasure whatsoever in her arrival. She hated to replace his smile with a glower, but she wanted to do it before she got inside. Annie Laurance's progress in the winning of enemies and antagonists. How did Peter McKimsey do it? Subtly, Annie my girl, and with charm.

"I wanted to talk to you before I went to see Chief Saulter."

"Sure. Be glad to help." He looked over her head as he stepped out onto the front porch. "Isn't that your young man's car out there?"

"He isn't my young man."

"Oh, so there's hope for us old dogs yet. Hey there, Darling. Come on up."

They found themselves shepherded briskly around the side of the house to the patio and offered mint juleps. Capt. Mac's patio was the ultimate in comfort, the white plastic webbed furniture scattered around the figure-eight pool, the shiny black, obviously new outdoor barbecue without any stains of weather or salt corrosion, the woven hammock which swung invitingly in the dappled shade of the spreading live oak. Not a single weed marred the perfection of the flowerbeds of late-blooming marigolds and zinnias. No effort or expense had been spared.

Capt. Mac returned with the juleps in frosted glasses. Sprigs of fresh mint poked over the rims. He was an eager host, providing bowls of cashews and peanuts.

"Now, what can I do for you?"

Annie was enjoying the julep, and she hated to ruin the pleasant moment. Max's eyes prodded her, but he cowardly dropped a handful of peanuts into his mouth and remained silent.

"You know that Chief Saulter thinks I killed Elliot."

"I keep telling Frank that's damn nonsense."

With every word, Annie grew more uncomfortable. Here he was trying to use his influence for her benefit, and she was steeling her courage to accuse him of some kind of buried wrongdoing, including, of course, four homicides.

"Annie and I are trying to clear it up ourselves," Max said firmly, to remind Annie why they were there.

Capt. Mac managed not to look too astounded, but his obvious surprise discouraged Annie, too. How could she and Max hope to solve the crime by themselves?

"I wish you'd help us," she blurted. She very carefully did not look toward Max. After all, Miss Marple sought the support of Sir Henry Clithering. Max should understand, if he weren't such a jealous pig.

"Sweetheart, I'll give you all the help I can."

If Max had been a toad, he would have swelled. Such is jealousy.

"We think Elliot was killed because of the Sunday night session. After all, we all knew he was getting ready to tell nasty secrets about everyone there."

Capt. Mac swirled the ice in his glass meditatively. "I wouldn't take all that too seriously. Elliot loved to be the center of attention. It wouldn't have amounted to anything."

"But it did. You see, he sent me a copy of what he was going to say, and he was right—people had plenty to hide."

Capt. Mac put down his julep on a side table and reached for a cashew. "Oh, he did?"

She plunged into her narrative. "Emma Clyde pushed her second husband overboard. Hal buried his wife. Jeff Farley is a wife-beater. Fritz Hemphill..." Annie paused, then created, "...was a crooked cop. And Kelly Rizzoli attacked a woman once."

Capt. Mac ate another cashew. "Maybe those things are true. Maybe not. Even if they are, could they be proved? Obviously most of them can't be proved in a court of law, or some of those people would be in jail right now. That's something a policeman learns early on. It takes a hell of a lot in evidence to bring a charge and to make it stick. Most of what Elliot had was stuff that could embarrass somebody, make it a little awkward at the Club if the word got around, but he didn't seriously threaten anyone. It's like what he had on me." Capt. Mac lifted the pitcher to replenish their glasses. "I imagine you don't think as well of me since you read that. And I wouldn't like to have it talked about." He shot Annie an uneasy glance, then averted his eyes from her. "Damned embarrassing. Of course, what can I say?" He shrugged his powerful shoulders "Nobody likes to be hit with a paternity suit. It ruined my marriage. I'm still paying for it—and I'll be damned if I think the boy is mine."

The three of them sipped their drinks, and no one said anything for a long moment.

For the first time, Capt. Mac looked angry, his face flushed and his mouth compressed. "I suppose it would have given him some kind of thrill to spill it in front of everybody." He ducked his head awkwardly toward Annie. "He knew I wanted you to think well of me. But I'll tell you for sure, I wouldn't have snuffed him to keep it quiet. I wouldn't have minded wiping that grin off his face with my fists. But I didn't get a chance to do that."

His flush faded, and he frowned. "I'll tell you, I don't see Elliot's big exposé as the crux of anything. So he insinuates that Emma gave her husband a push. So what? Who can prove it? And that's what you have to remember, accusations without proof are bullshit." He nodded toward Annie. "Pardon me, my dear. But that's how I feel about it. Elliot was a pain, all right, but that's as far as it went. Now maybe he could have queered things for the Farleys. I know they're up for the National Book Award. But for the rest of them, I don't take it too seriously. The only thing Elliot's performance proves is that he was a heel. When you think about that, it occurs to me that maybe you should take a look at his ex-wife."

Max and Annie stared at him blankly.

"But somebody at Death On Demand killed Elliot," Annie said.

"Did they?" Capt. Mac shrugged. "Maybe. Maybe not.

The back door was open." He paused. "His ex-wife is my next-door neighbor, Carmen Morgan. And is she a pistol."

They stood beside the Porsche.

"Look, Max, it's right next door. And Capt. Mac's pretty perceptive. He was a cop for a long time, and his instincts are good."

"He probably tried to put the make on her, and she turned him down."

"Max!"

"No kidding. We've got a platterful of solid suspects, and now he comes up with somebody who wasn't even there."

"He's smart enough to pay attention about the back door. I kept telling Saulter."

Max's voice rose in disgust. "How could this ex-wife know enough about your Sunday evening sessions to plant the dart and fix the lights?"

Annie didn't like being patronized. Who did Max think he was? Colonel Primrose?

"If she was mad enough to murder him, she'd find out. It would be a stroke of genius, wouldn't it, to kill somebody in front of a bunch of people with hot motives?"

Turning on her heel, she stalked toward the house next door.

The lawn was well kept, the house recently painted and guttered. That would be the work of the Halcyon maintenance company. The house had no touches of individuality, no hanging plants or flower beds.

Annie had just touched the bell when the door opened.

Capt. Mac was right. Carmen Morgan did look like a pistol. Silver-white, shoulder-length hair, a cerise tank top cut to the navel that emphasized a Dolly Parton cleavage and a Southern belle waist, and fingernails that must make thumb and finger precision difficult. Mike Hammer would have loved her—before he blew her away. A smell of camphorwood incense eddied from the dim living room.

She fastened shrewd, baby-blue eyes on Annie.

"I know who you are. Elliot got knocked off in your place." She smiled thinly. "Wish I'd been there."

"Were you?" Annie shot back, pleased at her own audacity.

"No such luck. Somebody say I was?" The baby-blue eyes narrowed. "You've been talking to that fat ex-cop next door. That jerk can't keep his nose out of other people's business."

"We thought you might have some idea who did kill Elliot," Max interjected smoothly, coming up silently behind Annie.

Carmen's face reformed as she looked at Max. Her pale eyes with their dramatic underscoring of lavender mascara widened in appreciation. This is the kind of reaction Magnum gets.

Annie felt her own face stiffen like plaster of paris.

The appraising eyes swept up and down Max's tall frame. "Why should you care, big boy?"

Big boy.

Gag.

"The cops have some dumb ideas. We're trying to set the record straight."

"You mean they want to pitch it on gumdrop here."

It took a minute to realize that she was said gumdrop. Annie opened her mouth to explode, but clever Max got there first.

"I'll bet they haven't even asked you for your help." He leaned revoltingly close to Carmen, oozing camaraderie.

"They didn't even bother to come tell me he was dead." Her porcelain pretty face turned brittle, and abruptly she looked a decade older. "I mean, I was married to the jerk for four years, three months and eighteen days, and nobody even tells me he's dead."

"That's awful," Max commiserated. "How'd you find out?"

"I got a friend at the police station."

Annie suddenly remembered the brawny motorcycle cop. A friend, indeed.

Carmen Morgan swivelled her platinum head to look again at Annie, a searching and not especially comradely look. "That's how I knew *she* was in a pickle. Bud, my friend, says they're going to arrest her tomorrow." She snorted. "Hell, you didn't kill Elliot. I can tell that by looking at you. You don't have the stuff."

While Annie was trying to decide whether to be complimented or offended, Carmen focused on Max.

"You come on in. I'll tell you what I can about my ex. The louse."

Annie moved in tandem with Max. She intended to stick to him like Nora to Nick, whether Carmen liked it or not.

The small hall was dingy with scuffed black-and-white checkerboard tile. A heavy smell of camphorwood combined with the two mint juleps to make her head feel dangerously unsteady.

"A beer, you guys?"

Annie started to decline, but Max grinned and said, "Sure. Let me help you," and he trailed Carmen into the kitchen.

Right on his heels, Annie followed. Max was not only a jealous pig and a sore-sport toad, he was now revealing himself to be a lecher of the first order.

Carmen opened three bottles of Dos XX's, and waved them to seats at the tan Formica-topped kitchen table. No light beer here. And apparently equally little cooking. The kitchen looked like a display in the home section at Sears, and just about as used.

Her body arched seductively toward Max, Carmen said, "What do you want to know?"

"Tell us about yourself." Max drew his chair closer to Carmen's. He would soon be on the same side of the table with her.

Annie gripped her bottle forcefully. Otherwise, she might have tossed it in his ingenuous face.

Carmen used both hands to fluff her long, silver hair. "True confessions?" she asked huskily.

Annie was delighted to note that Max looked a tad uncomfortable. He lifted his beer and drank.

"How about where you're from and how you met Elliot," Annie suggested tartly, smirking at Max's discomfort.

"I'm a dancer. I was working at a club down in the Keys, and Elliot came in. He was one big spender. Anyway, he was writing a book." She squinted reminiscently. "He told me I was like Sadie somebody, and I was wonderful material." She sipped at her beer and peered coyly and fuzzily at Max. The old bat was too vain to wear glasses.

Annie translated this: Carmen was a stripper in a joint,

and Elliot was playing another role, macho novelist à la Hemingway.

"And you got married?" She cringed at the naked astonishment in her voice.

"Yeah. We went on a big party, and it seemed like a good idea."

Wonder what kind of idea it seemed to Elliot when he sobered up?

Carmen's mouth tightened. Annie added another five years to her age.

"Have you been divorced long?" Where had Max suddenly acquired his vast reserves of sympathy?

"Six months."

"Why are you staying here? Why don't you go back to Florida?"

Carmen swung on Annie furiously. "Why should I? I've got as much right to live here as anybody."

Max finished his beer, smacking his lips in pleasure, then broke the uncomfortable silence. "Did you know about the writers' meetings on Sunday nights at Death On Demand?"

"Yeah. Sure." Her eyes flicked over Annie's face. "You people give me the creeps. Death On Demand. Why don't you have a nice little shop that sells pretty things? You know, painted sea shells and birds in glasses. That kind of thing?"

"My uncle died and left me the bookstore," Annie replied in a strangled voice.

Carmen shrugged. "You gotta go with what you got. That's what I've always done." Consciously or unconsciously, she raised her arms and stretched her body sensuously.

Max leaned forward. "Did you know Elliot was going to say a lot of bad things about the other writers the night he was killed?"

"Oh, hell yes. He told me all about it."

"He did?" Annie shot Max a triumphant glare. "When did you see him?"

"He dropped by Friday afternoon. About five. To bring my alimony check. He was trying to chisel like always, two hundred bucks short. Said he'd lost a bundle on the commodities market, but he'd get the rest to me next week." She tugged at the cerise tank top, redistributing the wealth. "Hey, how do you suppose I can collect my money?"

While Max enthusiastically explained the law of probate, Annie thought furiously.

"Carmen, what did he tell you about the other writers?"

Elliot's ex-wife took a dainty sip of beer. "This and that. He loved to snoop around. I mean, he really liked to get the dirt on people."

"Did he tell you what he was going to say Sunday night?"

"Oh, sort of. I didn't pay a lot of attention. I wanted to talk about the money he owed me. I mean, try living here without a lot of bucks—"

Max leaned across the table and turned on a two-hundred-watt smile. "Try to remember. It could mean a lot."

"To you?" Carmen inquired huskily.

"To everybody," Annie interjected in an arctic tone. It would be hard for Carmen to remember. Her attention span was obviously limited solely to matters of importance to her.

But, with Max cheering her on, the woman dredged up some interesting information.

Some of it they knew—about Emma, the Farleys, and Hal. Some of it they didn't.

"Elliot said Fritz Hemphill was an idiot not to pay his wife alimony. I told him I sure agreed with that. Guys who don't pay their alimony are real geeks." For the first time, Annie noted the diamond-studded hoop earring hidden beneath the platinum hair.

"Is that all he had on Fritz?"

Carmen snorted. "Naw. That was why he had stuff on Fritz. Seems like his ex-wife is no chum, and she unloaded a bellyful to Elliot."

"What?" Max asked.

Carmen smeared the moisture from her beer bottle with a deadly fingernail. "Something about watching your back-side with Fritz, not letting him come up behind you with a gun. Something like that."

A gun. That sounded more like it. Annie remembered Fritz's squidlike eyes.

"As for that jerk next door," and Carmen tilted her

platinum head delicately toward Capt. Mac's house, "Elliot said he was a cool bastard all right, one who'd learned to keep his mouth shut."

It figured that Capt. Mac wouldn't broadcast information about a paternity suit.

"How about Kelly Rizzoli?" Max prodded.

"Nutty as a fruitcake, he said," Carmen replied, twirling an index finger by her temple significantly.

"Nutty how?" Annie asked, then thought, *Now I'm beginning to sound like her*. As if he could read her mind, Max grinned teasingly. She ignored him.

"Something about some tricks she'd played. Nasty ones, like killing somebody's cat."

Annie's skin crawled. *Psycho. Hallowe'en II.* Highsmith. Rendell. There were people who did things like that. But could they include Kelly, who had such a sensitive face and such an air of vulnerability?

Annie's recoil didn't escape Carmen's notice. "Yeah, you were sure having a swell party Sunday night. Lots of fun people there." Her pale eyes glinted maliciously. "Then there's the scoop on you. Elliot found out all about Santa Fe." Carmen's lip curled. "You think I'm just a cheap bitch, but I'd never do anything like that." She glanced over to Max. "You ought to ask her about Santa Fe sometime."

Santa Fe. What would Max think about Santa Fe? It had spelled the end for her and Richard. Thank God.

Annie looked directly at Carmen. "Yes, I can tell Max about Santa Fe."

There was a short, sharp pause, then Max interjected smoothly, "Carmen, did Elliot play the commodities market very often?"

Annie could have hugged him.

The widow grimaced. "Like clockwork. The sap."

"So maybe he really needed money."

"He *always* needed money," Carmen said seriously. This was obviously a subject close to her heart.

Annie turned to Max. "See, I thought there might be blackmail involved. I don't care what you say, he was extorting money from Emma Clyde..."

"Wait a minute," the blonde interrupted. "What makes you think so?"

"As soon as I made it clear I knew what Elliot was going to say, Emma asked me how much money I wanted. That must mean she was already being blackmailed."

"Not by Elliot." Carmen lost interest in Annie's theory. "No way."

"Why not? If he needed money, and you said he did, why wouldn't he take money to keep quiet about something like that?"

"Not Elliot. He was a chiseler, yeah, but he wasn't a crook. He told me once he thought blackmailers were slime, real slime. No way. You got to understand"—she got up and wriggled to the refrigerator—"he was a rat, but he really hated killers and bad cops and nasty, underhanded people. You know his favorite detective, Josh Hibbert, well, all that stuff was really him. The trouble is, he wanted to shove people's noses in their little messes. He liked to push people. That's why I dumped him. Cat and mouse, always a little push here, a shove there. I wouldn't take it. I told him to stick it." She squinted into the refrigerator thoughtfully. There were no more Dos XX's. "I guess he pushed somebody too hard."

"I think she's kinda cute," Max said, gunning the Porsche.

"You and every male in South Carolina."

"That is a sexist remark."

"You bet it is." Annie gently massaged her temples. "Wow, beer on top of two mint juleps. But it's a good thing we talked to her. She did know Elliot was going to speak Sunday night, and she knew why. She could easily have hidden the dart and tampered with the lights."

"Oh, Annie. Admit it. You just don't like the girl."

Girl. That was a laugh.

"She's about as girlish as a female anaconda."

"But to the right male anaconda . . ."

"I wonder how Elliot left his money?"

Max slowed the Porsche to swing back onto the main road. Massive yellow pines crowded the road, and through the open sunroof came the scent of sunbaked pitch. The scaly orange trunks rose ruler-straight.

"According to Carmen, he'd commoditied out of money."

"Sure, that would be her story. But wouldn't you think ?ce about that sweet girl if it turned out she inherited?"

Reluctantly, Max nodded. "That's an oversight, all right. We need to find out who gets his money—if there is any to get. That could make a difference."

"You know the motives for murder. Hate, revenge, fear, and greed."

"Or a combination thereof. Where do you suppose Kelly Rizzoli fits in?"

On the surface, their interchange was just as usual— light, flippant, and fun. Annie sensed an undertone, though, whether or not Max did.

She reached out and touched his arm. "Before we see Kelly, I want to tell you about Santa Fe."

Fifteen

I've never been into true confession," he said drily. "What counts is now. Today." His dark blue eyes met hers directly.

Dear Max.

"I want to tell you. I know I don't have to." She couldn't quite resist reaching out to touch his cheek. "Let's go over to Indigo Beach."

She directed him to a rutted sandy lane.

Low hanging vines scraped the top of the Porsche as Max eased it around a fallen palmetto. He cringed for the paint job. "They could use a little machete work down this way."

Resurrection ferns laced the branches of a spreading live oak, and cinnamon ferns flourished beside a pond to the left. The undergrowth suddenly erupted with a flurry of movement, and a dusky gray white-tail deer plunged fleetingly across the narrow track to disappear into a thicket of bayberry.

A fallen southern red cedar blocked the track twenty yards short of the beach. They left the car and walked over the hummocky, sandy ground to a narrow boardwalk, half-covered by drifting sand.

Head-high sea oats, October brown, rippled in the onshore breeze. Nutgrass and sandspur rustled knee-high. As they stood at the top of the dune and looked over the littoral at the gentle surf, a ragged line of cormorants passed overhead. They walked down the dune to the flat-packed gray sand along the water's edge.

Annie reached down and touched an eddy of warm water.

"You don't have to tell me anything," Max insisted. "I know everything I need to know about you."

"I want to tell you." She frowned, picking her words. "Elliot must have talked to Richard."

Max was silent.

"I've never told you about Richard. It was right after I got out of school. I was living in Dallas and working as a model." She turned and began to walk up the beach, and Max paced with her. "Richard is a banker." She laughed. "That's not fair, really. I know there are all kinds of bankers, but Richard is like all of their worst qualities rolled into one. He is extremely cautious, extremely careful. He believes there are rules for every situation. We were engaged." She shook her head in self-surprise. "Actually, I can't believe now that I ever considered marrying him. Richard is extremely nice, extremely handsome, extremely . . . dull."

"Dull," Max repeated. "At least, you've never called me dull."

"Never. Anyway, Richard and I were engaged. Then a very old friend called me. She was in real trouble. She asked me to come to Santa Fe with her and not to tell anyone. So I told Richard that I had to leave town immediately, and that I would be back in a week.

"He wanted to know why. I told him I couldn't say." Annie winced at the recollection of the acrimonious dispute that followed. "Richard wasn't pleased. But I lost my temper, told him off, and went. A week later, when I got back, I wouldn't tell him why I'd gone, or what I'd done.

"Three days after that, he showed up at my apartment, and he was livid. He had a report from a private detective. It said that Anne McKinley Laurance entered a private nursing home on Sunday evening, gave birth to a son that night, and was discharged the following Wednesday."

"Your friend used your name."

"Do you know, that never occurred to Richard? He demanded to know how I'd hidden my pregnancy, since he knew damn well he hadn't gotten me pregnant, and who the hell was I sneaking around with?"

Max raised one blond eyebrow. "Is his bank on the FDIC worry list?"

"No, Richard is very bright about numbers."

"But, thank God, not very bright about people."

"That's what Elliot found out. The baby was immediately given up for adoption."

"Why did it have to be so secret?" he asked.

"You are perceptive, aren't you?" She bit her lip.

"You don't have to tell me any more."

"No, I want to tell you because I know what I did was illegal. You see, Emily was married. That wasn't the problem at all. She had hidden the fact she was pregnant from her husband. You have to understand, her husband was the oldest son of one of Texas's most powerful families—and a kind of crazy mean family, too. She didn't know it until she married Quentin, but his father controlled all of them, and I mean that literally. Everyone in the family kowtowed to that horrible, domineering old monster. It was just like Mrs. Boynton in *Appointment With Death*. Quentin and his sister both used cocaine. Their mother was an alcoholic. It was just an awful way to live—and all Emily could think about was getting her baby—the only grandchild—into a safe, *normal* family. So we went to Santa Fe, and she went into a clinic using my name, and three days later I signed the adoption papers to a wonderful couple who had wanted and prayed for a baby for years."

She half-turned and looked out over the surging green water. "I've always been so glad I did it. Emily and Quentin were killed in a plane crash a year later, and that little baby would have been swallowed alive by Quentin's father."

"Good for you," Max said warmly. At her look of surprise, he said almost roughly, "Richard may have been a damn fool, but I'm not, Annie."

"You don't care that I was a party to—I don't know what to call it. Fraud? Conspiracy?"

"I think you're wonderful. I've always thought so. I'll always think so." He couldn't quite resist adding, "Even if I don't have a serious job—like a banker."

They stopped at Death On Demand en route to Kelly Rizzoli's. Max insisted there was plenty of time before the ferry left to organize what they'd learned and then interview Kelly. He reached out to pat the glossy black head of the stuffed raven in the entryway.

"What's his name?"

"Edgar, of course."

Ingrid greeted them wearily. "Everything's okay. I think the rush is over. But I sold $689 worth. And you're out of Christianna Brands." She patted the stack of receipts proudly. Her eyes darted solicitously from Max to Annie before she added reluctantly, "Chief Saulter's been by twice, looking for you, and Mrs. Brawley phoned three times."

Bad news and good news. Annie stepped close to give Ingrid a hug. "Let's close up for now. And don't worry, Ingrid, Max and I are working on it."

Ingrid's face brightened. "Like Pam and Jerry North."

Not quite, but Annie wouldn't have minded a martini. Although that might be the final blow, after the mint juleps and beer.

Ingrid put up the Closed sign and locked the front door as she left. "I'll open up in the morning."

Did she think Annie would be in jail?

Max made himself comfortable in the largest wicker chair with the softest pillows.

"It's time to organize what we have." He propped a yellow legal pad on his knee.

Annie wandered restlessly around the store: the coffee area, the exhibit of watercolors, the central corridor with

the soft gum bookcases angling away, the cash desk, Edgar
with his glossy feathers and sightless eyes.

Sanctuary. That's what Death On Demand had been for
her in the days following Uncle Ambrose's death. She'd
always been so happy here, felt so safe. Had Saulter come
by to arrest her? Carmen Morgan had thought the arrest
would come tomorrow. How much time did she have left?
The clock in the tall Queen Anne walnut case next to
Edgar read 3:07. Time, time, she was running out of
time.

She whirled around and started down the central
corridor, then paused abruptly, her eyes on a level with
the top shelf of the True Crime section, which held all
the works of Uncle Ambrose's favorite author, Clark
Howard. Howard, a 1980 Edgar winner for his short
story "Horn Man," wrote everything well—short stories, novels, television and movie scripts, and nonfiction
crime books.

Annie stared at the books until the titles scrambled in
her mind.

They were losing sight of the most important fact.

"Max!" she yelped. She veered to her right, tangled
with a fern, and slid to a stop beside his chair.

Agatha erupted from the base of the fern next to Max,
stared reproachfully at Annie, and shot toward the dimness
of the coffee bar.

Annie flapped her hands at Max's sheaf of paper. "What
did you do with the stuff you put together on everybody
when I was being bopped at Elliot's?"

Max riffled through his stack and pulled out several
typewritten sheets. Annie grabbed them.

"We've got to fine-tooth-comb this stuff and see who's
connected to a killing that Uncle Ambrose was investigating. Don't you see? It all goes back to Uncle Ambrose.
That's important, not this penny-ante stuff like Capt. Mac
and his paternity suit."

"First, we have to organize our material." Max looked
extremely judicious, a non-eggshaped Hercule Poirot.

Annie didn't dignify this with an answer. Instead, she
grabbed the dossiers. Quickly, she scratched out a list of
people and places.

ANNIE'S GEOGRAPHIC CHART

Emma Clyde	Hal Douglas	The Farleys	Fritz Hemphill	Capt. Mac	Kelly Rizzoli
Billings	Wiesbaden	Columbia	Long Beach	Ft. Walton	Ft. Smith
Cincinnati	St. Louis	Kansas City	Saigon	Jacksonville	Ozark
N. Africa	Hollywood	Broward's Rock	Loma Linda	Camp LeJeune	Fayetteville
Memphis	Lake Tahoe		Los Angeles	Korea	Broward's Rock
New York	Broward's Rock		Broward's Rock	Miami	
Boca Raton				Silver City	
Broward's Rock				Broward's Rock	

As she studied her chart, she felt her first qualm. On the surface, not a single one of these people had any connection with Uncle Ambrose's famous cases. But she didn't know enough about the three cases Uncle Ambrose had been investigating.

Fifteen minutes later, her hand cramped from note taking, she put down the phone.

Max came up behind her and reached down to massage her tight shoulders. "What did you plug into? Today's devotional?"

"The crime reporter at the Atlanta *Constitution*. His name's Sam, and he asked me out for a drink the next time I get to Atlanta." She swivelled around to look at the clock face. Oh, God, 3:22. Here they sat, Max scribbling another damn list and she trying to forge some link between Uncle Ambrose's missing manuscript and the suspects. And, darn it, nothing was working out.

Max bent over to look at her work.

"Nothing," she said bitterly. "Oh, obviously he was on the right track, but there isn't anything to link those crimes to anybody here." She ticked them off on her fingers: "Alden Armbruster stepped into his Lincoln Continental to drive to work. He turned on the motor and kerboom. There had been labor trouble at the plant (they made plating for artillery shells). They suspected Alden Armbruster Jr., who had made a recent trip to Miami, where he could easily have purchased the plastic explosive used to blow up the car. No fingerprints. No proof. Case never closed. Alden Armbruster Jr. lives and presumably thrives in New York City. No other suspects, and nobody here could be Alden Armbruster. The Vinson suicide: Amalie Vinson, the tire heiress, was found one June morning in her Waikiki penthouse, dead of a cocaine overdose. Could be accident. Could be suicide. There was a note. A scrap, actually. The classic—*I can't go on*. As any fool knows, find a written regret to an invitation, tear it artfully, and you have a picture-perfect suicide note. Worked beautifully in *The Moving Finger*. Chief suspect—her third husband, Bobby Kaiser, who doesn't live on Broward's Rock. Finally, the Winningham case. Cale Winningham, heir to a tobacco fortune, was known as a brutal, spoiled womanizer. Somehow, he'd married a nice girl, Sheila

Hammonds. In the middle of a November night, Winningham killed her with a shotgun. His story was that they'd
had trouble recently with prowlers. A month before, they'd
been robbed. He heard a noise, got up, crept out into the
hall, shouted, 'Stop or I'll shoot!' There was no answer, so
he blasted. When he turned on the light, there was
Sheila. He was devastated. He married another woman
two months later. But Winningham didn't live long to
enjoy his new wife. They were killed when his private
plane crashed on takeoff a few months later. The FAA
found sugar in the gas line. So Cale Winningham can't be
on Broward's Rock. Unless he's a ghost."

Annie shoved her hands frenziedly through her hair.
"Dammit, there's no link to Broward's Rock."

Max held up his legal pad. "Here's what really matters."

Max's list:

1. Emma Clyde gave Ricky a shove. Who saw the dirty
deed? Check the Coast Guard.

2. Hal Douglas's wife ran around on him. According to Hal,
she also ran out on him. Where is Lenora Harris Douglas?

3. Jeff Farley beats his wife. Would he or Janis kill to
keep Jeff's brutality a secret?

4. Fritz Hemphill is apparently trigger-happy, with a
past he was determined to keep buried. What did his
ex-wife know?

5. Capt. Mac keeps his mouth shut. Did he hide
anything more dangerous than a paternity suit?

6. Carmen Morgan knew about the Sunday evening
session. She knew that everyone there would have a
motive for shutting Elliot up. Does Carmen inherit? Where
was she Sunday night?

7. Kelly Rizzoli. Elliot said she played some nasty tricks.
What were they?

Max reached for the telephone.

3:33. She tugged Max's sleeve and pointed at the clock.

He covered the receiver. "Plenty of time," he soothed,
as he dialed.

Agatha moved like a black shadow, jumping up to the top of the counter. She looked at Annie with her deep yellow eyes.

"What do you think, Agatha?"

The cat made a soft, throaty sound.

"If you could talk, you could tell us who came in here Sunday morning."

Agatha began to clean her face, licking her right paw daintily, then scrubbing furiously at her cheek.

Annie reached out, petted the silky fur, and tilted her head a little to listen to Max.

"Lieutenant Ferrill, did you investigate the drowning of Enrique Morales a couple of years ago?"

"Yes."

"This is Max Darling, attorney-at-law. I'm involved in a wrongful death suit, and I need to get a copy of the report on Morales's death. Could you send it to me by Federal Express?"

"Yes, I suppose so." A puzzled pause followed. "Wrongful death? That death was ruled an accidental drowning."

"There's some question of liability on the part of the yacht manufacturer, Lieutenant. Too low a railing on the afterdeck."

"That'd be hard to prove," Ferrill said drily. "The railing was four feet high."

Max swept ahead. "Did you interview the steward and the cook of *Marigold's Pleasure?*"

"Of course. Neither was aboard that evening."

"So Mrs. Morales and her husband were alone?"

The lieutenant paused. "Mrs. Clyde, that's what she calls herself. She and her second husband were alone."

But someone somewhere saw something, if Annie's blackmail theory were correct. "Wasn't there anybody else around?"

"We talked to the owner of another boat anchored close by. He corroborated the information we received from Mrs. Clyde. I think you're barking up the wrong tree. There wasn't anything wrong with the railing on that boat."

"Possibly not," Max agreed placidly. "But please send me the report."

After giving Ferrill Annie's address, Max hung up,
marking a series of fat, black question marks by Emma's
name. Annie was right. There was something there—or
Emma wouldn't have immediately suspected her of a
blackmail attempt. Maybe there would be something in
the report, at the least a few more names to call.

He tracked down Jeff and Janis Farley's editor, just
returning from lunch at The Four Seasons.

"This is Max Darling. I'm writing an article for a
library journal, and I'm trying to get some information
on personal factors that can affect book sales. You were
recommended to me as an extremely knowledgeable
observer of children's publishing. Anything you may tell
me will be confidential. I'm not using anybody's name in
this story."

"What do you want to know?" Her voice was clipped,
level, and noncommittal.

"What would be the effect upon sales for a children's
writer who was convicted of drunk driving?"

"Mr. Darling, that is a very peculiar question."

"There's been some concern among librarians that there
is an inverse censorship at work affecting the children's
market that isn't at work in adult writing. In other words,
does the behavior of children's writers make a difference in
their likelihood of sale? So, I'm asking you whether a
D.W.I. conviction or wife-beating charge or anything of
that nature could make a difference."

"I won't be quoted?"

"Never."

"Then, off the record and between you and me and the
wall, it makes a hell of a difference. If children's writers
have nasty personal lives, they'd damned well better keep
them under wraps."

"Do you think it's possible for a writer to win a national
book prize if something like this became public?"

"Forget it."

Annie was madly deciphering his cryptic notes as he
finished the call.

"My turn," and she took the receiver out of his hand
and dialed information for the alumni office at Washing-

ton University at St. Louis. It took patience to get the name of Lenora Harris Douglas's sister, Mrs. Bennett Berry.

"Mrs. Berry, I'm calling about your sister, Lenora Harris Douglas..."

There was an excited cry. "My God, do you know where she is? Where is she? My God, who is this?"

Annie felt a constriction in her chest. Martha Berry's cry told her almost everything she needed to know.

"Mrs. Berry, I'm sorry, you've misunderstood me. I'm calling to see if you have your sister's address."

"Oh. Oh, for a minute I thought..." Martha Berry took a deep breath. "No, no, I don't know where Lenora is."

"When did you last hear from her?"

"A postcard. Two years ago. From the casino at Lake Tahoe." Her voice quickened. "Do you know Lenora? Do you know somebody who knows her?"

"No, I'm sorry. I was calling about a reunion of our college class. That last address we have is a rural box number in California. We didn't get any answer."

"No answer. That's all I ever got. I went out, looked for her, but that cabin's empty, and I've never found a trace of the guy she married."

"Do you know anything about him?"

"His name is Harold Douglas. That's all we know. He took Lenora out to Hollywood with him, and that's the last we ever heard. She told me, the last time we talked, that he was crazy jealous. I asked her to come home, but she laughed and said it would be all right." Martha Berry paused. "Listen, if you do find Lenora, please tell her to call us. Tell her we've been worried sick because... well, she's a good girl but... All Lenora ever wanted to do was have a good time. We don't know why she hasn't called or written."

Annie hung up and drew a gallows with a noose. Girls just want to have fun.

There was no answer at the home of the former Mrs. Fritz Hemphill. Her office said she was out of town on a business trip and could be contacted that evening at the Vanderbilt Plaza in Nashville, Tennessee. Annie glanced at the clock. 3:50. They couldn't wait until evening. It was a wonder Saulter hadn't been by again—this time with a warrant. And they still needed to talk to Kelly and get Harriet's film to the mainland to be developed.

She watched the clock hands move as she waited on hold, but she was finally connected to the LAPD chief of detectives. He wasn't very forthcoming.

"Yeah. Hemphill was with us. For about ten—maybe a dozen—years."

"Why did he quit?"

"Ask him. By the way, who did you say you were?"

"I'm writing a feature on mystery novelists," Annie invented. "I understand he quit because he got in a little trouble."

"He quit because he inherited some money." The voice was flat. "If you want to know more about it, you might call a Mrs. Cynthia Harmon."

Cynthia Harmon ran a beauty shop in Long Beach.

"Who told you to call me?"

"Horace King."

"Horace— So you want to know about Fritz Hemphill." Her voice harshened. "Yeah, you called the right number. I'll tell you about Fritz. Horace can't say anything. He has to watch out, or they'll hit him with a slander suit. Me, I don't give a damn. Yeah, I can tell you about Fritz. He's a murderer."

"Who did he kill?"

"His best friend. Isn't that something? His best friend, Mike Gonzalez. He shot him in the back and then stood there and watched him bleed to death."

She was crying now.

"I'm sorry," Annie said feebly.

"We all ought to be sorry. A good man like Mike. I never liked Fritz, never, but I didn't say anything to Mike because a man doesn't like for a woman to knock his friends. But I always thought Fritz had cold eyes, like a snake. And that's what he was, a snake in the grass. See, Mike saved Fritz's life one time when they faced down some creeps in an alley, and one of them pulled a gun and was going to shoot Fritz. Mike got him first, saved Fritz's life. They were good pals then. Fritz was divorced, and Mike's first wife died of cancer and they didn't have any kids, so Mike made up a will and left everything he had to

Fritz. He should have known... Anyway, Mike had this beach house he inherited from this spinster aunt, a beach house in Carmel, and you know what kind of money that is. Mike never even liked the place, said the people were too ritzy for him, but he made up a will, left it all to Fritz. Then he met me, and it was great, it was wonderful. I finally met a nice man, a man I could really care about, and Mike liked my kids, everything. We were going to get married in two months, and he went hunting with Fritz, and he died with the back of his head blown away."

"An accident—" she began.

"Accident! Lady, cops don't have accidents with guns."

Annie hung up, started to report to Max, then saw the time. "I'll tell you on the way. We'd better hurry. It's almost four."

"Don't you think I have time to do some phoning on Capt. Mac?"

The front door rattled. Chief Saulter stood on the verandah, peering into Death On Demand.

Without a word, Annie and Max dropped to the floor.

Sixteen

She'd never realized how hard heart pine floors were when crossed on hands and knees. Had Saulter caught a glimpse of them? But the door was mullioned and that would make it difficult for him to see.

She didn't draw an easy breath until they'd tiptoed out the storeroom door, darted up the back alley, and skulked on the far side of the hibiscus to Max's Porsche. As they roared off, she looked over her shoulder. No one followed. Of course, Saulter could find her, if he looked hard enough. But every second gave them another chance to find out more. And they had to catch the six o'clock ferry and develop that film.

Magpie Plantation was hidden deep from the main road; enormous, thick-leaved live oak trees and their dangling swaths of Spanish moss shrouded the tangled undergrowth, enclosed the narrow, dusty gray road. It was like driving in a terrarium, moist, green, dim, and somber.

"All we need is a crow on a fence post," Max muttered.

The Porsche curved around the crumbling remains of old Fort Hendrix, an earthwork fortification built in 1862 by the occupying Union forces to overlook Abelard Creek. They rattled over a narrow wooden bridge, and Annie said in a hushed voice, "There's the house."

Magpie Plantation was old, a lovingly restored antebellum survivor of sea cotton days. The railings of the broad double verandahs and the slender Doric columns glistened with fresh white paint.

With the motor off, a funereal silence enfolded them.

Max raised an eyebrow. "I'll bet they laugh a lot here. My God, the place looks like a cross between a southern Wuthering Heights and the summer home of the Addams family."

The silvery Spanish moss hung motionless. The onshore breeze didn't penetrate the thick stand of live oaks. The sound of their footsteps on the oyster-shell path was distinct in the brooding stillness.

Annie remembered Magpie Plantation from summer hikes with Uncle Ambrose. It had been a derelict then, untenanted, dank weeds choking the drive, the second-story verandah sagging. She'd known, of course, that Kelly had bought and restored the old house. But why wasn't it included in the spring tour of plantation homes? Most owners of the antebellum mansions gloried in showing off their prizes.

They were starting up the rose-bordered front walk when a scream, high and rising higher, pealed through the heavy air.

"My God, what's that?"

Max was squinting at the house's beautiful facade. "There,"

he shouted, and pointed to the second-floor verandah, where two figures struggled near the railing, one trying desperately to squirm free, the other, smaller one holding on tenaciously.

Max leapt up the steps and yanked on the heavy front door. It didn't budge. He sprinted down the verandah to the end and an ivy-laden lattice. He started up, Annie close behind.

"It won't hold both of us," he shouted in warning as the framework quivered.

Annie dropped back down and craned to see.

The larger woman broke free to clamber awkwardly up onto the railing. The smaller figure, Kelly, grabbed and clung. The two teetered precariously. Then Max was up and over the railing, and the three figures disappeared in a melee of arms and legs.

The scream sounded again, piercing and shrill, then abruptly broke off, followed by brokenhearted sobs.

"Max," Annie yelled, then she climbed up on the railing to start up the lattice.

He peered down from the second story. "Hold on, Annie. We'll be down in a minute."

By the time the front door swung open, Annie was standing beside it and breathing almost normally.

Kelly stepped back and motioned her inside. Her dark red hair was disheveled, her face pale. Max had an angry scratch on his right arm, and his shirt pocket was torn.

"We'll go in the living room." Kelly's voice was as soft and unhurried as usual. They might have been joining her for afternoon tea.

The living room was lovely. Delicate, white molded cornices decorated fourteen-foot-tall ceilings. A magnificent three-tiered crystal chandelier hung from a center medallion. Pale gray walls set off the draped turquoise hangings over the huge arched windows. The room was shadowy, but Kelly didn't turn on a light. Annie thought of the approach to the house. It was all of a piece, quiet, spooky, sinister.

Their hostess waved them to an American Chippendale sofa, then sat in a small but very fine Queen Anne wing chair, upholstered in rose and white.

Annie felt a curl of uneasiness. This was *Knight's Gambit* territory. Antebellum perfection below and a madwoman above.

Kelly turned politely toward Max. "I do owe you a very great thanks."

"No problem." Max took up two-thirds of the sofa, overwhelmingly masculine in a feminine room. "I became quite skilled in ascending and descending lattices in my younger days."

Annie filed that one away for further reference and possible inquiry.

Kelly didn't smile. She nodded soberly and continued to gaze at Max with haunted green eyes. "It's great luck you happened by. We are rather isolated here. What can I do for you?"

It was a courteous way of asking what the hell they wanted, and a clear indication the verandah episode was closed.

Kelly wasn't Carmen or any of the others they'd talked to. If anyone were capable of out-thinking the world, it was Kelly Rizzoli.

"It's Elliot," Annie began, beating Max to the punch.

"Elliot?" Kelly echoed coolly.

"He sent me a copy of what he was going to say Sunday night."

"Oh, he did? Would you suppose he had a presentiment?"

Annie shrugged. "I doubt it. Maybe more on the order of insurance."

"It lapsed, didn't it?"

Annie could swear there was a sick glimmer of amusement in Kelly's gorgeous eyes, but she plunged resolutely on. "I don't really want to tell Saulter what he was going to say about you."

"So you came to see me instead?" Kelly wore a shamrock-green turtleneck and boxy white slacks. She looked very slight in the delicate wingback chair. Slight but somehow imposing.

Annie nodded.

"If I can persuade you that what he had on me wasn't sufficient motive for murder, you will protect my good name. Is that right?"

"Right." Certainly Kelly didn't seem discomfited by her threat to go to Saulter.

Kelly looked away, her gaze seeming to fasten somewhere near the delicate Adam mantel. She spoke dreamily. "It's funny what can serve as motivation. That was part of Elliot's thesis, you know, that a writer's reality serves as the basis for invention. I find motivation quite fascinating." She shifted a little in her chair, looked at Annie. "In my latest collection of short stories, there's one I like particularly, 'Gideon's Morning.'" Her voice had a singsong, musical quality like the faraway fall of water. "It is his last morning, you see. His mother splits his skull with an axe as he sits at the breakfast table."

Max and Annie sat quietly, scarcely breathing.

She tilted her head like a bird observing a worm. "It's really quite understandable. She'd told him and told him and told him not to track mud across her clean kitchen floor when she'd just mopped it."

The vision of a blood-drenched country kitchen hung in the shadows of the room.

"Motivation. Yes, Elliot was right. We use everything we've ever known or seen or felt when we write. Sometimes, we pick up pieces of people's lives, like a crow attracted to the shine of a broken brooch. We take it all and put together something new and different, but it does spring from our past, our collective past."

"And your past," Annie said softly.

Kelly nodded. She looked childlike, sitting in that straight-backed old chair, her hands folded primly in her lap, her shoulders narrow beneath the green turtleneck.

"My past—and Elliot. That's what you came to talk about. My past and my present. You know, Elliot was right and wrong about me."

"Can you tell us?" Max urged, his voice low and careful.

Pensively, Kelly nodded. "It's interesting. Motivation again. Elliot didn't understand that it didn't matter to me if he told everyone—right or wrong. He got the story from one of my classmates, I suppose. It happened at the College of the Ozarks." She turned to Max. "Have you ever been to southern Arkansas? You might understand better if you've been there. Did you know you can go back in the Arkansas swamp country and go to a lake that's hooded by trees—and there will be snakes hanging from the branches?"

Again that slow, dreamy smile.

"Think about that, picture it. The darkness among the cypress and the still, emerald water and the thick-bodied water moccasins dangling from the branches.

"Arkansas—it can be very still and dark and ingrown. Very ingrown. Many families have kept to themselves for a long time. My family, too. But my sister, Pamela, and I went together to college. I knew Pamela wasn't quite right, but we thought she could go if I were there." Kelly's dreamy eyes looked beyond them, to a past and place they couldn't see. "We rented a tiny room in a boardinghouse two blocks from the campus. Pamela took art classes." Her voice was suddenly animated. "She can really draw quite well. When she's happy, she paints smiling children. When she's unhappy . . . They found the dog first, the dog next door. His throat was cut. Then a parakeet was strangled. Our landlady had a pet cat, a beautiful cat who had her own silk cushion and special foods." Kelly moved her hand, as if stroking a cat.

Annie didn't ask what had happened to the cat. She didn't want to know.

"Pamela?"

Kelly's eyes slowly focused on Max. "I told them I did it. I said it was an experiment in the psychology of stress, and I promised to make restitution. Do you understand why?"

"To protect your sister?"

"They would have put her away, and she wouldn't be able to bear it. I never make her stay locked up. I let her go out when she wants, but I watch her very carefully. Upsets like today don't happen often, but I think she sensed I was disturbed about something. That affects her. She'll be all right, now that she's had a sedative. She'll sleep until tomorrow, then get up and be cheerful, and we'll walk along the beach and search for a perfect sand dollar."

"Why not get her to a doctor? She's sick, Kelly. You should know that. You majored in psychology."

Kelly's green eyes didn't look the least dreamy when she turned them toward Annie. "You do know a lot about me, don't you?"

"Why don't you get her into a hospital?"

Kelly's skin was almost translucent, the veins blue-black near the surface. "Never. You don't know what it would be like. Have you ever been in a mental hospital? Tan walls and cement floors, people with empty, staring eyes, figures in green coveralls, and doctors who ineptly try to treat illnesses that no one understands." She paused, then spoke so low Annie found herself leaning forward to hear. "She would be so frightened, so terribly alone."

"It must all be in your college records," Max said briskly. "About the animals. And that's what Elliot had. You said you didn't care if he told it?"

"Why should I?"

"Because someone might discover the truth about Pamela and insist she be put away."

"I won't let that happen." Kelly lifted her head regally.

She was cold and obdurate and a dangerous adversary. And very, very clever. She was also supremely confident of her cleverness.

Those shrewd, beautiful eyes watched Annie warily.

"Look, Kelly, I'll tell you the truth. Chief Saulter is going to arrest me tomorrow. He believes I murdered Elliot because he was threatening to raise my rent and drive me out of business. He even thinks I pushed my uncle into the harbor last summer, just to inherit· the bookstore."

For the first time, Kelly looked surprised. Annie wondered immediately if it were consummate acting or if it had never occurred to her that Ambrose Bailey's death had not been accidental.

"That's absurd. You wouldn't have done that."

"Well, thanks. I'm glad you don't agree."

Kelly wasn't listening. Instead, she studied the diamond pattern in the turquoise rug.

"Ambrose murdered." Her gaze swung back to Annie. "Why?"

Annie briefly described the true-crime book and the missing manuscript.

"Oh hey, Annie." Max was impatient, irritated at this diversion. "You and Saulter both are way off base. Your uncle fell. I'd bet on that."

"So what happened to the manuscript?"

"You probably lost a box when you moved the stuff from his house."

"Lost a box? Do you think I'm a nitwit?"

"Do you lose things sometimes?"

What a low blow. "Just because I mislaid that script."

At least he had the grace not to bring up the fact that it had almost cost him a producer.

"Where did we find it?"

"Okay, okay. I left it on a park bench. But a silly damn script is not the size of a box with a manuscript." Annie was tired of this battle. She turned to Kelly. "Anyway, my neck's on the block, and Saulter won't even listen, so Max and I have decided to find out everything we can to solve the crime. Will you help us?"

"How can I help you?" Kelly was still cautious, but interested. And perhaps tempted?

"Sure you can help. You know these people; you are extraordinarily perceptive. Maybe you'll see something we've missed." Max was busy exercising his charm. Max was world class when it came to wheedling. He could wheedle a seat five minutes before takeoff on a sold-out People's Express. He could wheedle a box-seat at game-time at the Super Bowl. He was *magic*, and Annie watched with reluctant admiration as Kelly received a concentrated dose.

"I might at that. Tell me what you have." A faint flush stained those marble-pale cheeks. Max was a marvel, and Annie was controlling a sharp impulse to give him an elbow in the ribs.

They started with number one, Emma Clyde.

When Max finished summing up, Kelly moved her hands, and Annie was reminded of seaweed swaying in water.

"Oh, yes. I can see it happening. Emma is quite capable of a carefully conceived, excellently executed plan. If she decided her second husband was a mistake—and she couldn't see any way of divorcing him without losing a great deal of money—I don't believe she'd hesitate for a moment to murder him. I find it quite revealing that she told you she had wanted to see him early the next morning about some investments. She was clearly thinking about him in terms of money. And it's very suggestive that she immediately assumed Annie's intention in bringing up the matter was blackmail. I consider that significant, too. I would almost feel certain she was already the victim of blackmail."

"If she can plan so well and won't stop at murder, why wouldn't she get rid of the blackmailer?" Max asked.

"But she did," Annie jumped in. "That's why she killed Elliot. He was blackmailing her, so she set it all up, stole the poison, killed Jill because she interrupted that, then hid the dart in my store and fixed the lights. It sounds reasonable to me."

"No, no," Kelly objected calmly. "You are misreading Elliot's persona entirely. My dear, he sought power, that was his overriding desire—to manipulate and coerce, to inflict punishment." A tiny smile rippled over her pond-smooth face. "He was not a very attractive person, dear Elliot."

"What's blackmail but a clear exercise of power?" Annie demanded.

"In a limited sense. Do you think, in Elliot's mind, that the receipt of money could compare in any way with the power and pleasure he would take from standing up in front of the Regulars and publicly stripping each person there emotionally naked?"

"By God, you're right," Max declared.

Where had Max acquired his perverted weakness for blond anacondas and redheaded vipers?

"So you think he meant every word of his threat to reveal all Sunday night?"

"Of course. I have no doubt that, had he lived, we would all have learned some fascinating particulars about each person there." Was there a touch of regret in her voice? Viper, indeed.

"So you agree that the motive for his murder must lie in his actions that night?"

"I have no doubt about it."

"How about his ex-wife? How about Ambrose Bailey?"

Neither of them even glanced Annie's way. Max was crinkling his eyes at Kelly, and she was responding on cue. Annie knew she would do well to remember his expertise in the future.

"You've certainly thought this through very thoroughly. Who are the other candidates?"

Max was spilling all to their new confederate. "The next person we talked to was Hal Douglas." Then his face abruptly went blank, and Annie knew he'd remembered her own comment that she suspected a romance between Hal and Kelly.

Kelly waited.

With Max struck dumb, Annie explained about Hal's emotional outburst.

Kelly was unruffled. "His wife could have run off with someone."

"Did you know he had a wife?"

"I knew there was an emotional block."

Annie stopped short of announcing her belief that Lenora was in an unmarked grave near that Lake Tahoe cabin. Instead, she skirted. "What do you think about Hal? Could he kill someone?"

"Hal is passionate. I can see problems if he loved someone deeply and discovered infidelity, but I have trouble imagining him cold-bloodedly killing Jill—or Harriet."

"Jill's death may not have been intentional," Annie suggested. "The autopsy revealed she had a very thin skull—and she was only hit once. Perhaps the killer simply intended to knock her unconscious." Annie reached up and touched the sore spot, still a little swollen, behind her ear. "As for Harriet, nobody really knows what happened. Maybe she saw someone go into Elliot's house and followed them. She may have accused that person of being the murderer and something happened to convince her she was right. The killer had no choice."

"That seems possible." Max nodded.

Kelly was skeptical. She stood and walked slowly to the mantel and lightly touched a piece of painted tinware. "Hal would do things in a rush. He might knock Elliot down or shoot him, but I can't imagine he would plan and carry out this complicated murder."

An attack on Hal made her uneasy. What might she do to protect Hal? Were she and Max naive? Did Kelly know all about Lenora, and was she determined to protect Hal at all costs? She'd already revealed that she would go to great lengths if she cared for someone. Witness her determination to shield her sister.

"Hal writes pretty complicated books."

Kelly merely smiled patronizingly and shook her head.

"How about the Farleys? Solo or together."

Kelly leaned back against the mantel, very much at ease now that Hal wasn't the subject. "They're possible, quite possible." Her dark red hair swung as she nodded. "There is repression there, and violence."

She wasn't at all surprised to learn of Jeff's attacks or Janis's protective response. But again, she thought outright aggression would be more likely for Jeff than the carefully premeditated death by dart.

"I wouldn't rule them out, though, psychologically speaking."

"What about Fritz Hemphill?" Did Max have to look as if he awaited a guru's pronouncement?

Kelly reached out and traced her fingers over the raised pattern in the upholstery of the small Queen Anne wingback. "Fritz is a dangerous man. What did Elliot have on him?"

"Apparently he blew away his best friend so he could inherit a valuable beachfront cottage at Carmel."

"Fritz is a planner, the kind of person who takes what he wants."

"Then there's Capt. Mac." Max's voice was as curdled as sour milk. "A paternity suit."

"At least he didn't kill somebody," Annie exclaimed protectively.

Kelly's green eyes darted from Annie to Max, brightly, perceptively.

Annie was getting pretty damn sick of perception.

"So Capt. Mac's libido caused him some difficulty. Not surprising. But he's capable and intelligent. A cool customer. Of course, that's what you would expect from someone who's headed a police force. Tough. Ruthless. Very savvy."

"Capt. Wonderful," Max said sarcastically.

Kelly slipped gracefully into the wingback chair and looked at him, amused. "You asked for my opinion. I didn't say I liked the man—either."

Max scooted away from that one. "Well, off the top of your head, who's the most likely suspect?"

Kelly gave them an enigmatic smile. "I'd rather know

what each of you thinks. Your choice will be so revealing."

Seventeen

The breeze through the open sunroof ruffled Annie's hair, which hadn't been combed in some time. As the Porsche rattled over the wooden bridge, and they left the ruins of Fort Hendrix behind, she blew out a whoosh of relief. "My God, that woman's enough to give you the creepy crawlies for life. I don't think Hal can be the good old boy everybody takes him for."

"I'm not taking him for a good old boy," Max said drily.

Her lips quivered in a smile. "I guess I have a perverse streak. I was pretty well set on Emma, until Kelly said she could be the villain. Now I keep thinking of Emma's good points."

"Such as?"

Annie laughed. "She's a nice guest. She brought extra chips and clam dip Sunday night."

"And a poisoned dart?" He gunned the motor, then turned right onto the blacktop.

"Hey, wait. Where are you going? Let's go back to the shop. I've got some ideas, and we have to hurry before the ferry leaves."

"I'm thirsty."

"Who do you think you are? Phil Marlowe? We can't spend the afternoon slaking your insatiable thirst. We've got work to do."

But he was already past the checkpoint and turning into Parotti's tavern parking lot when a siren sounded behind them. The Porsche smoothed to a stop, and Max turned an indignant face toward the big motorcycle cop. "I was going twenty-eight miles per hour. A motorized wheelchair could have passed me."

Annie recognized the young giant as the second of the Broward's Rock force, the one who'd dusted for fingerprints in Death On Demand after Elliot was killed. Now he placed ham-sized hands on the doorsill and ignored Max to fix her with a gimletlike stare out of his beady eyes. She started to bristle even before he spoke.

"Just a word to the wise, Miss Laurance." He radiated a thick scent of spicy cologne.

Was there ever a phrase better designed to incite rebellion?

"You'd better stay put. The chief told me to keep an eye on you."

Before Max could pull on his barrister's wig, Annie attacked. "Do they pay you extra to be officious?" she demanded, gray eyes glittering dangerously.

Max held up a hand, clearly a warning to cease and desist.

"Sure, I'm official," the cop retorted.

"Officious," she repeated loudly. "As in rude, overbearing, and gratuitously self-important. Just like Inspector Slack."

The young giant's face turned a dull plum color. "You can talk just as fancy as you like, lady. But you better watch your step, or you're going to jail." With that, he swung on his heel, remounted his motorcycle, and roared off in the direction of the village.

Annie slammed the front door to Death On Demand so hard the front window quivered and a display copy of *Break In* tumbled down. "I'm *mad*."

"Cool down, Tiger." Max moved down the central aisle, carrying the sack from their side excursion to Parotti's tavern.

Flicking on the lights, she followed, too infuriated to take time to pet Agatha, who registered her contempt with a resentful yellow glare.

Max put two six-packs of Bud Light on the coffee bar, then opened the refrigerator.

"Want a beer?"

"I'd rather have that cop's head on a platter."

"Annie, Annie," he said mournfully. "What are we going to do with your temper?" He lifted the beers from their cardboard cartons and put all but two away. "I'm doing my best to keep you out of jail, and that famous Laurance temper's going to get you tossed in the can before nightfall. Honey, didn't you ever learn it's easier to sweet-talk your way out of trouble?"

She banged a stack of *Sugartowns* into a neat pile. Some of the flush began to die out of her cheeks, and she could almost smile. "Okay. So I've got a short fuse."

"That's not all bad—depending upon what you're triggering." His dark blue eyes glinted meaningfully.

She reached up and ruffled his hair. "Stow it, lecher."

"Seriously, sweetie, you're going to have to button your lip. The chief isn't like that director you reamed out when they were casting 'Sailors Ashore.'"

"That sorry clown took his feebleminded script too seriously." She put her hands on her hips, ready to do battle. "At least Saulter hasn't made a pass at me." Her brows drew together. "I wonder why the hell not?"

Max laughed uproariously. "My God, you can't have it both ways."

"Well, just let him try," she said in a steely voice.

He opened two beers and handed one to her. "Come on, chum, cool off. You waste too much energy being mad."

She tilted up the brown bottle, then set it down without tasting its contents. "You know something, we are incompatible."

"Just because I believe in avoiding trouble?"

"That's one reason. But it typifies..."

He grinned and reached across the coffee bar to touch a finger lightly to her lips. "Typify's the kind of word Kelly Rizzoli likes. She could undoubtedly draw up a list of incontrovertible reasons why you and I should avoid interpersonal relationships." His hand traced the line of her cheek. "But she'd be wrong."

She should firmly push his hand away, but another kind of short fuse was ticking.

"Everyone says it's foolish to pursue relationships that

will deadend—" She didn't finish. Max's lips got in the way. The coffee bar was an obstacle, but neither paid any attention to it. Who moved first? Who cared? Their lips met, and Annie stopped analyzing, analogizing, and pontificating.

The phone rang.

Annie didn't quite have her breathing under control when she answered.

Max looked savagely at the phone.

"Yes, Chief?" she said icily.

"Understand you and that pet lawyer of yours are out bothering people."

"It's a free country. Or so I thought."

"You have no call to go around interviewing people. Mrs. Morgan resents it."

"The ex-Mrs. Morgan knew all about the Sunday night session—and she was pretty annoyed that Elliot wasn't forking over her alimony on schedule," Annie said furiously.

A voice broke in. "Hey, you people better leave Carmen alone." She pictured a meaty face with beady brown eyes.

"Butt out, Bud."

So that was Inspector Slack's name.

"Ms. Laurance, I'm calling to give you another chance. You keep your face out of my investigation. I've got enough trouble on this island without you and your boyfriend playing detective. Bud was just giving you some friendly advice."

"I have some friendly advice for Bud," she retorted. "His pal, Carmen, is a real pistol, and she wanted money—"

"Hey, lady, you watch your mouth about Carmen. What d'you mean, she's a pistol?"

"And, furthermore, Chief, have you found out who inherits Elliot's money?"

"Of course."

"Who?"

"That's no business of yours."

"If you're going to slap me in chains tomorrow, you can bet my lawyer will *make* it his business."

Finally, Saulter spoke, and there was just a hint of consideration in his voice. "He hadn't changed his will."

"So Carmen inherits?"

"Yes."

Bud was still fuming. "Hey, wait a minute. Nobody's going to hang a rap on Carmen. Me and her were on the beach Sunday night."

Not Inspector Slack, Annie decided. Mike Hammer on a vacation.

"Bud, get off the line." After an instant, there was a click. "Okay, Ms. Laurance, you and your boyfriend have your fun—but I'll be over to talk to you in the morning. And you better have some good answers." He hung up.

She replaced the receiver. "The tumbril's going to roll first thing in the morning." Her voice was light, but she glanced up at the clock. "Oh Lord, we've got to get cracking. It's ten after five. Come on, Max, let's split up the work. You summarize what we learned from everybody, and I'll call around and see if I can find out where everybody was when Harriet was killed."

Max spread out his notes from the day on the table nearest the coffee bar. He draped himself comfortably in a chair, took off his brown cordovan loafers, wiggled his toes, and drank some more beer.

She called Emma first.

"Yes?" The mistress of mysteries was not cordial.

"Emma, where were you between five and six P.M. Monday?"

There was a chilly pause. "I understand Harriet died about then," she said finally. "Is that what prompts this call?" She laughed softly. "You are indefatigable, aren't you? I was here, my dear. In my office. Working."

"I thought you wrote in the mornings."

"That's right. And in the evenings, too, when I'm close to the finish."

"How about 9:45 Sunday morning?"

"Now that's something new." Her tone was assured and amused. "Is there a corpse no one's told me about?"

"No. That's when the murderer hid the dart in Death On Demand."

"Oh my, you and Mr. Darling do seem to be clever at discovering things. I'm sorry I can't be more helpful. I was working. The next time I get involved in a murder, I'll be sure to order my time better."

Emma sounded quite good-humored now. She certainly didn't feel threatened by their investigation so far.

Annie took a flyer. "How about ten-thirty P.M. Wednesday, July seventeenth?"

"Is there any semblance of reason behind that question?"

"Somebody pushed Uncle Ambrose off his boat."

"Interesting that you know the exact time."

Annie would have given a hot reply, but Emma swept on.

"Sorry, dear, I don't keep a diary—and I wasn't skulking around the harbor that night." The line went dead.

It didn't take long to ring up her list.

Hal Douglas didn't seem affronted by her question. "Yeah, I was jogging about the time Harriet was killed, but I took a path through the bird refuge. I didn't see a soul," he said cheerfully. "As for Sunday morning, I was asleep. And I don't have any idea about last July." His voice dropped. "Do you really think somebody murdered your uncle?"

Annie was relieved when Janis Farley answered rather than Jeff. She replied to the questions in a low, uneasy voice. She and Jeff, she insisted, were at breakfast together Sunday morning and were playing Scrabble Monday evening. Annie could imagine her looking over her shoulder as she spoke.

Fritz Hemphill listened, then said distinctly, "Go to hell."

Before he could hang up, she threw out, "Do you still have the rifle you used to shoot Mike Gonzalez?"

"Funny thing, Annie. Dead men don't talk." His voice continued, cold and uninflected. "Neither do dead women. Sure, I got that gun. I still hunt with it."

Capt. Mac was encouraging. "Have you found out anything?"

"A lot. Some of it, you wouldn't believe."

"I'd believe it. I was a cop for a long time."

It wasn't hard to ask him. "Where were you when Harriet died?"

"In and out. No alibi, unfortunately. I'm transplanting some crape myrtle, so I was around the patio most of the time. You know, the privacy on Broward's Rock is great, but sometimes I wish I had a nosy neighbor."

"There's Carmen Morgan," she offered.

He chuckled. "The lady doesn't spend a lot of time in her garden."

The bedroom was her more likely habitat, but neither of them said it.

"Have you talked to Saulter about Harriet?" she asked.

"Yeah, but there isn't much to report. Place was wiped clean of fingerprints. Saulter thought that was interesting. I did, too. It might indicate the killer was caught by surprise. Otherwise, you'd think he would be wearing gloves."

Capt. Mac said he was probably in the shower Sunday morning. He remembered that he'd spent the evening working on his car the night Ambrose drowned.

Annie rang Carmen Morgan.

"Monday afternoon? Geez, I don't know. I don't keep track of my time like a shop girl."

"That was just yesterday," Annie reminded her in a long-suffering tone which caused Max to look up and grin.

"Sure. Yeah. Well, probably I was watching a game show. That's what I was doing."

Sure.

"What're you going to do with the money Elliot left you?"

"Money? What money?"

"You know. He never changed his will. You'll inherit. Just like a widow."

"Gee, I didn't know that! Gee, that's great." Her effort to sound surprised was as fake as her spiky eyelashes. Annie was glad she didn't have to act for a living. She claimed to be asleep Sunday morning and probably was playing bingo on a Wednesday night in July.

Kelly Rizzoli sounded dreamy. "Around six? I don't know, really. I sometimes walk down by the rock garden. It's peaceful as dusk comes."

Just Kelly and the earthworms, Annie thought.

Max was exhibiting, for him, great industry, shuffling papers and occasionally writing in spurts, so Annie, despite her meager results, stubbornly drew up a chart.

She carried her work to his table and plopped the chart on top of his papers. "Can you believe this?"

He studied it.

ANNIE'S ALIBI CHART

	9:45 Sunday	6 p.m. Monday	10:30 pm Wednesday July 17
Emma Clyde	working	working	?
Capt. Mac	showering	transplanting crape myrtle	car repair
Farleys	breakfast	playing Scrabble	don't remember
Fritz Hemphill	—	—	—
Kelly Rizzoli	?	walking in the garden	?
Hal Douglas	asleep	jogging	don't remember
Carmen Morgan	asleep	game show	bingo?

She ran her hands distractedly through her snarled hair. "These jerks would never make it in a Freeman Wills Croft book." She thumped the table in disgust. "Look at that. Not a single one has an alibi. How can that many people be invisible every time a murder takes place?"

"Everybody says writers are loners. Maybe it's so."

"Not only loners, weirdos," she muttered. "Every time I talk to Kelly Rizzoli, I feel like I'm in a deserted cemetery at midnight, consorting with a vampire."

"You can't expect charts to solve anything," Max continued with irritating placidity. "Life doesn't imitate art. Old mysteries can't help us solve this."

"Sure they can. Why, I'll bet I figure it out before you do. I know a lot more about murders than you ever thought about."

He gave her a smile that could only qualify as patronizing in the extreme, pushed her chart aside to pick up his top paper, and waggled his paper, filled with his dark, sloping scrawl. "Here's what we have to find out."

She ignored the proffered sheet. He quirked an eyebrow, still looking superior and amused, then swung his feet to the floor and stood.

He held his papers high as he moved up the central aisle. "When I get the answers to these questions, we'll know everything that matters." He picked up the phone at the cash desk.

Annie paced back and forth in the coffee area, pausing occasionally to look up at the watercolors. Of course she knew more about murders than Max! He had the usual male conceit, so certain he knew more than she did. By golly, she would show him. The little gray cells, that was the ticket. In all of this mishmash of information, there had to be a key to the villain. No alibi. That indicated a great deal of confidence on the murderer's part, didn't it? Confidence— Okay, she had confidence, too.

But she did prick up her ears to hear his half of the conversation. Fair was fair. After all, she'd let him see her alibi chart.

He was as slick as the hide of a greased pig.

"...calling from Beaufort County, South Carolina. We

have a homicide here, actually a triple homicide, and we need some information on a Miss Kelly Rizzoli. You've got her down for a couple of misdemeanors, around '78, '79. If you can pull it up on your computer, we'd appreciate the help. Sure, I'd be glad to hold."

"So if you get some stuff on Kelly, then we'll know about everybody," Annie kibitzed.

He covered the receiver. "Except for Harriet. And that's moot."

"I know that one. Elliot accused her of lifting a plot from somebody."

Max gave a small shrug. "We know she wasn't the killer. But that would hardly be reason enough."

She remembered Harriet's contorted face that day at Death On Demand. Max was wrong. That day, Harriet was mad enough to kill.

Annie spread her hands out. "How can we guess what's reason enough? Remember what happened to Gideon in Kelly's short story?"

Max waggled his hand for her to be quiet. "That's right," he said into the receiver. "That's the one. What've you got—well, I'll be damned. Sure. Listen, we appreciate your help. If we can ever give you a hand—"

He hung up, then turned to Annie, his blue eyes gleaming with excitement. "He remembers, all right, and he thinks Kelly is just as nutty as her sister. In fact, he believes Kelly did every bit of it herself." He scrunched his face in distaste. "She forgot to mention the chicken house. Apparently, she—or Pamela—set fire to the chicken house behind the place where they boarded."

"Ugh."

"Yeah. So maybe Kelly had more to lose than some embarrassing talk about her crazy sister."

"Maybe Pamela's not crazy. Maybe she's a *prisoner*—a variation on *Flowers in the Attic*."

He didn't laugh. "Actually, nothing about Kelly would surprise me." He ran a hand through his thick blond hair. "Maybe Carmen summed up the party pretty well. Annie, did you have any idea what your Sunday Night Regulars were like?"

She tried to remember back before Sunday. Sunday seemed a thousand years ago.

"I always thought Emma Clyde was a lot smarter than she acted. You know, she looks like the average housewife shopping in the housewares section at Winn-Dixie."

"That's on a par with calling a cobra a house pet."

"I really liked Hal Douglas. He has such an all-American face."

"Just your average neighborhood wife-killer," Max sang.

"And Kelly seemed so vulnerable, like a coed at a bad hangout."

"Very bad, but she's the den mother."

He lightly touched her elbow, and they started back down the central aisle.

"I never did like the Farleys. They give me the willies."

"Another all-American pair." Max walked behind the coffee bar, honing in on the refrigerator.

As he lifted out another beer, she mused, "Nobody much liked Fritz. He's such a cold fish."

Max carefully fitted the church key to the bottle cap. "Then there's Capt. Wonderful," and he shot a sly look at Annie.

She leaned against the coffee bar. "Why do you hate him so much? He's the only normal one of the bunch."

The cap snapped off, and foam rose over the lip of the bottle. "No cop is normal."

"That's not fair. Besides, he has a piddly motive."

Handing her the first bottle, he uncapped the second. "Keeping a paternity suit quiet doesn't seem worth a poison-tipped dart. But a man who'll cheat on his wife will cheat anybody. I intend to nose around him a little more."

Annie took a delicate sip of beer. She'd better ease up on her quaffing. She needed a clear head, especially if she were going to show Max up. He thought he was so smart. Of course, if the murderer's picture were on Harriet's film, neither—

She popped straight up. The beer jostled and overflowed as she gestured wildly at the wall clock.

"My God, Max, it's almost six!"

Eighteen

The Porsche leapt forward. Annie clung to the red leather rim of the dash. The clock flashed 5:52.

"Don't worry, this girl can fly. We'll make it. Besides, Parotti probably doesn't leave on time."

"Yes, he does," she yelled back over the whip of the wind through the open sunroof. The live oaks passed in a blur. "He's a little martinet. You'd think that damned ferry was the *Queen Elizabeth* the way he acts about her schedule."

In answer, Max pressed harder on the accelerator.

Annie thumped back against her spine. They had to make it. They had to.

The Porsche zoomed around the last curve and roared toward the checkpoint. He braked hard, received a pass-through wave from a startled Jimmy Moon, then floorboarded it, and the sports car burst forward like a two-year-old headed for the winner's circle.

Success was theirs! The car screeched onto the dock just as Parotti gave the preliminary toots announcing imminent departure. The ferry horn mingled with the high, abrasive whine of a siren.

Annie twisted in her seat and saw the motorcycle turning off the blacktop.

"Hurry, drive onto the ferry!"

Max twisted to look, too. The Porsche didn't move. "A work farm is not my idea of a pleasant way to spend the rest of October."

As the motorcycle drew alongside, she glared at Max in bitter disappointment.

Once again, the massive young policeman loomed beside the car. A waft of spicy cologne tickled Annie's nose. "Eighty-six miles per hour. You people think this island is a goddamned racetrack?"

Annie jounced in the seat. They had to hurry! The ferry always left on time. The clock flashed 5:59. She could see Parotti peering at them from the ferry cabin.

"Officer, I apologize," Max began smoothly, "but we have important business on the mainland."

"You may have business there. But she don't," and he jerked a thumb at Annie.

"Wait a minute—" she began angrily.

Max spoke out of the side of his mouth. "Stop snarling. Let me handle this."

"She ain't leavin' the island."

"She isn't under arrest so—"

The squinty-eyed giant smiled. It was as charming as a barracuda doing ballet. "I got a warrant right here." He thumped his brown khaki chest. "You get on that ferry, I arrest her."

Parotti yanked the whistle. Final call.

Annie glared at Bud, then leaned forward as if to kiss Max goodbye. At the same time, she pulled open her purse, fished out the roll of film, and jammed it in his hand.

"Go ahead," she whispered in his ear, then slid across the seat, opened the door, and jumped out.

Max looked from her to Bud and back again.

"Max, go!"

The Porsche jolted forward and rolled onto the ferry. The horn tooted, and the ferry chugged out into the sound.

Annie, arms folded, faced Bud.

His meaty face furrowed. "Hey, what was the big hurry?"

"Wouldn't you just like to know?"

Annie rented a battered chartreuse bicycle at Henry's Bikes By the Day or Week, picked up tacos-to-go at Maria's Cantina, and pedaled furiously back to her tree house, taking the shortcut across the Forest Preserve, cool and dim now as dusk settled over the sea pines. She pumped vigorously, treating the bike path like a Le Mans speedway, to help ease some of her frustration. What a lousy deal. She *deserved* to be in at the kill. Or, if not actually the kill, the moment of truth when the murderer's identity was revealed.

Parking the bike beneath the outside stairway, she ran lightly up the wooden steps, unlocked the front door, and carried the take-out sack to the kitchen. She wiped her face, flushed from exertion. She felt like a piece of salt-water taffy that had been dropped in the sand. It was easy somehow to picture Max lounging comfortably in the Porsche, enjoying the cool sweep of water off the sound—and carrying in his pocket the solution to their mystery.

She plumped two beef tacos in the microwave to warm, ducked into the bathroom to wash her hands and face, retrieved the tacos, liberally doused them with hot sauce, and poured orange Gatorade into a yellow plastic cup. Carrying her meal into the living room, she settled comfortably in the wicker divan with a soft red cushion behind her. As she ate, she imagined Max's reaction to this feast (utter horror) and studied her ceiling-high shelves filled with her own very favorite mysteries, many of them quite valuable and difficult to find. She had most of the Constance and Gwenyth Little books. All but one contained the word *black* in the title. Her favorite? Probably *The Black Shrouds*. There were the Leslie Ford, Mary Roberts Rinehart, Mary Collins, Eric Ambler, and Patricia Wentworth titles. Plus Phoebe Atwood Taylor, Rex Stout, and all the Christies, of course.

She finished the first taco, drank some Gatorade, and was reaching for the second taco, when her hand paused. Almost every one of these books, except the Ambler titles, contained magnificent denouements where the detective faced the circle of suspects and, *voilà*, through brilliant ratiocination, triumphantly revealed the identity of the murderer.

Hercule Poirot in *Towards Zero*. Asey Mayo in *Out of Order*. Nero Wolfe in *The Zero Clue*.

Why not Annie Laurance at Death On Demand?

A trap. All she had to do was set a trap for the murderer—

The second taco forgotten, she jumped up and hurried to the telephone. It rang the instant before she reached it.

Bother. She licked hot sauce from her fingers, picked it up, and barked an impatient hello.

"Has the Revolution begun?"

"Huh?"

"You sound beleaguered. Uptight. Stressed." Max dropped his bantering tone. "Is that cop bothering you?"

"Oh, no. No, no. Listen, I've got a great idea!"

"Whatever it is, wait until I get back. I'll—"

"There isn't time. I've got to trap the killer before Saulter comes after me in the morning. And you can't get back until tomorrow."

"I'll be back at nine tonight."

"Did you take your water wings? The ferry doesn't run again until ten tomorrow."

"Mr. Parotti and I are drinking beer at a tavern down the block from a one-hour photo shop in Savannah. We are in hearty agreement that the rich get richer, the poor get poorer, and the working man gets screwed every time." George Jones sang "He Stopped Loving Her Today" in the background. "So cool it till I get back."

She ignored that. "Max, this is *genius*. I'm going to phone everybody and tell them I've just found a diary of Uncle Ambrose's at the shop, and now I know the truth. I'll act all upset and frantic, then I'll break the connection."

George Jones's wail carried clearly over Max's thundering silence.

She practically danced with eagerness. "It's perfect. The murderer will have to come after me. I'll call Saulter and have him watching."

"You think somebody as smart as our killer is going to fall for the oldest trick in the book and come running with a marlin spike?"

"Sure. Yes. Hell, yes. It *always* works for Nero Wolfe."

"Annie, it's all well and good to read those books, but you can't take them so seriously." You'd have to be deaf to miss the patronizing tone of his voice. "Flee, all is discovered. Lordy." He chuckled. "Okay, you have fun, and I'll be back about nine with the goods. I've got to go buy Parotti another beer."

She replaced the receiver very gently. She was in control. Otherwise, she would have thrown the entire instrument into the marsh. She glowered at the phone and wondered how Grace Latham had resisted bloodshed through her years of association with John Primrose.

She'd show him. Nine o'clock. She reached for the receiver, then paused. Maybe he did have a point about the flee-all-is-discovered ploy. She nibbled thoughtfully on her thumb. Oh. She turned an idea over in her mind and smiled. Sure. That would work. She would entice everybody back to the Scene of the Crime, then, just like Miss Marple who drew on her experiences in St. Mary Mead, she would cull from the recesses of her mind the appropriate parallel to a fictional murder, and the answer would be clear. Annie reached for the phone.

Saulter's lip curled as he picked up the mug of hot milk. Dammit, his stomach felt like somebody'd dropped in a handful of live coals. This case was becoming a coast-to-coast sensation. Three murders since Saturday night, and what did he have to show for it? One autopsy report that sounded like something out of John Dickson Carr. God, now he was beginning to think like those bloody writers. But who'd ever heard of killing anybody with succinylcholine? And why'd medicines have names like Hungarian dancers? Damn crazy thing. Well, he wasn't going to be fooled. This was a setup, from first to last, trying to make it look like a nutty writer'd done it. Murder, when you got down to it, was always simple.

This time it was murder for money. That little sunstreaked blonde didn't want to lose the shop she'd murdered to get. She didn't have a penny until Ambrose drowned, and she inherited from him. She'd plowed every cent of his estate into the store, and she wasn't about to lose it.

Saulter gulped some milk and winced.

He'd made it pretty clear he was going to arrest her tomorrow, and now all he had to do was sit back and wait for her to do something foolish. Too bad Bud stopped her from taking the ferry. If she'd made a run for it, he'd have had all the proof he needed.

The problem was, he didn't have any evidence.

Just give him one tangible piece of evidence to tie her to the crime scene. Of course, her fingerprints were all over the circuit breaker box at the store, but her smartassed lawyer would make mincemeat of that. And so far there wasn't anything at the vet's or the Edelman murder.

Evidence. Something to put the nail in Annie Laurance's coffin. Or anything else that would tie her to Morgan. He glared at the last two boxes of papers from Morgan's house. He was sick and tired of reading this guy's stuff. But a careful cop keeps looking.

The phone rang, his hand jerked, and hot milk sloshed over his fingers. God, if it was another of those reporters... He lifted the receiver.

"Saulter here."

"Chief, you've got to get over to Death On Demand. I've called a meeting of all the suspects there in half an hour. We'll catch the murderer tonight!"

The pain in his stomach flared. He'd get this wise-guy little murderess if it was the last thing he did on Broward's Rock. "Ms. Laurance, if I come over there, I'll have a warrant for your arrest in my pocket," and he slammed down the phone.

That little dingo. As if he didn't have enough troubles without her horning in on his investigation.

Annie took a two-and-a-half-minute shower, dried off quicker than pelican diving for mullet, and dressed in a flurry—white linen slacks, a yellow cotton pullover, and yellow flats. She glanced at the clock as she raced out the front door. Everyone was due at Death On Demand in fifteen minutes. She needed to make coffee and organize her thoughts. It took a minute to start the Volvo. She had hardly driven it since Max arrived. Her golf clubs rattled in the back seat as she drove up the rutted road toward the blacktop. Not even a sliver of moonlight pierced the thick canopy of the swamp. When she reached the main road, she picked up speed until she turned into the oyster-shell lot behind the harborfront shops.

Her footsteps crunched loudly across the broken shells. It was a soft Carolina night, the air as silky as Agatha's fur. She unlocked the front door of Death On Demand, flicked on the lights, and hurried toward the back. Agatha peered inquisitively after her, then jumped lightly to the floor and padded toward the coffee bar. Annie poured a twelve-cup measure of Kona beans into the grinder, then turned it on. Good hostess prepares to receive murderous guests. She grinned and took a deep breath, delighting in the heady mixture of freshly ground coffee and old, musty books.

She glanced around the coffee area. Oh, good grief. She must clear out Max's papers. No point in letting the suspects know just how much they had on them. She gathered up the sheets and paused to read Max's list of questions.

1. Whose goose would have been charbroiled if Elliot had finished his talk Sunday night?
2. Why did the murderer show up Johnny-on-the-spot when Annie was in Elliot's tree house?
3. Was Elliot blackmailing Emma? Annie says yes; Carmen, no. Carmen should know. (*Thanks, Max.*)
4. Were Carmen and the dumb cop really on the beach when Morgan was killed? Pretty convenient timing.
5. Did Harriet score twice with her camera? What if she didn't?

The coffee finished dripping into the pot. Annie found her favorite mug, *The Yellow Room* (Rinehart, not Leroux), poured a cup, and leaned against the coffee bar to think.

Her guests began arriving promptly at eight.

Annie greeted them cheerfully, but her perspective had indeed changed since Sunday evening.

Emma Clyde's cornflower blue eyes scanned the coffee area with the same shrewd intensity. Her dress, a swirling mixture of orange and magenta, contrasted as sharply with her stiff bronze curls. But Annie would never again see her as a clever housewife. She didn't carry chips and dip tonight.

"So you've called a meeting of the island residents who are most knowledgeable about crime," Emma observed. "I feel so flattered to have been included." Her tone was tart.

Kelly Rizzoli and Hal Douglas came in together, spookily reminiscent of their arrival Sunday. Then she had seen them as incipient lovebirds. Now it was difficult not to see Grace Poole and Bluebeard.

Capt. Mac came down the central aisle, his tanned face grim. He looked at Annie questioningly. The Farleys stood at the edge of the coffee area. Janis tried to keep her bruised face in the shadows, but Annie saw Emma's eyes widen.

Fritz Hemphill arrived last. He gave no greeting to anyone, and his dark eyes sparkled angrily in a set face.

"Grab a cup of coffee," she offered. "Then if you'll take your places—where you sat Sunday night—we'll get started."

They moved around the coffee bar, but there was no repartee as they took their cups to the tables.

"Now that we're all here—"

"Not quite." Hemphill's voice rasped like a rusty gate. "Where's the boyfriend? And your twittery clerk, Ingrid?"

"Nobody could possibly think Max and Ingrid had anything to do with Elliot's murder. Max never met him until that night, and Ingrid wasn't on Elliot's list."

Hemphill wasn't deflected. "So Ingrid's not in the party. Okay, I buy it. But where's the boyfriend? Searching our places while we sit here?"

"Of course not," she objected hotly. "He's not even on the island."

"That's true. I saw him take the ferry at six," Hal agreed. "But what happened on the dock with you and the cop, Annie?"

Annie stood with her back to the coffee bar and felt control slipping away.

"No big deal," she responded quickly. "Max had some errands to run in Savannah, and I didn't go with him."

"So how come you got left at the dock?" Hal pressed.

"Because that charming cop was going to arrest me if I left the island." Her voice wasn't so good-humored now.

Emma attacked. "So you want us to figure out the crime and save your skin."

"Everybody will breathe easier if we solve the crime. I see no reason why anyone should oppose that—except the murderer."

No one said a word. Seven pairs of eyes watched Annie stonily.

It was time. *En garde.* Annie pointed at the nearest table. Color blazed in Jeff Farley's pale cheeks above his sleek blond beard. His thick horn-rimmed glasses glittered in the overhead light. His chest moved beneath his caramel-colored sweater as his breathing quickened. Janis, her shoulders hunched, pressed her knuckles against her mouth.

Her thick, pancake brown makeup was designed to hide the ugly bruise on her cheek. Instead, it emphasized the alabaster fairness of her neck.

"Jeff Farley couldn't afford to let Elliot Morgan live," Annie began.

Emma Clyde leaned forward, her eyes intent on Jeff's face. The others sat as quietly as mice when a cat nears.

"Jeff is sick." Her voice shook a little, because this wasn't nice. It wasn't fun to peel away the protective layers to a wounded core. "He hurts Janice. Elliot knew this, and, if he put it in a book, it would be the end of everything for Jeff as a writer."

Farley stumbled to his feet, the chair clattering to the floor behind him.

"Jeff, no. No!" Janis's voice rose in a desperate cry.

Capt. Mac was across the brief space in two strides, pinning Jeff's arms to his side. Without a struggle, Farley sagged against the stronger man.

"Sit down, and don't move again." Capt. Mac gently pressed the younger man back into his seat, then turned toward Annie, his face rock hard. "Don't you think this is a little much? Let's leave the investigating to the cops."

"Only the murderer should object," she said steadily.

"People don't like having their dirty laundry spread out in public."

"This isn't public. We were all here Sunday night." She looked from face to face. "We are all under suspicion until we find the murderer."

"That's quite true," Kelly said mildly.

"Go for it," Hal joined in.

Capt. Mac, his face tight with disapproval, shrugged and returned to his table.

Annie knew she didn't have a friend in the house.

"Emma."

The square-faced, sharp-eyed woman nodded curtly. "Here." She took a deliberate sip of coffee. "Good brew. As we used to say, the atmosphere is stimulating. I wouldn't have missed it for the world."

"You don't miss much, do you?" Annie demanded. "You know, if you aren't the murderer, I'll bet you know who did it."

Those keen blue eyes regarded Annie without a quiver. But Annie knew she'd hit the truth. "What do you know, Emma? Why don't you tell us?"

Again, Emma sipped her coffee, taking her time. She smiled, but it was as artificial as a potted plastic plant at a gas station. "I know one thing."

They all turned toward Emma and waited expectantly: Jeff Farley, his hands balled in fists, his face still flushed; Janis Farley, her eyes enormous, her arms crossed tightly over her chest; Kelly Rizzoli, her dark red hair falling softly around her face, her green eyes not the least bit dreamy; Hal Douglas, his pudgy face closed and empty; Capt. Mac, his dark eyes watchful, alert.

"I know a fishing expedition when I see one," Emma said caustically. "You don't know a damned thing, Annie."

Annie eyed her adversary. "But you know a lot of tricks, Emma. You're the smartest one in the room. You know the best defense is a good offense—and you know damned well you pushed your husband over the side of your yacht."

Something moved in those calculating, observant eyes. "I know I can afford a slander suit. One more crack out of you, and I'll call my lawyer."

Annie ignored her and leaned her elbows back against the coffee bar.

"Murder will out, whether it's ever proved or not. Nobody can prove it, but there are some people in L.A. who know Fritz Hemphill blew away his best friend in a so-called hunting accident so he could inherit some property in Carmel."

As usual, Fritz looked the part of a Broward's Rock islander: pale pink cotton broadcloth shirt, a blue ribbed pullover, gray slacks. So civilized. Except for those dark, hot eyes.

Annie met that gaze boldly. "How many cops have you ever known to have an accident with a gun, Fritz?"

When he made no answer, she nodded slowly. "Elliot knew. He knew about Jeff and Janis, Emma, and Fritz. And he knew about Kelly and Hal."

That ideal couple watched her unblinkingly.

"Kelly keeps her sister a prisoner. She claims the girl is mentally ill. I wonder what the truth is? Maybe somebody should talk to her sister. As for Hal, nobody's ever seen his wife since she disappeared from their cabin at Lake Tahoe. He didn't like the way she ran around with other men."

Hal looked like he'd been jabbed in the throat. His head swung toward Kelly. Her face was as placid as a tidal pond, and she reached out to touch his hand.

Capt. Mac slammed his palm hard against the table where he sat alone. Harriet had been his companion Sunday evening. Coffee slopped out of his mug and ran in a slow trickle across the table. He ignored it. "Goddammit, you've gone too far. And I'm not going to sit here like a schoolboy waiting to be scolded." His face, dark with anger, turned toward the others: "I'm next. What did Elliot have on me? A paternity suit, if any of you give a damn." He rose and faced Annie. "I've tried to be helpful to you. I don't think you killed Elliot or Harriet. Or Jill Kearney. But I do think you've let your so-called mystery expertise go to your head, young woman, and I've had enough of it."

He snatched up his soft cap and started down the central aisle. Other chairs scraped. Everyone was leaving.

Her denouement was collapsing like an overcooked soufflé. Now was the time—if she were Hercule Poirot or Nero Wolfe or Asey Mayo or Miss Marple or Miss Silver— when she would raise her hand and point at the guilty party, and the curtain would ring down.

There was one small problem.

She didn't know who in the *hell* the murderer was.

Her suspects were moving with stiff alacrity up the central aisle, and nobody was saying what a good time they'd had.

Emma Clyde paused at the head of the pack, looked back, and taunted, "I assure you, Annie, Marigold Rembrandt would have done it better."

That was the last straw.

Dammit, one of them was a three-time—no—four-time murderer, counting Uncle Ambrose.

"All right," she called out angrily. "You can all laugh now. But I'll have the last laugh tomorrow when I give Chief Saulter a photograph of the murderer."

The exodus stopped.

"Where in the hell did you get a picture of the murderer?" Emma demanded.

"The murderer's not so damned smart. Did it ever

occur to any of you that Harriet had a clear view of Elliot's house? And she was up in her widow's walk Monday afternoon—with her camera."

Nineteen

Max tapped a Scott Joplin intro with his fingers on the glass counter and watched the clock. In another five minutes, he'd know what Harriet had captured in her film. Would it be Annie? And someone else?

That reminded him of his list of questions. Elliot had collected information about the Sunday Night Regulars, and he had intended to blab everything he knew. When Annie pretended she knew about Elliot's information, Emma immediately suspected her of blackmail. That suggested she'd been blackmailed before. But Carmen insisted her ex-husband wasn't a blackmailer—Max stood up straight. Blackmail. Why did people blackmail? He thought about it with growing excitement, and he thought about everyone who'd been at Death On Demand Sunday night and the traditional reason for blackmail.

"Your pictures, mister." The clerk shoved the package across the counter with exquisite boredom.

Max grabbed them. There was Annie, climbing in the kitchen window of Elliot Morgan's house. And there—by God. It was the face he expected.

"Can I use your phone?" he yelled at the startled clerk.

He made a long distance call, using his Sprint number, but the line at Death On Demand rang busy.

It was very quiet in Death On Demand. So quiet Annie could hear the click of Agatha's claws as she glided up the central aisle to see why her mistress stood by the front door.

"Agatha, I may have blown it."

Curious bright yellow eyes stared at her unblinkingly.

"Emma made me mad." She spoke conversationally. Max had always warned that her temper was going to land her in deep trouble someday. Just because Emma had taunted her with that crack about Marigold Rembrandt was no excuse to have let slip about the film.

Her face furrowed in concentration. But no matter how hard she thought, it didn't change the truth of the matter. She'd told them about Harriet's camera—and she'd said she'd turn the film over to the chief tomorrow.

The bookstore was quieter than a graveyard at midnight. She swallowed, lunged across the few feet of space, and shoved home the deadbolt.

She gulped some air, then jumped to one side, her heart racketing in her chest as she stared wildly down to see what had touched her leg.

Agatha lifted a dainty paw and swiped again at her shin, thoroughly enjoying this new and active game.

God. A murderer somewhere outside and a cat with lousy timing inside.

Annie moved precipitously again, dashing to the cash desk and pulling open the drawer. Agatha flowed up to the counter and crouched, purring deeply. Annie scrabbled through the drawer. A letter opener. Wonderful to slice butter. Rubber bands. Band-Aids. Aspirin. Paper clips. A new package of golf balls. She ripped open the package and stuffed the three hard balls into the pocket of her slacks. It wasn't much, but they hadn't called her Dead-Eye on the softball team for nothing. She would at the very least go down firing.

Okay. She had some ammunition in case the killer broke in this minute, and now she'd call the chief. He *had* to listen this time.

She reached for the phone and realized her hand was shaking. She'd always felt absolute disdain for the wumpety conduct that landed gothic heroines in a pickle up to the top of their lace nighties. She had always been confident that she would never be guilty of repairing to the second tombstone at midnight in the company of a man with a mustache. Not she.

And here she was, trying to breathe silently so she could listen for the telltale noises that would signal the murderer's approach.

Her hand rested on the receiver. A faint frown touched her face.

Why wasn't the killer poking a rifle through a window and blowing her away? Or unleashing another poisoned dart? Or wielding a handy cosh?

Indeed, why was it as quiet as the proverbial graveyard? Nobody was trying to break in.

Was someone lying in wait for her outside?

She lifted her hand from the telephone and rubbed her knuckles thoughtfully against her cheek.

Let him—or her—lie. She wouldn't stir a step until Max came, and nobody could handle the two of them.

She breathed more easily, and checked her watch. Max and Parotti might be boarding the ferry this minute. It wouldn't be long, and when he got back, they'd take the pictures straight to Saulter.

But if nobody were reacting to her startling revelation about Harriet's camera—it meant nobody but Annie was pictured in those films. That's why the doors remained closed. No one knocked. No one called.

"Dammit."

Agatha stopped purring.

"Not you, sweetheart." Annie stroked the silky fur, but Agatha twisted away and dropped to the floor.

If she alone were pictured in the films, she and Max were back to Square One.

The whole evening was a fiasco. Perhaps the only solution was to look at everything with a fresh eye. Start at the beginning—with the murder of Uncle Ambrose. She paced down the central aisle, her eyes scanning the bright jackets to her right and left with disappointment. Her books had let her down. She *should* have been able to turn and dramatically unveil the villain, but her denouement had fizzled like day-old champagne. She passed the espionage/thrillers section and noted an Ambler title, *The Light of Day*. She felt just about as competent as Arthur Abdel Simpson.

She tucked her hand in her pocket and gripped the first golf ball. Maybe she should retire as a mystery bookseller and concentrate on her golf.

Reaching the coffee area, she stared up at the five watercolors, without experiencing the usual spurt of pleasure in them.

The old lady with faded blue eyes stared at approaching death without surprise as the heavy car hurtled closer in watercolor number one. The ancient servant strained to see in the second painting. The third pictured an active man's closet full of trophies and sports equipment. The young man exhibited disgust as he handed the letter to his sister in the fourth picture, and guests watched as their host raised a glass in a toast in the fifth.

What good did it do to know all about murder and murderers and be caught wanting when it mattered?

She knew these stories backward and forward. The sporting man who opened his library window on a snowy evening to someone he trusted—

Someone he trusted.

Annie stood very still and stared up at the third painting.

Trust.

Uncle Ambrose's murder.

Uncle Ambrose himself.

She stared at the painting and could see her uncle, his thoughtful, intelligent face. He had been smart, savvy, tough, perhaps a little cynical from his years as a prosecuting attorney in Fort Worth. He knew just how bad people could be. He knew that murderers were dangerous predators.

He was researching *murders*. He would never have turned his back on someone he suspected of being a killer.

Uncle Ambrose was nobody's fool.

So he had been killed by someone he trusted, just as was the man whose closet was pictured.

It was exactly as Hercule Poirot always insisted: the character of the victim revealed the identity of the murderer. Staring up at that painting of a jumbled closet, remembering her uncle, knowing the Sunday Night Regulars, she knew who had committed the four murders on Broward's Rock.

Swinging around, she ran up the central aisle, and grabbed up the telephone receiver. Agatha flashed into the darkness, seeking sanctuary beneath her favorite fern. Annie held the receiver to her ear, then stiffened.

The line was dead.

Max leaned sleepily back against the car seat and enjoyed the breeze lifting off the water as the ferry chugged peacefully across the sound. He felt a great sense of satisfaction. He'd tell Annie how he'd figured it out even before he got the pictures. All it required was an orderly mind, the ability to shuck away the extraneous and focus on the important. Poor Annie and her flee-all-is-discovered ploy. He shook his head and smiled, then smothered a yawn. Almost there. Well, he'd be tactful with her.

The lights went out in Death On Demand. Annie moved away from the switches and ran swiftly down the central corridor, a golf ball clutched in her right hand. She slid like a wraith into the storeroom and felt her way across the floor to the back door.

This was the tricky part.

The murderer must be waiting for her outside. That dead phone line was no accident. It was intended to prevent her from calling the chief, which meant, in turn, that the films did contain the murderer's picture. She had no intention of remaining in Death On Demand like one of the Ten Little Indians.

She edged open the back door and peered out into the alley. It was darker than the dirt heaped beside an open grave. As quietly as a water moccasin slipping through a marsh pond, she eased out of the screen door and crept up the alley, every nerve end alert for a betraying rustle. Reaching the end of the alley, she surveyed the broad expanse of lawn, dotted with sea pines, that lay between the shops and the parking area. Her blue Volvo sat in solitary splendor near a clump of wisteria. God, what she would have given at that moment for a little urban clutter and excitement. The shops and their parking lot, closed at night, were separated from the houses by the golf course. The nearest habitations were the marina condos, several hundred yards to her left. Lights shone cheerfully from several of the condos.

Could she scream loudly enough to get help?

Not in time. The Broward's Rock murderer liked to bash his victims. It behooved her to avoid all contact. If she could just reach her car—

Darting from palmetto palm to azalea thicket to palmetto palm, Annie plunged into the shadows nearest her Volvo and fell headlong over a body.

She didn't have to see to know it was a body. She could *feel* it. Her first, panicked, instinctive fear was for Max. But he couldn't be back yet. Frantically, she felt the still form, found the slowly beating pulse in the throat. A man's throat. A familiar smell. Cologne. My God, it must be *Bud*. Maybe Saulter had listened and sent Bud to keep an eye on her, but obviously the murderer had spotted him. She patted his pockets. Keys. A lighter. Shielding it with her hand, she flicked it on. Yes, it was Bud, with a smear of blood at the side of his head.

And no gun in his holster.

Annie crouched by the unconscious policeman, then hurtled toward her car, yanked open the door, jumped in, slammed and locked the door. She poked the key in the ignition, turned it, and nothing happened.

The phone dead. Bud knocked out. Her car disabled.

She was one sitting duck.

The murderer could get her now. The slam of the car door was unmistakable. He had to know where she was.

Minutes ticked by. Nothing happened.

She gripped the steering wheel. Okay, the murderer was after the film—

"Oh, God!"

Annie unlocked the car door, jumped out, started for the shop, stopped, flapped her hands frantically.

How could she have been so dumb?

She wasn't the target. The killer was after Max! Max's trip to the mainland had received full play at her abortive denouement—and this murderer thought fast and moved faster. The ferry would be back any minute, and the murderer would be there, waiting, ready to attack.

Car dead. Bud out. Phone off.

She had to get word to Saulter.

By the time she could knock at a condo, persuade someone to let her in, call the station, get Saulter, and convince him, it would be too late for Max.

Forever too late.

Her watch gleamed in the dark.

Five minutes to nine. The ferry was due back at nine.

Annie set off in a jog toward the condos. She'd find a bike. Steal one. Nobody locked up their bikes on Broward's Rock. Then she saw a gleam of metal in the bushes near where Bud lay. She tore at the branches of wisteria. It took only a moment to get the keys out of Bud's pocket. As she kicked the motorcycle to life, she remembered those long-ago summer outings on dirt bikes with Uncle Ambrose and gunned the motor.

Had anyone seen her race across the island, it would have been the stuff of legends: "Listen, my child, you shall hear of the night Annie Laurance flew by here." But instead she took the bike trail across the Forest Preserve, which, understandably, was not heavily populated at nine o'clock on an October night, and erupted into public notice at the checkpoint.

Throttling down, she squealed the cycle to a pause and shouted at a startled Jimmy Moon, "Call Chief Saulter. Tell him the murderer's after Max at the ferry landing and to come quick!"

The motorcycle jolted forward. Annie careened through the village streets and curved around the last corner to see the ferry bumping into the dock. She killed the motor and let the machine roll to a stop, then jumped down and began to run. She dared not call out. The killer had Bud's gun. The murderer much preferred a quiet knockout, but the gun would be used if necessary. She had no doubt of that.

She ran up the blacktop, her flats slapping against the pavement. The Porsche bumped slowly off the ferry.

A dark figure stepped out into the road and hailed Max.

The Porsche stopped.

Annie was close enough to see a figure bend near the window.

She gripped a golf ball, raised her arm and let fly.

Twenty

Her golf ball struck Capt. Mac square on the temple just as Max slammed open the car door and creamed him across the chest.

The police car, red light whirling and siren snarling, slid to a stop on the dock. The lights from the police car showed Capt. Mac struggling to get to his feet and reaching beneath his black turtleneck sweater.

"He's got Bud's gun!" Annie shouted as Max turned to dive toward McElroy and Chief Saulter reached for his own gun.

Her second golf ball bulleted into Capt. Mac's hand just as he drew out the pistol. Then Max's flying tackle dumped the older man on his back.

Chief Saulter trained his gun on the two of them, retrieved Bud's gun, then gestured for Max and his quarry to stand with their backs against the patrol car.

Parotti stumped off the ferry, his head jutting forward pugnaciously. "What the hell's going on here? Can't a man drink a beer in peace and quiet after a hard day?" Then he squinted at Max. "You still here? Got car trouble?"

Max jerked his head toward Capt. Mac, then rubbed his neck. "Ouch. Capt. Mac's the murderer. He tried to jump me. Didn't you see it?"

Parotti grumbled, "I was down below, but you people are making enough noise to raise the dead."

Capt. Mac kept trying. "Saulter, I was going to make a citizen's arrest. Darling's the man you want. He's—"

"Give it up," Max advised. "I've got the pictures, McElroy, showing you on Elliot's steps. Harriet had a talent for photography."

Capt. Mac slumped back against the police car, his face stolid.

Max yanked on his pullover sweater which had twisted around his chest in the struggle. The whirling red light on the police car revealed an ugly scratch on the side of his face.

Annie was preparing to move forward, offer a handkerchief, and make sympathetic coos when Saulter, snapping handcuffs on Capt. Mac's wrists, said, "So you solved it, Darling."

She stopped in midstride. "Oh, no," she objected energetically. "I solved it. I figured it out and came to save Max's life."

"Save my life! Hell, I knew it was Capt. Mac. Why do you think I rammed the door against him? I probably dented the hell out of it—"

"You just stopped in the middle of the road, and he was getting ready to cosh you. If it hadn't been for me—"

"For God's sake, I *had* to stop. He called out that he had you at his place, and if I ever wanted to see you again, I'd better cooperate."

"You just looked at Harriet's pictures," she said derisively. "I *deduced* it."

"Oh yeah! How?"

She described the third watercolor at Death On Demand. "And, of course, once I *thought* about it, it was easy. It had to be Capt. Mac." She leaned forward to explain. "You see, it was just as Hercule Poirot always says. The character of the victim is all-important."

"Look, Annie, admit it," Max urged, "you made a lucky guess."

"Guess, my monocle. It was an exercise in *reason*. One: Uncle Ambrose was smart. He was writing a book about murderers. He knew how dangerous killers are. He spent his life putting them behind bars. Would he turn his back on somebody he thought was a murderer? Hell, no. So that meant he wasn't afraid of the person who killed him. Two: What was Uncle Ambrose going to do the very next week? He was going to make a trip to do some research on his book. His first stop was to have been in Florida. Silver City." Annie turned to look toward the heavyset man in handcuffs. "You told us you didn't have anything to do with the Winningham investigation. You know something, Capt. Mac, I'll bet that's not true."

McElroy's face looked like a slab of rough-cut stone in the whirling red flash from the police car. He stared back at Annie with an ugly glint in his eyes.

"He trusted you. And you killed him."

"You don't have any evidence," Saulter objected.

"When you investigate, you'll find out," Annie insisted. "Once you know where to look, it will all come apart."

"A lucky guess," Max repeated disdainfully. "I'm the one who figured it from information we received. Emma Clyde was the key. Obviously, she was being blackmailed. That's the first thing she expected when Annie pretended to know what Morgan was going to spill Sunday night. And Carmen insisted Elliot wasn't a blackmailer. So where did that leave us? There was a blackmailer on Broward's Rock. And who was the only person in that bookstore Sunday night who lived in a two-hundred-thousand-dollar house and didn't have fat royalties to pay for it?" He pointed at the sullen figure of the ex-cop. "There he is. Living in a rich man's house—but retired from a police force. Where did he get the money to buy a place here and live like a man of leisure? I wonder how much Winningham paid him? Somehow he knew something that would convict Emma of murder. He lived like a king by keeping things quiet for money. That's what Morgan figured out. If an investigation into McElroy's finances ever began, he would be finished."

"Yeah." Saulter nodded. "I finished up going through Morgan's papers tonight. He'd gotten a copy of the Coast Guard report on the investigation into the drowning of Emma's husband.

"It didn't mean anything by itself. But it fits into your theories real nice. Guess who was in the boat anchored next to *Marigold's Pleasure*? Guess who told the Coast Guard there were no cries for help that night?"

"So," Max declared grandly, "I figured it out."

"Oh no." Annie shook her blond head. "I did it."

Heads lowered, hands on hips, Max and Annie glared furiously at each other.

Chief Saulter stood just inside the bookshop door. He peered at Edgar.

"Pretty nice place here."

Annie forbore to remind him that the last time he came in, he thought she was a murderess.

"Nice cat." Saulter reached out to pet Agatha. Instead of streaking away as any perceptive feline would, Agatha rolled over on her back and kneaded her paws.

Annie leaned on the cash desk and pondered feline intelligence. Then she looked up and down the empty aisles of Death On Demand. Where were all those customers who'd thronged the place when they thought Annie was killer-of-the-week? Ingrid had opened the store that morning and left when Annie arrived because it was crystal clear the rush was over. There wasn't a single person present to see Saulter eat crow.

Saulter opened his mouth, closed it. Apparently crow wasn't delicious.

She was too kindhearted to let him suffer. "How's Bud?"

Saulter's saturnine face twisted in a genuine smile. "Can't be too uncomfortable," he said drily. "Carmen Morgan's got him in bed." He paused and added stolidly, "Resting up from his head wound."

She and the chief looked at each other with mutual understanding.

Saulter shifted his weight from one big foot to the other. "Thought I'd let you know everything's falling into place against Capt. Mac. It's just like you and that young man thought."

She started to bristle. How could Max try to take credit?

"You figured it right. Capt. Mac couldn't afford to let Ambrose go to Silver City. I've been on the phone this morning. You know how he told you he didn't have anything to do with the Winningham investigation?" Saulter snorted in disgust. "Not much. He just ran the whole thing. Seems the chief then, Al Canady, why, he was a drunk. The city manager told me Capt. Mac was a great guy the way he ran the department and never seemed to mind that he was just the assistant chief." Irritation roughened his voice. "Who knows how many times he got paid off? Course, he really hit it big with the Winningham case. Then he anchored next to Emma when she pushed her husband over. We'll never prove that, 'cause Mac's not saying a word. But it's pretty clear she was paying off somebody, and we can bet it was Mac. That's why Mac murdered Elliot. And he had to kill Dr. Kearney when she caught him at the clinic, stealing the—" He paused; it was still too hard to say. "—stuff. And Harriet was watching Elliot's place and saw you and Mac arrive." The chief shook his head disapprovingly. "Breaking and Entry. You shouldn't of done that, Ms. Laurance."

"I know," she said humbly. "But you seemed so suspicious of me, I felt I had to look out for myself."

"Guess you were pretty upset about the investigation," he said uncomfortably.

She toyed with the spike holding phone messages (four from Mrs. Brawley).

He peered intently at the floor. "I really liked old Ambrose. Kind of lost my cool when I figured somebody pushed him overboard. Should have known it wasn't you. I always did wonder why nobody heard a splash in the harbor. Think I've figured that out, too. Ambrose must've gone over to McElroy's house that night for a drink. Bet Mac hit him from behind, then dumped him into his saltwater pool to drown. When he was—when he was finished—he hauled the body out and took it to the harbor." He rubbed the back of his hand against his nose. "Anyway, should've known you didn't do it."

Annie surprised herself. She reached out and patted his arm. "I can understand. Uncle Ambrose was a wonderful person."

The chief finally looked at her directly. "So anyway, no hard feelings?" He stuck out a callused hand.

She shook it. "Chief, what about the others?"

"We're scratching around. I've got the Tahoe people looking for a grave by that cabin, but I don't expect anything to come of it. Too much territory. Fritz Hemphill—he got away with murder, I don't doubt it. It'll never be proved. As for Mrs. Clyde—Capt. Mac won't say a word, so she's still out of our reach. I sent the district nurse to talk to the Farleys and Miss Rizzoli. The Farleys have agreed to some counseling. That Miss Rizzoli—she's a nut case, isn't she? Some little group of friends you had there."

He squinted at her. "You intend to have any more of those Sunday night meetings?"

"God. I hadn't thought about it."

She ticked the survivors off in her mind: Emma, the Farleys, Fritz, Kelly, and Hal.

Saulter grinned. "There'll be more writers coming to Broward's Rock. I'll bet you can start them up again in a few months."

She knew that was the most generous gesture he could have made.

"And that boyfriend of yours can help keep everybody in line. Especially if he sets up down the boardwalk from you."

"Sets up?"

"Yeah. He's measuring the empty shop right now."

"What for?"

"His detective agency."

As Saulter left, Max came in, grinning smugly and carrying a tape measure and notepad. The two men exchanged chummy greetings in the doorway. Saulter promised to take Max fishing.

Annie opened her mouth to attack, but Max spoke first.

"I'm only doing what you asked me to."

He was odiously pleased with himself. He draped the tape measure around Edgar and tied it in a bow, then grinned at her.

"I *asked* you—Max, I never asked you to be a private

detective. That's ridiculous. You can't be serious. How could a private detective agency have any business on a little island like this?"

"Why not? When word gets around how ingeniously I solved these murders when the authorities were stymied, people will flock to my agency."

He solved the murders! She'd get to that absurd proposition in a minute. "Dammit, Max. You are impossible. When we talked about you doing something, I meant something *real*. This is just the same old thing. Max, can't you be serious?"

He reached out and took her hand and drew her near. She came reluctantly.

Then a little closer.

"Max," and her indignant voice was muffled against his shoulder. "Why can't you—"

"Annie—"

The bell above the door jangled. They leapt apart guiltily as Mrs. Brawley poked her head inside. Her foxlike nose twitched and her bright eyes glinted, but there were more important matters than love. She darted to Annie, took her firmly by the sleeve, and started down the central aisle toward the coffee bar.

Annie was irresistibly swept along, and Max followed.

". . . called and called. I know I'm the first one. Now, here're the answers."

Mrs. Brawley pointed to the first watercolor.

"That's from *Easy to Kill*. And the next one's *Funerals Are Fatal*. Then *Murder at Hazelmoor, The Moving Finger,* and *Remembered Death*. All Agatha Christies. My dear," she chided, "is that quite fair?"

Design for Murder

FOR PHIL, PHILIP, AND SARAH,

WITH ALL MY LOVE.

THE TYPIST NODDED. It was finished, as neat a design for murder as could be envisioned. Murder with malice. To be enjoyed by a select group. Well, wasn't it deserved?

For an instant, the writer hesitated. Was public humiliation deserved? There was no question as to the answer. And perhaps the effect would be to break the pattern of silken domination, to end the ruthless manipulation masked by charm.

A gloved hand gently loosened the last sheet from the typewriter. It was an agreeable irony that the plan should be typed on the old machine that sat in the corner of the director's office of the Chastain Historical Preservation Society. Should these pages ever be linked to this particular typewriter, it would reveal only that the manuscript had been produced on a machine easily accessible to the cream of Chastain's social hierarchy.

When the pages were neatly folded and placed in the waiting envelope, the writer read the cover letter again, then painstakingly traced a signature. It took only a moment to slip the letter inside and seal the envelope. Everything was in readiness. As soon as the mystery expert was officially hired, the letter could be mailed.

The writer looked up at a wall calendar which pictured the Prichard House, one of Chastain's oldest and loveliest antebellum mansions. A crimson circle marked April 7.

2

IDELL GORDON TUGGED restlessly at her sheets. She should have gone to the dentist. Well, too late now. The upper-right back molar throbbed. She kept her eyes squeezed shut, hoping for the blessed release of sleep. But sleep wouldn't come. Finally, wearily, she struggled upright and levered her ungainly body to the edge of the bed, peering at the luminous dial on the bedstand. Almost three o'clock. Swinging her legs over the side, she slipped into her scuffed pink satin houseshoes. Oh, her jaw, her jaw. She padded across the room to her bath and reached up for the brown plastic vial of Valium tablets. One of them might help her sleep. She filled a bathroom cup with water and swallowed the tiny pill, then suppressed a groan. It would take a while for the drug to help. She almost walked to her easy chair, but she knew she would feel better if she kept moving. She crossed the room, dodging the potted plants and the rocking chair and the rickety maple whatnot, and opened the French window to step out onto the second-floor balcony. The soft night air swept over her, soothing and calming. It was almost warm enough to walk out in her nightdress, though it was only mid-March, but she grabbed up a shawl that she'd thrown over her rocking chair earlier that evening. The moonlight speckled the grounds below, hiding the burgeoning weeds in the beds along this side of the Inn. She sighed. Her back always hurt when she hoed, but she couldn't afford to hire a gardener this spring. Occupancy of the Inn had been down, and it was going to be touch and go on the bills. A little flicker of panic moved in her chest. What was she going to do if the Inn failed? It would be jammed for the house-and-garden tours in April, but that wouldn't make up for empty rooms later in the summer. She paced up and down on the balcony, gingerly holding her jaw and trying not to whimper, and careful, too, to step quietly so as not to arouse any of the sleeping guests. Then, sharp and harsh as a peacock's cry, the gate to the grounds of the Historical Preservation Society squeaked open. Idell recognized the sound at once. She'd known it for years, the sound of the gate that marked the boundary between her Inn and the Society grounds. But why would the gate be opening? And at this hour? She bent to peer over the railing. How curious! How strange! She would have to ask— fiery hot pain lanced her jaw. She gave a soft moan and turned to go back inside.

3

CORINNE PRICHARD WEBSTER stood in front of the or-molu-framed mirror. Despite the dusky, aged glass, her reflection glistened as brightly as crystal. She always enjoyed her morning encounter with her own image. Beauty was her handmaiden and had always been so. She felt confident that to men she represented the unattainable goal of perfection. Once, when she'd asked Tim if he'd like to paint her, he had been silent for a long time, then he'd said, even if grudgingly, "You're like the first streak of rose at sunrise." Tim was almost as poetic as he was artistic. It sickened her to realize that he'd been beguiled by Sybil, who was no better than a slut for all the glory of her old name and her wealth. Well, they needn't think she would let Tim take his paintings from the museum. After all she'd done for him, he must realize that it was his duty to stay in Chastain. Her mouth thinned with determination, then curved in a humorless smile. They thought it was settled, but he couldn't very well have a show in New York without any paintings—and the paintings belonged to the Prichard Museum.

She lifted a slender white hand to touch the tightness between her eyes, and the tiny wrinkles disappeared. She stared at her face appraisingly. Her eyes were still as vividly blue as always, her skin as smooth and soft as a young girl's. She felt a flash of satisfaction. She did so despise women who let themselves go. Lucy's face popped into her thoughts. Skin like leather from too many hours in her wretched garden and no more imagination in fashion than one might expect from a librarian. Boring, that was how Lucy dressed, although she could look quite nice when she chose. On Sundays, for example, she always wore a well-cut silk dress and a hat and gloves. Corinne shook her head. Hat and gloves. Almost no one wore them nowadays—except Lucy. It certainly dated her. Corinne looked at her reflection in continuing satisfaction. No one could say that about her. She was always *au courant*, and no one thought she was as old as Lucy, either. It was certainly a good thing she'd been firm years ago. It wouldn't have done for Cameron to marry Lucy and make her a Prichard, not a girl whose father ran a clothing store. The Prichards had never been small shop-keepers. The Prichards owned plantations and, long ago, sailing ships and warehouses.

Her eyes narrowed, and she no longer looked at her reflection so she didn't see the transformation. At one instant, the mirrored face was soft and beguiling, almost as beautiful with its classic bones, silver-blonde hair, and Mediterranean blue eyes as on her wedding day at nineteen almost forty years before. Then, as Corinne Prichard Webster thought about her niece, Gail, and the manner in which she was behaving, throwing herself at a totally unsuitable man, the face hardened and looked all of its fifty-nine years, the eyes cold and hard, the mouth thin, determined, and cruel.

The phone rang.

Corinne didn't move to answer it, but she looked across her bedroom, past the silken canopied bed and the Queen Anne dresser to the compass rose desk which sat in an alcove, the blue velvet curtains unopened yet to the morning. The white and gold telephone, a French reproduction, rang again. Corinne waited, certain she knew the caller.

A gentle knock sounded at her bedroom door, then Marybelle stepped inside.

"The call is for you, ma'am. Mr. Roscoe Merrill."

Corinne nodded. "I will answer it, Marybelle."

As the maid softly closed the heavy door, Corinne moved to the telephone. Picking up the receiver, she lifted her chin. If Roscoe Merrill had been in the room, he would have recognized that stance. It was Corinne at her most imperious.

"Yes, Roscoe." She listened, then said impatiently, "The private man reveals the public man." He spoke again, but Corinne was shaking her head. She interrupted sharply, "It won't do any good for you to take that tone with me. I will do what I feel is right. You should have considered the consequences of your actions. I certainly feel that Jessica has every right to know." At his angry response, she depressed the cradle. Her face was implacable as she replaced the receiver.

The green and pink porcelain clock on the mantel delicately chimed the quarter hour. Vexed, Corinne shook her head. She was running late this morning, and there was much she had to do. There was that

matter of the clinic and John Sanford's foolish plan to
expand it. That would draw more country people into
Chastain, overburdening the hospital with the kind of
people who couldn't pay. John must be made to see
that he was out of line. Corinne yanked on the bell
pull. She would have time for Marybelle to draw her
bath, then she must hurry. So many things to attend to.
That silly mystery program, for one. She felt a surge of
irritation. Such a cheap idea. For once she agreed with
Dora, but it had been obvious that the Board was going
to approve Roscoe's stupid proposal. She'd voted yes,
even though she was seething inside. After all, she
couldn't let it appear that the Board was taking such a
major step without her approval. At least, as president,
she'd retained control of hiring the mystery expert.
That was another reason to make Roscoe pay for his
actions, which she certainly intended to do. There was
a proper way to act and an improper way. That reminded her of Gail. She would talk to Gail without
delay. Corinne sighed, overburdened. There were so
many demands on her time and energy. Then she
straightened and looked toward the dusky mirror, her
face again soft and unlined. After all, she was Corinne
Prichard Webster. People depended upon her, so many
of them. What would they do without her?

4

WANT ALL OF them. Every last one of them."

The penetrating voice grated on Annie Laurence's ear drum. Her hand tightened on the receiver, but she kept her reply light and cheerful. Think of it this way, she lectured herself, every demand by Mrs. Brawley translated into a cordial hum on the cash register.

"I don't believe they've all been reprinted yet. But I'll be glad to order them as they're scheduled."

"Hildegarde Withers is *wonderful*! It's a crime they've been out of print all these years." The tone was accusing.

Annie didn't quite see it as a capital offense, but she murmured agreement. "Don't worry, Mrs. Brawley, I'll order them for you. And, if you like, I can round up all the Stuart Palmer titles second-hand—"

"I want *new* books."

"Oh, certainly. By all means. Now, I have your number. I'll let you know as soon as the first title arrives."

It took several seconds more to end the conversation. Mrs. Brawley's singleminded pursuit of a goal ranked high on any all-time list, neck-and-neck with Carrie Nation, Johnny Appleseed, and Zsa Zsa Gabor.

Once free of the phone, Annie returned to a jollier pastime, reading mystery reviews in *Publishers Weekly*. The latest Robert Barnard sounded marvelous. And there was a new book by Sister Carol Anne O'Marie. She would—

The front doorbell sang. Annie dropped the magazine on the wicker table, pushed up from her favorite rattan easy chair, the one with the softest red and yellow cushions, brushed by a flourishing Whitmani fern, and stepped into the broad central corridor of Death on Demand. She hurried past the angled gum shelving with the various mystery categories toward the front desk and the rather stunning woman who was surveying the interior of the bookstore as if it were a Peruvian slum.

Annie's smile tightened. You don't have to *like* customers, she reminded herself, although, as a general rule, she did. Mystery readers, as a class, were bright, well-informed, and articulate. This well-preserved blonde was a stranger to her. Maybe she'd just moved to Broward's Rock. She certainly looked prosperous enough to afford the island's casual but expensive lifestyle. Annie swiftly appraised the elegant cream suede suit, the crimson silk tie, the brown alligator pumps and handbag, and a wedding ring that glittered like the Waldorf chandelier.

"Good morning. May I help you?"

Deeply blue eyes flicked disdainfully from Edgar's sleek feathers to a splashily bright poster affixed to the

True Crime section, which advertised the latest book on the luckless headmistress with the unfortunate love life. Carnelian lips thinned in disgust.

Annie could feel a rush of heat to the back of her neck. Steady, she thought, foreseeing lurid headlines. MYSTERY SHOP OWNER BLUDGEONS OBNOXIOUS CUSTOMER.

"I'm looking for a Miss Annie Laurance." The tone indicated the same eagerness that might be experienced upon searching for a boa constrictor.

"I'm Annie Laurance." And to hell with you, lady.

"Oh." Frosty eyes scanned her. The artfully darkened blonde brows drew down in a delicate frown. "You're very young."

Tempted to respond with a combative, "So?," Annie evinced exemplary restraint, and merely said again, a little more insistently, "May I help you?"

"I'm Corinne Prichard Webster."

Annie waited.

"From Chastain."

"Chastain. That's not far from Beaufort. I understand it's a lovely old town."

"You've never been to Chastain?" Incredulity lifted the well-modulated voice.

"Not yet," Annie admitted, her smile now unforced.

"Oh, well. I don't know what to say."

Annie was beginning to feel trapped in a surrealistic conversation. It was time to hack her way out of this encounter. Maybe this expensive blonde was a nut. "Are you looking for a particular book?"

"A book. A mystery? Oh, heavens, no. I don't read them." Her moral superiority was clearly established.

"This is a mystery bookstore."

"Yes, I know. I'm here on behalf of the Chastain

Historical Preservation Society. One of our Board members, Roscoe Merrill, recommended you."

Merrill. Merrill. Then she remembered him, a stocky lawyer with a shiny bald head and humorless brown eyes. But he liked Rumpole, so there had to be a spark of humanity beneath that pinstriped exterior. What on earth, she wondered, had Merrill recommended her for?

Mrs. Webster didn't seem cheered by the recommendation. "Are you familiar with the annual house-and-garden tours in Chastain?" She looked at Annie doubtfully.

Recalling the chaste gray and pink poster she'd seen in the hallway of the Broward's Rock Public Library, Annie nodded.

"It has been suggested—" The smooth voice thinned just a trifle, and Annie detected a ripple of irritation. "The Board decided that we could enhance the success of our annual house-and-garden tours if we offered a further enticement." She enunciated each word as if she were sucking a lemon.

The Board of the Chastain Historical Preservation Society must be hard up for support if it'd sent an emissary all the way to an off-lying island. Annie was looking forward to an unctuous refusal to harbor promotional material, something on the lines of, "This is a mystery bookstore, and we only offer information of interest to mystery readers," when the magic words "some kind of mystery program" registered.

"Mystery program?"

"Yes. Now, of course, if you don't feel that you can handle an assignment of this nature, it would be understandable. After all, you certainly are very young, and there isn't much time to develop it. We would need to have the scripts, if that's how it's done, by next

Thursday. If you feel the time is insufficient, I will explain to the Board and perhaps another year—"

"Mystery program?" A happy surge of adrenaline tingled from her ears to her toes. "You mean, figure out the plot and create the clues and run the whole thing? Oh, God, I'd kill to do it!"

When the door finally closed behind Corinne Webster's trim figure, Annie unclenched her hands and felt the tightness ease from her neck and shoulders. What a poisonous creature! A Gila monster would have a certain charm in comparison. But the chance to run her very own mystery nights program was too exciting to lose, so she'd ignored the Board president's clear distaste for the entire idea. Something funny there. Obviously, the little tyrant had been maneuvered into approving the Mystery Nights. Be interesting to meet the other Board members. Well, she'd have her chance on Thursday when she presented them with her wonderful Mystery Nights program. And she could thank Roscoe Merrill for suggesting her for the job. Annie felt utterly confident that she would indeed create a super-duper mystery. How could she miss? She'd read every mystery from *Les Misérables* to *Death From a Top Hat*. Her mind teemed with ideas—a mannequin which turns into a body, babies switched at birth, letters hidden in the attic. Grinning, she reached for the phone and called Ingrid to see if she could work full-time for the next few weeks. Then, she hurried down the aisle to make a fresh pot of Kona coffee. The better to think with.

Ingrid arrived before the brew was finished. Annie filled mugs for both of them, and Ingrid settled in behind the front desk, emitting enthusiastic coos as Annie described her new project.

"The House-and-Garden tours start Monday, April 7. I'm going to put on a mystery program the first four nights, and end up with a Denouement Ball on Friday night. And they're going to pay me $1,000!"

Ingrid applauded.

Delighted with herself and the prospect, Annie freshened her mug and wandered happily among the shelves. There were so many *interesting* ways to commit murder. Douglas Clark used castor-oil beans in *Premedicated Murder*. V. C. Clinton-Baddeley took honors for originality when he created a poison of ant's brew in *Death's Bright Dart*. H. F. Heard opted for a swarm of deadly bees in *A Taste of Honey*, and Elspeth Huxley aimed a poison-tipped stick in *The African Poison Murders*.

And think of the fascinating variety among victims: a charming, likable woman with good intentions in Dorothy Simpson's *Last Seen Alive*, the narcissistic coed in Jane Langton's *Emily Dickinson Is Dead*, an arrogant braggart who made the fatal mistake of collecting killers in Agatha Christie's *Cards on the Table*, a woman who married too many times in Raymond Chandler's *The Long Goodbye*, and the socially impeccable Cogswells in Virginia Rich's *The Baked Bean Supper Murders*.

Where to begin? With victim or detective? Margaret Truman recommends starting with the victim, and Robert B. Parker insists the point of mystery fiction is the detective, not detection.

Should her mystery take advantage of its setting in one of South Carolina's oldest coastal towns, as Leslie Ford milked the atmosphere for every last drop of Spanish moss in *Murder with Southern Hospitality*? Or should she appeal to the mystery addict's interest in faraway places, as Mary Stewart did in *My Brother Michael* and James McClure in *The Steam Pig*?

She bent to straighten the row of Ruth Rendell titles. Now those kinds of stories wouldn't do at all for this genteel group. No, better something more on the order of Mary Roberts Rinehart or Louisa Revell. Or perhaps—The bell above the door rang. She stepped into the central aisle, looked toward the front, and saw Max peering at her determinedly from the doorway. Ingrid beamed at Max, then shot her a shamefaced glance. Ingrid was the most wonderful employee in this or any other bookstore, but she was clearly on his side now.

The newcomer grinned at Ingrid, but his eyes were on Annie.

She waved her hand at him. "Come on in. The floor isn't mined." He was obviously girding for battle, still confident that he would prevail. Dammit, she loved him, the silly ass, but she wasn't going to be swayed.

He still stood, half in and half out of Death on Demand, and she thought about Calvin Gates's first encounter with Mr. Moto in *Mr. Moto Is So Sorry*, the two at cross purposes, Calvin tenaciously pursuing his destiny, and Mr. Moto intent upon his own ends. Even the enormous stuffed raven beside the door seemed to be looking at Max sympathetically. Was everybody, dead birds included, on Max's side? And Agatha, of course, was moving languidly toward him. Where was her sense of loyalty? Didn't she know who her mistress was? But the small, silky-furred black cat was already twined gracefully around his leg. Absently, he reached down to pet her, then cleared his throat decisively.

She hurried to forestall him. She wasn't up to another discussion today. Besides, even though they were at odds, Max would be delighted at her good fortune.

"Guess what? I get to plan my own murders. For

money! And I can't decide between cyanide or electro-
cution or maybe defenestration. But don't you think
cyanide in champagne has a lovely ring?"

"In a glass or bottle?" he inquired mildly. He finally
came all the way inside. Ingrid patted his arm as he
passed her and was rewarded with his sexy grin. Annie struggled to concentrate on her immediate task, but
she felt the old familiar thrill, the unmistakable tingly
delight at his presence. He looked freshly scrubbed, as
if he'd just stepped from a shower and into his crisp
white shirt and gray poplin slacks. Was there a hint of
dampness in his thick blond hair? For a moment, she
thought about Max in his shower, the water slapping
against his tanned, muscled chest, then she firmly
brought her mind to heel.

"What's the difference?"

"Cyanide in a bottle, if mixed in a punch, could fell
hundreds. Are you and Ingrid planning a reception for
the store?"

"I prefer to entertain my customers, not kill them,"
she retorted. She glanced around. Actually, the increase in customers at Death on Demand this spring
had been phenomenal—and she didn't believe it had
anything to do with her notoriety as half of the team
which solved the first murders in modern times on
Broward's Rock. At least not much. They came because
they wanted to see the shop. Some wanted books. After
all, she carried the best selection of mystery and suspense novels this side of Atlanta. Some were readers
who relished matching the painted scenes on the back
wall to favorite books. Local artists vied for the right to
paint new scenes every month, and the contest successfully lured patrons in month after month. And, of
course, all the area mystery writers liked to come, too,
though they'd been a little slow to return after last fall's

excitement. Hopefully, everyone was starting to forget about the murder in the shop.

"I guess I'd better put the cyanide in a glass."

He moved so close she had trouble concentrating on her topic.

Casually, she stepped back a pace, then realized she was wedged between Max and the romantic suspense section.

"Whose? Anybody I know? I thought I was the only person you were mad at right now." He managed to look both injured and appealing. Dammit, why did he have to remind her of a Brittany spaniel? What was there about Max that she found so irresistible? Well, she was going to avoid any further discussion of their dilemma, no matter how pathetic he managed to look. It was a pose, of course. He was a bullheaded, insensitive, money-flaunting brute.

"Come on and have some coffee," she said brusquely, wriggling past him into the aisle and leading the way to the back of the shop. Behind the coffee bar, several hundred white mugs sat on shelving. Each mug carried the name of a book which had earned recognition as an all-time great in mystery fiction. She poured Max a fresh cup and refilled hers. Max lifted his mug and sniffed it suspiciously.

"What's wrong?" she asked.

"Just making sure the cyanide hasn't popped from the champagne to the coffee."

She laughed. "I'm not that mad at you. I'm thinking about cyanide for the Chastain Mystery Nights." She described Mrs. Webster's visit. "Although it's going to be a royal pain to work with Her Highness."

Max took time to see which famous mystery title was written in red script on his white mug (*The Lone Wolf*). He raised an eyebrow quizzically.

She hastened to reassure him. "Nothing profound is intended. My mugs are not fortune cookies." And she waggled her own, which carried the legend, *The Beast Must Die.*

He lounged comfortably against the bar, drank some coffee, and sighed.

It was wonderful the way good coffee could improve his disposition. She must remember that for future mornings together—if those mornings ever materialized. The prospect didn't look so good at the moment.

"So you're being unleashed to develop a murder program. Do they have any realization they may have uncapped a bloodthirsty genie from a bottle?"

She felt a surge of relief. She had successfully deflected him from the purpose of his visit. With luck, she could keep the conversation on cyanide and murder and away from the dangerous topic of September.

She put her mug on the yellow formica top of the coffee bar and smiled at him rapturously. "It's going to be so much fun. Max, do you want to help?" she asked eagerly. "No kidding. We can do it together." She ignored the quick gleam in his eye. "I mean, like Frances and Richard Lockridge. Or the Gordons. Or Per Wahloo and Maj Sjowall." She bent over the bar, fished out a notebook and flipped it open, then scrounged vainly in the pocket of her white slacks for a pen. Max obligingly handed her one. "Look, what do you think? Should we do a locked-room mystery like John Dickson Carr's *The Hollow Man* or Clayton Rawson's *The Footprints On the Ceiling*? Maybe we should consider psychological suspense like Helen McCloy's *The Slayer and the Slain* or Charlotte Armstrong's *Mischief*. Or an academic murder, like Amanda Cross's *Death in a Tenured Position* or Gwendolyn Butler's *Coffin in Oxford*. And there're always sporting murders. Let's see, it was archery in *Death at St. Asprey's School* by Leo Bruce, bullfighting in *Puzzle for Pilgrims* by Patrick Quentin, running in *Dead Heat* by Linda Barnes, basketball in *The Giant Kill* by Kin Platt, golf in—"

"Annie. Annie. ANNIE!"

She paused, images still flashing in her brain like neon on a rainy Saturday night.

"Quiet now. Take a deep breath."

Obediently, she breathed. Then she shook her head impatiently. "I'm not choking."

"I thought you were hyperventilating. Take it easy. Approach it logically." His voice was low, deep, soothing, and extraordinarily irritating.

"I am fine, thank you. It's just that there are so many wonderful possibilities—"

Max was trying hard not to laugh. He set his mug down and reached out to ruffle her hair. "Annie, love, I do enjoy you so."

She looked at him skeptically. "Are you making fun of me?"

"I'd never do that," he said virtuously, but the corner of his mouth twitched suspiciously.

They both laughed, and she realized this was the happiest she'd been in weeks, immersed in mysteries and laughing companionably with Max. Agatha leaped gracefully up to the bar to join in the merriment. Annie stroked her and felt ridiculously happy. It was almost as if she and Max hadn't quarreled. Well, it wasn't exactly a quarrel. But it was a disagreement. In spades. This moment forcibly reminded her in what direction happiness lay. But she had to retain her independence.

Oblivious to her unspoken soliloquy, Max reached for the notebook and took his pen.

"Okay. First things first. Who will play the role of the suspects?"

She understood at once. "Oh, sure. That limits some of the possibilities." Her mind ran over and discarded murder in the Himalayas, on a submarine, or while deep-sea fishing. "The roles will be played by members of the Historical Preservation Society."

He quirked an expressive eyebrow. "If they are anything like the women in my grandmother's bridge club . . ."

"Allowing for cultural distinctions between Connecticut and South Carolina, I would imagine they are soulmates."

Devilment glinting in his dark blue eyes, Max leaned forward. "Hey, I've got a great idea. Make the victim a Hollywood producer in 1926 and have the suspects be a bunch of young starlets. Oh wow, can you see these old ladies in vamp clothes and beads and bangles . . ." He melted in laughter.

She laughed, too, then mused, "Actually, I can see casting that horrid Mrs. Webster as an aging star, who everybody hates. Maybe an old folks' home for retired actors and actresses, and she has a chance for a big role, and all the other old-lady stars are jealous and one of them spikes her bedtime toddy with cyanide."

He shook his head, half in awe, half in despair. "You do have a fertile mind, love, but let's skirt any possibility of slander. Your Mrs. Webster probably wouldn't like that role at all."

His caution surprised her. Max could act like a lawyer most unexpectedly. But how marvelous that he wasn't predictable. Now, what was she doing mooning on about Max? The mystery was the thing.

"She's not my Mrs. Webster. But, you're probably right. I'd better not use her as the victim." Absently, her face scrunched in thought, she stood on tiptoe and stretched. Her mind worked better when her muscles were loose. "Okay, we're going to build a story that centers around upper-class, middle-aged suspects."

He poised the pen over the notebook. "How do we go about it?"

"Just like Agatha Christie did. We *think*." She ran her hand excitedly through her short blonde hair. "Did I ever tell you my favorite Christie story?" She charged ahead: "One day when walking in her garden with a friend, Christie abruptly announced her book was finished. This excited her companion, who had always wanted to read one of Agatha's books before it was published. The friend asked for permission to read the manuscript. Dame Agatha looked very surprised, then responded, 'Oh, I haven't *written* it yet.' "

"Oh, that's great."

"So we have to do the same. We have to figure everything out." Her eyes narrowed in concentration.

He tapped the paper with the pen. "How do we do it?"

"Here's what we need," she explained confidently. "Victim. Five suspects. Motives. Alibis. Clues." She traced the outline of the title on her cup. "I mean *real* clues, like half of a torn letter, a smudged postmark, cigarette butts, a box of insecticide. I'll scatter clues around the crime scene for the detectives to find."

"Who's the victim?" He scratched at his thick blonde hair with the stub end of the pen.

She pressed her fingers against her temples for a long moment, then nodded. "How about a bank president? Think of the lust, greed, and general hatred that can swirl around a bank president." She pictured Roscoe Merrill's shiny bald head. Any prosperous lawyer could look like a bank president.

"Dark secrets in the hallways of high finance," Max intoned.

"We'll call the bank president Thompson Hatfield—and we'll use Kansas as a setting. Agricultural banks are nosediving all over the place in the Middle West. Now, here's what happens," and she leaned close to Max. They were elbow to elbow as he wrote furiously to keep up with her bullet-fast pronouncements. "Motives *abound*. His wife's in love with another man, he's about to foreclose on a huge ranch run by his brother-in-law, his stepson's been embezzling, the vice president of the bank wants his job, he's going to fire the PR director, and he's the only man who won't agree to merging with another town bank to save it from going under."

"And somebody slips cyanide into his coffee thermos," Max suggested. "See, there's your cyanide."

Clues to be found at the murder scene: The name of his wife's lover written in his appointment book, the torn foreclosure notice for his brother-in-law's ranch, a key chain belonging to the vice president who wants his job, a gun registered in the name of the PR director, a Stetson hat that belongs to the president of the rival, failing bank, and a strand of hair belonging to his wife. (She is a redhead.)

"Well, now that that's settled," Max began, and once again he had that determined, bullheaded *September* look in his dark blue eyes.

She threw herself into the breach. "Oh, no, we've just started. We have to figure out the information to give to the suspects."

The phone rang at the front desk, but Annie knew Ingrid would answer it.

"Let's see, we'd better draw up a timetable, then we'll decide who was where and—"

"Max," Ingrid's voice warbled cheerfully. "It's for you."

He reached for the extension behind the coffee bar. "Hi, Barbie. Sure, I'm free. I'll be right back." He hung up and whistled. "Barbie said this guy's waiting to see me, and he's talking a thousand-dollar retainer."

Annie was tickled. Max actually sounded interested. It wouldn't be the money, of course, but the chance to have a job. Perhaps he was reforming. Max excited at the prospect of work!

He paused at the front door and called back meaningfully, "I'll be back in a little while. We've got to talk."

She stood by the coffee bar, her arms folded. Ingrid, her springy gray hair in tight curls from a new permanent, bobbed down the center aisle like a curious but ladylike bird. She had decided opinions on Annie and Max's disagreement, but she practiced her own brand of tact. After she poured both Annie and herself fresh coffee, she said, "Sounded like you were having fun for a while."

"Yeah." She refused to meet Ingrid's eyes.

Ingrid gently touched her arm and once again backed into her subject. "You know the old saying about pride. Well, pride is a mighty cold bedfellow. And people, if you hurt them too much, you can lose their friendship. And that would be a shame."

Annie felt a sick ache in her heart. Lose Max? It seemed such a small thing, really, to want to plan the wedding her own way. A simple, small ceremony here on the island, paid for by her. But Max was obstinately insisting on a magnificent, grandiose, *immense* wedding in his hometown, at his expense.

She took a gulp of the hot coffee. "I'd better see if

that delivery's come," and she carried her coffee mug past the scattered tables to the storeroom.

"Call me if you need any help," Ingrid offered, before turning up the central aisle to the cash desk. Annie knew she was offering more than assistance with unloading boxes, and she was torn between affection and irritation. Darn it, did *everybody* think Max was right—except her? She put her coffee on the worktable and attacked the unopened carton of used books, bought from a collector in California. Wrestling the box open, she started pulling out the wads of crumpled newspaper. The top volume, well-wrapped in plastic, was an autographed first-edition copy of *The Thirty-Nine Steps*. It was a wonderful find, but she didn't enjoy the usual flip-flop of pleasure. Instead, she slapped the cardboard carton shut, retrieved her coffee mug, and wandered back out into the bookstore. She'd not thought in terms of *losing* Max. Why, any fool could see how much fun they had together.

Even the excitement of working on the upcoming Mystery Nights waned as she considered Ingrid's unsettling but well-meant warning. Restlessly, she paced into the American Cozy area, full of rattan chairs, wicker tables, and tangly ferns in raffia baskets. But the mingled smell of recently watered greenery and both musty and new books lacked its usual charm. Absently she noticed that Agatha had been chewing again on the fern closest to the Christie shelves. On a normal day, she would steal a half hour at least to look at her newest acquisitions, and perhaps succumb to the temptation to forget all duties, pressing or otherwise, and just curl up with one. Only yesterday she'd received a mystery she'd been seeking for years, Sax Rohmer's *Fire-Tongue*. This was the famous book that he started without a solution, couldn't solve himself, and finally had to ask his friend Harry Houdini to solve for him.

But not today. *Fire-Tongue* could wait until she'd completed the Mystery Night scripts—and stopped brooding about Max.

Come on, Annie, she instructed herself sternly, don't be a gothic wimp. Everything would be all right with Max. She felt a flood of good cheer, with just a faint undercurrent of apprehension. Okay, she'd get back to work on her very own murder. Humming "Happy Days Are Here Again," she returned to the coffee bar, put down her mug, and reached for the notebook. Now, what would cast members need to know about their characters to portray them successfully? She leaned against the bar and stared upward, and her eyes paused on the watercolors pinned to the back wall. By golly, these were a triumph.

In the first watercolor, a large, slope-shouldered man in a gray suit knelt beside a long, thin body in a black overcoat. The kneeling figure, with the face of a blond Satan, gripped a flaming cigarette lighter in his left hand. The flame flickered close to an open, immobile eye. His empty bloodstained right hand was raised. A football-shaped parcel wrapped in brown paper lay beside the body.

In the second picture, the strong-jawed, brown-eyed private detective in a wet trenchcoat clutched his dripping hat in one hand and looked impassively at the young, slim, naked woman sitting stiffly, in the pose of an Egyptian goddess, in a highbacked teakwood chair. Her eyes were opened wide in a witless stare. Her mouth was agape, her small, pointed white teeth as shiny as porcelain. Long jade earrings dangled from her delicate ears. A corpse lay face up on the floor near a tripod camera. He wore Chinese slippers, black satin

pajama pants, and his embroidered Chinese coat
seeped blood from three wounds. Strips of Chinese
embroidery and Chinese and Japanese prints in wood-
grained frames decorated the brown plaster walls of
the low-beamed room.

Annie's eyes narrowed thoughtfully. Maybe they
were too easy.

In the third sketch, a body lay sprawled on the floor
of a cabana overlooking surging ocean waters, a single
crimson bullet wound in the head. A husky, dark-
haired man with a scraped and bruised face and weary
gray-blue eyes looked questioningly at his friend in the
doorway and the .32 target pistol in his hand.

In the fourth painting, a yellow jeep with a front-end
blade accelerated directly at the big, aging jock standing by an open pit in a subtropical pasture. Visible in
the pit was the glossy, red-brown body of a dead horse.
The driver of the jeep was shirtless, a mat of black hair
on his tanned, muscular chest. He wore a white canvas
cap and oval aviator's sunglasses. His quarry,
crouched by the pit, ready to spring out of the jeep's
charge, had light eyes and dark hair. He wore boat
pants, sandals, and a faded white shirt. A vulture
hovered overhead in the yellowish sky.

In the final painting, an athletic, savvy-looking man
stood poised in the archway of the living room of an
old apartment, a gun in his hand. Velveteen hangings
covered the walls. Skulls flanked an altar. A naked girl,
her body painted with cabalistic and astrological signs,
was tied to a cross, which hung from the ceiling. The
cult's almost naked priest, wearing only a hood, stood
near the cross, brandishing a stubby stick.

The old-familiar thrills coursed through her. Mysteries, the stuff of life. She bent over the bar and began to
write, as fast as her hand could fly. By golly, this was

going to be a wonderful mystery. And all her own. She whistled cheerfully as she worked. The Mystery Nights would be a smash and everything, of course, would ultimately come right between her and Max. He would see reason and agree to her plan for the wedding.

As Annie would later say, had she but known. . . .

5

MAX HELD A FRESHLY sharpened No. 2 pencil between his index fingers, but he didn't write a word. The yellow legal pad lying in solitary splendor on his leather blotter was blank. Nor did he offer refreshments to his prospective client, though he knew good, strong coffee pilfered from Death on Demand steamed in his stainless steel Krups coffee thermos. Max felt neither receptive, sociable, nor agreeable. Max didn't like Harley Edward Jenkins III.

Harley Edward Jenkins III sat in the red leather chair as if he owned it, Max, and the island. Only the latter was partially true, since he did control forty percent of the stock in Halcyon Development Inc., the real estate investment holding company which had created the luxury homes and condominiums on Broward's Rock.

"So get on it today." Jenkins started to rise, which wasn't especially easy for someone of his bulk. He bulged, despite the deceptive embrace of an artfully tailored navy blue Oxford suit.

Max held up his hand. "Just a minute."

A frown creased Jenkins's porcine face, and he pursed his fat lips impatiently.

"I want to be certain I understand you."

Jenkins jerked his head in acknowledgment and balanced on the edge of the chair. Max thought he resembled a rhino in a hurry to get out on the savannah and gore some fresh meat.

"You're in a business deal," Max summed up. "You want to buy some land cheap. The guy who owns it is running around on his wife. You want me to follow him, get some choice pictures, and hand them over to you. Right?"

Jenkins wet his thick lips. "I don't quite like the way you put that, Darling. Let's say I merely wish to improve my position in negotiations, gain some leverage."

Max slapped the pencil crisply on his desk and leaned forward. "I've got some advice for you, Jenkins."

The businessman's red-veined face turned a mottled purple.

"Why don't you go after money the old-fashioned way, Jenkins? Why don't you *earn* it?"

He was grinning as the door to his office quivered on its hinges as Jenkins, livid with fury, slammed it shut.

He couldn't wait to tell Annie about this encounter, even if he did owe a little to Smith Barney for his bon mot. He wished he'd had a camera to capture the shock on that sorry bastard's face.

Then he sighed. Dammit, he hadn't had a job for three weeks. Not that it mattered financially, of course. It's not as if he'd ever have trouble paying the rent. But

Annie did like for him to be busy. That girl must have been frightened by a Puritan spirit in her cradle.

Actually, he felt that his office was an artistic creation able to stand on its own merit without any need for utilitarian justification. He looked around in satisfaction. The room was large. An elegant rose-and-cream Persian rug stretched in front of the Italian Renaissance desk. Annie's tart observation had been that the desk deserved at least a cardinal's red robe for its owner. Glass-covered bookcases, filled with statute books and annotated treatises, lined one wall, though he made it very clear to clients that he was not practicing law. In fact, clients were usually more than a little puzzled as to his exact role, which suited him fine, since he had decided upon reflection that he didn't care to be bothered to take either the South Carolina bar or to obtain a private investigator's license. In his view, it was cruel and unusual punishment to require anyone to take more than one bar exam. He had manfully (if that weren't sexist) passed the New York bar. As for a private investigator's license, the sovereign state of South Carolina required either two years of work in an existing licensed agency or two years as a law enforcement officer before one could be obtained. Hence, his office window bore the legend, CONFIDENTIAL COMMISSIONS.

As he had earnestly explained to a skeptical Annie, it was his aim to help his fellow man (or woman), and to that end he was willing to undertake any mission which was both legal and challenging. After all, he didn't have to be either a lawyer or a private detective to ask questions and solve problems. A discreet but inviting ad ran in the Personals Column of both the *Island Herald* and the *Chastain Courier:*

*"Troubled, puzzled, curious? Whatever your problem,
contact CONFIDENTIAL COMMISSIONS, 321-1321, 11
Seaview, Broward's Rock."*

At this very moment, however, he was glumly debating why he ever thought this was going to be fun. And the one thing he was absolutely, positively, without question convinced of was that anything in which he engaged be first and foremost fun.

That did not include skulking about with a camera in hopes of obtaining blackmail material. Still, he wished it had been a legitimate case.

He reached out and picked up a silver photograph frame from the corner of his massive desk. He held it up to the light, and Annie smiled at him.

Wonderful, marvelous Annie with her short blonde hair streaked with gold, her serious, steady gray eyes, and her gentle, kissable mouth—the most exasperating, mule-headed, aggravating female he'd ever encountered. By God, didn't every woman want her wedding to be special? And wasn't that what he was offering? Hadn't his mother been at her most charming and least flamboyant when he and Annie visited her in Connecticut at Christmas? And Mother, with three superbly married daughters, had buckets of experience in planning weddings and would be delighted to help.

The trouble with Annie—one of the troubles with Annie, he corrected himself sourly—was her stiff-necked pride which confused money with independence. What he needed to do was to make it clear to her that money, when you had it, must never be master. The best way to keep money in line was to treat it as disposable and spend it. This theorem was Darling's Law of Finance, quite on a par and in happy contrast (at least in intent) to Veblen's Principle of Conspicuous

Consumption. Veblen had no sense of humor. He took money very seriously indeed. As did Annie.

What to do about Annie?

Max folded himself comfortably into his well-padded, high-backed swivel chair, which could be tilted almost horizontal and contained a vibrator and heating element. He flipped two switches and relaxed as the chair lowered and began to purr. Propping his Cordovan loafers on the gleaming desk top, he regarded the portrait. Time for an end-around run. When opposition held the middle ground, the smart general foxed his way to an unprotected flank in the manner of Leonidas Witherall, the erudite sleuth created by Phoebe Atwood Taylor writing as Alice Tilton. He shook himself. There he went again. Obviously, he was beyond help. Annie's approach to life had infiltrated his mind.

Max thought cheerfully for a moment about unprotected flanks, then concentrated.

If he couldn't persuade Annie of the merits of a grand wedding, which were undeniable, then he must beguile her. How best to do that?

She could not be bribed, heaven forfend, but perhaps she could be inveigled. What could he do that would persuade Annie that he, Max, was the world's most wonderful man, and should, of course and as a matter of justice, be deferred to? He spent several delightful seconds imagining Annie in a posture of deference.

She loved surprises.

His eyes narrowed, his face furrowed in thought. Surprises—the shop—Agatha—

Raising the picture high, he let out a whoop. Of course! Why hadn't it occurred to him sooner? He flipped the chair's switch. Upright, he plopped the picture next to the phone, yanked up the receiver, and

punched a button. "Barbie, dial international information, then get Sotheby's on the line."

The object of this deliberation was at that moment
braking as she coasted onto the ferry. Hers was the first
car aboard. Stumpy Ben Parotti waved to her from the
cabin. As the ferry lurched away from the dock, Annie
pulled on her cherry-red cable-knit cardigan and got
out of her aging blue Volvo to stand next to the railing.
The cool April air was perfumed with fish, saltwater,
and tar. She breathed deeply. Broward's Rock was the
best place in the world to live, an unspoiled island with
civilization's amenities. Pity those poor deprived millions who called someplace else home. Leaning on the
metal railing, she shaded her eyes from the noon sun
and looked across the softly green waters of Port Royal
Sound at the mainland, then fished a thin book from
her pocket. The guidebook, which had been published
by the Chastain Historical Preservation Society, contained a succinct but detailed history of Chastain, its
most famous houses and people.

She smiled a little at the history's opening sentence:

*Chastain was never the center of commerce and art that
was Charleston or even the shipping haven that was
Beaufort.*

The writer apparently harbored a sense of inferior-
ity. Had no one ever suggested accentuating the positive?

She continued reading:

*Nor can Chastain rival Charleston (founded in 1670 at its
earliest site) or Beaufort (founded in 1710) in age, but Chastain, first settled in 1730, proudly claims its place in the sun
as the favorite coastal hideaway of South Carolina's lowland
plantation owners, who sought its healthful breezes during*

*the deadly fever months of May through October, and in so
doing built and maintained some of the loveliest antebellum
mansions extant. Chastainians then and now feel themselves
blessed above all others in the gentility, beauty, and grace of
their city, secure on its bluffs above the Broad River.*

*Chastain was first settled by Reginald Cantey Chastain,
who received a grant from King George the year after the
Province was returned to the King by the Lord Proprietors,
Carolina's first rulers. Chastain's prosperity was great in
these early years as she offered a safe port, stable government, and only occasional harassment from the Indians.
During the Revolutionary War, when Charleston and the
surrounding countryside suffered greatly, Chastain was little touched. What seemed great misfortune when the city fell
to the British early in the war turned out to be her greatest
fortune, as she was spared fighting and destruction. Indeed,
Chastain was apparently favored by Heaven. During the
War Between the States, she was early occupied by Federal
troops, and therefore escaped the horror of Sherman's torch,
although her loyal sons and daughters found it painful to
endure the sequestering of their enemies within their homes.
However, this indignity was ultimately to preserve for the
glory of the present the grandeur of yesterday. Some of the
oldest homes in South Carolina survive in Chastain, including the famed Prichard, Chastain, McIlwain and Benton
houses.*

The horn alongside the cabin gave three toots,
Parotti's signal that landfall neared.

Slipping behind the wheel, she dropped the guidebook on the seat. Sea gulls moved in a rush of wings
from their pilings as the ferry thumped against the
buffering rubber tires, and Parotti lowered the ramp.
First on was first off, so she quickly put the Volvo in
gear and bumped onto the dock, then negotiated the
ruts in the lane for a half mile and turned right onto the

blacktop. A weathered sign announced: *Chastain 13 miles.*

She drove with the window down, enjoying the clear, fresh air with its underlying sourness of marsh and bay water leavened by fragrant Carolina jessamine and pine resin. The greening marsh grass announced the coming of spring. Pale green duckweed scummed the roadside waters, and fiddler crabs swarmed over the mudbanks. Tall sea pines crowded the shoulders of the road. Pine pollen coated the road and the shoulders and everything else in the lowlands with a fine lemony dusting from the yellow-purple spring flowers. As she neared Chastain, a stand of enormous live oaks screened a plantation home from view. Only glimpses of tall red-brick chimneys revealed its presence. Delicate swaths of Spanish moss hung from the low, spreading limbs.

Her first view of Chastain was unprepossessing, a fast-food hamburger joint, three derelict wooden houses, a jumble of trailer homes. She judged these with a jaundiced West Texas eye—one good wind would level them flatter than squashed pop cans. By the second Kentucky Fried Chicken, she spotted a plaque announcing the Chastain Historical Area, with an arrow to the right. Stuck behind a smoke-belching chicken truck, she chafed at the slowness of the traffic and kept a wary eye peeled for the eccentric driving common to small towns (mid-block stops, unheralded turns, and blithe disregard for stop signs).

She turned on Mead Drive, followed it to Montgomery, found another plaque and finally reached Ephraim Street, which ran along the high bluff. A half dozen lovely old homes sat on large lots to her left. The river, sparkling like beaten Mexican silver, slipped seaward to her right.

She drove to the end of Ephraim Street and parked in a neat graveled lot on the point, appropriately named Lookout Point. She locked the car, being sure to scoop up the guidebook with its map of the historic homes, her camera, and an extra roll of film. She paused to admire a flock of stately brown pelicans diving toward the river and a luncheon snack of mullet, then turned to survey the street. Just opposite rose a squat, buff-colored, square building which housed the Chastain Historical Preservation Society. From her guidebook, Annie knew the building was originally a tabby fort built in 1790 when the country raged to join with the French against England and other European powers as the French battled to protect their Revolution. However, Jacobism languished when the French Revolution banished Lafayette. She imagined for a moment the bustle and effort that had resulted in the fort, the grounds churned by wagon wheels, and the smell of lime and crushed, burned oyster shell hanging in the air. Now a smooth carpet of grass lapped against flowing banks of brilliantly red and yellow azaleas. A brick wall separated the Society grounds from Swamp Fox Inn, which boasted that Lafayette had slept there during his triumphal tour of the South in 1825, an old man remembering the glories of his youth, still tall, lame in one foot, but with electric, crackling black eyes and a gentleman's charm of manner. The three-story frame Inn was an amalgamation of additions. Its center had been built in 1789.

She studied it with interest. Mrs. Webster had explained that the Inn was providing a room for the mystery expert in return for promotional mention in the House and Garden Week brochures. Annie had called that morning to reserve an adjoining room for Max, her helper, as she explained to the innkeeper. She sighed as she noted the paint peeling from the second and third story pillars, the untrimmed live oak trees, which threatened to poke holes in the weathered exterior, and the unkempt stretch of lawn visible through the sagging wooden fence.

Although nice surprises certainly could arrive in plain packages, it was her experience that poorly maintained motels, hotels, and inns featured hard beds, lousy food, and were either too hot or too cold. And she knew how fastidious Max could be. He was every bit as particular as Koko, the kingly Siamese in *The Cat Who Could Read Backwards*. Her heart sank. Oh well, it would be good for Max to traffic with hoi polloi. She pictured him arising from a lumpy bed and stepping into a lukewarm shower. Grinning, she crossed the street, her goal the famous Prichard House which would be the site of the Murder Nights entertainment. She was ready to survey the setting and figure out the practical elements. Where should the corpse be found? Where would the suspects be placed? And the Investigation Center? What clues should she strew at the Scene of the Crime?

Fortunately for her sanity and the logistics of the week, the three featured homes were all here on Ephraim Street, right in a row. As she understood it, ticket holders would first tour the ground floor rooms in the three featured houses, then gather on the lawn of the Prichard House for a buffet dinner to be followed by the coup de grace, the Mystery Program.

She stopped in front of the wrought iron fence to look at the Benton House. A two-story frame built in 1798, it glistened with recently applied white paint and looked as crisp as Tom Wolfe in a fresh white suit. Double porticoes flanked three sides, supported by simple Ionic columns. Black shutters framed the windows. Stubby palmetto palms were spaced every ten feet along the fence, but the magnificence here was in the grounds. Annie's eyes widened. *SOUTHERN LIVING* should see *this* garden. Lady Banksia, yellow jessamine, honeysuckle, pittisporum, a long shimmering arc of wisteria across the back of the deep lot, dogwood so brilliantly, pristinely white that it glittered in the sunlight, and azaleas—single blossoms, double blossoms, hose-in-hose blooms, in vivid splashes of color that included salmon, pink, orange-red, yellow, purple, and white.

Although an occasional car had passed as she made her way slowly from the Lookout Point bench past the Society Building and the Inn to this first historic home, Annie soon realized this part of Chastain didn't exactly teem with activity. The Benton House reflected back the early afternoon sunlight. The venetian blinds were closed, and the many windows offered no hint of its interior. Just then a middle-aged man came briskly around the corner of the house, pushing a wheelbarrow. He looked like a competent, no-nonsense gardener. If he were in charge of this garden, he deserved kudos indeed.

She propped her purse and the guidebook against the base of the fence. Removing her camera from its case, she held it up and took a series of shots. Returning the camera to its case, she picked up her belongings and continued down the sidewalk to the entrance to the grounds of Prichard House.

Each house along Ephraim Street sat far back on a large lot. This provided a great deal of space for the gardens and, the guidebook informed, accounted for the plantation-like appearance of many of the older homes.

When Annie saw the Prichard House, she realized it

SKETCH OF HISTORIC AREA

LAFAYETTE STREET

PARKING

CHASTAIN HISTORICAL PRESERVATION SOCIETY (FORMER TABBY FORT)

1790

LOOKOUT POINT

BLUFF

PARKING

HOT TUB

PATIO

OFFICE DOOR

GATE

SWAMP FOX INN (3 STORY)

ALLEY

TENNIS COURT

GARAGES

ROSE ARBOR

BENTON HOUSE

1798

POND

CANE THICKET

GARAGES

(GREEK REVIVAL)

PRITCHARD HOUSE

1834

GARAGES

McILWAIN HOUSE

(GEORGIAN)

PALLADIUM PORTICO

1765

EPHRAIM STREET

BROAD RIVER

N
W E
S

fitted Mrs. Webster perfectly. There was nothing casual, downhome, or unpretentious about the Prichard House. It was a two-story, brick, Greek Revival mansion, with six immense octagonal columns supporting the double porticos. Pale pink plaster coated the exterior walls. A five-foot-high decorated parapet topped the second portico and four massive octagonal chimneys thrust up from the roof. Shining marble steps led up to the main entrance. Enormous and ancient live oak trees, festooned with long, silky strands of Spanish moss, dominated the front lawn. Most of the action would take place here. There could be few lovelier homes in all the South. Prichard House was, as Mrs. Webster had advised and Annie had nodded gravely, the jewel in Chastain's architectural crown.

The Prichard House garden featured a natural woodland with live oaks, mimosa, and magnolias interspersed with wildflowers and colorful banks of azaleas and yellow jessamine. Far to the back of the property, a tall stand of cane guarded a pond, providing only a tantalizing glimpse of dark water.

It was so imposing that she felt a twinge of hesitation in poking her camera through the wrought iron fence to take photographs. Thanks heavens, with the lovely speed of a .35 mm., it only took a few seconds.

The third historic home rivaled the Prichard House in beauty. McIlwain House was a lovely Georgian mansion, two stories, again on a high foundation, with a delicate extended front portico with slender columns supporting the second story partial verandah. Formal gardens ruled here, beds of roses flanked by dogwood, crepe myrtle, and azaleas.

Once again, she shot a series of pictures, then, returning to her vantage point in front of the Prichard fence, she made a rough sketch of the Historic Area.

Dropping the drawing into her purse, Annie pushed through a gate to the oyster-shell path that led to the grand entrance of Prichard House. She walked slowly, appreciating the soft crackle of the shells beneath her feet, the mixture of scents, jessamine, honeysuckle, and wisteria, and the silky freshness of the afternoon air. There was going to be plenty of room. She could order tents put up, three of them in a row, on the wide expanse of lawn embraced by the circular drive. What she needed now was to determine The Scene of the Crime, but she could only accomplish that by nosing around the gardens, and she had no intention of trespassing in these sacred precincts without permission. She wondered if Mrs. Webster would be surprised at her prompt appearance. Hired in the morning, at work by afternoon. Well, it should only endear her to the Board president.

It was a long walk to the shining marble steps. She was midway up when a car churned up the oyster-shell drive, spewing a plume of gray dust. Annie glanced toward the sound and glimpsed the face of a pale girl whose pretty face was contorted by fury. Then the gray Continental and its driver were beyond the house and only the cloud of oyster-shell dust hung in the air.

Annie's insatiable curiosity was piqued. Obviously, the girl must belong in this magnificent house. Only an inhabitant would have the effrontery to drive like that on grounds such as these. Who was she and why was she so angry? And on such a beautiful day.

Mounting the steps, she rang the front door bell and, faintly, deep within the house, heard a somber peal.

The gleaming white double doors rose nine feet tall. They opened in a moment, and a middle-aged woman in a maid's uniform nodded politely at her.

"Yes, Miss?"

"I'm Annie Laurance, and I'm helping Mrs. Webster with plans for the—"

A reverberating crash sounded from the back of the shining hall.

Startled, the maid swung around.

The driver of the car burst into the main hall. She was tall and willowy, with strikingly lovely auburn hair which she wore in an old-fashioned chignon. Her face was delicately boned and slender; her pale blue eyes were enormous. She would qualify as a beauty except that her face was white and pinched, the lips quivering in distress.

She ignored Annie. Perhaps, in her anger, she didn't even see her. She spoke to the maid, her voice shaking with fury.

"Where is Corinne?"

6

SUNLIGHT FLOODED THE old and elegant hallway from the open doorway to the left. Tall double doors were open, revealing a drawing room decorated in muted blues and grays. Annie, standing frozen at the entrance, glimpsed an English Sheraton cabinet filled with leather-bound books, a decorated Adam mantelpiece with bronze candelabra, silk-upholstered sofas and chairs, and pieces of Meissen and Sevres china. Matching double doors opened to the right into the dining room, which had walls of Williamsburg green. Silk damask curtains, a lighter green patterned in yellow, hung from the tall windows.

French wallpaper from the 1820s decorated the hallway, and sunlight spilled in a warm golden pool across the wide-planked floor. The young woman was as clearly limned as if by a spotlight, her spectacular auburn hair glistening like the flank of a sundrenched

Kentucky colt, her delicate, anguished face a study in anger. And something more. Heartbreak?

It seemed so unlikely a place for drama. Or melodrama. The long hallway was immaculate, the floor glistening. A French Empire card table with dolphin feet sat beneath an ornate Chippendale mirror with a gilt eagle at its apex. A smell of potpourri, crushed roses and ginger, mingled with the homelier odors of freshly baked bread and floor wax. And the girl seemed an unlikely candidate for passion, with her patrician face and tasteful yet understated dress, a crisp white cotton cambric blouse with a high neck, front tucks, and long sleeves, and a mid-calf length cotton skirt with an aquamarine stripe. But her face was twisted with emotion, and her breathing was ragged.

"Where is she, Marybelle?" she demanded hoarsely.

"Miss Gail—" The older woman, clearly upset, reached out a hand. She was in her early fifties, attractive in her highly starched pale brown cotton dress with white ribbing at the collars and cuffs.

A soft, cultivated voice sliced through the emotion-charged atmosphere as cleanly as a surgeon's knife.

"Gail, you forget yourself."

They all looked up, like obedient marionettes, at Corinne Prichard Webster. She stood at the landing of the stairway, one hand lightly touching the mahogany handrail, her face composed, her lips parted in a Mona Lisa half-smile. The Palladian window behind her provided a dramatic frame for her cool loveliness. Her silver-blonde hair was softly waved, her face smooth and unlined, her cream suede suit the last word in elegance. She was beautiful, and she knew it. She wore that knowledge as a knight might flaunt a royal coat of arms.

"Miss Laurance, how nice of you to call. I want you

to meet my niece, Gail Prichard." Her blue eyes blazed
a warning at Gail.

The girl turned reluctantly toward Annie. She still
breathed unevenly, with the half hiccups that signaled
extreme stress. Her eyes slowly focused.

Annie watched innate good manners and long ad-
herence to social norms struggle with emotions too
deep to be ignored.

Corinne reached the foot of the stairs, and nodded
toward the maid. "Thank you, Marybelle."

The maid pulled her pitying eyes away from the girl
and turned away silently, her rubber-soled shoes
squeaking a little against the highly polished wood
floor.

Trying to spare the girl, Annie rushed into speech.
She would have recited "Thanatopsis" to distract the
blonde viper from Gail Prichard.

"I wondered if I might look over the gardens, Mrs.
Webster. For the Murder Nights. If it's all right, I'll take
some pictures, too."

"Of course, Miss Laurance. You are welcome to poke
into every nook and cranny. We want you to feel very
much at home while you work on the festival program.
But we must observe the amenities before business.
Gail, this is Miss Annie Laurance, who has so kindly
consented to help us publicize the spring house-and-
garden tours."

It was worse than watching a butterfly squirm to its
demise against the hurtful intrusion of a pin. Watching
Corinne Webster force her niece to make the proper
response, no matter what private agony the girl was
enduring, was as ugly a demonstration of raw power
as Annie had ever witnessed. It put her right on a par
with Mrs. Boynton in Agatha Christie's *Appointment
with Death*.

Gail swallowed jerkily. She managed to hold out her hand and speak. "Miss Laurance—I'm glad—to meet you."

As Annie touched that slim, shaking hand, she felt a white hot bubble of anger. If Max were here, he would recognize the signs. He knew her, knew that she could erupt, and the devil take the hindmost, when she was pushed too far. This vicious, golden woman was coming perilously close to pushing Annie Laurance too far. Who the bloody hell did Mrs. Sainted Webster think she was to subject her to this paralyzing scene? At that moment, she would have been delighted to be teetering on a hanging bridge over a Borneo chasm, if a magic carpet could have whisked her there.

With a Herculean effort, she held onto her temper and began to back toward the door. "I won't trespass on your time. Thank you so much." She groped behind her for the hamhock-sized silver handle.

"Of course you aren't intruding." Corinne lifted a perfectly manicured hand, the nails sleek and blood red, and gestured toward the drawing room. An enormous purplish blue sapphire in an antique gold setting flashed like a Hessian's dress uniform. "You must have tea with us. I insist. I know Gail will enjoy telling you about the work she has done in planning the programs this year at the Prichard Museum."

Gail's face was the color of gray Sheetrock. Her anguished blue eyes looked like smears of rain-puddled ink.

Corinne smiled blandly at her niece.

A poison-ring tipped into Chablis would be far too good for Corinne Webster. That being out of the question and beyond her purview, Annie's immediate goal was to remove herself from the poisonous presence of Corinne Prichard Webster without succumbing to the temptation to tell the woman just how beastly she was. Her hand found the doorknob and turned it.

"Thanks so much, but I'm due back at the island for tea shortly." She tried to sound as if afternoon tea were an activity in which she unfailingly engaged, and her social calendar was filled *weeks* in advance. "I'll just take a few shots and be on my way." She waggled the camera at them, stepped out onto the front piazza, pulled the door shut, then turned and plunged down the gleaming marble steps as if pursued by the hounds of hell.

She didn't look back until she'd crunched down an oyster-shell path and ducked behind a line of palmetto palms. Her chest heaving with exertion, she skidded to a stop by a wooden bench and paused to listen.

A lawnmower whirred in the distance. Nearer at hand, a blower tidied fallen pine needles into flower beds. She peered around the splintery gray trunk of the palm at the front door of the Prichard House. It didn't open.

She had escaped without exploding.

And she had held her breath, too. She let it out with a rush and, for an instant, an infinitesimal space of time, wondered if she'd overreacted. No, Mrs. Webster rated on a scale with pirahnas, cobras, and Moriarty. Definitely not a choice for gentlewoman of the year. What a pleasure it would have been to let her have it.

That poor girl. Funny. She thought of her as a girl, though she must be about Annie's own age. But there was something young and vulnerable about Gail Prichard. What could have happened to upset her so dreadfully? What had Corinne Webster done? For it came down to that, without doubt.

But it wasn't any business of hers.

Her business was to create a successful mystery program, and she wasn't going to accomplish that by standing flat-footed staring at a door that remained closed. Good. She didn't want it to open. She wanted to mark the entire episode closed.

The temptation to march right back up those marble steps, punch the doorbell, and tell Mrs. Corinne Prichard Webster to stick it was almost overwhelming. To hell with the thousand-dollar fee. To hell with the Chastain Historical Preservation Society.

But she had given her word. If she didn't provide the script for the Murder Nights, the Chastain Historical Preservation Society would be left dangling in the wind, as they said in Texas. She felt, too, that she owed a good job to the faceless individuals who made up the membership of the Society. Mrs. Webster may be president, but surely the Society consisted of other and, more than likely, worthier Chastainians. Besides, Mrs. Webster clearly was lukewarm about the mystery program. By God, she was going to have one—and a bloodcurdlingly marvelous one—like it or not.

Duty wrestled hotblooded temptation. Duty won.

She turned away from the mansion to study the geography of the garden. A long sweep of springy green lawn was embraced by the circular drive. There was certainly room for three tents, as much to mark various activities as to provide shelter. And no one would even admit to the *possibility* of rain. The mystery would begin promptly at seven P.M. with the introduction of the suspects and an explication of their relationship to the victim. The mystery buffs would be divided into ten teams, each with a maximum of ten members. After electing a Detective Captain, the teams would, one at a time, be taken to The Scene of the Crime, where they would be instructed to follow good police procedure, i.e., prepare a detailed sketch of the premises, careful not to disturb any evidence, and list all possible clues. The teams would then repair to the tents. The first tent would house Police Headquarters. There team members could study the medical examiner's report on the victim, the laboratory analysis of physical evidence, and obtain copies of statements which had been given to the police by the suspects. The second tent would provide areas for the interrogation of each suspect by the teams. In the third tent would be tables where teams could huddle to discuss the progress of their investigations.

Ducking beneath the low limbs of a gnarled live oak, she paced out the position of the tents. Then she scuffed a mark in the grayish dirt with her sandal. This would be a good place for the Death on Demand table. She could picture the table now, heaped with bookstore mementos, including blood-red, stiletto-shaped bookmarks, a stock of t-shirts with the store name, or pictures of favorite mystery sleuths, such as Hercule Poirot, Miss Marple, Sherlock Holmes, or Nero Wolfe, or slogans, such as I'D RATHER BE DETECTING, CRIME DOESN'T PAY ENOUGH, or POISON IN A PINCH.

Her irritation began to fade. She always enjoyed planning new and novel ways of spreading the good word about Death on Demand. And just think, most of the people signed up for the Mystery Nights must be mystery lovers. Why else would they come? She brushed away their interest in old houses and lovely gardens. These were *crime* enthusiasts, ready to swap knowledgeable tidbits about their favorites, ranging from *Bleak House* to *Home Sweet Homicide*.

And she had just had the marketing idea of the century. The watercolors! They were the first things everybody checked out at the store. The competition to be the first to name author and title was fierce. What would it cost to have the watercolors run off as posters and offer them for sale, too?

Whipping out a notepad from her purse, she scrawled a reminder to check the cost and confer with Drew Bartlett, this month's artist.

"Genius," she murmured to herself complacently. "Sheer genius."

Okay. Practical matters. Order the tents, tables, chairs. Make up instruction sheets for the teams.

The teams would be racing against the clock in their investigations. As soon as a team was certain it knew the murderer's identity, the Team Captain would write this information, along with the incriminating evidence they had detected, put the information in an envelope, seal it, and turn it in to Annie, who would initial it and stamp the time on the outside of the envelope. At the climax of the grand Denouement Ball Friday evening on the tennis court of Prichard House, the winning team would be announced. The winner would be the team which discovered the murderer in the shortest time, no matter which evening the team competed. A team which turned in its correct answer at 9:03 P.M. Wednesday would defeat a team which handed in the correct answer at 9:15 Monday night.

Now, where to put the body.

She looked again at the smooth lawn, bounded by beds of lavender-pink and rose-red azaleas, then paced along a wide oyster-shell path to the back of the enormous lot. Here a woodland garden bloomed with tangled dogwood, redbud, and wisteria. The snowy white of the dogwood contrasted brilliantly with the purplish red of the redbud. The path wound past a twelve-foot tall thicket of cane and emerged in a small clearing. A black water pond, ringed by clumps of royal purple

irises, lay in the sculpted shadows of immense, dark, knobby cypresses and graceful willows. Annie took a deep breath, enjoying the faint, sweet scent of the irises, barely distinguishable against the stronger smell of the still water. It was a secluded spot. She felt a rising sense of excitement. Rapidly, she discarded her original plan for Thompson Hatfield's body to be discovered in his bank office and substituted the background of the annual bank picnic. The Victorian gazebo among the willows would be a superb spot. Of course, this change would entail a whole new set of clues, but she could manage that easily. She got out her notepad and sketched The Scene of the Crime. Oh, it was perfect.

The body. A dummy? A store mannequin? She must attend to that today, also. She glanced at her watch. Almost two. Somehow, between fending off Max and traveling to Chastain, she'd missed lunch. She'd noticed a chili dog stand on her way into town. That would do nicely. But first, she'd drop by the Historical Preservation Society and leave some information to be stapled to the brochures. Mrs. Webster was clearly uninterested in promoting the Mystery Nights program, but she needn't think Annie Laurance was going to be fobbed off or ignored.

She was feeling fairly combative as she pushed through the massive wooden door of the old fort.

Two-foot-thick walls, inset windows, low ceilings, and forty-watt bulbs in wall sconces recreated the dungeon-like atmosphere the place must have had almost two hundred years before. The musty smell from long years of dust hung in the damp air. A wooden rack filled with pamphlets and brochures ran along the brick wall to her left.

"Good morning." An elderly woman with the soft,

slurred speech of a native South Carolinian smiled and
looked up at Annie with interest. She had masses of
faded blonde curls and wore a shapeless baby-blue
polyester dress and matching beaded earrings, but her
heavy face radiated good humor and an unquenchable
enthusiasm. She sat behind a mahogany Chippendale
writing table. Both she and the old Remington on a
typing stand behind her looked incongruously modern.

"I'm Annie Laurance, and Mrs. Webster has hired
me to plan a Mystery Night program for—"

"The house-and-garden tours. Oh, I do feel this is
going to be so thrilling. And such a wonderful idea. I
think it was Mr. Merrill who thought it up. He and his
wife went to a Murder Weekend in Atlanta last year
and just had a wonderful time." She heaved herself up
and came around the desk. "I'm Louisa Binning, the
secretary. What can I do to help?"

What a difference in blondes, a gorgeous viper and a
frumpy delight. Annie began to nurture kindly feelings
for the Chastain Historical Preservation Society as Louisa, who turned out to be not only chatty but efficient,
loaded her down with brochures, provided the names
of caterers and equipment rental companies, swiftly
took down the details of the Mystery Nights program,
and promised production, "Oh, by next Monday at the
latest," of a promotional blurb to be included in the
previously printed House and Garden tour brochures.

"As for the body," she riffled through a stack of
papers on the writing table and handed Annie a Red
Cross brochure, "you can stop on your way out of
town and talk to Edith Ferrier, one of our very nicest
Board members. I'll call ahead for you. I just know
she'll be glad to help out."

Adding the brochure to her stack of pamphlets, she

said gratefully, "Mrs. Binning, I can't thank you
enough for all your help."

"Oh, I love doing it. And it's my job." She beamed.
"Now, about the slip-ins for the tour brochures. We can
manage one color on our mimeograph machine. Do
you think a dagger dripping blood?"

"Fantastic," Annie crowed.

"Disgusting," a voice hissed from the cavernous
dimness of a bricked archway behind the secretary.

Annie jumped, but mellow Louisa merely turned her
head and said, "Oh, there you are, Miss Dora. Come
meet our young mystery expert, Annie Laurance. Miss
Laurance, this is Miss Dora Brevard, who is the mainstay of the Society. No one knows more about Chastain
and its history than Miss Dora."

A tiny figure, more like a gnome than a woman,
poked out of the shadow. Shaggy silver hair framed an
ancient face, the skin crumpled in cross-hatched lines.
But the deep-set eyes, dark as raisins, peered out with
ferocious intelligence. Dora Brevard wore a heavy
black silk dress that rustled around her high-topped
leather shoes and a rakishly tilted cloth hat with a purple feather. She gripped an ebony cane in one withered
hand, but she moved with surprising speed, thumping
across the stone floor to look up with keen suspicion at
Annie.

"The goal of the Society is to preserve the heritage of
Chastain." She tapped the cane to the stone for emphasis. Her voice had a crackly, dry quality like the rustle
of old paper. "Adding these Mystery Nights," the
words sounded like an epithet, "can do nothing but
detract from our mission."

The secretary interceded quickly. "Now, Miss Dora,
this young lady has come here today to get materials
about Chastain. She's *very* interested in our history.

And she wants to help us raise as much money as we can."

"Desecration," the old lady muttered. "That's what it is. All these people tramping through our houses—"

Louisa patted the bony shoulder soothingly. "Tourists come because they want to understand the past."

The old lady shrugged away the secretary's hand. Her beady eyes glittered with anger. "Cheap, that's what the world is today. Everything tawdry and false. And I won't stand for it here in Chastain. Do you hear?" She thudded the cane against the floor. Then, in a swift and disturbing about-face, the wizened features reformed in a cunning smile. "So you're interested in our history, are you, young woman. That's as it should be. And I'll see that you aren't filled with jiggery and pokery. You can walk me home, and I'll tell you about Chastain. Here now, you can carry my bag for me," and she thrust a crocheted receptacle into Annie's hands. It was surprisingly heavy. She glanced down and saw it was crammed to the brim with books, papers, and photostats.

"Records." Miss Dora stabbed a gnarled finger at the bag. "Deeds, land grants, birth and death certificates, and wills. That's the heart of the matter, wills." She cackled and darted toward the heavy door, the cane a staccato accompaniment. "Come along now. I don't waste time."

Annie glanced helplessly toward the secretary, who said meaningfully, "Miss Dora is Secretary to the Board."

"Secretary," Annie repeated blankly. "But I thought you—"

"Oh, I just work here. Miss Dora is *permanent* secretary to the Board."

And Annie was employed by the Board. She got the

message, hefted the bag, and followed the tip-tap of the cane.

Out on the sidewalk, Miss Dora paused long enough to dart a malevolent glance down Ephraim Street. "I suppose Louisa gave you the brochure that describes the houses on the tour?"

"Oh yes, I have all the material on those houses." Annie was surprised to find her hands sweating. She found Miss Dora unsettling, to say the least. There was too much force and intelligence in those piercing brown eyes to dismiss her as merely dotty. It would be easy to imagine her as a Salem witch or Florentine poisoner.

"It's poorly phrased," the old woman snorted, "but accurate. So we'll walk up Lafayette." One hand tapped the cane and the other gripped Annie's elbow like a marsh hawk clutching a juicy rodent. The raspy voice swept ahead relentlessly, unfolding the pageant of the past. Annie, despite her wariness, was caught up by the vividness and pungency of the old lady's descriptions, and, unexpectedly, she glimpsed visions of long ago: The huge grave they dug for the yellow-fever victims. The glorious night when General Washington came for a ball. "That was in the Smiley house. It stood on the bluff over there where the fire station is." The devastating fire of 1756, which started on the docks, a careless match thrown into bales of cotton. "A new bride ordered the slaves to dip all her tablecloths and linens in the river and cover the roof, so the Mainey house was saved." The duels, the horse races, the elegant and civilized parties. The long, heartbreaking Federal occupation, and the grim days that followed the War when the homes of most old Chastain families were sold for taxes.

Miss Dora paraded Annie up and down Federal

Street. "The first Episcopal Church stood just there. The present St. Michael's and All Angels was established in 1760, after the fire." She dismissed the stuccoed business buildings erected in the late 1800s as uninteresting, but grudgingly admired the Prichard Museum. "Built in 1843 by the Chastain Thursday Night Society. Men have always loved gaming." She bracketed the word, "Men," much as Miss Silver did when discussing the eating and drinking habits of the male species. But she wasn't as genial as Miss Silver, by a long shot. Then, the indefatigable Miss Dora led her back to Ephraim Street and they followed the curve of the River past Lookout Point. More lovely old homes fronted the bluff. "They built them on high foundations of tabby, that's the cement made from burning oyster shells to make a lime, then mixing it with crushed shells and sand. Two-story homes with front and side piazzas to catch the prevailing breezes from the southeast. It was hot in the summertime, mind you, but the open central hallways made the rooms as cool and fresh as the little airconditioned boxes they build today. There's the Cannehill house, eight fireplaces and a fine double verandah. Early 1800s. That's the Hapworth House, built in 1850, belonged to a doctor, sold for taxes after the War. A Board member, also a doctor, lives there today." Then the old lady, her wrinkled face twisted in a fierce scowl, paused to lean against her stick and glare at a magnificent Greek Revival mansion with a portico that rivaled the Prichard House in grandeur. A quartet of huge Ionic columns rose two stories and supported a gleaming white pediment. A luxurious, classic yellow Bentley lounged in the drive, the kind of automobile that proclaims its owner's wealth and cockiness.

"What a lovely home. And what a magnificent car," Annie said admiringly.

"She defiles her heritage," the raspy voice intoned.

Startled, Annie looked down at her tiny, black-clad companion.

"No better than a common whore, and I don't care if her name is Chastain."

"Really?"

The black eyes darted up at Annie, who hastened to explain, "I mean, really a descendant of the original Chastain?" She doubted if she could count high enough to figure out how many generations that spanned.

"Evil. That's what Sybil is. A Jezebel. It was a grave mistake when the Board made her a member, despite her lineage." Then, again disconcertingly, the rat's nest of wrinkles smoothed into a high, mirthless cackle. "But she makes them sit up and take notice. Especially Corinne." Her voice dropped to a subterranean hiss as she spoke the name, and hatred eddied in the perfumed air.

Miss Dora's house was two past the Chastain mansion. She snatched her carry-all from Annie at the gate. "Now, this mystery you're planning. Tell me about it."

Quickly, Annie sketched the saga of the banker.

Miss Dora bent her head forward, her reptilian eyes squinted in thought. When Annie finished, she jiggled her head and the straight silvery hair undulated under her hat like wisps of cirrus clouds. "Businesslike," she muttered. "But boring. Not like Peter Dickinson." Then she opened the gate and thumped up the walk, without a backward glance.

Annie stared after her. She couldn't decide whether to laugh or be angry. But, as she slowly retraced her path to Lookout Point and her parked car, she decided the old devil would certainly add some spice to her assignment.

And maybe she had something there. Boring. Maybe she should give the mystery program a whole new look, come up with some juicier characters, more original motives. But first things first. It was time to see about the body. Back in her Volvo, she consulted a street map of Chastain, which looked somewhat as though a child had taken pick-up sticks and flung them across the page. She had a little trouble finding the Red Cross office, which was tucked back on a side street between a French bakery and a U-Haul lot. She parked outside the bakery and virtuously resisted the temptation to succumb to an éclair stop. Business first. The door to the Red Cross office opened into a boxey room that smelled of yeast from next door and of ink and slick paper from the pamphlets stacked on a cardtable.

Three women were at work in the room. Annie had no trouble singling out the honcho. She smiled impartially at all three, but dismissed the overweight receptionist and frizzy haired typist from her thoughts and focused on the gaunt-faced woman with golden hoop earrings, deep-set green eyes, and red-gold hair piled atop her head in copious curls, moving to greet her.

"I'm Annie Laurance. I'm hoping you can help with some plans for the house-and-garden week."

"Certainly, certainly. I'm Edith Ferrier." She spoke in a hurried staccato. "Louisa called and explained about your needs. She thought our CPR doll might suit," and she pointed across the room at the five-foot-tall rubber doll lounging in a wicker chair next to an old-fashioned bottled water cooler.

"Oh, she'll be perfect. Though I might have to come up with a new mystery. I'd planned on a male murderee, but I can always think up a murder with a female victim."

The pleasantry slid right by Mrs. Ferrier, who peered at Annie intently. "Now, it's important that Rhoda— that's what we call her—Resuscitation Rhoda—not be treated roughly. It would be very expensive to replace her."

"We'll take excellent care of her," Annie promised quickly. "She'll be behind police tape marking the scene of the crime, so no one will touch her."

"That's all right then." Her head jerked back, and Annie recognized the sharp, unconscious reflex of a nervous habit. This taut redhead was strung tighter than a violin string.

"I'll run by and pick her up the morning of the seventh."

At the door, she thanked Edith Ferrier again. "It's really a great piece of luck that you are both the Red Cross coordinator and a member of the Historical Preservation Board."

"I'm busy. Very busy." There wasn't a glint of humor in her face.

"Mrs. Webster is going to be pleased that it's all worked out."

A short, taut pause, then, again, that quick, involuntary movement. "Yes, I suppose Corinne will be pleased. Things always do seem to work out when she is in charge."

They parted in a friendly fashion, Annie turning for a last wave as she climbed into the Volvo, but the smile slipped from her face as she turned the corner. She prided herself on sporting a fine set of antenna, guaranteed to sniff out subtle nuances in behavior and attitude. That instant's pause after her mention of Corinne —Annie's antenna quivered to attention. So here was someone else who didn't care at all for Corinne Webster. But what else was new? Miss Dora didn't like her. Mrs. Ferrier didn't like her. And she had yet to meet the evil Sybil, who apparently didn't like her either.

She pulled into the parking lot of the chili dog stand. As she ordered, a cool breeze rustled the fronds of a nearby palmetto palm. A black cloud slid over the face of the sun, and it was suddenly cool. Although she wasn't susceptible to omens, if she were a gothic heroine, she would be looking over her shoulder. Instead, she munched on the dog and studied her list, checking off the notation: *Arrange for body.*

I T WAS A NIGHT THE angels made, just enough offshore breeze to caress and refresh, a hint of coming summer in the warmth captured by the wooden slats of the deck chair, the languorous wash of water against the pilings, the faint strains of "Some Enchanted Evening," and the nearness of Max.

Undoubtedly, a moment of human perfection, fleeting, impermanent, and precious.

And Annie almost succumbed. It was delightful to share a deck chair with Max and feel the warm weight of his arm around her shoulders, and know that in an instant or two, she could half-turn, raise her face, and his lips would meet hers.

She almost succumbed, but her mind still worked. For weeks now, she and Max had been butting heads about September, but ever since he had picked her up at seven, all the way through the magnificent Beef Wellingtons at the Island Hills Clubhouse cypress-paneled dining room, up to and including their hand-in-hand stroll along the harbor front, he had made no mention at all of the wedding.

Instead, he had smiled cherubically and acted as though they were in harmony on all planes.

Annie turned her head.

Max turned his.

Eyeball to eyeball, she demanded, "Why are you being so agreeable?" It was the same tone an American negotiator might use upon receiving the latest Soviet arms proposal in Geneva.

"Annie, that is unworthy of you."

His injured tone confirmed her suspicions. He was up to something.

She sat up, removing her face from such dangerous proximity to his. "All right, what's going on?"

"What do you mean?" He was as bland as cottage cheese. "I'm spending a very pleasant evening with my girl. Dinner. After-dinner drinks. A stroll along the harbor. And looking forward to what was once called a romantic interlude. You. Me. One deck chair and—" His hand tugged her closer, his face bent nearer.

She placed her hands on his chest. "Wait a minute. You've been hounding me for weeks to agree to a spectacular for a wedding, including everything but a brass band and fireworks, and now you're acting as if everything's agreed upon. I don't get it." She peered at him. "Are we dis-engaged?"

"Hell, no." He kissed her decisively. Then he grinned. "I hadn't thought of that ploy, but I'll tuck it back in case it's needed." He silenced her hoot of outrage with another kiss. "No, rest easy." His arms tightened around her. "I merely experienced a moment of enlightenment today."

Her mind skipped back over the day. What had he been up to? All right, she would get to the bottom of this, but he was continuing, unperturbed and still cherubic.

"I realized that everything would come out right."

She waited.

He reached out and traced the line of her cheek.

She shook her head, unwilling to be distracted.

"Why?"

"Because."

Annie gritted her teeth. What a day, dealing with a woman who turned out to be a blood sister to Attila the Hun, surveying the beauties of Chastain in the tow of a formidable eccentric, now faced with this disconcerting behavior from Max. But he was looking at her with an unmistakable gleam in his eyes, and his next actions were predictable. As for his sudden enlightenment, it must mean that he was seeing things her way, but, being Max, he would never, of course, admit to that. Well, that was all right. She could be gracious, too. When they next discussed September, she wouldn't revel in his defeat. As she moved closer to him, she spared one final thought for Mrs. Webster. The woman obviously was a snake, but that would come out all right, too. Besides, she didn't have to deal with Mrs. Webster until Thursday.

As for now, the night was young.

Her first instinct was to shred the letter.

Her second to hire a howitzer and blast Prichard House and its occupants into oblivion. What the Yankees had not accomplished, one mad Texan would achieve.

"Annie. Annie, honey, whatever is the matter?"

She heard Ingrid's worried chirp through a blood-red haze, but she was too angry to manage even an outraged squall. Wordlessly, she flapped the thick stationery until it sounded like an avalanche on a 1930s radio drama. Ingrid snatched up one of the newly arrived posters of the back wall paintings and began to fan her. "What's happened?"

"I've worked my guts out!" Annie pounded on the cash desk and the skull-and-crossbones No-Smoking sign skidded sideways. "And now, the day before I'm supposed to make my presentation to the Board, Mrs. President, Mrs. Corinne Prichard Prissy-Ass Webster, sends me *her* outline for a mystery. How about my clues? How about the instruction sheets for the suspects? How about the autopsy report and suspects' statements? I'll have to redo everything! I could murder that woman!"

Annie parked at Lookout Point on Thursday morning and stared grimly across the street at the square fort, home of her present employer, the Chastain Historical Preservation Society. She was still close, blazingly close, to telling the Board members, individually and collectively, to go to hell. Ingrid had soothed; Max had counseled. And, they did have a point. A weak point, Annie felt, but a point. She would still have the fun of creating the clues and running the Mystery Nights, even if she did have to use Corinne's plot. But the thrill was gone. She'd wanted to have her very own mystery, and now she was saddled with that odious woman's creation.

From her vantage point, she could see the front of the old fort and the entry to the parking lot behind it. A cream-colored Mercedes turned into the drive, fol-

lowed by a faded gray Volvo older than her own,
driven by the gaunt redhead she'd met at the Red
Cross. Ferrier, that was her name.

Annie took a deep breath. The Board members were
gathering. Time for her to arrive, too. And she might
still present Madame President with her crumpled letter, now smoothed and stuck into a green folder, and
tell her to run her own Mystery Nights. She locked the
car, then checked both ways and paused to watch the
approach of the magnificent and unforgettable Bentley
she'd seen the day Miss Dora took her on a tour. Miss
Dora, when not breathing fire and brimstone, had indicated that the Bentley's owner was also a Board
member. A sinful one, apparently. Annie glimpsed luxuriant dark hair, enormous tortoise-shell sunglasses,
and a slash of bright red lipstick. The car turned onto
Lafayette, then slowed to make a left into the lot.

That's the one who gave Corinne a hard time. Annie
was all in favor of that. Maybe she could start an insur-
rection, persuade the board that her original plan was
better, get them to okay her mystery and dump Corinne's. Because, actually, it was pretty snappy. Hmm.
It would all depend upon how she presented it.

With a decisive nod, she started across the street.

A brown Ford Tempo squealed around the corner
and jolted to a stop in front of the Society. A stocky,
well-built young man with thick, curly brown hair
slammed out of the driver's seat. He had a crooked
nose which looked as though it might have been
drubbed into football turf more than once. He carried a
notebook and a pencil. A couple of extra yellow pencils
poked out of the pocket of his short-sleeved white
shirt.

She reached the sidewalk at the same time. He saw
her and smiled appreciatively, his mouth quirking up

in good humor and lessening the predatory look of his misshapen (football?) nose. His admiration was so unstudied that she grinned back. Then he looked past her. His face hardened, hooding his dark brown eyes.

Curious, Annie half-turned and knew her own face toughened, too. America's sweetheart stood on the sidewalk, pointing at the Tempo.

"What is that vehicle doing here? Move it along. You're blocking the entrance to the Society."

From her tone, Corinne Webster might have been addressing the driver of a garbage scow.

The stocky young man ignored her and began walking up the sidewalk.

"Young man, do as I say. Move that car."

He turned as if aware for the first time that she was speaking to him. "Press, lady."

"But you can't come in here." She waved her bejewelled hand toward the Society building.

"Sure, I can. It's a city agency, funded by the city, and there's an open meeting law, lady." He pivoted and continued briskly up the sidewalk.

"You've never come to any of our meetings before." Corinne hurried up the walk after him, her face pale with anger. "If you've come to cause trouble because I spoke to you last week—"

He paused and swung toward her. A muscle twitched in his taut face. "Oh, yeah." His tone was sarcastic. "Gee, I didn't recognize you either. If it isn't Mrs. High-and-Mighty Webster. Sure, you're the dame who offered me money to get out of town. Yeah, I remember you now." There was utter contempt in his dark eyes. "Don't worry, lady, I'm not here on your account. I'm here because the news desk got a tip this was going to be an interesting morning."

He moved on up the sidewalk, yanked open the heavy front door, and disappeared inside.

Corinne Webster stood frozen, her hands gripping the handle of her dhurrie purse so tightly that her fingers turned a waxy white. She wore a black-and-white linen dress this morning and a heavy, beaten-gold necklace with a shiny opal drop. She stood stiffly for a long moment, then stalked forward. Annie glimpsed her face as she opened the door. When it closed behind her, Annie felt her tight shoulders relax. Ah, Chastain, this sundrenched, idyllic coastal hideaway. What next?

A squeal of tortured metal raked the morning quiet. Miss Dora, dressed this morning in a full-skirted bombazine with puff sleeves, turned up the sidewalk, pulling a child's rusted red wagon. A black pillbox hat with a jaunty green plume topped her flyaway silver hair. The raspy voice rose above the scrape of one bent tire against the bottom of the wagon.

"Open the door there, girl."

Obediently, Annie hurried up the walk and pulled open the heavy wooden door and watched in fascination as the gnome-like figure, cane in one hand, maneuvered the wagon. A large hammer rode atop a pile of placards attached to two-foot white stakes, pointed on one end.

Footsteps sounded behind them, and a tall, slender woman reached down to help.

"Good morning, Aunt Dora. It looks like you're all ready for the tour week." Then she straightened, smiled at Annie, and held out her hand. "I'm Lucy Haines, a member of the Board. You must be Annie Laurance, our mystery creator."

Annie took her hand and liked her at once. Her grip was cool and firm, her face serious, her manner formal, but friendly. She wore a gray-and-white striped seersucker skirt and an unadorned white blouse and looked wonderfully normal in contrast to Corinne and Miss Dora.

The heavy, blonde secretary joined them in the entryway. "I'll put the wagon in the storeroom, Miss Dora. I think everyone's here. They're all in—"

The voice full, throaty, and deep, carried as clearly as a Broadway actress's delivery to the farthest stall.

"You've gone too far, Corinne. I won't tolerate this."

Even in the dim entryway with the weak illumination from the wall sconces and the pale squares of sunlight from the deepset windows, the malicious curve to Miss Dora's smile was unmistakable. "Sybil."

Annie felt a quick march of goose bumps across the small of her back. Miss Dora's sandpaper voice oozed simultaneous disgust, pleasure, vindictiveness, and amusement. The secretary peered toward the archway, her eyes wide with distress. The sensible Lucy Haines frowned, and gnawed her lip.

Sybil's deep, vibrant voice quivered with rage. "It is unspeakable."

Miss Dora wheezed with laughter, revealing blackened, uneven teeth. "Come on, girls, let's not miss the show," and led the way through the bricked archway and down a narrow hall to a wider archway that opened into an equally dim, very large room, which held an ornately carved walnut refectory table. One man unknown to Annie sat at the table, but she recognized Gail Prichard, her sometime customer Roscoe Merrill, and the red-headed Edith Ferrier. No one noticed their arrival. All eyes were riveted on two women.

Corinne stood beside the speaker's stand at the far end of the table. Her blue eyes glittered like a southern sea on a blistering day. Annie realized with a twist of shock, however, that Corinne was *enjoying* herself. There was no sense here of a woman beleaguered or defensive. To the contrary, she stood by the table, upright as a goddess on the prow of a Roman ship, and just as arrogant and supercilious.

"Really, Sybil, your attitude is surprising." Her voice was cool, amused, untroubled. "It's a matter of contract, you know. All very clear. You can ask Roscoe."

All eyes, Annie's included, switched to Sybil, posed dramatically in front of the Flemish tapestry that covered a third of the bricked wall behind her. At her first full view, Annie thought simply, "Wow." Voluptuous described Ruebens' nudes and Sybil. And Sybil had the edge. A bitch in heat could not be more frankly sensual. A diamond clip glistened against her midnight black hair. Violet eye shadow emphasized the depth and hunger of equally black eyes. She wore a green jersey dress with a sharply plunging neckline that clung to every generous curve, revealing a cleavage guaranteed to galvanize every male present. She made every other woman in the room look about as attractive as a praying mantis. She turned now and stretched out a hand tipped by talon-sharp, vermilion nails. A diamond large enough to rival the Kohinoor weighted her third finger. A great square emerald glittered in an antique gold setting. Matching emeralds gleamed in a bracelet. "Roscoe, is this true?" The contralto voice vibrated. "Did you have anything to do with this unconscionable exploitation?"

Roscoe Merrill was obviously wishing fervently that he were somewhere else, maybe a far outpost of the Foreign Legion. A fine beading of sweat glistened on his bald head. His expressionless brown eyes avoided both Sybil's probing gaze and Corinne's confident stare, peering down instead at the legal pad on the table. He cleared his throat. "The Museum, of course, felt it imperative to protect its own interests. And, since the paintings have been executed on Museum time and using Museum materials, it is only equitable and reasonable that the Museum should have title to the paintings."

"I can't believe that contract." Sybil stepped closer to the table and bent down to grip his shoulder.

He glanced up, then jerked his eyes away from that enticing cleavage to stare determinedly at the legal pad. A dull red flush spread over his face and bald head.

"It's disgusting. Not only to steal the poor boy's work, but to forbid him to take part in an exhibition! To sabotage his career! Roscoe, you ought to be ashamed." Then she whirled toward Corinne. "And you, you're a jealous, conniving bitch. Just because you're a dried-up, dessicated old woman, you resent anyone who's truly alive. But you needn't think you've won. Just you wait and see!"

For the first time, Corinne's control wavered and an ugly flash of hatred moved in her eyes, but she retained an icy smile. "The Museum's position is irreproachable. And now, it's time for—"

"Mrs. Giacomo, I'm Bobby Frazier, reporter for the *Chastain Courier*." The stocky young man who had smiled at Annie outside pushed away from the wall, and approached Sybil.

Annie put names together. Miss Dora had said she defiled her name, that she was a Chastain. So, Sybil Chastain Giacomo. What price an Italian count?

"Can you tell me a little more about your disagreement here? Is there a problem at the Prichard Museum?" His pencil poised over his notebook.

Corinne reached out and gripped the speaker's

stand. "You have no right to come in here and ask questions—this matter is not of public concern."

The reporter ignored her rising voice and, admiration evident, addressed Sybil. "You're a director of the Prichard Museum, aren't you? Can you tell me what's going on?"

Sybil absorbed his interest automatically, instantly recognized a way to embarrass Corinne, took a deep breath, and let fly. "Why, certainly. Of course I can, Mr. Frazier. I know all about it. Tim Bond—you know his work, of course—is a curator at the Prichard Museum. Actually, he does *everything.* He makes most of the reproductions and cleans old pictures and he paints. Everyone knows he has a *great* future. Corinne snatched him up, because she always wants to own everyone. She told him he could work at the museum and paint all he wanted and he'd have a salary and not have to worry about money at all. But she didn't tell him the contract he signed made all his paintings belong to the museum—"

"That isn't true at all." For the first time, Corinne's voice was strident. "He read the contract. He understood."

"You told him the Museum would be happy to loan his paintings out for exhibits, and there was no question of the Museum keeping the paintings here until Corinne found out that Tim and I—" Sybil's shoulders shifted, and Annie could almost hear the whisper of satin sheets—"are friends. She resents his having friendships. Now, he's had this wonderful offer from a gallery in New York. They want to show all of his paintings in September, and it could absolutely launch his career—and Corinne won't give him permission to take his work to New York!"

Frazier wrote rapidly in his notebook, then turned

toward Corinne. *"Has* the Museum refused Bond permission to show his works?"

"The paintings belong to—" Corinne began angrily.

Merrill intervened smoothly, "Mr. Frazier, this matter is still under consideration by the Museum Board and no final determination has been made. I understand there will be further discussion of Museum policy in regard to loan exhibitions at next month's meeting, so it would be premature to announce that a decision has been made."

"Tim Bond's future is at stake," Sybil thundered magnificently, "and I for one do not intend to let the matter drop. Most Chastainians will support me." She paused. Her face was slowly transformed from petulant anger to malignant pleasure. "I'm going to launch a petition drive. I'm going to ask everyone to sign who wants Chastain's most talented young painter to have a chance to achieve success."

"When will you start the petition drive, Mrs. Giacomo?" Frazier was egging her on, well aware that his every question further infuriated Corinne.

"Today. Right now." She reached over Merrill's shoulder, snatched up the yellow legal pad, and brandished it over her head. "Here. I'll start it now." Grabbing a pencil from Frazier's pocket, she scrawled in block letters: PETITION TO FREE TIM BOND'S PAINTINGS. With a triumphant glance at Corinne, she flung the pad down on the table in front of Merrill and handed him the pencil.

Not a muscle moved in Merrill's heavy face. He was as expressionless as a poker player who'd made his last draw. He read Sybil's scrawl, then said temperately, "Obviously, both Lucy and I as members of the Board of the Prichard Museum which would, I presume, be the recipient of the completed petition, are precluded from signing this."

Sybil's sultry eyes traveled slowly from the shiny top of his head to a visible portion of his glistening black leather shoes. Then she drawled, "You never did have any balls, Roscoe." Without waiting for an answer, she shoved the pad down the table toward Edith Ferrier.

Corinne moved like a flash, darting past Sybil to snatch up the pad.

Sybil lunged toward her, grabbing one end.

A sharp crack resounded through the room, and, for an instant, no one moved.

Annie absorbed the tableau: Miss Dora with her ebony cane still upraised, ready to pound the table again; Lucy Haines, lips parted, brows drawn in a frown; Gail Prichard, her hands tightly clasped, watching her aunt in horrified fascination; Corinne Prichard Webster, the bones of her face sharpened by anger, her mouth a thin, taut line; Sybil Chastain Giacomo, triumphant, her tousled black hair an ebony frame for her flushed face; Bobby Frazier grinning, reveling in Corinne's discomfiture; Roscoe Merrill, his shoulders bunched, rigidly controlling his anger; Edith Ferrier wary, her green eyes flicking from face to face; and the sharp-visaged man, whom she hadn't met, beating an impatient tattoo with the fingers of one hand.

Miss Dora broke up the moment, circling the table like a dragonfly, then raising the cane again to bring it down with a decisive whack against the legal pad, still held on either end by Corinne and Sybil. The blow tore the pad from their hands, and it fell to the floor.

"Sybil, sit down. There. By Edith. Corinne, you get yourself up to the table and start this meeting." She swung toward Annie and Lucy. "And you two. Take your places over there." Everyone did just as instructed.

Corinne reached the lectern and began to riffle through a thin sheaf of papers. Her breathing was rapid and shallow. The room pulsed with hostility.

Lucy Haines's low, pleasant voice was in odd counterpoint to the seething atmosphere. "Corinne, we should introduce our guests."

Corinne looked at her blankly.

"Mr. Frazier and Miss Laurance."

Corinne's eyes narrowed, but, after an instant's pause, she brusquely presented them to the Board. "And our members: Gail Prichard, Roscoe Merrill, Sybil Giacomo, Edith Ferrier, Dr. John Sanford, Dora Brevard, and Lucy Haines."

Dr. Sanford. Annie looked at him with interest. The corner of his ascetic mouth turned down in disdain. He had floppy gray-streaked dark hair that curled untidily over his ears, a hawk nose, and impersonal eyes. He sat at the end of the table beside Edith Ferrier, but he ignored her. Edith watched Corinne somberly, and her dour expression contrasted sharply with her cheerful, almost girlish dress, a cyclamen-pink floral print.

Sanford brushed back a drooping lock of hair. "Can't we get this show on the road? I've got to get back to the hospital."

Definitely a Type-A personality. She wondered why he'd become involved in a historical preservation group, which might be expected to pursue a leisurely course guaranteed to drive a man of his temperament mad.

Corinne cleared her throat and briskly described the progress of plans for the tour week. She had herself well under control now. Only the tiny white spots at the corners of her mouth indicated her anger. As her introductory comments wound down, Annie picked up her green folder. She was going to have one swell audience, no doubt about that.

"And now it's time for us to hear from Miss Laurance, who will explain the program she has put together for our house-and-garden-week tours. Miss Laurance."

Still not calling them Mystery Nights. The thought ignited Annie's smouldering anger. How infuriating! Corinne Prichard was such a meddlesome know-it-all that she'd taken over the mystery program, but she still refused to even mention the word mystery. How obnoxious. She had to take a moment, when she reached the lectern, to tamp down her explosive juices.

"Thank you, Mrs. Webster." It wasn't easy to say, and her voice sounded like thin steel. "It's a pleasure for me to be here."

Fun, fun, fun, the imp in her mind chanted.

"I'm looking forward to the Mystery Nights. I believe we can offer a program that will attract a great many participants."

"How many?" Dr. Sanford barked.

"About a hundred a night," she shot back. The Board members looked startled, but, by God, she'd had enough. "The evenings will begin at six with a tour of the three houses and gardens, followed by a buffet supper on the lawn of the Prichard House. Promptly at seven, the participants will divide into teams and go to The Scene of the Crime. The teams will then study evidence available in the police tent, interview the suspects, and confer to decide who they believe is the murderer."

Dr. Sanford cracked his knuckles. "All right, all right. The mechanics seem sound. Give us a rundown on the murder, then we can okay it."

"It's a Southern Mystery." Not my mystery, she wanted to say. She flicked a brief glance toward Corinne. "We must thank Mrs. Webster for our plot. Our victim is Mrs. Meddlesome Moneypot, owner of the fabulous Familytree Plantation. Mrs. Moneypot is extremely proud of her social position and determined that everyone in her family shall behave as she believes they should. She ruined her brother's romance. She's alienated her husband and niece, and has also made many enemies in town. Her husband wanted to have a career in the foreign service, but she made him resign and come home."

A sharply indrawn breath was magnified by the taut silence.

Annie paused. Was her sardonic reading alienating her audience? Damn it, the room quivered with hostile vibes. She tried to smooth out her tone. "Her husband's been drinking too much for years, but everyone in town is whispering that he's met another woman. Mrs. Moneypot's niece is seeing a man she considers very unsuitable, and—"

A chair moved against the planked flooring, making a sharp high squeak.

"—there are people in town who have reason to hold a grudge against her. She's trying to ruin the life of a young artist—" Annie stumbled over that sentence. How odd. "—she's threatening the marriage of a prominent attorney, the career plans of a doctor, the club election of a society woman—"

Annie paused. Something very peculiar was happening to her audience. As she well knew from her earliest acting days, every audience has its own personality. She would always remember the summer night when she played Honey in "Who's Afraid of Virginia Woolf?" in an outdoor amphitheater in Dallas.

It was sultry and thunder rumbled in the distance. The smell of dust, freshly mown grass, and buttered popcorn hung in the still, hot air, but the audience responded on an elemental level to the passion on the stage. It was an audience linked soul to soul with the players, and it was as near exaltation as Annie ever expected to reach.

That was the pinnacle. There had been other memorable audiences, for good or ill. But there had never been an electric silence quite like this. What the hell was going on?

She stumbled to a stop and stared at her stunned audience. Gail pressed the back of her hand against her lips. Roscoe, looking like a watchful turtle, assessed Annie very carefully indeed, his pale brown eyes narrowed to slits. Sybil was frankly delighted, wide mouth spread in her malicious smile. Edith glared furiously, a bright patch of red staining each hollowed cheek. Dr. Sanford scowled, his restless hand spread flat against the table top. Miss Dora peered at Corinne. Lucy shook her head, as if bewildered.

Corinne's face was as white as ivory, and her dark blue eyes blazed. She pushed back her chair so abruptly that it tumbled to the floor. "I'll sue you," she shrilled at Annie. "You and that disgusting creature." She whirled toward the stocky reporter. "This is your work—and I'll make you pay for it."

Frazier cocked a black eyebrow. "Not me, lady. This isn't my show—but it's a hell of a lot of fun." He turned toward Annie. "Listen, I need a copy of your script. Maybe the *Courier* will run the whole thing." He smiled gleefully. "I'll say you've come up with a Southern Mystery. What did you say the victim's name was? Mrs. Rich Bitch? And who're the suspects?" He looked around the refectory table. "The leading lights of the town?"

The room exploded.

Sybil crowed. "Oh, you got it this time, Corinne. Jesus, I love it. Hey, I didn't know Leighton was up for grabs. I'll have to take a look. He's always been a good-looking man, and if he's developed a backbone, he'd be worth at least an afternoon."

Miss Dora's wizened face turned plum colored. "Sybil Chastain, don't you know your mama's turning in her grave right this minute, hearing you talk like a harlot."

"I hope she's spinning like a dervish," Sybil said coolly.

Dr. Sanford looked like an enraged eagle. "I don't know what kind of attack is being mounted. But I don't intend to tolerate it. My professional reputation is unassailable."

Gail flushed to the roots of her auburn hair and averted her gaze from Bobby.

"I find it quite unbelievable that I should be held up to public ridicule." Edith's voice trembled with outrage.

"Please, please everyone." Lucy's well-bred voice rose above the babble. "There must have been a mistake of some kind."

Roscoe pounded on the table, calling for quiet.

Not even the urbanity of a John Putnam Thatcher could salvage this board meeting.

"It's a conspiracy. That's what it is. A conspiracy to embarrass me. Well, I won't let them get away with it." Corinne flung out a hand toward her niece. "Don't you see how vile he is?" She glared at the reporter. "He's behind it. He and this girl. He's probably been sleeping with her, and they—"

"Mrs. Webster, you'd better stop." Annie had never realized that she could bellow. "And you'd better apologize—or I'm the one who will sue. I don't know what the hell is going on here. What's wrong with everybody?"

That brought a moment's stunned silence.

Finally, Lucy spoke apologetically. "It's your murder victim, Miss Laurance. Corinne thinks you're talking about her. It's such an odd coincidence."

"Coincidence!" Corinne's narrow chest heaved.

"Just a few home truths about Chastain's leading bitch—" Sybil began.

To forestall another furious outburst from Corinne, Annie held up her hand. "Let's get a few things straight. I didn't write this murder plot."

"Oh, yes, you did—you and that despicable muckraker!"

"Mrs. Webster, I gather you don't care for Mr. Frazier. That's your problem. I've never met him, never talked to him, and he had nothing whatsoever to do with this murder plot."

"You do too know him. I saw him *smile* at you outside."

The little flicker of fury lapping at her control blazed higher. Annie moved away from the lectern, pushed past the reporter, and stood inches from Corinne.

"Listen very closely. I'm going to say it once. I had never seen this man until I arrived here this morning. He likes pretty girls, so he smiled at me. I smiled back. That's too innocent and genuine an action for you to understand, isn't it, Mrs. Webster? Now, let me make myself perfectly clear. I don't like you, but I also don't like being used. Clearly, I'm the patsy here today. I was set up for this." Moving back to the lectern, she picked up the plan she had received from the Chastain Historical Preservation Society. "Somebody sent this to me. I thought it came from you. The cover letter's signed with your name."

Corinne snatched the six typewritten pages, then scanned the cover letter. "That signature is a forgery." She looked around the room. "This was written on Society stationery."

The implication was plain.

Lucy objected immediately. "That doesn't mean a thing. Everybody in town drops in here from time to time."

"No member of the Society would do such a dreadful thing," Miss Dora insisted.

"I'm going to find out who did this." Corinne's voice was metallic with determination. "And when I do—"

"Best thing is to let bygones be bygones," Roscoe Merrill interjected persuasively. "It doesn't do to take this kind of thing too seriously. You know, women get their noses out of joint, and—"

"What do you mean by that?" Edith demanded shrilly.

"Not a thing, not a thing," he said quickly. "Obviously, this has been a foolish prank." But his voice was worried and tense.

Annie eyed him with interest. Roscoe obviously didn't like this situation at all, and he was determined to get past it.

He held both hands up. "I suggest we get back to the object of this meeting. Our guest has been put in an extremely difficult position. We will have to hope that she will overlook this episode. Ms. Laurance, we agree that you have been victimized, but hopefully we can go forward from here. As I see it, the main problem—"

"The main problem is to determine who perpetrated this outrage." Corinne glared again at the reporter.

Frazier spread his legs and rocked back on his heels. "Nope. Guess again. I wish I'd thought of it. More fun than a whorehouse on Saturday night. But you'd better look among your snooty friends, Mrs. Webster. Who knew enough to dig all this dirt?"

"Young man, your attitude is reprehensible," Miss Dora scolded.

Corinne bit into an idea and clung. "Why did you come this morning," she demanded of Frazier, "if you didn't have anything to do with it?" Then she bent a sharp look at Gail, who began to shake her head in negation.

Frazier's good humor fled. "So now you want to slice Gail up, too?"

"Bobby, don't," Gail pleaded.

He ignored her. A vein throbbed in his neck. "Listen, lady, I'd rather stack crap than have anything to do with you. I'm here today because the city editor got a note in the mail saying all hell was going to break loose. Frankly, I thought he had a screw loose. You people are usually about as interesting as yesterday's obits."

"A note in the mail," Corinne repeated sharply.

"I'll look into all this." Peacemaker Roscoe held out his hand for the letter. "I promise you, Corinne, I'll get to the bottom of it, if at all possible."

But Annie reached out and plucked the letter from Corinne's hand. "Nope. This letter was sent to me. It's mine. And I'm going to do some investigating myself."

"Young lady, I appreciate your concern, but this is a matter for the Board," Roscoe insisted, flushing.

Who did he think he was? Antony Maitland?

"We can all investigate," she said drily. "I'll send you a copy of it."

"This is all very well and good, and I understand

why Corinne and Roscoe and Miss Laurance will pursue this matter, but I do think we must face up to our immediate problem," a reasoned voice urged.

Everyone looked at Lucy.

"After all, the Mystery Nights have already been advertised as part of the house-and-garden tours. I mean, we have only a little over a week before the festival begins."

"Lucy is hewing to the main point," Roscoe agreed. "Ms. Laurance, will you overlook this unfortunate contretemps and create a murder for us?"

8

ANNIE REFILLED MAX'S white coffee mug (*The Red Thumb Mark*), then her own. Contrary to her usual habit, she shoveled a heaping teaspoon of sugar into her cup and stirred briskly.

It didn't escape him, of course. "Well, old dear, you must be frazzled." He stretched out comfortably, tilting the straight back chair on its rear legs.

Annie looked up from her ragtag collection of papers containing bits and pieces of possible Mystery Nights. "Have you been reading Sayers again?"

He grinned. "Nope. But maybe you should."

"Civilized mayhem as opposed to Southern discomfort?"

"Right." Then his dark blue eyes grew serious. "Actually, why don't you jump ship? Working for those people is like afternoon tea at a nuthouse."

"Quit *now*? Why, I can do any mystery I want to."

Visions of plots danced in her head. "Maybe a movable corpse. Like *The Trouble With Harry*. Honestly, Max, did you ever in your life see anything funnier than Harry? Every time somebody buried him, somebody else dug him up."

He rubbed his check with his knuckles. "It's comments such as that which make me wonder about you sometimes."

"Oh, my God, it was *wonderful*."

"It wasn't one of Hitchcock's successes."

"Dumb audiences," she said stubbornly. She took another swallow of the sugar-laden coffee. "Or I can do an academic mystery, something on the order of *Seven Suspects*."

"Not unless you want to bore everybody into a coma." He took a big swallow of coffee.

"Or I could go for a grim background, like Moscow in *Angels in the Snow*."

She suddenly felt warm and cozy. Was it the sugar and the caffeine, or the wealth of possibilities that lay before her?

Max tipped the chair upright and leaned his elbows on the table. "What's wrong with good old Thompson Hatfield, the late, unlamented president of the bank? You already had suspects, clues, et al."

"Oh, no. I'm not going to do any mystery where the victim or suspects could by the stretch of anybody's wildest imagination have any relationship to anybody in Chastain, S.C. No, sir." She shook her head decisively. Then she paused and rubbed an ink-stained finger to her nose, resulting in a distinct smudge. "You know, if I didn't have so much to do for the Mystery Nights, I'd hit Chastain like Kinsey Millhone and shake some teeth until I got some answers."

His eyes glistened. "Would you wear tight jeans?"

"Don't be sexist." But it was an absent-minded put-down, and her frown pulled her brows into a determined line. "Dammit, I don't like being used—even if the end result was to take a cut at la piranha."

"Do you think it was a Board member?"

"I don't know. That was my first thought, but I talked to Lucy on the way out, and she said the Board had reported to the Society at the general meeting last month about the plans to have the Mystery Nights, and my name was mentioned then. I do think it must have been done by someone who belongs to the Society. Lucy said people drop in to the office all the time, but I'll bet they parcel out their creamy stationery like gold plate. It's that kind of place."

"Sounds like a good lead. Who had access to the stationery? Let me see the letter for a second."

She rooted around in her piles, found the green folder, and slid it to him.

He read it carefully, then announced, "First, it was typed on a typewriter, not a word processor, because the capital *B* jumps up half a line and the lower case *r* is worn."

"Bravo."

He ignored her sarcastic tone. "Moreover, the typist isn't skilled because the pressure is uneven, resulting in erratic inking."

"Ah, The Thinking Machine at work."

"The allusion escapes me, but I will assume it is apt. Even though machines don't think."

"You, not the typewriter. The Thinking Machine was Jacques Futrelle's detective."

He clapped a hand to his head. "How can I not know of him?"

"Probably because Futrelle went down on the *Titanic*

before he had time to write more than two volumes of short stories."

But Max was still analyzing the letter. When he spoke again, the lightness had left his voice. "This is heavy stuff. Somebody *really* doesn't like your Mrs. Webster."

"She's not *my* Mrs. Webster." She sipped at the hot, sweet coffee. "But I don't have time to worry about that mess. I've got to get the Mystery Nights ready to roll—and come up with a plot that can't possibly have anything to do with anybody, living or dead, in Chastain. Listen, how does this grab you? I'll make it a South Sea Island and one of those New England missionaries and he gets involved with this languorous beauty—Max, you're not listening."

He was staring at the letter, his eyes unaccustomedly grim.

Annie whistled.

Startled, he looked up.

"Hey, it isn't all that bad."

"I think it is." His voice was grave. "I don't know. I have a funny feeling."

She quirked an interested eyebrow. "Are you coming all over psychic? Like the tweenie in a Christie country house murder?"

"It doesn't take any psychic powers to pick up bad vibes from this." He tapped the letter. "It's more than an ugly incident. It's dangerous."

She didn't laugh. "I agree," she said reluctantly. "It's just like the *The Moving Finger*. The villagers dismissed the anonymous letters as nasty but meaningless. And they were dreadfully wrong." She picked up the heavy stationery, squinting thoughtfully at the first page. "But surely this was nothing more than an effort to embarrass Corinne Webster. That's all there was to it—and certainly I was a kind of innocent bystander."

Max slammed his fist on the table. "Annie, tell the Chastain Historical Preservation Society to go get screwed."

She laughed aloud. "Oh, my. What a vision that conjures." Then she shook her head. "Nope. They're counting on me."

"I mean it. I think you should drop the whole thing."

"Oh, I couldn't do that. Really. I promised." She reached over the table and ruffled his hair. "Come on, don't gloom. It'll be okay. The letter writer can't fool me—or anybody—twice."

"That's right," he said slowly. "But, I think I'll nose around Chastain, see what I can pick up. That might discourage any further activity."

"Oh, that's a good idea." Once again, she spoke absently, and she gave an abstracted wave as he departed. She could do a Victorian mystery, such as Peter Lovesey's *Wobble to Death*. Or dart back to the days of Richard the Lionhearted as Victor Luhrs did in *The Longbow Murder*. Or attempt the clever twist achieved by Selwyn Jepson when he presented a modern Macbeth in *Keep Murder Quiet*. Or emulate Edward D. Hoch's talent for the preposterous, exhibited so well in *The Spy and The Thief* when his master criminal, Nick Velvet, stole an entire major league baseball team. Or perhaps she should go for that perennial favorite, an English country murder, à la Catherine Aird, Reginald Hill, or Elizabeth Lemarchand . . .

Max floorboarded the red Porsche off of the ferry. As he drove toward Chastain, gray dust boiled in the car's wake. His urgency surprised him. Damn. Why did Annie have such an indomitably Puritan conscience? He was the New Englander, and he'd never had any difficulty in persuading himself to do whatever he wanted. He thought for an instant of that wonderful *New Yorker* cartoon of the devil explaining to some newcomers that after all, down here it was whatever worked for you. Annie would never receive *that* advice. He sighed. So he might as well stop trying to talk her out of putting on the Chastain Murder Nights. But, dammit, it didn't feel right to him. Maybe if he just sniffed around, the letter writer would lie low—at least until he and Annie were out of town.

The place to start was the Chastain Historical Preservation Society. He followed the plaques into the historic district, took one wrong turn into a dead end, but finally ended up at Lookout Point. He locked the Porsche, dodged through Chastain's version of five o'clock traffic (one milk truck, a station wagon filled with a wild-eyed mother and nine Cub Scouts, a stripped down Ford Mustang, and three Lincoln Continentals) and pulled on the front gate. It didn't budge. He read the gilt sign. *Hours: 10 to 4.*

Sourly, he wondered why Fletch always found somebody to talk to.

Okay. Four-thirty and nobody home. He kicked the gate. That shut off at least until tomorrow any inquiry into disbursement of the letterhead stationery. But he sure didn't intend to go back to the island without accomplishing something.

Annie had described all the participants in the morning brouhaha. He leaned back against a brick pillar, pulled a small spiral notebook from his pocket, and studied the list of names.

Corinne Webster, the object of attack. An ice maiden

busy leeching the vitality from everyone around her. She probably wouldn't talk to him and would be better left for later, in any event.

Sybil Chastain Giacomo. Max's eyes gleamed. Annie described her as a Ruebens nude in an Oscar de la Renta dress. With the mouth of a termagant. Awesome.

Lucy Haines. Sounded nice. Annie said she looked rather serious. A lean, tanned woman with a firm handshake. A librarian.

Roscoe Merrill. A stalwart of the community, obviously. Treasurer of the Society. A lawyer with a face that kept its own counsel. He'd promised La Grande Dame Webster he'd look into the letter, but all the while he kept stressing that it was better to drop the matter.

Dr. John Sanford. Intense, self-absorbed, arrogant. And something in the letter made him mad.

Edith Ferrier. The letter made her mad, too. Why did she take it personally? And she didn't like Corinne. Why?

Miss Dora Brevard, permanent secretary of the Board, and Chastain's ancient historian in residence. But she seemed to aim her venom at Sybil, not Corinne.

Gail Prichard. The letter writer said Mrs. Moneypot's niece was seeing a very unsuitable man. Obviously, that was a reference to the combative reporter. Max ran down the list again. If he had his druthers, he'd drop in on the luscious Sybil, but he had a feeling—just a faint niggle of warning—that Annie might take that amiss. And the letter seemed far too subtle an approach for Sybil. So, checking the map Annie had loaned him, he began to walk down Lafayette street toward the heart of town.

.   .   .

"She wants the one with the nun who detects."

Annie looked blankly at Ingrid. "Nun?"

"Mrs. Canady. She's called twice, and she insists she wants the new book with a nun."

Dragging her mind back from the depths of its involvement in the rapidly burgeoning plot for the Mystery Nights, she repeated, "Nun?" Then, in a burst of animation, she rattled off, "Sister John and Sister Hyacinthe? Sister Mary Teresa? Sister Mary Helen?"

"A new series," Ingrid offered helpfully.

Annie squinted her eyes in concentration. New series. Oh, yeah. An *ex*-nun. "Ask her if she wants Bridget O'Toole in *Murder Among Friends*?"

As Ingrid loped back to the telephone, Annie gathered up the strands that had been swirling together in her mind: A weekend at an English country home, croquet, tea, and murder. Perfect. Move over Sheila Radley and Dorothy Simpson.

Audubon prints of a red-shouldered hawk and a wood ibis hung against the Williamsburg green wall. Heavy brown leather furniture offered soft-cushion comfort and the aura of a good men's club. A faint haze of autumn-sweet pipe smoke hung in the air.

Roscoe Merrill met Max at the door, offered a brief handshake and an appraising look, then guided him to the oversized wingback chair that faced the desk.

"So you are helping Ms. Laurance with the program for our house-and-garden week." Merrill settled back in his padded swivel chair, his face bland, but his eyes wary.

Max fashioned a genial smile. "Yes, she's hard at work on the nefarious-doings plot now. However, both she and I were disturbed at the trick that was played on her."

Max's good-humored sally evoked no helpful response. The lawyer merely stared intently and said noncommittally, "Unfortunate. Very unfortunate. But just one of those things."

Max quirked an eyebrow. "Does this sort of thing happen often within the Society?"

"No. Oh no, of course not. You misunderstand me, Mr. Darling."

Max waited.

Merrill's dry voice was unemotional, a nice match for his measuring eyes. It was easy to imagine him in settlement conferences, cautious, careful, and calculating. He would never give the store away. His pale gray suit fit him perfectly, and he wore his suit coat even in his office. Not a shirt-sleeve man. He had the air of authority to be expected in the senior partner in an old-line law firm. The law books ranged on the shelving behind his desk were leather bound and had been there for a century. The law firm had borne his family name since 1820. Merrill, Merrill, and Merrill.

"Not at all a usual occurrence, of course. I can't think, in fact, of any other example where the Society letterhead has been misused. A shocking episode, upsetting to all of us. No, Mr. Darling, what I referred to was the—" Merrill paused as if in search of precisely the right word—"the proclivity of women, perhaps, to be a trifle more emotional in their responses to certain situations than men. And, of course, the fact that women, because they are not creatures of business, do not realize sometimes the seriousness of what might otherwise pass as a prank."

Max briefly fantasized about Annie's probable feminist response to Merrill's pre-1940 view of women. *Ka-boom.*

"As I told Corinne, it will be very much for the better if we all overlook this incident, painful as it was. To seek to discover the perpetrator would avail nothing. Of course, Corinne has a legitimate complaint. Her signature obviously was forged to that missive, but making this a matter of law would bring an importance to it that it certainly doesn't deserve."

Max had a collection of relatives who specialized in obfuscation, so he sorted nimbly through the verbiage. "You think a woman did it. And you don't think it matters."

The lawyer leaned back in his chair and regarded Max over steepled fingers. "I wouldn't go so far as to put it that directly."

Max grinned. "No, I wouldn't say you put it too directly, but that's the substance, right?"

Slowly, Merrill nodded, his pale brown eyes alert.

"Why a woman?"

"It seems to me that it is a distinctly feminine attack." Merrill rubbed his blunt nose thoughtfully. "Obviously, the letter was planned to humiliate Corinne in front of the Board. And the note to the newspaper editor seems an essentially feline touch."

Max was tempted to describe some very feline men he'd encountered in his time, but instead concentrated on prizing loose information. "Did you check on that?"

Merrill pondered for a moment. He obviously didn't relish imparting any information, but finally he conceded. "I spoke to Ed Hershey, the city editor. He received a note typed on plain white paper. No signature. He didn't save it."

So that was that. "Did Hershey print anything?"

"Not much," Merrill said grimly. "Libel *per se,*

young man. But the paper carried a general report of plans for the house-and-garden tours and a brief story quoting Sybil about the question of Bond's paintings being exhibited in New York." His mouth compressed.

"What's going to happen there?"

The pale brown eyes regarded Max with about as much enthusiasm as a Republican dowager opening the door to an ACLU pamphleteer.

"That is hardly relevant to the question of the forged mystery plot."

"No?" Max leaned back comfortably in the luxurious embrace of the soft leather. "I'd think it might have some bearing. You suggest the perpetrator is a woman. Maybe Mrs. Giacomo was ticked off enough to put the show together."

For the first time, interest flickered across Merrill's face, followed immediately by dismissal. Max realized with a surge of excitement that Merrill felt certain of the letter writer's identity.

The lawyer said drily, "Mrs. Giacomo is capable of a rather alarming number of rash acts—but this is much too devious—too quiet—for her."

"You know who did it."

Merrill immediately assumed the bland expression of a sunning crocodile. "Absolutely not. I have no more information than you, Mr. Darling." He paused, then reached out and pensively selected a cherrywood pipe from a rack. Opening a wooden canister, he picked out a thick clump of aromatic tobacco and methodically tamped it in the bowl. When the tobacco was lit and drawing, he regarded Max through the smoke. "I assume we can speak confidentially, Mr. Darling."

"Ms. Laurance and I work together."

He blew a cloud of bluish smoke toward the ceiling. "Let me put it this way." How many settlement confer-

ences had the canny lawyer begun with just that tone?
"It is inevitable that jealousies arise when women
work too hard and too fervently in organizations." He
smiled with all the warmth of a robot. "My wife has
described situations to me that would shock you, Mr.
Darling. I am confident that the unfortunate incident
this morning was a direct response to this kind of pressure."

Max wondered if he were being led down the primrose path, but he dutifully responded to the lure. "Did
Mrs. Webster clobber somebody in the Society?"

"It could be viewed in that light. There may be some
heartbreak here, Mr. Darling. Let us assume, hypothet-
ically, of course, that a woman member has given herself heart and soul to the Society, served it in every
capacity, devoted days and nights to its advancement,
and then found herself refused the one office she desired. Now," and he spoke precisely, "I wish to make it
clear that I am not and will not be construed as refer-
ring to any particular individual. But that," and he
sucked on his pipe, "could be the answer to it."

"How bitter is this woman?"

"What do you mean?" Merrill asked cautiously.

"How likely is she to sabotage Annie's Mystery
Nights?"

"That won't happen. I'm confident that this was an
isolated occurrence. It is over and done with. I'm sure
of it."

"I don't want Annie embarrassed—or hurt in any
way."

"Mr. Darling, you can rest easy. I assure you it's a
closed chapter. The only thing that could cause more
trouble would be for you to continue to pursue this. I
feel that very strongly. And I'm asking you, as an of-

ficer of the Board, as a member of our Chastain community, to let it rest. Will you do that?"

Salt water stung Max's eyes, but, blurrily, he could see a familiar—and oh so shapely and touchable—body, or the half of it, beneath the surface. He stroked nearer and reached out and slipped his hand delicately up the back of her leg.

Annie shot out of the water like a Yellowstone geyser, bounced back down in the surf, and flailed wildly toward shore.

Max came up, laughing so hard that he swallowed a mouthful of salt water and began to choke.

She paused in mid-lunge. "You rat! I thought it was a shark." She squinted at him. "How did you get here?"

"I drove back from Chastain, parked, changed in the cabana—"

She slapped her hand down against the water. "No, I mean *here*. I didn't see you come."

"Actually, my love, a school of hammerheads could have surrounded you. You were staring at the horizon in total absorption. I came up behind you, then swam underwater. The better to pretend I was a shark."

"Max, will you ever grow up?"

"Hell, no." He splashed to her and picked her up in his arms.

"Put me down."

"Hell, no," he said again, enthusiastically.

They toppled backwards, the water roiled, and they came up again, sputtering with laughter.

His report on Chastain could wait until later.

Much later.

.   .   .

Annie put a big red X on the paper tablecloth. "And that's where I'll put the corpse."

Max moved his Bud Light for a better view.

The waiter arrived with two Caesar salads. She motioned for hers to be put to one side of the red X.

With true sophistication, the waiter didn't change expression when she said, "I'm going to have her bashed over the head with a croquet mallet."

"Oh, good going," Max murmured, avoiding the waiter's eye.

She leaned back and said in satisfaction, "So, I did pretty well today."

The waiter cut his eyes toward her as he moved away.

"That's great, honey."

"And what happened in Chastain?"

When he finished his report, Annie speared an anchovy. "Are you going to drop it?"

Max scooped up a garlicky chunk of cheese. "I don't know. I guess I'll decide in the morning."

MAX WAS SITTING with his tasseled loafers resting on his Italian Renaissance desktop when Barbie buzzed. He flicked on the intercom.

"A lady to see you, Mr. Darling. About a missing painting."

Work.

If he didn't exactly feel a transport of joy, he did feel a moderate stirring of interest. But he hesitated. Did he want to take anything on? He certainly could delve further into the matter of the Forged Murder Plot. But that would just be depressing if it turned out as Roscoe Merrill predicted. Well, it wouldn't hurt to talk to this prospective client. A missing painting.

"Send her in." Max rose and straightened his tie as Barbie opened the door for a little old lady with faded blue eyes, fluffy white hair, and an anxious expression.

"Mrs. Hilliard," Barbie announced.

As Max solicitously directed her toward a chair, he felt her arm tremble under his hand. As he took his place behind the desk, he studied her.

She wore a navy-blue silk dress with a white ruffled lace collar. A brown and white cameo sprouted from the lace.

"What can I do for you, Mrs. Hilliard?"

She looked around nervously. "Do you make records of everything in your office, Mr. Darling?"

For a moment, he was puzzled. "Records?"

"Recordings," she amplified.

So the old darling watched TV.

"No, I don't tape record anything."

"So our conversation is confidential. Absolutely confidential?"

"Yes, of course."

She paused, looked around once more, then said, in a voice scarcely above a whisper, "Mr. Darling, a painting has been stolen from my home. A very valuable painting." Her strained, fuzzy blue eyes avoided looking at him directly, focusing instead on the silver letter opener that Barbie had arranged artistically in the dead center of his desk. "I believe it has been—I think the expression is—hocked. Can you investigate for me, and discover who sold it to this antique shop?"

"Mrs. Hilliard, if your property has been stolen and sold, you should contact the police."

A flush crimsoned her plump cheeks. She clasped her hands together. "The police. Oh no, no, Mr. Darling. Never. Not the police. I just want to know what happened."

It took another ten minutes to soothe her down, obtain the rest of the story, and discover her objective. She wanted him to interview the antique shop owner, get a description of the person who sold the painting, and obtain a sworn statement from the shop owner. That was all.

He stared at her in puzzlement. There was something a good deal more complicated here than a simple theft. The old lady was clearly distraught—and not about a painting. He was intrigued, but if he took this on, it meant he would have to drop his inquiries in Chastain, just as Roscoe Merrill wanted him to. Max had a congenital dislike of doing what others desired. Actually, he hated to miss out on a session with Sybil the Magnificent. And Miss Dora might have an interesting perspective on Corinne and Chastain society. Moreover, Merrill obviously had an axe to grind. He didn't want any more turmoil touching his precious Society. But he was probably on point in his assumption that nothing more untoward would happen in Chastain, and this frail old lady was waiting for his answer as if her life depended upon it. What the hell.

"I'll check into it," he promised.

His new client took a deep breath, as if an irrevocable step had been taken. "Thank you, Mr. Darling." She gathered up her purse and rose. At the door she hesitated. Again, she didn't look at him, but stared down at the floor. "Now, don't forget. Not a word to anyone—like the police. I just want that written statement."

When the door closed, he scribbled down the gist of their conversation, studied it for a moment with a puzzled frown, then nodded decisively. He picked up the phone and dialed.

"Death on Demand."

"Hi, Ingrid. Annie there?"

"She's gone to Chastain to rent the tents and check the mystery inserts for the tour programs."

"Okay. Tell her I've got a new case, but I'll call her

later. Oh, and Ingrid—tell her I decided to drop the letter inquiry. I'm sure the only murder that will take place on the Murder Nights will be the one she's planned."

Dress rehearsal.

Or the next best thing. The meeting room at the Chastain Historical Preservation Society lacked the musty smell of a theater, and the upcoming session wouldn't have the stomach-wrenching sensation of imminent disaster that Annie associated with the night before an opening, but she still quivered with anticipation. Tomorrow was The Day—the opening of Chastain's Fifth Annual House and Garden tours, and the launching of Annie Laurance's first mystery program. She could hear the cheers now. This might signal the beginning of a lucrative sideline to Death on Demand —if the Mystery Nights succeeded.

If. The old rhyme about a horseshoe nail flickered like a ticker tape in the back of her mind, even as she finished putting copies of the character sketches at each place around the refectory table. Damn, if anyone ever had to deal with the incalculability of the human personality, it was she. It had sounded so easy. Put together a plot, drill the cast, plant the body and, bam, start the show. That simple scenario had failed, however, to take Corinne and Sybil into account.

In fact, she had seriously considered canceling tonight's rehearsal. After all, they'd met twice, and the cast members were bright if unschooled in acting. If she'd been able to restrict the rehearsals to cast members, all would have gone swimmingly. The difficulties came from the presence of Corinne and Sybil. She'd made it clear the sessions were intended for the players, and the presence of other Board members wasn't required. Edith and Miss Dora had gracefully, and perhaps gratefully, stayed away. Not so Corinne and Sybil, and Annie could see no way of barring them, especially since Sybil would ignore any polite subterfuge and claw her way with public clamor to the real reason—and that would be appalling. Although Corinne certainly was white meat. It should be obvious to her that Sybil's honey-voiced pursuit of Leighton was calculated solely to infuriate. If Corinne would just ignore her, the game would cease to be fun and a bored Sybil would promptly drop it. But no, Corinne puffed up like an enraged cat, so Sybil smiled and intensified her campaign.

But Annie had a few tricks up her sleeve, too. She would place Sybil as far as possible from Leighton, and she'd persuade Miss Dora to attend tonight, which might slow Sybil down. She wished Max could have come, but he was finishing up his investigation into the missing painting.

"Nothing funny about murder." The hoarse voice scraped Annie's nerves like chalk on a blackboard. She just managed not to leap into the air, but turned to greet Miss Dora, who stood in the archway, peering into the meeting room, her head poking out of a ruffled collar like a turtle surveying the surface of a pond. Tonight she wore a brown bonnet trimmed with dove feathers and sturdily tied beneath her bony chin. "Idle minds are the devil's workshop." She lifted the watch hanging from a thick gold chain around her neck and stared at it accusingly. "Five minutes after eight. Is no one else here?"

Annie was saved from answering as the others arrived in a flurry. She directed Leighton to a seat at the head of the table and put Corinne to his right and Miss

Dora to his left—and felt her heart lighten. She grabbed
Sybil's arm, managing not to be overwhelmed by the
intentionally heady whiff of Diva perfume, and deftly
maneuvered her to the chair at the opposite end of the
long table. Sybil gave Annie a concentrated look of
dislike, then leaned forward, revealing more bust than
a lingerie ad, and spoke to Leighton as if the two of
them were the sole inhabitants of a desert island.
"Leighton, the most exciting discovery!" Her throaty
voice promised pleasures known only in the watches
of the night. "I've found Great-great-grandfather's diaries—and they start the year the War began, when he
was twelve. I can't *wait* to share them with you."

Leighton came up out of his chair, like a silvery six-
foot tarpon hooked by a skilled fisherman, and Annie
knew a table length wasn't far enough. With Sybil Giacomo, a football field wouldn't suffice.

Corinne looked every day of her fifty-nine years, her
cheekbones jutting against her skin, her mouth drawn
so tight that hairline wrinkles marched on her upper
lip like a stockade fence.

Annie moved to intercept Leighton. She couldn't
care less if Sybil bedded him in the foyer, but, right
now, her concern was for the Mystery Nights.

She reached out and touched his tweed-clad arm.
"Mr. Webster, we're ready to get under way now." She
gently nudged Corinne's husband back to his place.
Actually, he was attractive enough to warrant Sybil's
interest on his own account. Although his face might
be a little ruddy from too many bourbons and water,
he still possessed an undeniable magnetism, brown
eyes, a boyish smile that hovered between diffident
and appealing, a big, burly fullback's build, and a
courtly manner. How the hell had Corinne landed
him? She realized her smile was almost too warm and

knew Corinne would have a stroke if she decided Annie were after him, too. Feeling Corinne's icy gaze on her back, she turned and flashed her a smile. "But first, we'll give Miss Dora some background," and she picked up her own copy of the character information sheets.

She raised her voice just enough to carry over the murmurs of conversation, which immediately fell away into well-bred silence. "Our mystery is set at Gemway Court, the country home of Lord Algernon Eagleton and his wife, Lady Alicia, who will be played by Jessica Merrill." Annie glanced down the table and smiled. Roscoe's wife was a pleasant surprise, vivacious and pretty, with shining black hair and eyes that were a curious catlike mixture of yellow and brown. Annie wondered what had attracted her to her reserved and balding husband, who sat beside her exhibiting all the personality of a possum in August. Then she directed her attention back to Miss Dora, hoping to restrain Sybil, who was beginning to move restively at her end of the table. "Members of the houseparty, in addition to Lord Algernon and Lady Alicia, are Nigel Davies, Matilda Snooperton, Susannah Greatheart, and Reginald Hoxton. They spend the afternoon playing croquet. Lady Alicia is a croquet champion, but she plays erratically and her team loses. People have commented lately upon her haggard appearance and generally nervous demeanor. The entire house party seems affected by an air of malaise; conversation is strained and disjointed at tea following the croquet. Everyone disperses to dress for dinner. Shortly before seven, Lady Alicia dashes into the upper hall, calling frantically for her husband, Lord Algernon. She announces that her famous ruby necklace, The Red Maiden, has been stolen. All the members of the house party gather in the upper hallway. Miss Greatheart clutches a handkerchief to her face. Mr. Hoxton looks shocked, then angry. Lord Algernon and Nigel Davies discuss calling the local constabulary. But, in the midst of the clamor, they realize that one of the party, Miss Snooperton, hasn't appeared. She is not in her room. Immediately, everyone begins to look for her. Hoxton announces he will check down by the river and dashes out. When she isn't found in the house and Hoxton returns saying there is no trace of her by the river, a wider search is organized and her body is discovered in the gazebo by the pond."

Annie paused for breath and for dramatic effect and scanned her listeners. Leighton smiled up at her with flattering attention. Corinne watched him, slit-eyed. Gail leaned her face against her hand, her thoughts obviously far away. Roscoe sat with his arm on the back of his wife's chair, his fingers resting on her shoulder. Jessica appeared absorbed in Annie's recital. Sybil opened her double-handled Vuitton satchel and drew out an embroidered cigarette case. Miss Dora's snapping black eyes shot Sybil a look of disgust, then moved to Annie with scarcely more enthusiasm.

Annie smiled determinedly at the old lady. "Mr. Webster plays LORD ALGERNON, a stalwart, soldierly figure, known in the village for his champion pigs. He doesn't have much to say, though the village whispers he's been neglected of late, since Lady Alicia spends all of her time playing cards, going to London for several weeks at a time to stay with different friends, playing bridge for money far into the night. He has been very attentive to one of their guests, Susannah Greatheart.

"Lucy Haines plays AGNES, Lady Alicia's maid.

Not much misses her notice. She is fiercely loyal to her mistress."

Lucy smiled and bent to whisper to Miss Dora, who pursed her lips and nodded.

"Roscoe Merrill is NIGEL DAVIES, who motored down with his fiancée, Matilda Snooperton, but Nigel, a reserved Oxford don, has been noticeably glum this weekend and was observed by Agnes in a quarrel with Matilda. In his pocket is a love letter from Susannah Greatheart.

"Our love interest, SUSANNAH GREATHEART, is played by Gail." Gail managed a faint smile. "She has known Nigel since their school days and has always adored him. She had expected they would one day marry and was shocked when his engagement was announced to the strongwilled and determined Matilda Snooperton.

"Our last cast member, Dr. Sanford, isn't here yet. He plays REGINALD HOXTON, a man about town in London. No one is quite certain how he earns his living and some men mutter, 'Cad,' when he is about. He's known to follow the races and is quite adept at cards and roulette."

Annie aimed her most charming smile at Miss Dora, whose dark eyes darted from face to face with reptilian swiftness. "Everybody a volunteer, I suppose?"

Taken aback, Annie nodded.

"Amateurs, all of them. And Jessica's much too pretty to play the part of a raddled old gambler. Should have got an older member." She cackled maliciously. "Why didn't you give Corinne a role?"

The juxtaposition wasn't lost on Corinne. Or on anybody else.

Annie wondered wildly why she'd ever thought

Miss Dora, with her unpredictable tongue, would be any help at all.

Sybil didn't lose any time. She blew a waft of perfumed smoke heavenward and looked like a wicked but pleased dragon. "Perhaps there should be some changes in the casting. After all, is Roscoe the right man to play a lover? Leighton should have that role."

Lucy trotted to the rescue. "Actually, Miss Laurance has done a superb job—not only in the casting, but the program as a whole. Why, it reminds me of my very favorite mystery writers, Christie and Allingham and Sayers and Marsh. It just couldn't be any better."

Corinne spoke in a carefully controlled voice. "I would under no circumstances consider playing a role in a murder program. I would find it degrading."

"Oh, now, Cory, that's too strong," Leighton admonished gently.

It was like hearing Dr. No called Doc.

He smiled reassuringly at Annie. "Of course the program's good. Very good. I just hope it doesn't take too much acting talent. But I suppose I can stand around and say 'Eh, what,' without too much difficulty. You've put together a good show, Miss Laurance."

Annie knew good-humored "Eh, whats?" wouldn't satisfy the mystery participants. She'd been to several murder weekends and knew the detectives took their tasks with utmost seriousness and fancied themselves as a composite of Holmes, Vidocq, and Maigret, with a dash of Peter Wimsey.

"Most of your time," she said quickly, "will be taken up with answering questions from the mystery night participants. Now, I have a sheet for each of you which contains information known only to you. You can, of course, lie to the detectives on critical points. You are forced to tell the truth only when a detective team formally accuses you of the murder."

"Oh, this is marvelous fun," Lucy exclaimed. "I think I already know the murderer."

"You can't possibly," Jessica objected. "That would outdo even Ellery Queen."

"Ellery Queen?" Leighton's voice was puzzled, and he thumbled through the sheets. "I don't see a character named Queen."

"Actually, this would be a perfect case for Miss Seeton," Roscoe suggested, with a mischievousness Annie would never suspect he possessed.

Miss Dora crisply explained Ellery Queen and Miss Seeton to Leighton, while other voices rose disputing the identity of the murderer.

"Hey, wait a minute. Who the hell are you? Oh no, come on in here." The brusque voice of Dr. Sanford cut through the goodnatured chatter.

Sanford came through the archway, his hand tightly gripping the elbow of a scrawny figure in a navy blue warmup, navy scarf, and grass-stained tennis shoes. "Who's this? She tried to run when I came in."

Despite the dark headcovering, Annie knew instantly. She stalked across the stone floor. "Mrs. Brawley, what in the world are you doing here?" As if she didn't know.

"Oh, Annie, I didn't know you were here."

Sanford released her bony elbow. "You know her?"

"Yes. Mrs. Brawley and I know each other well."

Freed from the doctor's firm grip, Mrs. Brawley gave Annie the look of a rabbit at bay, then bleated, "I was looking for the Inn and made a mistake." She took two quick steps backward. "It could happen to anybody." Then she whirled around and fled.

Corinne arched a thin golden eyebrow. "What was that all about? Was that woman a prowler?"

"Nothing so dramatic. One of my more active customers. She loves to win, and I suppose she couldn't resist the temptation to learn something about the Mystery Nights ahead of time. Actually, no harm done. She didn't hear anything that would give the mystery away." Annie frowned. "I don't like it, though. I'm running an honest Mystery Nights program. Damn, I wish that woman could channel her competitiveness into something useful—like stamping out pornography."

Corinne's face had all the warmth of a Steuben glass polar bear. "I don't see that this is a matter for levity."

"I'm not laughing," Annie replied sourly.

"A flippant remark doesn't hide the seriousness of the situation. Obviously, if the program is compromised, the Board must meet its responsibility."

Annie had a funny feeling, like catching herself on the edge of a twelve-story drop.

"Just exactly what do you mean, Mrs. Webster?"

"The Board of the Chastain Historical Preservation Society represents the community and is responsible to the community for the probity of its programs. We cannot offer a contest in which an unfair advantage has been given to a customer of yours." Corinne pushed back her chair and stood to her full five feet six inches, which gave her the advantage of height over Annie. She stared down arrogantly. "In fact, I believe it must be clear to all the members that this unfortunate and foolish attempt to mix entertainment with our serious exposition of history is a failure and should be dropped."

.   .   .

"All hell broke loose then." Annie pushed back the lock of hair that struggled over her forehead. She still burned with fury. Usually, the serenity of Death on Demand at night with the book jackets gleaming in the dim light could smooth away even the most difficult of days. But tonight's unpleasantness had been scorching.

"I hope you told her to go to hell." Max's normally pleasant face reflected her own anger.

"Oh, I did. In a choice assortment of words." She paused, recalling her tirade with a tickle of pleasure. She hadn't minced words with Mrs. High-and-Mighty Webster. "Of course, I'm not sure how much she heard, because everybody else was yelling—even nice Lucy Haines. But Morgan settled Corinne down in a hurry. He made it clear that we'd signed a contract." Annie grabbed Max's hand. "That was smart of you to insist we do it that way."

He gave her hand a warm squeeze. "Always put it in writing. I knew that before I went to law school." But he was pleased at her gratitude. He lifted his bottle of Bud Light. "Are you still going to go through with it?"

"Go through with it? I intend to put on the Mystery Nights program in Chastain if I have to play every part, answer every question, explain every clue, and play the corpse all by myself." The tightness in her shoulders began to ease. "But I don't have to do it alone. Everybody rallied—and, of course, that hacked her, too. It wasn't the jolliest session I've ever coached, but we worked on the roles for an hour, with Corinne pulsating like a toad and Sybil trying every trick in the book to get closer to Leighton. Honestly, she did everything but unzip his pants."

"Damn, I've *got* to meet this woman."

Annie wasn't amused. "Your father should have warned you about females like her."

"He might have," Max said blandly.

"If he didn't, I am." She sighed wearily and looked around the dimly lit coffee area. "Golly, I'm tired, and I still haven't put all the stuff for tomorrow in my car."

"I'll do it."

"We'll do it together."

Annie drove the Volvo into the alley and parked it by the door to the storeroom. They perched their beer bottles on the car roof and carried the pre-packed boxes from the storeroom. As she lifted in the last one, she said, "Hey, with all the fireworks in Chastain, I forgot to ask about your painting case. Did you solve it?"

Max pushed down the trunk lid. "Yeah." His voice sounded oddly flat.

She peered at him in the golden shaft of light from the lamp at the end of the alley. "What's wrong?"

"It wasn't much fun."

"What happened?"

He reached up and retrieved the beer bottles and handed one to her, then leaned against the trunk. "I feel like a rat. But, I had to put a stop to it. Dammit, love can sure screw people up."

"What's love got to do with a missing picture?" She tilted her bottle and welcomed the sharp taste of the beer.

"Everything. You see, old Mrs. Hilliard is dead crazy about her nephew. She's had a young girl named Edie keeping house for her and running errands. Her nephew, Alec, met the girl and fell for her—and Mrs. Hilliard doesn't think the girl's good enough. The usual objections. No education. No background. Too much make-up. And Alec's the pride of her life. She sent him to college, and he's a rising young junior executive at the bank."

"Did Edie rip off the painting?"

"That's the picture." He grinned a little as Annie winced. "I went to the antique store. Got the description of the person selling it. Right enough, it's Edie. I got the signed statement from the owner."

"So why do you feel like a rat? Looks like Mrs. Hilliard—"

"Sure that's what it looks like. Simple case, right? One more confidential commission executed. But I sat on that statement for a couple of days. I decided to nose a little harder. I hung around outside Mrs. Hilliard's, waited 'til Edie came out and followed her. I struck up a conversation. In a nutshell: her story is that Mrs. Hilliard asked her to sell the painting, and she turned the money over to the old lady."

"I don't get it."

"Neither did I, so I nosed around some more. Found out Alec isn't the sort of fellow to look past the obvious."

Annie understood. A signed statement. Once lovestruck Alec saw it—

"What did you do?"

"She's a sweet old thing. Crazy about that guy." He cleared his throat. "I told her I was on to the scam, and it was no deal."

"So why do you feel so bad?"

"I told you. She's a sweet old thing, and the funny part of it is, I think she's right about Edie."

"When good people do bad things," Annie said quietly.

"All because of love," he concluded.

He upended his bottle, finishing his beer.

She patted his shoulder. "Come on, let's go take a swim. Tomorrow, we'll be caught up in a script, and we won't have to worry about real emotions."

10

IN THE ORDERLY CONFINES of her imagination, Annie had pictured the opening day of the Chastain House and Garden tours: the weather would be April idyllic, soft puffy clouds dotting a turquoise sky; the participants would be genteel, interchangeable with an audience at, say, Sotheby's, and there would be a general aura of Southern elegance, like a debutante's garden party. That was how the month-long pageant unfolded in Charleston's Historic District.

She got it right about the weather. The sky glittered like a blue enamel bowl, and the air was as soft and smooth as Scotch House cashmere. But half a mile from the historic area, she realized the Board of the Chastain Historical Preservation Society had neglected to inform her of some of Chastain's native customs. Cars that had enjoyed their youth in the Truman administration, mud-splashed pickups, and a rickety hayrack pulled by a green John Deere tractor and carrying a bevy of bony teenage girls in long white dresses clogged Montgomery, the main artery (it actually boasted four lanes) to the River. There was a lengthy pause at Montgomery and Federal for the passage of the Chastain High School Marching Band in purple and black uniforms. The musicians were belting out a fairly good rendition of "The Saints Go Marching In" except for the proclivity of one clarinet to squawk on the high notes. Every parking place on both sides of Montgomery was taken. Energetic hucksters held up hand-painted signs, PARKING $5, offering five to ten spots per front yard. Pedestrians thronged the brick sidewalks. They didn't look like garden party goers to Annie: farmers in high-bibbed overalls and women in freshly starched print cotton dresses; teenagers in so many layers of clothing, shirt on sweater on pullover on sleeveless jersey, it was difficult to imagine, much less determine, sex; and tourists of all sorts and shapes, fat, thin, tall, and tiny, but identifiable by the profusion of costly cameras and camera accessories that hung around their necks, including light meters, zoom lenses, filter cases, and even collapsible tripods.

It took twelve minutes to inch across the intersection once the band played past. Annie feared asphyxiation from the bilious fumes roiling out of the Mercedes Diesel in front of her. It didn't improve her humor to recognize the driver as Dr. Sanford, who blasted his horn every foot or two. In a damn big hurry, wasn't he? But he hadn't made any effort to arrive on time for the rehearsal last night. Halfway up the block, he signaled and turned left. By the time she realized he was turning into the alley behind the historic houses, which provided access to the parking lot at the Historical So-

ciety, she was past the opening and fated to continue
her snail-like inexorable progress forward.

Ephraim Street stunned her. Where yesterday there
had been an occasional car and the placid calm of an
unhurried backwater, there was today a chaos that at
first glance resembled the deployment of several thousand extras in a Steven Spielberg spectacular. Sightseers milled about the street. Booths filled every inch of
space along the river bluff, except for a broad space
directly across from the Prichard House where workmen tussled with scaffolding to erect a grandstand
overlooking the river. In the booths, Annie glimpsed
painted wooden ducks; a Statue of Liberty fashioned
from fused Coke bottles; hundreds of quilts; shiny
wooden signs that announced The Joneses, People
Love My Kitchen Best, Use It or Lose It, and Daddy's
Girl; stacks of Canton Blue china (manufactured in Tai-
wan?), and potholders shaped like roosters, cats, baseball mitts, and starfish. Hot dog stands dispensed
coneys, chili, and pop, while vendors hawked barbecue, fried shrimp, cotton candy, and egg rolls.

She was halfway into a left turn, although realizing it
would be slow going up Ephraim Street because of the
crowds, when a whistle shrilled. Jamming on her
brakes, she poked her head out of the window.

The uniformed policeman had patches of sweat under his armpits, and he looked like he hadn't smiled in
a millenium or so, the frown lines were so deeply en-
graved on either side of this mouth.

"Closed for the crafts fair. No left turn. NO LEFT
TURN, LADY!" The whistle scalded the air.

"I've got to get to the Society parking lot. I'm already
late—"

He held a hand behind his ear, then chopped a fist to
her right. "Right turn, lady. RIGHT TURN."

She tried again, yelling like a trader in the closing five.

Swiping sweat from his forehead, he lunged to the car. "Lady, no exceptions. The street's closed."

"I've got to get to the Prichard House. I'm in charge of the murder."

"No need to get ugly," he yelled back. "I didn't make the street plans. You turn right, or you go to jail."

Twenty-eight minutes later, after a circuitous route that rivaled the complexity of a maze, Annie wedged the Volvo between a yellow Winnebago (Wisconsin plates) plastered with stickers—*Yellowstone's for the Bears, Take Me Back to Texas, My Heart Belongs to San Francisco,* and *Chattanooga Choo-Choo Me Home*—and a black Toyota pickup that smelled strongly of chicken manure.

She unlocked the trunk and looked at the boxes, none of them small, then sighed, and hefted the first one. It was awkward to carry, and she could scarcely see over it. She was rounding the corner when her knees came up hard against a metal obstacle, and she fell heavily forward.

"Here now, Papa, the lady's fallen," a soft country voice called out.

A large calloused hand reached down and lifted her as easily as setting a broom upright, but a hoarse voice howled angrily: "My placards. Don't let those fools stomp on my placards. Clumsy idiots."

And Annie was clambering around on her hands and knees trying to scoop up the mystery sheets which had tumbled from the box. Then she realized she was eye-to-eye with an enraged Miss Dora, equally vigorously pursuing the contents of her upended wagon, which had brought Annie down.

It sorted out in a moment, two friendly Georgians

forming a blockade against the crowd. Soon Annie's box was full and Miss Dora's wagon and her placards restored.

Miss Dora gave Annie a venomous glare, then hunkered down and resumed pounding on the placard-adorned stake at the corner of Lafayette and Ephraim streets.

Annie read the message, written in a fine Spencerian script on white posterboard and covered with a protective sheet of Saran wrap:

"Here stood the waggon yards from 1802 to 1825. Cotton was unloaded here and sold for shipment abroad. Due east of this site rose the shops which served the planters, offering clothing for slaves, shoes, harnesses, groceries, satin, laces, and India china."

In the background, pounding continued on the grandstand, holiday banter rose in a Niagara-like roar, and vendors shouted.

Annie rubbed her bruised knees, sighed, picked up her box, and set out for the Prichard mansion.

It was not an auspicious beginning.

Where the hell were the tables? With her luck, they'd been sucked into the crafts fair booths, never to surface again, or perhaps to reappear laden with tinware, log cabins made of matchsticks, or pictures painted-by-the-number of iron-gray Traveller with his black mane and tail. But she had to have tables—

"Miss Laurance."

Annie pivoted. Corinne stood at the top of the marble steps to Prichard House. She wore a sky blue satin-finish wool gabardine that emphasized her youthful figure and the satisfied expression of a chatelaine who's caught the maid snitching a bonbon.

"You certainly took your time getting here this morning. I've been watching for you, and I must say, you're very late."

The box of mimeographed Mystery Nights instructions weighed at least twenty-five pounds. Annie had lugged it from the parking lot, survived her encounter with Miss Dora, and maneuvered through tourists clotted like Devonshire cream on the sidewalks. Her once crisp mid-calf navy skirt and cotton cambric blouse with a deep frilled shawl collar clung limply to her aching body.

She glared up at Corinne. "Why the hell didn't anybody tell me this place would be like Atlantic City when the casinos opened?"

Corinne stiffened haughtily. "Obviously, Miss Laurance, you lack the necessary experience to take part in a House and Garden week. I want to make it clear that I will certainly urge the Board to withhold full payment of your fee if the Mystery Nights are inadequately produced."

Annie's eyes slitted like Agatha's on the approach of a blue jay. "Mrs. Webster, if anything turns out to be inadequate, it won't be the Mystery Nights," and she turned on her heel.

At three o'clock that afternoon, Annie wondered if her brave words could be fulfilled. Clutching a box of clues and a croquet mallet, she stood indecisively on her left foot, and tried to read her smudged list.

Tents.
Chairs. Tables. Platform.
Speaker's stand.
Audio equipment.

Death on Demand display.
Crime Scene materials.

The candy-striped tents were in place, three of them: black-and-white, red-and-white, and green-and-yellow. A large poster was affixed to the main entrance of each: POLICE HEADQUARTERS (black-and-white), SUSPECT INTERROGATIONS (red-and-white), and DETECTION TEAMS CONFERENCE AREA (green-and-yellow).

Where the *hell* were the tables? She'd called three times, and they had yet to arrive. The long conference tables were to be set up in the headquarters tent to hold clues and copies of the suspects' statements, and the round tables capable of seating ten in the other tents.

If there were six of her, it might all come off on schedule. As it was, she felt a frantic urge to race into the Society building to check on the audio equipment and an equally frantic urge to hotfoot it in the opposite direction down the shell path to the pond and strew clues. This inability to decide where to leap next accounted for her storklike wobble on one foot. Fortunately, she did have help. Max had arrived late, of course, held up by the traffic, but he was busy now talking to Harry Wells, the police chief, who had agreed to serve as technical advisor, and Edith Ferrier, obviously in her element, was crisply ordering about the extremely slow-moving minions from the rental company that was providing the tents, chairs, and platform, but that had, as yet, failed to come up with the tables. Meanwhile, Society members fanned out up and down Ephraim Street, making last-minute checks on contents of the rooms to be shown in the three houses. Every so often, Edith introduced Annie to another docent, and she'd now perfected a response to "Isn't it *scary* to plan a murder?"

As she tried to decide which direction to spring, Annie heard Edith's high, rather humorless voice admonishing a catering employee to be careful in firing the butane-fueled steam ovens which would be used to roast the oysters. Out of the corner of her eye, she spotted Corinne making yet another foray. Annie turned to look down the path toward the gazebo. It would be better for her blood pressure if she didn't tangle with Corinne again today.

Then she spotted one of Miss Dora's placards. It was better than Kilroy Was Here, and it gave her an excuse to keep her back to Corinne. She crossed several feet of lawn to read it.

"The earliest home at this site was erected by Morris Prichard in 1746 for his bride, Elizabeth. It was a two-story frame structure built on a stuccoed brick foundation with a hipped roof and a small portico facing the river. It was lost in the Great Fire of 1831. Old Chastainians claim that a grieving spirit, Abigail McNeil Prichard, may sometimes be glimpsed crossing the lawn at dusk in early spring, searching for her husband, Donald, who was killed by the British at the Battle of Fort Balfour, April 13, 1781. The present Greek Revival house was built in 1834 by Abigail's grandson, Nathaniel."

Annie looked across the freshly mown lawn, much of it hidden now by the colorful tents, and she wondered what Abigail's ghost would think of the brightly striped tents, the fluttering groups of women in pastel dresses, and the harried caterers frantically shoving together the last of the serving tables. Tables. That reminded her—she swung around and wished she hadn't.

Corinne stood beside Edith, one hand on the younger woman's arm, the other gesturing at the serving tables arranged on the drive east of the tents.

"I thought we'd included the she crab soup in the menu."

"The Women of Old Chastain are serving the soup and shrimp salad sandwiches this week in their booth."

"Oh." The monosyllable hung like a block of ice between them. "I suppose it's difficult to decide to whom you owe your loyalty, Edith, when you are active in so *many* organizations. But I do believe you should have remembered that the Chastain Historical Preservation Society is the oldest and most important society in Chastain—and we should, of course, during the Tour Week be offering the best low country food at our buffet." Corinne lifted her shoulders in a delicate shrug. "However, it's too late to make any improvements in the menu now, so I—"

"The menu doesn't *need* any improvement." Edith's deep-set green eyes burned in her sallow face. She looked like a Picasso pastiche animated by hatred: arms akimbo, sunken cheeks touched with fire, black-and-white silk dress, a half-dozen gold bracelets.

Annie held her breath, almost expecting the woman to explode, like a tangle of wire and steel blown apart by dynamite.

Edith's tight, controlled voice rattled off the foods. "We have okra, shrimp, and crab gumbo, oyster pie, shrimp pilau, stuffed flounder, roast oysters, corn on the cob, black-eyed peas with bacon, orange halves stuffed with sweet potato, cheese soufflé with oyster sauce, hush puppies, cheese popovers, lemon chess pie, sweet potato pie, and Carolina trifle."

Even Corinne looked impressed. "Well, that sounds

very good." Her cherry red lips formed a patronizing smile. "Edith, you certainly do have a talent for organizing kitchen work. I do hope that you will continue to be willing to exercise your abilities for the good of the Society. I know it was a disappointment when you weren't named to the slate for president, but I'm sure that you will continue to find your natural level." Then she looked past Edith and raised her hand to wave. "Jessica, wait a moment, I want to talk to you."

As she hurried away, Edith remained by the last serving table, staring after Corinne, her face rigid with fury. Annie tucked the croquet mallet under her arm and moved closer, reaching out to touch her arm.

"Hey, don't let her get to you. She's just a bitch."

Edith slowly turned, and Annie was disturbed to see the glitter of tears in her eyes.

"Someday someone is going to kill that woman." She lifted her hands, pressed her palms against her burning cheeks. "Sometimes I wonder why I don't just leave, just say to hell with it all, but Paul and I were so happy here." She tried to smile, but her lips were trembling. "My husband. He died last year, and ever since I've spent every minute with my organizations. But I've always loved it, you know, loved the history and the wonderful old houses and the people, since we first came here when Paul was stationed at Parris Island. Corinne's not typical, thank God. She never lets you forget it if you aren't a native, and she manages to make so many people miserable. Like me. I guess they've told you how she screwed me out of being president of the Society. And it shouldn't matter a damn—but it does. There are so many things that need to be done—"

A soft voice interrupted. "Edith, I know how hard

you're working. I brought some lemonade for you and Annie."

Gail Prichard held out a silver salver holding two frosted glass goblets with sprigs of mint poking over the rims, and her gentle eyes offered amends.

Edith smoothed back her curly hair and managed a smile. She had the worn look common to so many redheads in late middle age, and Gail's shiny youthfulness and sleek auburn hair emphasized the contrast. "Thank you, dear. You're very thoughtful."

"It looks marvelous. Let me put my stuff down." The clues could wait for a few minutes. Annie hurried over to the Police Headquarters tent and tucked the mallet and the box of clues behind a folded card table she intended to use for the Death on Demand display. Then, with a grateful smile, she took the goblet. "Thanks for thinking of us."

"I was watching from the verandah. Is everything coming along all right?" Gail's glance at Edith was uneasy.

"Oh, just fine," Annie said quickly. "Except the tables haven't come. I'm going to call again in a minute. The lights aren't working, and I can't get the audio hooked up yet—" She clapped a hand to her forehead. "My God. I forgot to pick up Resuscitation Rhoda! Edith, is the Red Cross closed? Can we get in?"

"She's sitting in the back seat of my car. Let me know when you're ready, and I'll go get her. I'm parked behind the Inn," and she waved her hand generally northward.

Annie nearly collapsed with relief. "Oh, thank goodness. Lord, what else do you suppose I've forgotten?" She dug in her skirt pocket, searching for her list, then panicked, checking her watch again.

"Relax," Edith admonished. "Believe me, I've put on

a hundred of these kinds of things. Miraculously, they always come off."

Gail nodded in agreement. "Everything will work out. What you both need is to take a break for a little while. Edith, why don't you show Annie through the Prichard House? She'll be too busy tonight to go through on a tour."

Annie didn't miss the byplay, the obvious flash of reluctance in Edith's eyes, Gail's attempt to reassure Edith that she was indeed welcome. Or the tacit admission when she added quickly, "Corinne's gone over to the Museum. Something more about Tim's paintings."

Annie was worried over losing the time, still concerned about the audio, the tables, and clue strewing, but refusal would thwart Gail's attempt at an apology.

They started in the kitchen of the Prichard House, returning their empty lemonade goblets and meeting Chloe, the cook, who had provided the refreshment. "Of course, this isn't the original kitchen," Edith explained. "As you know, kitchens were separate from the main houses to avoid fires, but this was added to the Prichard House in 1880. The blue Delft earthenware has been in the family since it was bought by a new bride on a trip to Europe in 1817."

As they emerged into the central hallway, Annie realized this was the way Gail had come the day she arrived to scout out the terrain for the Mystery Nights. She recognized the French Empire card table with the dolphin feet and the Chippendale mirror topped by the gilt eagle. Once again the wide double doors on either side of the hall were open. Annie glanced uneasily up at the curving staircase. Today it was empty. Presumably, Corinne was wreaking havoc at the Museum.

Edith led the way into the big drawing room, giving a rapid-fire commentary. "Look at the overmantel with the short pilasters and broken pediment above. Those are original to the house. Note the stucco reliefs of classic figures. And, of course, the decoration in this room is glorious, the dentil cornices and the ornamental plasterwork on the ceiling."

Her deep-set green eyes sparkled as she pointed out the English Regency chairs and an eighteenth-century portrait of Abigail Prichard, who entertained the English general quartered in her house during the Revolution while sending information to Marion's troops by an overseer of one of her plantations.

Looking up at the smooth, young face in the portrait, Annie imagined her listening with grave courtesy to the general, while her heart churned with worry for her absent husband.

In the dining room, Edith pointed out the silk damask curtains, gold-and-cream patterned Aubusson rug, Hepplewhite sideboard, and reddish-brown mahogany dining table and chairs. "Notice that wonderful Chippendale mirror hanging between the windows."

At the front door, they thanked Gail for the visit, and Edith led the way out. Midway down the marble steps, she paused to gesture at the massive octagonal columns. "Pure Greek revival, of course, and what outlanders always envision when you talk about a Southern plantation house. Actually, not many of the Low Country plantations look like Tara, although that style is common in the South. We're fortunate to have houses of three very distinct types here that have survived to today, and part of the very great charm of Chastain is that the old homes are freestanding on large lots. Many of them are counterparts of true plantation homes. A few, in fact, were boxed up and moved to town by planters trying to escape the bad air. That's what they attributed malaria to, of course. Bad air from rotting vegetation.''

It was obvious that Edith adored her adopted home. Annie was impressed by her fund of knowledge and enthusiasm for her topic, even when the house she was describing in such admiring terms belonged to a woman she obviously loathed.

"How long have you lived in Chastain?"

The sparkle dimmed in her companion's eyes. "We came to stay about six years ago, but we had lived here several times over the last twenty-five years when Paul was stationed at Parris Island. He was career military. A lot of military people retire here. We were from Indiana originally. Paul loved to fish and hunt, and I guess there's no better place in the world for that." The emptiness in her eyes echoed her grief. "And now that he's gone . . . I don't have anywhere else to go. No family." She tried to smile. "Most people here are very gracious and welcoming. But the natives, even the nice ones, always know who belongs and who doesn't. It reminds me of an anecdote by Mrs. St. Julien Ravenel in her book about Charleston. She is talking about a man whom everyone in town liked and admired very much. Then she comments that he was a stranger among them for eighteen years.''

"Oh. Wow. And I suppose she said it in all seriousness?''

"Oh, yes, but she meant it quite kindly. Not like Corinne." She glanced back at the Prichard House. "What amazes me is how sweet Gail is. And Corinne tries to run her life, too, of course. If Gail doesn't get free of it, she'll end up warped, just like Leighton. But I don't know of anything short of death that will stop Corinne." She drew her shoulders in, then turned away from the mansion. "Well, let's see. Shall we go

left or right? The McIlwain House is quite lovely. It
was restored by Lucy Haines.''

''Restored?''

''It was a boarding house from the early thirties until
she bought it about twenty years ago. Of course, it
doesn't have family pieces, but she has purchased
some very fine antiques, many of them authenticated
to some early families. She inherited a great deal of
money from a bachelor brother, and she's really enjoyed working on the old house. It is an example of
absolutely lovely symmetry. At one time, it belonged
to some distant cousins of hers, so I suppose it's family
in that sense.''

Annie looked across the lush sweep of the Prichard
lawn. Through the low spreading limbs of live oaks,
she glimpsed portions of the exquisite Georgian mansion. ''A boarding house. That's hard to believe.''

''Oh, my dear, if it weren't for the Historical Preservation Society and *very* hard work by its members, we
would have only a handful of old houses still standing.
You see, this part of town—'' her wave encompassed
the McIlwain, Prichard, and Benton houses ''—has
long been encroached upon by the commercial. Over in
the next block, past the alley, it's all commercial, although much of it is old, dating at least to the 1840s.
Doctors' offices, lawyers. And the library is on the corner directly behind the Historical Preservation Society.
That makes it very convenient for Lucy.''

An orange WE-RENT-IT truck rattled into the circular drive, jolted to a stop by the buffet tables, then
grated screechingly into reverse.

Annie gave one look, leaped down the remaining
steps, and hurtled toward the truck, yelling, ''Stop.
Stop!''

The truck shuddered to a standstill not more than

three feet from the yellow-and-green DETECTION TEAMS CONFERENCE tent.

Panting, she reached the cab. The driver squinted down sourly at her. "Yeah?"

"You just about knocked down the tent. Do you have the tables?"

"Gotta get 'em close enough to unload, lady."

"You're within three feet—and they won't do us any good without the tents. Put the long conference tables in the black-and-white striped tent and the round tables in the other tents."

Edith joined her. "Now you're all hot again."

"It's all right." She looked around. "You know, I'm almost afraid to say it, but it's taking shape."

And it was. Order was emerging out of chaos. Black and gold balloons tied to the open front gate bobbed in the gentle afternoon breeze. Similar clumps of balloons marked the entrances to the Benton and McIlwain houses. The truck driver and several helpers were efficiently unloading and setting up the tables in the proper places. Servers were unloading food from the caterer's two pink vans.

And Max was industriously arranging the Death on Demand display in the Police Headquarters tent.

Her spirits zoomed. Suddenly, nothing seemed difficult. She beamed at Edith. "I'd love to see the other houses with you, but I'd better check with Max. How about tomorrow?"

As they parted, Annie called over her shoulder. "Would you bring Rhoda to the police tent?"

Yes, it was all falling into place. She might even begin to have fun. Especially if she could avoid Corinne.

Max stood a few feet back from the card table. As she joined him, he shook his head solemnly. "Why just one card table? We need a lot more space."

We. What a nice word it was.

"We've got t-shirts, bookmarks, and the posters." He threw up his hands. "There isn't room for the posters."

"You're right." She looked around and waved energetically at the rental employees. "Hey, bring one of the long tables over here."

"Terrific," Max crowed. "We can hang the t-shirts around the edges, then use the t-shirt boxes to prop up the posters." He opened a box and held up a t-shirt.

A throaty laugh, like the gurgle of an overfed pigeon, sounded behind them. When they turned, Sybil read the legend on the t-shirt. "Let Me Haunt Your House. Oh, God, that's wonderful. Save one for me." She spoke to Annie, but her eyes devoured Max, who was proving a theorem she vaguely remembered from basic biology, something about living plants bending toward the source of light. If Max leaned any farther forward, he was going to topple on his handsome nose.

"Max, this is Mrs. Giacomo, a member of the Board. Max Darling."

Sybil was already past Annie and a scant inch from her quarry. She held out both hands, magenta-tipped nails today and yet another array of gems, two rubies and a winking diamond surrounded by a glint of emeralds. "Max Darling." If her voice went any lower, it would slither on the ground. "I want you to come over here in the shade and tell me all about yourself."

"I know he would just *love* to do that," Annie said sweetly, "but he's promised to go get our victim for us." She eyed him sternly. "The CPR doll."

Max shot a fascinated glance at Sybil, then grinned lopsidedly at Annie. "Sure. I was just on my way. Mrs. Giacomo, I'll look forward to visiting with you later."

As he moved off toward the parking lot, Annie and

Sybil exchanged measuring glances. Each understood the other perfectly.

"I'll be sure and save a t-shirt for you, Mrs. Giacomo. And now, if you'll excuse me, I must go strew clues."

Annie crouched in the gazebo, peering at the floor. It was a little on the order of playing Hide the Thimble. Clues must of necessity be in plain view, but not so obvious they bleated. She yearned for the skill of E. C. Bentley, who was a master of slipping unremarked clues into his narratives. She'd stuck the croquet mallet into a clump of reeds by the pond, the handle clearly visible. But it was more difficult in the gazebo. She twisted to look toward the steps. The detection teams would be limited to a view from the steps. Couldn't have them stepping right into the gazebo, or they would mess up some of the clues. And the red herrings, of course.

She opened her clue box, lifted out the crumpled handkerchief with the initials SAG marked in red ink in the right-hand corner, and dropped it near the bench.

"What the hell are you doing here?"

Her head jerked up.

Bobby Frazier, the broken-nosed, abrasive reporter, glared across the placid green waters of the pond at Gail, who stood framed by the dangling fronds of the willows, looking ethereal, vulnerable, and anguished.

Neither saw Annie, still on her hands and knees in the gazebo. Before she could reveal her presence by clearing her throat, Gail replied, "I saw your car. I knew you'd be here."

"Right. I *work* for a living."

The girl jammed her hands into her skirt pockets and

looked at him sorrowfully. "Money's awfully important to you, isn't it?"

"Is that what your aunt told you?"

"She told me—" She pressed one hand hard against
her trembling mouth.

"Did she tell you I'd called? And called back all
week?"

"No."

"The last time I called, she said you never wanted to
see me again."

Tears began to slip unchecked down her face. "Just
tell me—is it true you took a check?"

"Yeah. Yeah, I did."

She turned and thrashed blindly up the path.

He stared after her. "Goddammit it to hell," he said
harshly. Head down, face working with anger, he
lunged past the gazebo, following Gail.

In the gazebo, Annie sighed. If anybody wanted her
opinion, and no one was clamoring for it, she thought
she detected the fine Italian hand of that good old
monster Corinne. Shaking her head, she arranged the
rest of the clues: the initialed handkerchief, a Turkish
cigarette stub, a crumpled note with no salutation that
read 'I can't come.' Her last item was an old boot
filched from Max. Carrying the clue box, empty now,
she paced to the edge of the pond and artistically
mashed the boot into the muddy bank. On her way
back to the tents, she glimpsed Gail and Bobby on the
path behind the Prichard House. They were deep in
conversation.

Annie stepped back to admire the five posters, displayed against the backing of the t-shirt boxes. Fabu-

lous. Nobody could pass by those colors without a second look. She only hoped she'd ordered enough—

The thud of running steps cut across the expected background noises, the low chatter of women's voices, the clang of oyster shells being dumped into the ovens, the muted hum from the crowds wandering Ephraim Street. Annie whirled, her pulses racing. Something was wrong.

The running man pounded up the marble steps of Prichard House to the immense front door, and the hammering of his frenzied knock echoed across the lawn. Everyone paused to look his way, the docents, the workmen for the rental company, the catering staff, Annie. And Corinne, who had just appeared, walking up the drive from the gate at Ephraim Street.

"Tim." Corinne's clipped, cool voice overrode the thunderous rapping. He stopped, one fist upraised, then swung around and clattered down the steps. He loomed over her, basketball-player tall, but thin to the point of emaciation. He had a mop of soft chestnut hair that curled on his shoulders.

"You can't take my stuff. You can't do it." His huge hands gripped her shoulders. "You can't do it, I tell you."

"Let go of me." Her tone was imperious, contemptuous.

His hands fell away. His Adam's apple juggled in his throat. "My stuff—all stacked up, ready to be boxed. Who said you could send my paintings away?"

"I am the director of the Prichard Museum. The disposition of our holdings is my responsibility—and I'm responding to a request from some sister museums for a traveling exhibit. You should be pleased, Tim. Your work will be on view across the Southwest for several months."

"We'll see about that." There was nothing sexy or soft about Sybil's voice this time. She faced Corinne with the intractable expression of Daddy Warbucks guarding a mound of gilt-edged bonds.

"I'll kill her. I swear to God I'm going to kill her." A sob hung in the painter's throat.

Sybil turned and slipped her arm around him, and it was oddly touching, the young, almost frail, too-tall young man with his soft, curling hair and the voluptuous, lusty woman. "It's all right, Timmy. Don't be upset."

"But she's—"

"No, she won't. I promise you. I'll get your paintings for you." Sybil looked over her shoulder, her face tightening like a leopard's upon attack. Her voice hung in the air, husky and penetrating as the warning rasp of a foghorn. "You haven't heard the last of this, Corinne," and then, gently, she steered Tim toward the street.

Corinne looked after them, a faint flush staining her porcelain-perfect cheeks.

Annie could have turned back to her display. The others dotted across the lawn were picking up the tempo of their interrupted activities. But Annie had had enough. "Do you eat babies, too?" she inquired.

Corinne turned toward her slowly. "What did you say?"

"You heard me. Obviously, you like to take candy away from babies."

"Museum policies are not your concern. You are hired solely to provide entertainment—and clearly that was a mistake."

"Go to hell."

Annie turned back to her display. Behind her, she

heard the scrape of Corinne's shoes as she crossed the crushed oyster-shell drive toward the booth.

"What are those hideous things?"

Corinne was looking at the five posters. Her eyes briefly touched each. The blond man in the gray suit kneeling by a body in a long black overcoat. The naked young woman sitting in the highbacked teakwood chair. The question in the bruised face of the man standing over the body in the beach cabana. The yellow jeep hurtling toward the big man with light eyes. The man with the gun bursting into the cult scene. Disgust was clear in the pinched line of her mouth.

"Copies of watercolors hanging in my bookstore," Annie said furiously. "I run a monthly contest. The first person to figure out the author and title represented by each painting wins a free book—and free coffee all month. If it's any of your business!"

"Get them out of here."

"Over my dead body, lady. Or yours."

ANNIE SHIFTED RESUSCITATION Rhoda from one shoulder to the other. Dressed in the rather voluminous folds of a lavender cotton eyelet dress suitable for a 1937 tea party, the rubber dummy was fairly heavy, but as soon as she, or rather the victim, Matilda Snooperton, was in place on the floor of the gazebo, everything would be done.

Everything?

Oyster shells crunched underfoot. A touch of spring coolness wafted out of the long shadows thrown by the live oaks. The air smelled of sun-warmed grasses, pond water, and iris. The serene calm soothed away the last vestiges of her fury with Corinne. By God, she wasn't going to let that poisonous woman ruin the Mystery Nights for her. She'd worked too hard to let that happen. No, she was going to be calm, cool, and collected and enjoy the evening. Which was almost upon her. Had she overlooked anything?

She ran through the list in her mind, checking off item after item. Yes, this was the last task. Perhaps there would be time for her and Max to repair to her room at the Swamp Fox Inn and savor a Bud Light from the cooler she had thoughtfully iced and brought with her. She paused and looked up at the twelve-foot cane stalks, permitting herself a moment to relish her own cleverness. What a quintessentially perfect spot for The Scene of The Crime, isolated yet romantic. She would give pride of place only to the misty, pine-shrouded finger of lake in Theodore Dreiser's *An American Tragedy*.

Shifting Rhoda to her other shoulder, she began to whistle, "Oh, You Beautiful Doll," as she followed the path around the cane thicket and into the grove of willows that encircled the pond. She headed straight for the gazebo, which graced a gentle rise about ten feet east of the pond. A Saran-sheathed placard, slightly tilted, had been hammered into the ground beside the steps since her last visit to the pond. Ah, Miss Dora.

"Superstitions of the Low Country: Danger awaits the unlucky soul whose path is crossed by a rabbit. (Jimmy Carter might believe that one.) Death follows the hoot of a screech owl. Plant corn and boil soap under a waxing moon. A blue-painted door wards off ghosts. Thirteen at dinner signals death. A bird flying into a house or a mirror cracking without cause presages disaster. Never christen a child, marry, or begin a journey on Friday."

Climbing the steps, she scanned the gazebo's hexagonal interior. Good. Nobody had messed with the clues. Kneeling, she stretched Rhoda out on her stomach, arms artistically outflung. She placed the railroad ticket in the pudgy, rubbery right hand, tucked the scrap of stationery with the scrawled, "I can't come," in Rhoda's pocket, the edge just visible. When she stood and surveyed the scene, she frowned. That initialed handkerchief was too visible. Picking it up, she stepped closer to the railing, and dropped it in the shadows formed by the westering sun.

What a delightfully sinister ambience, the lengthening shadows, the brooding quiet, the black, still water. Her eyes narrowed. What was that clump of sodden cloth among the reeds at the marshy edge of the pond? Had it been there earlier? Her gaze traveled out from the bunched cloth, and she saw a hand languidly floating.

Annie didn't give herself time to think. She moved, vaulting over the side of the railing and dropping five feet to the leaf-strewn ground, sprinting to the far side of the pond, then stumbling over knobby cypress roots to splash into the duckweed-scummed water. Her feet stirred rotting vegetation on the mucky bottom. She grabbed at the torso, then her hands recoiled at its lifeless weight. Gritting her teeth, she reached down again, fastened her hands at the waist and tugged. It was hard work. The sticky bottom sucked at her feet. Razor-sharp reeds slashed at her skin, and sweat filmed her face, dripped into her eyes. The cloying stink of dank water sickened her. And sometime during the hideous exercise, she began to scream. She heard her own voice, high and frantic, as if from a long distance.

The body was so damned heavy, and the reeds snagged it, holding it, impeding her. Then, blessedly, there was help, other hands, and, suddenly, they stumbled out onto the bank, and the body lifted from the water, too.

Annie struggled to catch her breath. Lucy Haines, her face gray with shock, stared down at the sprawled figure. "Oh, my God. It's Corinne."

Gasping, Annie dropped to her knees and reached to check the slack mouth for obstruction. Then her hand fell away. CPR wouldn't help here. A concave depression, about the size of the bottom of a glass, disfigured the crown of the blonde head above the right ear. A rusty stain streaked the pond-drenched hair.

Annie looked up at Lucy, whose wide eyes mirrored horror and the slow dawning of fear.

"This is dreadful. Leighton . . . Gail. Oh, my Lord." Her lean hands twisted together. Today, probably in honor of the house-and-garden tours, she wore a sprightly figured silk dress with pink and rose flowers and matching low pink heels, dress and shoes now stained with mud and water. The lovely spring dress was in stark contrast to her putty-colored face and the tightly twisting hands with their fresh coat of pink nail polish.

Annie stood and repressed a shudder. "We have to get help."

"I'll go call." Lucy stepped toward the path, then turned back. "I'm sorry. You won't want to stay here. If you go that way," she pointed to a well-defined gray path that curved out of sight behind a screen of willows, "you'll come to the gate into my grounds. I live next door, the McIlwain House. You can call—"

"No, that's all right, Lucy. You'd better go. It will save time. I don't mind staying." That wasn't true, of course. She would have given anything to leave that silent place of death, but it was clearly silly to send a stranger to find a phone and make the proper calls.

Time might not be of the essence, but there was no point in squandering it.

Time! Annie glanced at her watch. Surprisingly, very little had passed since she had blithely whistled her way to the gazebo earlier. It was only 5:35. But the tours were scheduled to begin at 6. Everything would be canceled, of course.

Lucy still hesitated, peering anxiously around the quiet, secluded spot. "Do you suppose it's safe? Perhaps you'd better come with me."

Her fear was contagious. Annie glanced, too, at the sun-glossed fronds of the weeping willows, the black, knobby, sinister cypress, the blackish water. Only an occasional rustle as some creature stirred in the reeds broke the silence. The faraway tattoo of a woodpecker sounded. "It's safe enough. I don't suppose there's a mad killer lurking around to bash me."

The brave words echoed hollowly in her mind after Lucy's reluctant departure. She backed away from the corpse, one step at a time, her eyes darting nervously into the thickening shadows. Every crackle of the cane, every vagrant rustle of the willow fronds made her skin prickle.

The sound of running footsteps brought a hot surge of adrenaline. She tensed, ready to run.

Bobby Frazier burst around the cane thicket. Skidding to a stop, chest heaving, he glared down at the sodden corpse. "So the old bitch got it. Where the hell's Gail?" Before she could answer, he gave an impatient jerk of his head, turned, and pounded toward the gazebo.

Annie sorted out the geography in her mind. The path past the gazebo was probably the closest route to the Prichard House.

A siren sounded, than another. Tires squealed; doors

slammed. Heavy footsteps came from the direction of the alley, and police spilled into the clearing, led by a heavyset man in a black broadcloth coat, tan trousers, and a white, wide-brimmed cowboy hat. He shot her a cold, measuring look, then approached the body.

No one moved or spoke as he studied the scene, his thick gray eyebrows bunched, his heavy jowls puffed in concentration.

The pond bank reflected Annie and Lucy's struggle to pull the body to land, drifted pine needles scattered, reeds bent and trampled. The corpse lay face up, eyes wide and staring, mouth gaping. That mushy depression in the skull—Annie searched the nearby area. Then she glanced at the pond, and tensed.

The croquet mallet—her very own croquet mallet— floated in the water a few feet from the bank.

"All right." The lawman's voice was a growl, deep in his throat, like a rusty gate opening. His team swung into action: a young, sandy-haired officer shoved short stakes into the sandy soil at four-foot intervals, then began to string yellow tape, a glum plainclothesman with a gimpy leg pulled out a dog-eared spiral notebook and began a painstaking survey of the crime scene, and a red-faced detective with a beer belly lifted a .35 mm camera to record Corinne at her final rendezvous.

The gaily colored lights strung on the gazebo roof for the tour week flickered into life, adding a garish glare to the twilight. Annie swallowed. So the lights were working. Turning them on was a duty she'd assigned to the Society secretary. Even now, bright yellow lights would be glowing in the tents. And all for nothing.

For a moment, there was no sound other than the clicking of the camera, the occasional crackle underfoot as the men moved about. The lawman gave a satisfied grunt, and turned toward Annie.

He walked ponderously, a bear of a man with heavy shoulders and a thick chest. His face was heavy, too, a bulging forehead, slab-like jowls, a triple roll of chins. His watery blue eyes were murky with the memory of too many crime scenes over too many years.

Annie felt the muscles tighten across her back. When he loomed over her, the world shrank to the space between them. She heard his labored, asthmatic breathing, saw the tracery of red veins in his eyes, and smelled a sour odor of tobacco.

"Harry Wells. Chief of police." His tobacco-roughened throat yielded the rasping introduction reluctantly. He looked at her without a vestige of warmth.

"Annie Laurance. I'm in charge of the Mystery Nights for the Houses and Gardens tour."

"What's your story?" Those dour eyes gazed at her unblinkingly.

Her story. The unease in her shoulders spread down her back. God, he was hostile, and she hadn't told him anything. She started out, then realized her voice was high and rushed. She took a deep breath and controlled her pitch. When she finished, he glanced toward the gazebo, then at the pond. "You brought the mallet?"

"A prop. It was supposed to be a prop."

"Turned out not to be, didn't it?"

She didn't like his words, or his tone.

"That's hardly my fault," she shot back.

He didn't bother to answer, merely stared at her.

"Look, she was dead when—" She broke off at the sound of approaching voices. Oh, God. She hadn't had time to wonder about Lucy, but she should have expected this.

"There's no mistake, Leighton. Please, you shouldn't—"

"Hurry, John." Leighton Webster came around the gazebo, his hand tight on Dr. Sanford's arm. "You'll see, Lucy, Corinne's just fainted. That's all. John will take care of her. No one would—" His deep voice rumbled to a stop. He stopped in mid-stride. Behind him were Lucy, whose face held no shock, and Gail, clinging tightly to Bobby's arm.

Everyone watched Leighton's approach in profound, stricken silence: Lucy, Sanford, Gail, Bobby, Annie, the police, and newly-arrived Max, Edith, and Roscoe, who had hurried around the cane thicket, drawn by the wail of the sirens and the inevitable groundswell of rumor already sweeping across Chastain.

But Leighton was oblivious to them all. He stared down at the crumpled figure of his wife, his face frozen in puzzled disbelief.

"Corinne?"

"Leighton." Lucy touched his arm, and then gently tugged, but it made no more impression than sea spume against volcanic rock. He stumbled forward and would have torn through the restraining yellow tape, except for the fresh-faced young officer who stepped between him and the barrier. "Sorry, sir. This is a crime scene now, and no one may enter."

Slowly, his stricken brown eyes settled on the detective's face, focused there. "We can't leave her. She's . . . We can't leave her there."

Chief Wells could move his bulk with surprising swiftness. "Mr. Mayor, I'll take care of Mrs. Webster. You can't do anything for her now. Go on back to the house. I'll come and talk to you as soon as I can."

Mr. Mayor. The note of deference was unmistakable. Wells did everything but pull on his forelock, and Annie's sense of isolation increased. Nobody demanded to know Webster's story. Mr. Mayor? My God, the interlocking power structure in this town was nothing short of incestuous. Did the Websters run everything?

Leighton's dazed face was gray-white with shock. "Harry, who did this? What happened to her?"

"Nobody knows." The massive head jerked in Annie's direction. "She raised the alarm. Claims she found her dead."

Leighton swiveled, looked at her. "Miss Laurance." His gaze swept the gazebo, and understanding moved in his eyes. "The house tours."

"We'll cancel them." Lucy spoke briskly. "We'll take care of it, Leighton. Please don't worry—"

"Cancel?" He shook his large head slowly, then with determination. "Oh, no, we mustn't do that. Corinne wouldn't want us to do that."

"Of course they must be canceled. They should never have been started," Miss Dora hissed. "Strangers tramping through our lives. I told everyone they were a mistake—and look what's happened—murder."

Annie stared at the wild eyes, the straight silver gray hair, the old twisted mouth working with excitement. Where had she come from? No one had seen her arrive, darting swiftly in those high-top shoes, her cane making no sound on the soft ground.

She lifted the ebony stick, pointed the silver tip at Annie. "Ask her about murder. She knows all about how to kill. Maybe she *likes* to kill."

"Oh, now, wait a minute." Max strode toward Annie, reached out and grabbed her hand. "That's damn silly."

"But we never had murder until *she* came." Miss Dora's head jerked and the black feather on her hat vibrated.

Everyone was staring at Annie, everyone but Max, who slipped a firm arm around her shoulders and glared angrily at Miss Dora. The watching faces looked inimical in the rose and yellow glow from the string of lights atop the gazebo.

Miss Dora rocked back and forth. "Cancel them. Yes, cancel them. Or a murderess will move among us to-night."

The hoarse chant had the sound of madness, but Miss Dora's eyes were as shiny and hard as new minted pennies.

Lucy cleared her throat. "Aunt Dora, you'd best go in now. It's getting late. We will cancel the evenings, of course, but Miss Laurance certainly can't be held responsible for this dreadful accident."

"No, no, we won't cancel." Leighton spoke with a dogged stubbornness. "Corinne wouldn't want us to cancel."

Silence hung over the pond and the oddly assorted people standing there. A dragonfly veered away from them to skim over the dark water.

"How can we continue?" Lucy sought out Wells. "A decision does need to be made. People must be arriving even now. The gates open in minutes." She looked at Leighton in distress. "But you won't want Prichard House to be on the tour. That wouldn't do at all."

But Leighton was determined. Perhaps the thought of the gala helped him escape from the reality of his wife's death—if only briefly. "It must go on. That is what Corinne would have wanted. Only the two front rooms are open, and Gail and I can stay upstairs so that will be all right. The tours last only an hour. No, I don't want any of it canceled."

Edith chimed in, "Leighton's right. It will devastate the work of the Society if we cancel."

"Harry, what harm can it do?" Leighton demanded. "And it meant so much to Corinne."

In the instant before Wells replied, even as Leighton once again insisted that the program continue, Annie surveyed the silent, watching onlookers.

Lucy stood by the distraught widower with brooding protectiveness, giving an oddly militant cast to a middle-aged woman in soiled pink shoes and a muddy dress. Her concerned face was gray beneath her tan, making her coral pink lipstick startlingly bright in contrast.

Gail looked shrunken. Her pale blue eyes were wide and staring, like a child who has wakened in terror from a nightmare. She averted them from her aunt's body and clung to Frazier's arm as she might to a lifeline in a turbulent sea.

The young reporter scrutinized Leighton and the police chief sharply, as if listening for words that weren't spoken. His muscular body seemed ready to spring, and there was about him the look and air of a crouched panther.

Rouge stained Edith's cheeks in bright patches, but her face was composed. Her white cotton pique dress gleamed fresh and crisp. Only her hands, balled into tight fists, betrayed her emotions.

For once, Sanford didn't appear impatient. His hawklike face jutted forward, the smooth skin and hooded eyes expressionless, the thin lips tightly compressed. Annie doubted very much indeed that the dark doctor was experiencing any emotion over Corinne's demise. Why then did he look so wary?

Miss Dora leaned on her stick and glowered malevolently at Annie.

Roscoe was as suitably grave as a mortician. Every

so often, he glanced up from the body to Leighton and back down again, but he said nothing.

Annie's eyes moved toward the body, too. How odd that so many whose lives had been affected by Corinne now stood assembled at her death. But no grief was apparent in that silent circle, except, perhaps, for Leighton's air of inchoate puzzlement. Instead, Annie sensed a strand of tension, verging on fear, joining them together.

"A vagrant," Leighton said abruptly. "That's what must have happened. Corinne startled someone, a robber perhaps, and she was struck down. We can't let it destroy the work of the Society. It meant too much to her."

Annie wondered if his plea rang as false to other ears as to hers, but the police chief was nodding.

"Be a damn mess with the crowds if they're thrown on their own," Wells said heavily. "Ephraim's jammed right now. All right, open up."

Open up. Just like that. Didn't anybody have any idea of the problems involved? Annie could keep silent no longer.

"Look, I understand Mr. Webster's feelings—and I'm sorry about the crowds, but it just isn't possible! The gazebo—" She didn't want to talk in terms of The Scene of the Crime. Not with Miss Dora's malignant gaze still pinned to her. Backing up, she started over. "All the clues are in the gazebo—and Mr. Webster and Miss Prichard had agreed to play the roles of two of the suspects. I don't think—"

Edith stepped forward. "Of course we can do it. There are others who will willingly take their places. In Corinne's memory, we will do it."

12

WERE THESE PEOPLE CRAZY?
  Was sudden death merely a piquant addition to their mystery lust?

Apparently so, because the Mystery Night program was a sellout despite the ripple of rumors about Corinne's murder, and tourists without tickets were pressed against the front fence, straining for a glimpse of police and any movement near the cane thicket.

Annie took a deep breath and climbed the steps to the platform facing the tents. She looked out over the cheerful spring scene. Pastel hues predominated in the encroaching dusk, women in pink, yellow, and white, men in light blue, gray, or tan. It might be any church picnic or annual firm outing except for the undercurrent of nervous excitement threading the hum of voices. The lights strung in the live oak trees and suspended inside the tents glowed a soft yellow. Most of the men and women were sitting around the tables under the Suspect Interrogation and Detection Teams Conference Area tents. A few heartier eaters were in line to refill their plates with Low Country specialties. Her stomach rumbled hungrily. She hadn't even had a bite of the Carolina trifle. She'd been hardpressed to scrub off the pond mud, change into a fresh strawberry-and-lemon striped skirt and soft pink cotton blouse, move the crime scene to the rose arbor just east of the house, drill Max and Edith, who were pinch-hitting for Leighton and Gail as suspects, and make it to the foot of the platform only ten minutes after the mystery program was scheduled to begin.

She looked down the path leading to the pond and wondered if Corinne still lay defenseless on the gray sandy bank, her once lovely face sunken in death, her immaculate wool gabardine dress soiled by water, mud, and blood. A policeman, scarcely visible in the growing dusk, stood guard, turning away venture-some Mystery Night participants. This was the first moment she'd had time to think about her gruesome discovery and its ramifications. That hulking police chief wanted to hear her story—and he had called Leighton Mr. Mayor. But surely he wouldn't cast her as the murderer just because she was from out of town. Her gaze skimmed the crowd surging closer to the platform, and Miss Dora's wizened face popped into view. Annie fought a feeling of panic as she stared into those brooding, hostile eyes. Why had the old lady turned on her? And the answer hung in her mind: because she was a stranger. Jerking her glance away, she stared down at her notes. She had so many things to remember when she made her presentation, including two gruff demands from Chief Wells. She glanced to her left. The Mystery Night suspects, most of them costumed suitably for an English house party in the late 1930s, stood in a line by the steps. They looked uneasy, their faces strained and subdued in the soft yellow light. And why not? Most of them were a good deal more concerned about the progress of the murder investigation unfolding a hundred yards to the northwest than they were the evening's entertainment.

A sharp voice wafted up from immediately below her. "Are you working on the real murder? Can I help?"

Annie looked down into the fox-sharp eyes of Mrs. Brawley.

Mrs. Brawley stood on tiptoe. "What time did it happen? Maybe I saw something."

"But the grounds weren't open then. What would you have been doing?"

For once, Mrs. Brawley appeared at a loss. Then she mumbled, "Oh, looking here and there. Interested in flowers. Irises." Glancing down at her watch, she yelped, "It's almost fifteen after. You must get started," and she turned and scuttled back toward the Suspect Interrogation Tent.

Swiftly, Annie translated. Mrs. Brawley had made a reconnaissance to get a jump on the other contestants and been prowling around the Prichard grounds. Obviously, she hadn't seen the murder or she would be regaling Wells and the world with an embellished account. But it meant she'd cheated on the mystery program, no doubt about it. However, in the scheme of things, she didn't at the moment give a bloody damn. Let Mrs. Brawley win. Just let this horrible, endless week be over, and then she would be free to return to Broward's Rock and the uneventful (usually) life of a mystery bookstore owner.

Still, it rankled. She'd gone to a lot of effort to create

a neat mystery, and everybody who paid their ten bucks deserved a fair chance to win. But any attempt to disqualify Mrs. Brawley would delay the beginning of the program yet again and create an emotional tempest.

So, she loosened the microphone from the stand. The crowd shifted in anticipation. Her gaze swept over the throng and rested for an instant on a very familiar figure, the redoubtable Emma Clyde, the most famous mystery writer on Broward's Rock. Emma's stiff bronze curls had a fiery tint in the fading light. She wore a lime cotton top and a multi-pleated orange skirt. Shell earrings with a matching necklace and three bracelets affirmed a spring outfit. She looked like a housewife enjoying Wednesday night bingo, except for the piercing cornflower blue eyes that even at a distance crackled with intelligence. For an instant, their eyes met and held. As always, Annie felt a quiver of unease in Emma's presence. The woman was so damned smart. Then Annie grinned and gave a little wave. If anybody could outwit Mrs. Brawley, it was Emma Clyde.

As she thumped the microphone, expectancy flickered among the crowd like summer lightning. She gave one last glance at her notes.

"On behalf of the Chastain Historical Preservation Society, I'm delighted to welcome all of you here tonight. It has been my pleasure to create a Mystery Night program for your enjoyment. Before we begin to delve, I want to ask: Did you enjoy your tours of the Benton, Prichard, and McIlwain houses and gardens?"

There was an enthusiastic chorus of affirmatives.

"Did you enjoy your Low Country dinner?"

"Yeees!"

"Are you ready to put together your mystery team

and begin the investigation of the English Manor Mystery, a k a 'Alas, A Sticky Wicket'?"

Cheers rose.

"Excellent. We are ready, too. There are a few official procedures to be followed. Participants are requested to form teams of not more than ten members and to elect a Team Captain Detective, who will officially represent the team in the investigation and pose questions to the suspects. The investigation begins after I describe the background to our mystery and introduce your suspects."

Looking out at the sea of eager faces, Annie described the functions of the three tents and the availability of materials in the Police Headquarters tent. "Each team, at the conclusion of the investigation, is to turn in a sealed envelope which contains: 1. The name of the murderer and 2. the reasons why the team accuses this suspect. Now," she leaned forward, slipping in Chief Wells's first order, "it is imperative that you list on the outside of the envelope the name of every member of your team, complete with address and phone number. Failure to include this information will disqualify your entry." Listeners nodded, and some scrawled in open notebooks. "Your entry will be received by 10 P.M. On Friday evening, you are invited to return here for the Denouement Ball, which begins at eight. You may dress as your favorite mystery sleuth or character. Prizes will be awarded for the five best costumes. At midnight, we will announce the winner, that is, the team which correctly identifies the murderer at the earliest time. Finally, one last warning." The low hum of excited voices ceased. These people were serious mystery fans, and they avidly waited to hear Chief Well's second instruction. She spoke distinctly. "The area open to Mystery Night detectives is limited to the tents"—she pointed to each tent in turn—"and to the area around the tennis court, which is just east of the Prichard House. If a member of *any* team is discovered anywhere else, that *entire* team will be disqualified." She smiled. "I know I can count on your cooperation. And now, Mystery Night sleuths, here is your crime."

Heads bent, hands flew, as Annie related the sequence of events at Gemtree Court, the manor house home of Lady Alicia and Lord Algernon: the disappearance of The Red Maiden, and the discovery of Matilda Snooperton's crumpled body beneath a rose arbor by the tennis court, not far from where only a few hours earlier the happy group had enjoyed croquet. "Detectives are encouraged to study the area near Miss Snooperton's body closely. From police reports, it will be learned that a tool shed near the murder scene has been broken into. There are no fingerprints on the broken lock to the shed.

"You will find in the Police Headquarters tent copies of the statements made by each suspect, the autopsy report, and a table containing replicas of the clues. Each team may make application for one—repeat, *one* —search warrant, which will be granted only if you can convince the magistrate—*me*—" she paused for the laughter which greeted her pronouncement, "that you have sufficient reason. You may sign up at the clue table for your turn as a team to visit The Scene of the Crime."

She tried to ignore a sudden vivid image of the pond and Corinne Webster's crushed skull. In the pause before she forced herself to continue, she heard a contestant mutter happily, "I just love stately home murders. Have you read *Blue Blood Will Out* by Tim Heald?" Her companion nodded enthusiastically. "Loved it. Another good one is *Lord Mullion's Secret* by Michael Innes."

Annie noted that both women, right on the front row, were plump and wore sensible tweeds and sturdy walking shoes. Mrs. Brawley faced sharp competition.

"Now, I'd like to present your suspects."

Suspects. Who would be the suspects in Corinne's murder? Other than herself, the stranger in their midst. Discomfort moved in her stomach, and it wasn't hunger. Would Wells remember to cherchez la femme? Or would that be lèse majesté to Mr. Mayor? But the police always looked first at the husband, didn't they? Maybe not this time. Worry gnawed a little deeper.

Jessica started up the steps. Despite her somber face, she was lovely in an ankle-length, leg-of-mutton–sleeved dress of pale yellow organdy.

Suspects. How about the distraught painter and libidinous Sybil? Or the perhaps more than merely eccentric Miss Dora? Or Gail and her unsuitable suitor? And Edith sure as hell—Annie's wandering thoughts quivered, then crystallized. That letter she'd received with the Mrs. Moneypot's mystery plot; it had been full of innuendos about people who hated Corinne!

"Annie."

Jessica's urgent whisper jerked her back to the platform.

"May I present Lady Alicia."

Jessica, her sleek black hair upswept in a chignon, addressed the crowd languidly. "After tea, I rested in my room. I'd quite a headache from our afternoon in the sun, playing croquet." She shaded her dark eyes. "I saw no one. When I was dressing for dinner, I opened my jewel case and found that my famous ruby necklace had disappeared, so I immediately raised the alarm. As for Miss Snooperton, I hadn't seen her since teatime. She was a dear girl."

Brava. An unexpectedly talented amateur actress.

"Lord Algernon," Annie announced.

Max shot her a brief, warning glance as he strode on stage. As always, he carried himself with élan, even in a borrowed tuxedo. He looked every inch a young English lord, tall, blond, and crisply handsome.

"Took a stroll down to the river after tea, but I didn't see anyone." Then he paused, timing it just perfectly to raise doubts among his listeners. "But there might have been somebody over by the arbor. Dashed hard to see in the mist. Damn shame about Matilda. Must've been the work of a tramp."

Leighton asserted that a robber must have murdered Corinne. Nature imitating art? Or had that fragment simply stuck in his mind from his suspect sheet?

Max stepped back beside Jessica, and Roscoe soberly moved forward. As always, he looked reliable, imposing, and excruciatingly boring. He waited stolidly for Annie's introduction.

"Mr. Nigel Davies, the betrothed of our victim, Matilda Snooperton."

Roscoe clipped his speech neatly, reading from his sheet and ignoring the enthralled crowd. "Appalled. Absolutely appalled. Not the sort of thing that happens in our set. Hadn't seen much of dear Matilda since we motored down. Tennis, then croquet. After tea, took a stroll toward the village. Didn't see a soul."

John Sanford stepped forward, quite natty in a light blue cotton suit and a boater hat.

"Mr. Reginald Hoxton, a friend of Lady Alicia's from London."

Unexpectedly, he threw himself into the part, speaking in an ingratiating, oily manner. "Only too glad to help in the investigation. Miss Snooperton a charming gal. First met her this weekend. Left my room after tea. Ran down to my car to get my shoe kit from the boot. Didn't meet up with anybody." He closed' with a toothy smile.

Edith was up to any challenge to protect her beloved Society. Though her deep-set green eyes were clouded, she threw herself with utmost seriousness into her role as the love-struck girl, Susannah Greatheart. Her abundant hair covered by a gay pink scarf, she stood with her eyes downcast, nervously twisting a white cambric handkerchief. "Such a shock. I did see Miss Snooperton after tea. I happened to walk down to the arbor, but she was quite all right, oh quite all right, when I left her." She paused, gnawing her lip. "Actually, she was laughing." She held the handkerchief to her face and stepped away.

Edith's rendition of counterfeit distress was outstanding. But the distress emanating from the final player was only too real, though ironically, it was critical to the success of her role. "Agnes, Lady Alicia's devoted maid," Annie announced.

Lucy had changed clothes, but obviously made no attempt this time to dress for a formal dinner at an English manor house. She wore a navy blue skirt and gray silk blouse, and her face scarcely resembled that of the cheerful woman who had been so friendly to Annie. Her eyes looked haunted, and her cheeks sagged. Annie knew her thoughts were far from this platform and felt immediate sympathy. Lucy clutched her suspect sheet in a white-gloved hand that trembled and read in a monotone.

"Happened to overhear Mr. Nigel having words with Miss Snooperton. That I did, early this morning. And later, after tea, I saw Mr. Hoxton with a tire tool, and he looked very disagreeable. And Miss Susannah was crying when she crept up the stairs this afternoon. And there's more that could be said about some of these fine ladies and gentlemen."

And wasn't that the truth, Annie thought grimly. She lifted the microphone and forced a lilt into her voice. "It's all yours, detectives. The suspects will repair to the Interrogation Tent, and I will be in charge in the police tent as Detective-Inspector Searchclue of New Scotland Yard. And—one last point, which I'm certain you will all appreciate—Mrs. Gordon at Swamp Fox Inn has volunteered her restrooms for use by the participants and staff of the Mystery Night. Also, the Inn coffee bar will be open until midnight."

The throng of eager detectives swept toward the tents. It wasn't quite a mad enough rush to imperil life and limb, but it bordered on the frantic. It matched the festival exuberance in Phoebe Atwood Taylor's *Figure Away*, but at least it lacked loon calls and shotgun blasts. The comparison was disturbing, though, when she recalled the fate of the person in charge of that celebration. She started down the steps and saw the dour face of the policeman who'd refused her entry to Ephraim Street that morning. Was he assigned to watch her?

13

I N THE LAST-MINUTE CRUSH around the clue table, Annie tried to answer a half-dozen sharp questions at once, keep an eye on Mrs. Brawley who was edging ever nearer the search-warrant stack, and accept entry envelopes thrust at her with demands for instantaneous time notations. It made the closing minutes on the floor of the New York Stock Exchange seem pastoral in contrast.

Team Captain #3, in his saner moments a courteous druggist on Broward's Rock, waggled his envelope a millimeter from her nose. "We're next!" He thrust an elbow militantly into the ribs of Team Captain #9. "By God, we're *next*."

Team Captain #9 bared her teeth. "I *beg* your pardon. Some people will do *anything* to win," and slapped her envelope on his.

Grabbing the envelopes, she scribbled 9:48:03 on

158   CAROLYN G. HART

both, stuffed them in the shoe box cradled beneath her arm, and reached out just in time to pin Mrs. Brawley's hand to the table. "One search warrant, Mrs. Brawley. *One.*"

"We thought you meant *one* for each suspect."

Annie reflected honor on her upbringing by overcoming the impulse to snort, "In a pig's eye." Instead, she gritted, *"One* search warrant to *each* team, Mrs. Brawley. Your team already received a search warrant for the tool shed."

That search yielded Mrs. Brawley's team a card with this information: "The broken lock on the hasp of the tool shed has been wiped clean of fingerprints. The tool shed contains tools and gardening and hobby equipment, including shovels, trowels, hose, putty, paint, the balls and mallets from the croquet game, drills, bits, flower pots, and sacks of fertilizers. Nothing appears out of place. Atop the workbench is a pile of sawdust. On the floor of the shed are found several pieces of gold filigree."

Mrs. Brawley shrieked over the hubbub. "Can we *trade* cards?"

A piercing whistle brought a merciful instant of silence, then Team Captain #4 demanded shrilly, "Is it true Lord Algernon bought that train ticket to Venice?"

Annie ignored him, too, and mustered the strength to shout, "Time, ladies and gentlemen, time!"

Annie stood guard by the trunk of the Volvo, still parked beside the Winnebago in the deep shadows of the Society parking lot. A faint glow from a single light on the back wall of the old building provided the only illumination. She scanned the shadows warily. Nothing would have surprised her at this point. Faked entries. A raiding party on camelback. An offer of a weekend in Rio in exchange for the name of the murderer. She had stationed Edith beside the Death on Demand display on the Prichard lawn while she and Max carried the boxes to the car for overnight safe-keeping. There was no point in trying to maneuver the Volvo down Ephraim Street. The booths were closed, but the street still teemed with departing Mystery Night participants, and the odds of finding a parking spot in the Inn lot were nil. Max was making the last trip. She didn't envy him his struggle through the ambling holidayers.

Bright white light exploded beside her. She jumped a foot.

A hearty laugh boomed. "Scared you that time. Just another couple of shots now. Hey, Ms. Laurance, give us the low-down on the murders—Miss Snooperton's and the real one." In the recurring flashes, she saw a walrus mustache quivering with good humor. "I told Mother," her tormentor jerked his head at a dumpling shaped face nodding in agreement, "this was just the best vacation idea we ever had. We'd planned to go to Europe this summer, wanted to be there for the Wedding, but Mother and I decided there was no time like now to stay home." Mother nodded sagely. "All those bombs. Why, a man would be taking his life in his hands. So Mother read about the house-and-garden tours, and then we saw the bit about the murder, and we just had to come. I'm a sucker for Perry Mason. And can you believe we've got your murder and a real one to boot!" He resheathed his camera, and leaned forward. Annie caught a strong whiff of fresh Juicy Fruit gum. "Tell us now, was that Miss Snooperton a blackmailer?"

Annie caught a flicker of movement at the foot of the Winnebago.

"Come right on out here where I can see you, Mrs. Brawley."

Without a trace of embarrassment, Mrs. Brawley sidled closer to the open trunk. "I had a little thought. If I could just see our entry, Annie, just for a teeny second."

"No." She snapped it with a satisfying sharpness, like the hiss of a plunging guillotine.

"Oh." Mrs. Brawley gave a nervous titter. "I guess Chastain's going all out for the Mystery Nights to assign a policeman to guard the entries," and she looked past Annie.

Annie knew before she turned and saw the sallow face of her favorite traffic cop. "How about that," she managed to say coolly. But her temper never let her quit when she was ahead. "I'm in Room 312."

"Yeah. I know."

She was still staring belligerently at him when Max arrived with the last container. He looked curiously at the newcomers. Annie was in no mood for introductions. She snatched the box from him, dumped it in the trunk, slammed down the lid, and grabbed his arm.

As they rounded the corner onto Ephraim Street and fought their way against the lemming-like stream of exiting gala-goers en route to whatever Bacchanalian delights Chastain afforded after ten o'clock, Max implored, "Hey, where's the fire?"

"Me. I'm mad. Dammit, I'm more than mad. I'm scared. Look behind us. Is that cop coming?"

He twisted his head and gave a low whistle. "Yeah."

"Oh, hell."

Annie stalked up the main walk to Swamp Fox Inn,

but Max took her elbow to detour her around to the side. "We'd better go in the back way."

"What's wrong with the lobby?"

"Honey, Refrigerator Perry couldn't heave through that crowd."

"Oh, *double* hell. Max, I'm so *tired*—and I'm starving."

"Not to worry. I spotted a back patio that isn't in use. Leave it to Papa."

She almost retorted sharply that she wasn't Mama (shades of the walrus mustache's Mother), but she had run out of steam.

But she had to admire Max's artistry as he charmed their landlady. Annie leaned against the spotted wallpaper in a back passageway and watched plump, exhilarated Idell Gordon succumb to his charm.

Fluffing her frizzy orange hair, she twittered, "Of course, I know how you feel. Ms. Laurance *needs* a restful dinner. And the coffee bar is packed!" She simpered at Max, thoroughly smitten. "I know what we can do." The "we" was so happily familiar that Annie beguiled herself with a vision of Max and Mrs. Gordon dancing a minuet. "I'll turn on the whirlpool in the patio, and we'll just put on a *tiny* little light, then no one will even know you're there."

As a general rule, Annie considered public whirlpools about as attractive as a lunch date with Typhoid Mary, but tonight her whole body ached with weariness. Manning that clue table had taken the perseverance of a hockey player and the manual dexterity of a card shark, and all the while she had worried about Wells and his stony attitude toward her. "Whirlpool?"

Mrs. Gordon nodded proudly, then heaved a sigh, her protuberant brown eyes mournful. "I had to do it. The Pink Cottage has one, and so does Harbor Lights.

And you have to have free wine in the rooms. All the inns do it."

When she checked in that morning, Annie had noticed the bottle of wine sitting on the high nightstand next to the modern-day version of a four poster rice bed. Italian. But there was no handy antifreeze gauge.

"You young people run on up to your rooms and change. I'll bring your sandwiches out to the patio."

As they walked up the hall toward the main stairway, the din from the jammed coffee bar buffeted them.

Annie felt a marrow-deep longing for her lovely, *isolated* tree house on Broward's Rock.

"It's going to be a long week." The worn treads of the staircase slanted to the right. As she started up, the banister wobbled under her hand. "God, a fire trap." And when she opened the door to 312, stale, hot air washed over her.

She turned on the window air conditioner. A faint eddy of slightly cooler air fanned her.

Max stood just inside her doorway, his face determined. "I'm going to see what I can get out of her."

"I doubt if she runs to roast duck."

"Annie, my God, do you ever think about anything but food! I'm worried about your neck."

But Max putting her fear into words triggered a stubborn ostrich-like response. "I don't have anything to worry about," she said loudly.

"Oh, no. Just two extremely public confrontations with Corinne hours before she was mortally bashed."

"Me and everybody else in town," and she told him about Edith, Tim, and Sybil. As she talked, she felt more and more confident. "And there's the infamous letter. Hell, I'm going to laugh when I hand that over to Wells. He can't ignore all those motives." She pushed

away the memory of venomous Miss Dora. "I don't
have a thing to worry about—and I'm too tired to gossip with a landlady who twitters."

The phone buzzed.

She yanked it up.

"Your sandwiches are ready, Ms. Laurance."

Food.

A nobler character might have gone to bed hungry
to thwart his quest for information. Annie stalked
down the slanting stairs.

Max continued to look grave as he pulled out a
webbed chair for her at a wrought iron table. Was he
trying to make her nervous? Yes, of course he was. She
ignored him, though that was hard as they'd both
changed to swimsuits, and Max in navy blue boxer
swim trunks excited another appetite.

The ham was paper thin, the Swiss cheese brittle,
and the white bread store-bought, but it was food. She
wolfed three sandwiches as he plied Idell Gordon with
questions. Annie shot them a bored glance, which both
ignored. My God, who *cared* when Corinne and Leighton got married? Or that Miss Dora was sister to Lucy's
mother? Or that Sybil had been married three times,
and the last husband was an Italian count who was
tragically killed driving a race car at Monte Carlo. She
toyed with a fourth sandwich, then picked up her glass
of Chablis (of dubious American vintage) and wandered around the shadowy patio. Even in the single
light mounted over the doorway, she could see pink
paint peeling from the stucco walls. The drooping ferns
in the fake blue-and-red Chinese porcelain pots needed
a stiff dose of Vertigro. Annie stopped beside the whirlpool, which smelled heavily of chlorine. She squinted
at the frothy water, almost sure she saw several bird
feathers and the carcass of a black roach. Sitting down,

she dangled her legs in the swift, steamy water. And drank some more Chablis, contrary to Department of Health instructions posted prominently on a nearby pillar.

"Of course, she made me so *mad*! So rude and overbearing, but always in this sweet, reasonable tone, as if you were the one in the wrong."

Annie slid over the side and sat on the first step. The water felt good. So Corinne wasn't beloved by Idell either.

". . . kept saying the Inn had to maintain standards . . ."

Too bad Idell hadn't listened.

". . . couldn't understand the economics of it. She was *always* rich. What do the rich know about money? I'm trying my best, but everything costs so much. And you can't get good help. One maid was drinking the wine in the rooms and replacing it with water!"

Annie flowed down the steps until the hot water lapped around her neck. The light mounted over the door turned into a nice rainbow when she squinted at it. She could never remember being so tired. And there were three more Mystery Nights ahead—and tomorrow she must persuade Chief Wells how ridiculous it was even to consider her as a suspect in Corinne's death.

"She and Dr. Sanford had the ugliest quarrel. A friend of mine was in one of the patient rooms, and she overheard. She peeked out the door, and she said Dr. Sanford looked *murderous*." Idell's laughter tinkled insincerely. "Oh, I didn't mean that." But her disclaimer was as phony as imitation alligator. "He really was awfully mad. He wants to expand the Chastain Hospital's program for poor people, and Corinne said that was nonsense, they could go to the county hospital. Dr.

Sanford said no, they couldn't for all the things they needed, and then they went at it hammer and tongs."

Annie floated in the bubbly water, and the words danced in her ears like kernels popping in a hot air machine.

"She even made poor Leighton quit the Foreign Service and come back here. He was so handsome then, and he just kind of went to seed." Her voice dropped conspiratorially. "But everyone's noticing how he's taken a new lease on life lately. Lost some weight and been out walking a lot. And sometimes you can't help but think that when a man spruces up, there has to be a *reason*."

Handsome man. He certainly was. She wiggled in the water. "Good looking," she announced.

There was a moment's strained silence from the table.

"Who?" Max asked stiffly.

"Leighton Webster, of course." Languidly, she pulled herself up, shivered as the cool night air swept over her damp skin, and sank down again. "Mrs. Gordon, do you think he and Lucy might have something going?"

"Lucy?" Her voice rose in astonishment.

"She was certainly protective of him this afternoon, at the pond."

"Oh, no." The landlady spoke with certainty. "No, no, no. Lucy and Leighton are old, old friends, but nothing more than that. Why, Lucy was head over heels in love with Cameron Prichard."

"Who's that?" Annie asked.

"Gail's daddy. You see, it happened this way. Lucy and Cameron fell in love the summer after he graduated from Princeton. They went everywhere together. And then, all of a sudden, Cameron went off to Atlanta. Corinne introduced him to some rich girl there, and he married her. That was Gail's mother. Cameron and his wife were killed in a private plane crash in Louisiana, and Gail came here to live when she was ten. Lucy's just crazy about that girl."

So Lucy didn't care about Leighton Webster. Just an old friend.

Heat coursed through Annie. She should get out of the whirlpool before she dissolved. She rubbed her eyes and stared fuzzily at Max and Mrs. Gordon.

"Of course, people will say anything." Idell's tone indicated her delight in this human failing. "I don't believe a word of it, but some think Corinne cared a little too much about young Tim Bond. Otherwise, why did she get so upset about Tim and Sybil when everybody knows it's right normal for a young man to enjoy an older woman? I think that's why Corinne wouldn't let him send his paintings to New York. She was just jealous."

Fragments of thoughts swirled in Annie's mind. Tim's paintings. The watercolors. Damn good this time, especially the yellow jeep. And the one with the big teakwood chair and the naked girl. Tim wanted to go to New York. Big kid. Why didn't he go? Enormous hands.

"Annie. Annie!"

The call punctured her reverie. Sleepily, she opened her eyes.

Max knelt by the side of the pool, and the rainbow light flickered over his face.

"Come on, honey. You'd better get out before you're parboiled."

"I've got a better idea," she said huskily. "Why don't you get in?"

Max stood on the front steps of the Swamp Fox Inn and relished the feeling of utter righteousness shared by early risers. The Broad River gleamed pale gray in the first pulse of dawn. No one stirred near the empty booths and the grandstand. Closer at hand, crumpled Pepsi cups and mustard-stained hot-dog wrappers littered Ephraim Street. He breathed vigorously, enjoying the fragrance of the purple iris blooming magnificently near the Inn steps. Do Annie good to get up and greet the sun. He was on the point of turning on his heel to go knock on her door, when wisdom prevailed. She would not be pleased. Moreover, she would not be sympathetic to his plan. Dammit, she was in a stubborn mood. What would it take to convince her that Wells was after her? Well, at least he saw the danger. Running lightly down the steps, he turned to his right. Fragile patches of mist rose from the river, swirling like strands of Christmas tinsel in the low branches of the live oak trees. The rhythmic slap of a solitary morning jogger's Reeboks against the sidewalk broke the early morning stillness. Max responded to his cheery good morning and strolled past the crisply white Benton House with its graceful double piazzas. He was intent upon the Prichard House, in all its Greek Revival glory, and what he could see of the extensive gardens. There, far to the back, stood the thicket of cane that screened the pond. He walked as far as the McIlwain fence, then retraced his steps, passing the Prichard House, the Benton House, and the Inn. On the east side of the Inn, on the corner, sat the buff-colored former fort that housed the Chastain Historical Preservation Society. Max turned left down Lafayette, passing the parking lot behind the Society. It was almost full, holding, he assumed, the overflow from the area inns. Halfway up Lafayette, a narrow, dirt alley opened to his left.

The alley was bordered on his left by brick walls or wrought iron fences covered with honeysuckle or shielded by towering pittisporum and banana shrubs. On the right, plainer iron or wooden slatted fences marked the back of business properties. Access was available on both sides for garbage pickup. At the back of the Prichard grounds, magnificent wisteria flowed up to and over the intricate iron fence. Max opened the gate and followed a curving path to the rear of the garages. The path forked there, one branch leading directly to the kitchen steps. He followed the other branch. In two minutes, he had reached the grove of willows and the gazebo. The pond looked dark and deep, sunlight still barred by the surrounding trees. Mist wreathed the trunks of the black-barked cypresses. There was an unearthly oppressiveness about the spot. A fit place for murder.

"Hey, you! Nobody can come through here. Crime scene."

"Sorry. Thought my dog came this way."

"No dog's been through here, buddy. Beat it."

Max lifted a hand and turned back toward the alley. He walked briskly back to Lafayette and turned left.

At the next corner, he started down Federal, his footsteps echoing in the empty street. The locked and shuttered buildings here backed up to the alley and to the houses on Ephraim Street—and to the dark, silent pond.

A granite slab inscribed with ornate cursive writing identified the golden-domed building on the corner as the Prichard Museum. The paint on the gilded dome glistened as the rising sun spilled down. So this would be the home of the paintings whose ownership was so bitterly contested. Tucking his hands in his pockets, he walked on. Next door was the Chastain Public Library, a cheerful yellow frame with cane-bottomed rocking chairs on the front and side piazzas. The final three adjoining buildings of rose, pink, and yellow stucco housed antique stores, a furniture shop, law offices, and medical offices. He'd already visited one of the buildings, the day he'd talked to Roscoe Merrill in the offices of Merrill, Merrill, and Merrill. Next door, in the pink stucco building, were the offices of Dr. Sanford.

A street-cleaning truck rumbled down Federal's brick paving. A battered pick-up passed with the radio blaring an Eagles tape.

Max found a narrow passage between the rose stucco building and the Chastain Public Library and turned into it. He swiftly crossed the alley and the parking lot of the Swamp Fox Inn and ducked beneath the arch that led into the patio. All nine tables were occupied with Inn guests taking advantage of the free Continental breakfast. Two tables were pushed together to accommodate an octet of chattering garden clubbers engaged in a synthetically sweet struggle over which walking tour to take that morning. "I declare, Beryl, you know I 'specially came to Chastain because my great-uncle Marcus is buried in the St. Michael's graveyard." "Gardens first, I say, gardens first!" "Now, girls, we can all just have a good time today without *any* hard feelings, I know we can."

Annie waved at him with moderate enthusiasm.

"My God," he exclaimed in tones of awe, which were clearly not appreciated, "you're awake."

She sipped coffee, then replied in a carefully modulated voice. "Mrs. Brawley telephoned at six-fifteen.

She wanted to know whether Reginald Hoxton's shoes were freshly shined."

"Fascinating the way her mind works." He dropped into the chair opposite her. "What did you tell her?"

She poured a fresh cup of coffee from the server. "This damn stuff's lukewarm. And the croissants are dreadful."

He waited.

"I told her I had no friggin' idea."

"You didn't!"

"*Six-fifteen* in the morning."

"Lovely hour. You should have been up with me."

"I hope you were having more fun than I was."

"I took a walk."

"Your voice is freighted with portent."

He looked over the table, picked up a dog-eared menu, dropped it hastily. "Do you have some paper? A pen?"

She found a crumpled renewal notice for *Time* with a tiny wooden pencil attached.

He looked at it in disdain. "I *think* this is a collector's item." Then, hunching over the table he drew a map.

When he was finished, he proudly handed it to her.

She studied it, handed it back, picked up a croissant, and bent it. "Spongy."

"Don't you see?"

"I see that Ephraim Street and Federal Street are parallel."

He poked at the map with a determined finger. "Don't you remember yesterday afternoon, how all those people showed up at the pond? Like a Greek chorus."

"So?"

"They were all within minutes of the pond. *Minutes.* Anyone of them could have clobbered Corinne."

She glanced back down at the map. "I guess so," she said slowly. "Anyone of them could have." Then she grimaced. "But so what? Why do we care? I'll tell you something, Max. I am not going to get involved in another murder hunt. I'm involved in the Mystery Nights, and that's enough to satisfy my blood lust for months." She warmed to her theme. "Correction: for *years*." She started to shove back her chair, then froze, looking over his shoulder toward the arch.

Chief Wells filled the brick entryway, his shoulders almost touching the curved walls. His slab-like face, pocked as old cement, looked ominously grim. Then his questing eyes stopped and focused on her.

14

IN THE SUDDEN SILENCE, his boot heels rasped loudly against the bricks as he crossed to their table. He didn't remove his cowboy hat, and Annie took an unreasoning dislike to the smooth, high, undented crown. Who did he think he was? A Canadian Mountie? He wore gray slacks this morning with his black coat. A black string tie drooped against a faded white shirt. His frosty eyes watched her like a hunter with a 22-inch mallard in his sights.

Whispers, soft as a summer wind in wheat stubble, rippled among the garden clubbers. Annie heard "chief" and "murder" and a sibilant hiss of meaningful "she's." She shared an impartial glare between the brightly curious women and the lawman.

"Ms. Laurance." He moved his pouchy jaws, shifting a wad of chewing tobacco from one side to the other, then gave Max a brief glance. "Mr. Darling."

The words sounded like they'd been scraped out of a rusting barrel. "Like to talk to you. At the scene of the crime."

Max smiled pleasantly, but his dark blue eyes were watchful. "Ms. Laurance gave you all the information she had yesterday, Chief."

"Did she? I didn't hear tell about her quarrel with Mrs. Webster." The tobacco bulged against one cheek. "Course, she can talk to me over there," the big head nodded to the west, "or at the station. Her choice."

Annie had always wondered what it would be like to be taken into custody. Her present feelings were as close as she ever hoped to come. She didn't like it, but, mostly, it made her mad. Max was sending an avalanche of silent messages, which she had no difficulty deciphering. They boiled down to: keep cool.

It was still too early for tourists, but an occasional car passed as they headed down Ephraim Street. A street cleaner paused in his sweeping to eye them curiously. No lights shown from the front windows of the Prichard House, and the morning paper lay midway up the gray marble steps. Annie had devoured the headlines in her copy of the *Chastain Courier* over her breakfast coffee. The lead story was topped with a 3 column 48 point bold head:

SOCIETY PRESIDENT MURDERED AT POND

The drop head read:

CORINNE PRICHARD BLUDGEONED;
WEAPON IS MYSTERY NIGHT PROP

How dreadful it would be for Leighton to read those blaring headlines. She felt hideously intrusive as the police chief gestured for her and Max to walk up the drive toward the tents, which had a forlorn, after-the-circus appearance this morning.

"Was it right about here?" Wells grated. He spat into the grass, but his eyes never left her face.

"Right about here what?" she demanded.

"That you threatened Mrs. Webster."

"That's unwarranted, Chief." Max's voice was as hard-edged as a meat mallet. "At no time has Ms. Laurance in any way ever threatened Mrs. Webster."

Wells transferred his glower to Max. "Were you here?"

"No. However—"

"Then butt out. I'm asking the girl here."

"That's fine. But I'm a friend of Ms. Laurance's, and I'm telling her that she doesn't have to answer any questions unless she has an attorney of her choice present."

"You a lawyer?"

"Member of the Bar of the State of New York."

Wells lifted a massive hand to scratch at his jaw. "That doesn't give you any right to mouthpiece here."

"Certainly not, and I don't hold myself out as practicing in South Carolina. But there's no law to prevent me from providing Ms. Laurance with counsel free of charge." Max had lost his aura of relaxed complaisance. As he faced Wells, he looked as tough and determined—and handsome—as The Saint at a denouement. Annie loved it.

Wells masticated his tobacco for a long moment, then without a word, turned back to Annie. She savored it as a victory, but realized with a sinking heart, that the skirmish was far from over.

"I got a witness, heard you tell Mrs. Webster she'd be a dead body if she didn't get off your case."

Annie seined through yesterday's encounters. Oh God, the watercolors . . . The entire infuriating scene sprang into her mind, and once again she throbbed with anger.

"She was really a bitch," Annie exploded.

Max sighed wearily and rolled his eyes heavenward.

Wells looked like a hammerhead positioning himself for the kill.

"I mean really! She insulted Edith Ferrier, who's worked her tail off for the Society, then she twisted the knife in that poor kid painter, and, finally, she went after my posters. I wasn't having any."

"So when you met up with her at the pond and she started in again, you picked up that croquet mallet and let her have it." His words bounced like boulders down a hillside, gathering force as they came.

Too late, Annie remembered Max's signals. So what the hell. She couldn't go head-to-head with Wells. He was too damned big, but she glared up at him and spit back, "Absolutely not. I didn't see her again until she was dead—and that wasn't my pleasure." Actually, her stomach gave a decided lurch, remembering that dented skull. "Look, you're off on the wrong foot. Frankly, I don't care *who* crunched that awful woman, but there's a big field out there."

"Nobody else threatened her. And you and she had a knock-down-and-drag-out fight at the rehearsal Sunday night, and she ticked you off first thing Monday morning 'cause you were late. It all got to be too much, didn't it?"

"Chief, that woman was ripe for murder. She'd infuriated everybody who knew her. She poisoned everything she touched. Have you bothered to look around? You haven't even asked me about the letter that listed all the reasons everybody wanted to kill her. What kind of investigator are you? If you've got so many big-mouthed witnesses, surely somebody's told you about the letter."

Wells looked exquisitely bored. "Yeah, I heard about it. That letter you *say* you didn't write."

"Obviously, she didn't write it," Max interjected. "How would she get stationery from the Chastain Historical Preservation Society? How would she know the dirt on everybody in Chastain?"

Wells shrugged. "That letter don't mean a thing. Just some woman with her nose in the air." So he'd talked to Roscoe Morgan. "I don't need any fancy-dan fiction to find a murderer when I got two people hot and heavy with Mrs. Webster."

"Two people?" At least she wasn't the only candidate for the county jail.

Wells paused to expectorate a long stream of tobacco juice, then rubbed a heavy hand over his mouth. "Yeah. You and that smart-ass reporter."

Two outsiders. Annie could almost hear the click of the cell door.

"How about Edith Ferrier? And Tim Bond? And Sybil Giacomo? And everybody else mentioned in the letter?" Hands on her hips, she glared at him.

"Little lady, I don't give a damn about that letter. Now you tell me this—who picked the pond for a murder spot? Who carried the weapon there? And who knows all about killin'?"

An ear-splitting roar echoed up from the river. Annie pressed her fingers briefly to her temples.

"The speedboat races," Max observed. "They get underway about eleven."

Sightseers eddied up and down Ephraim Street, drawn to the booths which were beginning to open.

"All this place lacks is a Coliseum with lions."

Max grinned and stuck his hands in his pockets. "Maybe next year."

"This year the sport's going to be feeding me and Frazier to the local gendarmes."

The high keen of a revving speedboat almost drowned out her words.

"Oh, good grief. Let's see if we can find a spot quiet enough to despair in."

But the lobby of the Inn teemed with culture-hungry tourists.

A fat lady stuffed into an orange polyester slack suit pouted in a corner. "I don't see why Mildred *always* has to have her way."

Mildred, prim and purposeful in a restrained gray shirtwaist, brandished her guidebook. "The McNeil gardens are second only to Middleton Place. And *that's* where we're going."

Idell Gordon spotted them, and gestured energetically at the message slot for Room 312.

Max made it to the ferry wharf with ten minutes to spare. He wriggled impatiently in his seat. He wished he were with Annie, but they needed that letter containing the Mrs. Moneypot's mystery plot. If the chief wouldn't investigate its origins, by God, they would.

The cellular telephone rang.

He snatched it up, then relaxed at the sound of his secretary's voice. God, he wouldn't put it past Wells to clap Annie in chains at any minute.

"London called."

"The Queen, or the Prime Minister?"

"Neither," Barbie replied seriously. Max admired her efficiency but regretted that her sense of humor was on a level with Agatha's. "Mr. Ronald Harrowgate called from Sotheby's. He said the matter could be concluded for 200 pounds."

"Great. Call right back. And tell them to send it Federal Express."

"Across the Atlantic?"

"Sure."

As he hung up, Max grinned. At least *something* good was happening this morning. It wasn't an expensive gift, but it was a momento she would cherish. And, when she was ecstatic with delight, well, that would be the time to spring his *new* plan for the wedding.

Three cheery toots of the whistle signaled the ferry's approach. Max looked across the sparkling water. As soon as he had the Moneypot's plot in hand . . .

Gail was waiting on the kitchen steps for Annie. She wore an ankle-length gray cotton skirt, a high-necked white blouse with a lacey front panel, and a pale yellow cummerbund. Her thick, shining auburn hair was twisted into a severe bun, emphasizing the circles beneath her eyes and her pallor.

"I'm sorry to ask you to come to the back. Leighton's in the drawing room with some cousins from Savannah." Her hands twisted nervously. "You're awfully nice to come at all."

Although she had her own objectives for this meeting, Annie couldn't have refused the piteous message Idell had handed her. *Please come. I need help.—Gail P.*

And Gail did look damned vulnerable, frail, and grief-stricken. For just an instant, Annie felt a flicker of irritation. Where was the girl's gumption? Then she thought of Corinne's steel strong will and the years she'd had to dominate this gentle creature.

"Certainly I've come. What can I do?"

"I saw you out in front. With Chief Wells. Did he say anything?" She waited tensely for Annie's answer.

Annie saw no point in advertising her own predicament. She replied judiciously, "He was interested in what Corinne did yesterday." Which was a very delicate way of putting it.

"Did he—did he mention Bobby Frazier?"

Annie couldn't decide how to field that one, and she waited long enough that Gail assumed the worst.

"Oh, I knew it." The girl clung to the wooden railing. "He's prejudiced against anyone different. I'm so afraid he'll try to blame Bobby."

"Being from out of town isn't sufficient grounds for a murder charge," Annie said firmly, mentally crossing her fingers.

Gail shook her head hopelessly. "You don't understand. Bobby and Corinne—"

"Why did she want him out of town?"

Gail stared at Annie as if she'd suddenly sprouted horns. "How did you know that? How did you ever know?"

The morning's on-shore breeze rattled the glossy magnolia leaves and whipped the frothy lace at her throat.

"Last week at the Society meeting, the famous one where I read the letter—" Gail nodded, her eyes never leaving Annie's face—"before we came in, Bobby and Corinne had a spat on the sidewalk and I heard him say something about her offering him money to leave town."

Gail gripped Annie's arm. "Did you tell Chief Wells?"

"No. But look, Gail, something like that can't be kept quiet. I'm sure I wasn't the only one who heard it. Lucy was coming up the sidewalk just then, too."

"Oh, Lucy would *never* tell. She knows how I feel about—" Gail flushed. "I mean, he's awfully nice. No, Lucy won't tell." Then her cheeks burned a deeper red, and she released Annie's arm. "I'm sorry, I can't ask you not to speak out. But it isn't nearly as awful as it sounds. If you just let me explain, you'll see it doesn't amount to anything!

"I met Bobby last fall when he came to do an article on the Museum. I work at the Prichard Museum. I'm the curator." Quiet pride shone in her eyes. "That's what I studied at school, art history. And I don't have the job just because of my family. Even Bobby sees that. He told me so." A smile touched her drawn face. "Bobby's not like anyone I ever met before. He's so strong and quick, and he says what he thinks, always." She looked at Annie with a flash of rare defiance that made her look radiantly beautiful for a fleeting moment. "I like that."

Annie knew directness could have its advantages. She thought of Max, whose mind was positively serpentine. And she enjoyed that, for all the frustration it could engender. Weddings with 500 guests indeed!

Gail's moment of courage faded. "My aunt didn't like him. She said he wasn't—" she jerked her head angrily "—wasn't a gentleman. She told me not to see him anymore." She darted a defensive look at Annie. "He kept on coming to the Museum. And we went out for lunch, and sometimes we met for dinner."

"Corinne didn't know?"

Gail lifted her chin. "I finally decided we weren't

going to sneak around anymore. I told her I was going to see him when I wanted to."

"Is that what prompted her performance the day I came to look at the grounds?"

Gail avoided Annie's eyes, staring down at the lake-blue amethyst ring on her right hand. "That was just Corinne being Corinne."

"Why were you so angry?"

"Because—because I couldn't believe what she'd done." An echo of that anger throbbed in her voice now. Her blue eyes enormous, the girl struggled to breathe, and Annie remembered the dreadful moments in the exquisite front hall of Prichard House. "She offered him money to leave town—and he took it." Gail looked at her imploringly. "You won't understand. I almost didn't understand, when I found out. I felt like a fool, that he hadn't cared for me at all, that he was just interested in money. Then, yesterday, he was mad, too, and he yelled at me to look at the canceled check before I made up my mind. I called a friend who works at the bank, and she checked for me. Bobby's endorsed the check over to the National Children's Fund."

"So he took the money, just like he was being bought off, then turned it over to charity? She must have been furious." Oh, what she would have given for a glimpse of Corinne's face when she discovered Bobby's doings!

"He doesn't care about money. When I told her yesterday afternoon, she said he was a thief and a cheat, and I told her she was an ugly, jealous old woman." The fire died in her eyes. "I didn't know anything was going to happen to her. I told her there wasn't anything she could do to keep us apart. She said if I saw him again, I wouldn't get a penny of my parents' estate. But when I told Bobby, he didn't care about that at all."

The back of Annie's neck prickled.

"This happened yesterday afternoon? You found out about the check and quarreled with Corinne, and then you told Bobby all about it?"

Gail nodded.

Annie approached from another angle. "How could she keep you from inheriting?"

"Oh, she could do it," Gail explained reluctantly. "She had the power under Daddy's will to decide if I should receive the bulk of the estate on my twenty-fifth birthday, or on my thirtieth birthday. Yesterday she said I'd never get any of it. But Bobby said she could take her precious money and—" She paused, blushing. "He didn't care at all! He said we'd do fine without a dime from anybody."

And Chief Wells would be as likely to believe that, Annie thought, as he would to believe in little green men serving pink champagne in the mansion gardens at midnight.

"What time did you talk to your aunt yesterday?"

Gail's face again looked shadowed and pale. The vivacity drained away. "It must not have been long before . . . it happened."

"But you were mad at Bobby when you talked to him at the pond."

Gail drew her breath in sharply. "Were you there?"

"I was putting some clues in the gazebo. Neither of you saw me. When you started talking, well, it seemed like a bad time to speak up."

"That was *before* I talked to Corinne. Bobby chased after me, and made me listen. That's when I called the bank, then I marched in to Corinne and told her she was trying to embarrass me and make Bobby look bad, but it wasn't going to work. Then I found Bobby out in the grounds, and we worked it all out. Afterward, I went to the Museum. It always makes me feel better to go to the Museum. I'm putting together a new exhibit of Victorian wallpapers. I love the names of some of the patterns. They're so grand. Bachelor's Pear Vine. Oglesby Damask. Fuschia Trellis. Hewes Parlor Paper."

But Annie scarcely listened. She was sorting out the timing.

1. Bobby and Gail at the pond.
2. Bobby follows Gail.
3. Gail and her aunt quarrel.
4. Gail and Bobby talk on the Prichard grounds. Gail tells Bobby, whee, all is fine, I'm being disinherited, but whither thou goest, etc.
5. Gail to the Museum.
6. Bobby where?

Wherever he was, he carried with him a gilt-edged motive. As did Gail.

Annie looked curiously at the girl, who had the relaxed air of someone who has told it all and found it less awful than expected. Didn't she have the slightest idea that she had now provided both herself and Bobby with enormously satisfying reasons to murder her aunt?

"So you see," she concluded, "once Bobby knew I was going to keep on seeing him, he didn't have any reason to be mad at Corinne anymore."

Annie nodded solemnly.

Then worry clouded the pale blue eyes looking at her so earnestly. "But I'm afraid Chief Wells won't understand."

Annie felt confident Gail's concern was thoroughly justified.

"So that's why I asked you to come over. Roscoe told

me that you and Mr. Darling have some experience with murders. The thing is, do you think you could help figure out what happened to Corinne?"

"I'd sure like to—" Annie began.

"Oh, that's wonderful! You're wonderful!"

Annie felt on a level with a charlatan advertising radio waves to rid a house of termites, but when she saw the effect of her response on Gail, she couldn't backtrack. The girl looked as if she had been suddenly reprieved from the gallows.

"There's no way I can ever thank you enough!"

"Please don't try," Annie said feebly, wondering how she was going to explain this to Max.

Gail had the grace to look embarrassed. "I was just sure you would help, so I've already called Lucy and persuaded her to talk to you. You'll go see her first, won't you?"

The lady in front of Max couldn't decide. Did she want "Chastain. Two Hundred and Fifty Years of History," or "Interiors of Low Country Plantations?" Then she held up "Southern Gardens, Their Majesty and Magnificence."

"That's the one," Max encouraged. "No one should come to Chastain and leave without that book. The gardens, you know."

She glanced up at him and the frost in her eyes melted. "Oh, do you really think so?"

"Absolutely. Cross my heart."

He smiled genially at her as she paid, received her change, and slowly yielded her place.

The Society secretary, eyes bleary with fatigue, looked up gamely.

"Yes, sir. What can I do for you?"

"Can I buy you a beer?"

Louisa Binning brushed back a tangle of peroxided curls. "That's the nicest thing anybody's said to me all day." Then she looked past him and sighed. "But I can't leave. You have to make hay, etc."

"You think they'll all buy books?" He tilted his head at the two-deep line that stretched behind him out the propped open door and all the way to the sidewalk.

"My dear, they buy *everything*!"

"I'll buy a stack of ten, any ten, you pick 'em, if you'll give me a few minutes time."

She laughed goodhumoredly. "Talking to you—and to everybody—is my job. You don't have to buy any books."

Max took out his wallet, picked out a bill, and dropped it into a wooden box shaped like the fort, varnished a golden brown, and carrying the painted legend, *Gifts for Chastain*. Then he reached into his inner jacket pocket, pulled out a thick envelope, and handed it to her.

"How did the writer of this letter get the paper and the envelope?"

She emptied the envelope, glanced at the cover letter, then stiffened. "Why, this is the letter . . ."

He nodded.

She was still studying the sheets, and her mouth formed a silent O.

Max had the silky feeling of delight akin to rolling up three oranges on a slot machine.

When she looked up, worry lines bunched around her eyes. She stared past him at the restless line of tourists, then pushed back her chair.

"Ladies and gentlemen, there will be a slight delay in filling your orders. Please feel free to look over our brochures, and you will enjoy walking through the fort. You will find musket slits in the east wall. I will reopen the desk as soon as I have restocked the books. Thank you for your patience."

Then, in a low voice, she turned to Max. "Come back to the stockroom with me, where we can talk."

15

As she climbed the shallow front steps of the gracious Palladian portico of McIlwain House, Annie couldn't resist a glance to her right, but banana shrubs masked the wrought iron fence, affording not even a glimpse of the Prichard grounds. The sweet scent of the shrubs mingled with the smell of freshly turned dirt in the flower beds by the steps. It couldn't be far to the pond, though, for Lucy to have heard her screams for help.

The front door was open. Annie rang the bell and looked through the screen door into the hall. Lucy came slowly, her footsteps heavy with fatigue. She seemed to have shrunk since that day they first met. Annie remembered a vigorous woman with a country road stride. The woman holding open the door seemed frail. Her voice was flat. "Gail said you might come. I don't know what you can do, but I'll help if I can."

The heart pine flooring of the entry hall glistened in the early morning sunlight that splashed through the open door of the dining room to the east. Lucy slowly led the way to the drawing room. Annie looked around appreciatively. No expense had been spared in restoring this room to grandeur. Bois-de-rose silk hangings framed the tall windows and emphasized the rose background of the Aubusson rug. The wallpaper was a rich floral print of peonies against a cream background. Rose and cream, too, dominated the upholstery of the Chippendale-style furniture. The most remarkable piece was a mahogany china breakfront, holding a Blue Canton dinner service.

Lucy gestured for her to be seated. "Won't you have some coffee?"

Annie accepted immediately. The morning offering at the Swamp Fox Inn had a taste like lukewarm dishwater with a dash of instant coffee. Lucy's coffee had the dark, winey taste of chicory, and the warm, homemade doughnuts she brought were superb.

Lucy smiled as she ate with relish, but didn't touch her own pastry. "This was a recipe of Corinne's. We made them often when we were girls." Her voice was controlled, but a sense of anguish hung in the room, not so much grief, perhaps, as sorrow at the passing of long ago days.

"You had known her for a long time," Annie said softly.

"A very long time." Lucy turned the small garnet ring on her little finger and shivered, then looked up apologetically. "I'm sorry. You want me to help. What can I do?"

Annie put down her coffee cup. "Tell me about her. What she was like?"

Lucy had large, expressive eyes. It was as if an

opaque curtain fell. "You met her. Corinne was what she seemed to be, a beautiful, willful, determined woman." Her voice was studiedly neutral. "She wasn't all good or all bad—like most of us. She had very decided views on everything, on life and love and what was suitable and what wasn't. Usually, she meant well —or thought she did. The only difference between Corinne and most of us was that she would have her way, at all costs."

"You were good friends."

"We grew up together."

"Is it true—that she kept you from marrying her brother?"

For a moment, Lucy's pallid face was absolutely blank, then a lopsided smile faintly touched her lips. "That old story. Lord, don't people ever forget anything? And Cameron's been dead now for a decade or more." She gave an impatient head shake. "People always think that if you never marry, it's because no one asked you. And that's not true. No, Corinne had nothing to do with my turning Cameron down." Her lips closed into a thin line. "And that's all I intend to say about that."

Again her eyes dropped to the garnet ring, and she moved it around and around.

Annie knew she was skating on thin ice. "That morning at the Society when I made my presentation, everybody—but me—knew the fictional victim was Corinne. The story listed a bunch of people who had motives for murdering her."

Lucy stiffened. It was so quiet Annie could hear the tick of the Dresden clock on the mantel.

"It said her husband was playing—"

"You can't pay any attention to that letter!" She leaned forward, gripping the chair arms. "Please, it was—oh, it's just a scurrilous piece of nonsense. I told Chief Wells this morning that it didn't amount to anything—and he agreed with me. Can't you just let it drop?"

"Let it drop? Why, it's the best lead we have! And obviously, the writer was right on target about Tim Bond and Sybil and Edith Ferrier. And certainly about Gail and Bobby. So why not—"

Lucy's eyes flashed. "Have you come here expecting me to tell you every nasty bit of gossip I know? I'm sorry, Ms. Laurance, but I'm not playing that game. That letter was just a meanspirited attempt to embarrass Corinne. To take it seriously would be absurd."

Annie tried to suppress her anger, but she knew her response was crisp. "Is it absurd? I don't think so. And I intend to find out the truth behind it."

"You must do what you feel is right." But Lucy's face was drawn into a tight frown.

"All right, I will. And I wonder if the Chief might be more interested in that letter when he finds out that on Monday afternoon Corinne threatened to keep Gail from receiving her inheritance, and Gail told Bobby? What kind of motive do you think that is?"

"Gail would never injure anyone, and certainly not Corinne." But the sick anxiety in her eyes showed how deep the barb had gone.

"Perhaps not. But she's crazy about Bobby Frazier—and Chief Wells is sniffing after him. And, as a matter of fact, after me. I'll lay you odds of ten-to-one he puts either Bobby or me in jail by week's end."

"That's dreadful." Lucy's eyes were wide and shocked.

"I think so, too. That's why I'm here. I've *got* to find out who hated Corinne and why." She leaned forward. "Won't you help me?"

Lucy picked up the silver server and poured a stream of fresh, hot coffee into Annie's cup. Her gaze roamed restlessly from the iris-filled Delft vase on a Chippendale table to the gleaming bronze andirons at the fireplace. "There isn't evidence enough to arrest Bobby—or you." Her eyes flicked to Annie's face. "It's all just circumstantial evidence—isn't that what they call it?"

"Juries have been known to convict on circumstantial evidence."

"Oh, it won't happen. It won't."

Annie was torn between compassion and frustration. Lucy was so evidently upset—and so determined to protect her friends and neighbors. But it was disconcerting to see her willingness to jettison Annie or Bobby.

"So you won't help me?"

"My dear," her voice was bone-tired and defeated, "I would help you if I could. But I can't."

Max refused to reveal his discoveries until they had eaten, even though it took a forty-five minute wait in a line that snaked from the marina parking lot to the restaurant, The Pink Carrousel, atop the bluff.

Annie brought him up to date on her talks with Gail and Lucy, then suggested, "We could go to a fast food stand."

"I do not eat fast food." There was a monumental dignity in his pronouncement.

"That's un-American."

"Did you know that the rate of heart disease in China is less than—"

She reached up and put a finger to his lips. "Love, I don't give a damn."

When they were finally seated in the outdoor garden, the table listed unsteadily to her right and gnats hovered in a friendly gray cloud.

The menu featured a jaunty merry-go-round, pink, naturally, on a beige cover and 12 pages of offerings.

Max sighed. "A menu this extensive presupposes a microwave."

"*Everybody* uses a microwave."

"Not in a first-class restaurant."

It only took twenty minutes for the harassed waitress to reappear for their order.

"Taco salad and a pink limeade."

Max avoided gagging and ordered, "Baked scrod, steamed broccoli, and a Bud Light, please."

She grinned at him.

"Taco salad is a gringo invention," he admonished.

"Don't try to sound authoritative about Mexican food. That's my province. And taco salads have an honorable history—"

"If you include junk food in culinary history, perhaps."

"Ah, refried beans, fajitas, sopapillas dripping with honey and powdered sugar. Heaven in Texas on a Saturday night."

"If we're going to talk about the components of a heavenly Saturday night, in Texas or—"

"Down, boy. We're talking food."

Their drinks arrived, and he averted his eyes from her gloriously red cherry limeade. She sucked noisily on her straw.

"I do have news," he said portentously.

"Better than mine, I hope. I didn't get any change at all out of Lucy."

Max pulled two envelopes out of his pocket, tossed them to her.

Annie felt the thicker one, poked inside, and recognized the famous mystery plot letter.

"I've seen—"

"Put it on the table. Then put the sheet from the other envelope beside it."

He crossed his arms and smirked in satisfaction.

She glanced at the new sheet, read: "The quick brown fox—" then exclaimed, "It matches. It matches! Where did you find it? How did you find it?"

"The old Remington at the Chastain Historical Preservation Society."

"Oh." Her voice sagged. "Hell, I thought maybe we'd learned something."

Max held his tongue until the waitress unloaded his scrod, which looked like it might rival the Sahara for dryness, and Annie's salad, which appeared disgustingly delectable, the guacamole a luscious green and the taco shell crisp and light.

"I found out a terrific amount." His fork stuck in the scrod. He yanked it free and used it as a baton, tapping the beer bottle for emphasis. "One: The letter must have been written between March 12, when your name was first mentioned as the prospective mystery expert—"

Annie poked at the bobbing lime in her glass and frowned at him skeptically. "And who told you that? A flea in the woodwork?"

"Louisa Binning, the Board secretary. She types up Miss Dora's meeting notes. It's all there, in black and white."

For the first time, Annie looked interested. "Okay, the letter must have been written between March 12 and—" she paused, figuring "—and say around March 24, because I got the letter on the 26th, and we have to allow time for delivery."

"It's postmarked the 24th."

A grin tugged at her lips. "Very good, Sherlock." She balanced a piece of shell heaped with taco meat. "But that gives us a ten-day period—so how does it help?"

"The Remington was at Crosswhite's Typewriter Repair Shop March 10 through the 19th. But here's the meat: Louisa insists the letter couldn't have been typed during hours when the Society is open and that includes the weekend of the 22–23rd when the Society hosted a local China painting display."

Annie chewed reflectively on a morsel of taco shell. "So somebody got in and used the typewriter at night on either the 19th, 20th, or 21st of March." She scowled. "How could anybody get into that place at night? The walls must be two feet thick."

"That's the point." His voice oozed satisfaction. "It would take a broadaxe to make a dent on those doors, and the windows are too small for anybody but a midget. Besides, there were no traces of a break-in."

"So how did anybody get in?" Her face brightened, and she answered her own question. "A key. Max, the typist had to have a *key*!"

Max interred the remains of the scrod beneath some watercress and prodded doubtfully on the mushy broccoli. "And who has keys?" he prompted.

"Okay, you're wonderful, Maigret. Share with me the results of your investigation."

"It's a nice, small list. The members of the Board and Louisa Binning."

"Oh, sure. Sure. It certainly figures. That means somebody was enjoying the hell out of my presentation of the Moneypot's plot." She wriggled her shoulders in distaste.

"Maybe. Maybe not. A Board member or anybody with access to a Board member's keys."

"Like Leighton."

"Or even Merrill's wife."

Annie pushed her plate away. "That brings up a critical point. Did the letter give somebody there a murderous idea? Or is the letter writer the killer?" She banged a small fist on the table and beer foamed over the top of Max's glass. "Why won't Wells listen to us? The letter is absolutely critical. Whether Lucy admits it or not, the woods are full of suspects, including Leighton, Dr. Sanford, and Roscoe Merrill. And if Wells won't investigate them, we will!"

The spicy smell of cedar potpourri didn't quite mask the underlying odors of burnt coffee, chlorine, and unswept corners. The bar of sunlight which flooded in as they opened the front door revealed, too, that the black-and-white tiled entry of Swamp Fox Inn was long overdue a good scrubbing. Annie thought longingly of the exquisite cleanliness of Death on Demand, but soldiers of fortune had to make camp at the battle site. At least it was quiet this afternoon; the indefatigable tourists were out thirstily absorbing Chastain culture.

"Miss Laurance. Oh, Miss Laurance!"

The foyer, with its scuffed tile floor, led directly to the old-fashioned oak counter. A desk littered with letters, brochures, empty soda cans, a greasy box with two soggy glazed doughnuts, and a flyswatter shared space with a Depression-era switchboard and a wall letter box with numbers affixed for guests' rooms. Idell Gordon stood on tiptoe behind the counter. She wore a dark brown cotton dress with speckles of lint from the dryer.

Reaching up to the slot for 312, she pulled out a

scrap of paper. "For you, Miss Laurance. Chief Wells left word for you to call. I have the number for you." She pushed forward the telephone that sat on the counter. Her protuberant eyes glistened with curiosity.

"Oh, thanks so much. I'll call from upstairs."

Annie was pink with suppressed giggles as she unlocked the door to her tiny room. "Did you see her face? She was *quivering* for me to use that phone so she could hear."

Max draped himself comfortably on her bed. "Either way, your call has to go through her switchboard, sport. I'll bet a scrod (you eating) that she listens in."

"I don't gamble," Annie countered righteously.

She pulled up a wicker chair next to the telephone stand and dialed. She was put through immediately.

"You called?"

"Oh, Miss Laurance." The greeting sounded like a dungeon door dragging against twelfth-century flagstones. "Thought you might be interested in the autopsy report."

"Yes, of course." Alarm tingled down her spine. Why tell her?

"The skull injury was caused by the end of the croquet mallet. But it wasn't the cause of death."

"It wasn't?"

"She drowned."

Annie remembered the heavy, wet figure face-down in the duckweed-scummed water.

"Medical Examiner figures someone struck her from behind, and she pitched forward into the water."

She tried to picture it. Corinne arguing, then swinging around arrogantly to walk off. No, Corinne must have turned away and faced the pond, and someone snatched up the mallet and flailed out.

She had a funny feeling of ESP when Wells's heavy

voice grated, "Hard to picture why she would turn her back on somebody, look out at the water."

There was something about him that brought out Annie's combative streak. "Oh, I can think of a lot of reasons. She and this person were standing there gazing across the pond, and the other person stepped back and let her have it."

"That's not the way I see it."

She didn't like his tone. At her frown, Max swung off the bed.

"No," Wells rasped. "I see it this way. She's quarreling with somebody and turns away and starts to leave, and then she's struck from behind and plops forward."

She didn't relish being his straight man, but she couldn't resist asking, "How could she have drowned, if she fell forward on the path?"

"Drowned?" Max mouthed.

Wells bulled ahead. "Her killer realized she was still breathing, but it's too late then to back down, so the murderer pulls her around and shoves her into the water and holds her head down." His heavy breathing echoed on the wire. "You were goddamned wet and muddy, weren't you?"

She got it then, like buckshot between the eyes. "Now, wait a minute, for God's sake. I was trying to get her *out* of the water."

He didn't say a word, just stood there and breathed, and Annie felt like a hapless soprano being stalked by the phantom of the opera. The *jerk*. Trying to use psychological warfare on her.

She opened her mouth for a withering reply, but he beat her to it.

"And the only fingerprints on that mallet are yours. Clear as a bell most places; smudged and partial on the grip."

She felt the icy calm that precedes panic. "Of course my prints are on it. I carried it down to the pond. I brought it to Chastain. I must have touched it hundreds of times."

A worried frown creased Max's face.

Once again, that infuriating, accusatory silence from Wells.

Her fingerprints. That simple statement indicated a great deal of police effort directed at her. "How did you get my fingerprints?"

"Frank Saulter. Broward's Rock police."

"You're a busy little man."

Max immediately began a frantic waggle of sign language.

"Too bad you're wasting your time and the taxpayers' money. Listen, Chief, I've got some information for you. The letter—you know which one I mean—the letter that lays it out about who hated Corinne and why—okay, that famous letter was typed late at night on the old Remington right next door from here at the Society. It was typed after hours on either March 19, 20, or 21. Now, nobody broke into that massive old fort—so what does that mean? The typist had a key. That's right. And you know who has keys to that building? Only the members of the Board of the Chastain Historical Preservation Society. I'm telling you that whoever wrote that letter was either the murderer—or has a hell of a good idea who the murderer is. And I think I know who wrote that letter."

Even in her fury and despite the chief's stertorous breathing, Annie heard a telltale gasp. So Idell wasn't missing out on much.

But she didn't care who heard what she said.

"I'll tell you who wrote that letter—Who knows *everything* that goes on in town? Who's a thwarted old spinster who hates *everybody*? Who's the only member on the Board who *wasn't* listed as a suspect? I'll tell you —Miss Dora!''

Max made an "Oh-God-I-can't-believe-it" face, then drew his finger across his throat.

But there was no stopping Annie now. "So you just keep on hounding innocent people and see how much good it does you. If you won't find out the truth, I will!''

16

MAX BELLOWED IN HER EAR. "We don't have time to do this!"

"We'll take time!" she insisted. Then, standing on tiptoe, she struggled to see over the bobbing heads. "For Pete's sake, what is that awful noise? And why are people jumping around?"

He reached up and grabbed a gnarled live oak limb and nimbly hoisted himself up. Dropping down in an instant, he yelled, "It looks kind of like a cross between square dancing and tap dancing."

"Oh, of course. The cloggers," she shouted.

"Don't be silly. They don't have loggers in South Carolina."

She gestured helplessly toward the side street, and, heads down, they fought their way into the less densely packed mob on Lafayette. The thunderous clacking was reduced from the roar of an approaching subway train to merely the thunder of nearby surf.

"Clogging," she explained. "I read all about it in the Chastain House and Garden Tour brochures. It originated in Ireland and Lancashire, England, and it's here by way of Appalachia. That bit of news was tucked next to the information about the magic shows on the hour at Prichard Museum. And the flea market in the Armory. And the praline eating contest in the basement of the Methodist Church." She grabbed his arm, and they broke into a half trot. At least they were moving against the traffic flow now.

"Is there any other excitement you're keeping from me?" He darted a worried glance at his watch. "Annie, your cast is going to show up in twenty minutes for a warm-up."

"They'll keep. And everybody did swell last night. This is more important."

She did slow for a moment, however, at the corner of Ephraim and Prince streets to point up a curving drive at the greenish-gray plaster of a Greek Revival mansion. "Lady Lust lives there."

"Sybil Giacomo?" It would not be inaccurate to say his tone quickened.

Annie shot him a disgusted look. "The one and only."

"Hey, why don't we talk to her now? We need to find out where she and Tim were when Corinne was killed."

Annie grabbed his arm firmly. "Tomorrow."

But when they reached the long, dark line of wrought iron two doors down, she felt a funny little thump in her chest. The late afternoon shadows threw deep pools of shade across this immense stretch of lawn. Spanish moss hung in ghostly filaments from the live oaks. The day was still and somber, and the sweet scent of the pittisporum hung in the air like a powerful perfume, dizzyingly.

She pulled open the gate with its ornate pineapple motif. The reluctant shriek of the metal was worthy of Inner Sanctum's finest hours.

Midway up the stately avenue of live oaks, she stumbled to a stop. "Look, there's another one." She might have been pointing out a tarantula.

This placard was bound with scratchy brown twine to an especially low and thick branch:

"This live oak was the site of eight recorded duels, only one of which resulted in death. The facts are these: Harold Anderson Chastain derided the conduct of Judge Arthur Winyard, declaring him to be the servant of the factor and disloyal to his duties as a magistrate. The judge's son, Thomas, sought out Mr. Chastain and, after a heated exchange, struck him with a riding crop. The men met in combat at the hour of noon on August 18, 1805, each walking twenty-five paces, then turning to fire. Mr. Winyard was mortally wounded and died at the scene. He was 22 years, 8 mos. and 6 days of age. Mr. Chastain suffered a grievous injury and passed from this earth on September 6, 1805, at the age of 32 years, 9 mos., and 17 days."

She shivered, and the chill came from more than the sunless dark beneath the trees.

"She's *crazy*," Annie whispered.

She took Max's arm again, purely for companionship, of course, and they continued up the shell drive. In the silence, oppressive after the roar near the riverfront, the sound of their footsteps carried clearly.

A low tabby wall enclosed the house, which was built of brown-toned plantation bricks. Four huge tabby-covered Doric pillars supported a two-story verandah and a flat roof with a balustrade around the top. They mounted the steps. A rattan rocker faced the front yard. Annie knocked vigorously.

They might as well have pummeled a tomb door in the Valley of the Kings. No sound. No movement. No response.

"Dammit, she can't accuse me of murder, then go to earth like a rat in a burrow."

But Miss Dora's house brooded in the light of the setting sun, impervious to Annie as it had proved impervious to intruders throughout its history.

Frustrated, Annie lifted both fists and pounded again, but with no more effect than before. They were turning to descend the steps, when she reached out, gripped Max's arm.

"Look. There. Did you see?"

"Where?"

"The window. That curtain *moved*. I swear it did."

Annie stared at the dusky folds of velvet, pressed against the pane. Was there a slit there, a fine line open to vision? Were malicious black eyes staring out at her?

They gave it up, finally, and started down the steps, but Annie knew she was engaged in a duel. A duel of wits that might prove deadly.

Annie was forewarned for Tuesday night. She had, after all, survived Monday night, the kick-off of the English Manor Mystery, a k a "Alas, A Sticky Wicket." Ingrid was on duty in the Police Headquarters Tent, emphatically instructed to be certain that each team received only one search warrant and warned to be suspicious of everyone, especially sturdy little old ladies with angelic expressions. Further, she was keeping a vigilant eye on the clue table. Tonight Annie intended to personally roam the Suspect Interrogation Tent to ensure that the Mystery Night detectives stayed within some bounds of reason.

After she made her brief speech introducing the suspects, she followed them and the charging crowd to the tents. She waved at Max, who was busy signing up teams to visit The Scene of the Crime, now moved to the rose arbor near the tennis court. Ingrid flapped her hands frantically. Annie started toward her. She was dodging her way around clumps of conferring detectives, when a piercing voice demanded:

"How about the real murder, Ms. Laurance? Are you snooping around?"

Walrus Mustache, beaming genially, hefted his camcorder and focused. Mother bounded forward, microphone outstretched.

Annie had often wondered what it would be like to be the cynosure of all eyes; abruptly, she knew. A hush fell, like the dead air at a hurricane's center.

"Understand you and the police chief had some words."

The intelligence-gathering capabilities of the Sticky Wicket detectives should be studied by the CIA for possible emulation.

"We have discussed the crime," she answered carefully.

"Come on, now, girl. Let us in on the real scoop."

"I don't really know very much—"

A disappointed collective sigh rose.

"—but I can tell you this much."

The quiet was absolute.

"It looks like the murderer is someone who had known Mrs. Webster very, very well." She waved her hand, smiled, and turned away. Let Chief Wells stuff that in his jaw and chew it.

She was in high good humor when she reached a besieged Ingrid and the clue table.

"Aren't there supposed to be *five* exhibits?"

She glanced down at the table, which held a train ticket, a crumpled initialed handkerchief, a Turkish cigarette stub, and a note that read *I can't come.*

She felt disgust but no real surprise. These addicts were capable of anything. "Somebody's ripped off a clue," she muttered to Ingrid. "I'll be right back." Thank heavens, she had duplicates of all the clues at the Inn. Replacement seemed simple enough, but she hadn't taken into account the limpet-like qualities of the detectives. She was accosted three times en route to the front gate, then had to struggle through the county-fair–strength crowd on Ephraim Street. This evening, the free entertainment featured a ventriloquist with a talking banana. Fortunately, the Inn was just the other side of the Benton House. She wormed through the coffee bar patrons, raced up to her room, grabbed the cast of a footprint, and hurtled back downstairs.

Idell poked her head out of the untidy office behind the counter.

"Miss Laurance, oh Miss Laurance!"

"Sorry, I'm in a hurry—"

"Miss Laurance, do the police think the person who wrote that letter to you is the same as the murderer?"

Halfway out the door and barely paying attention, she yelled back. "Maybe. Maybe not."

She replaced the pilfered clue, then began to circle unobtrusively. At least, this investigation was proceeding smoothly, although not everyone appeared enchanted with her Stately Home murder. A skinny man in black-checked trousers perilously held up by yellow suspenders snarled to a fat woman in pink tights, "This is a sissy kind of murder. As far as I'm concerned, you need a hero." He paused, then said gruffly, "Down these mean streets—" "Oh, my God," his companion groaned, "if you're going to quote Chandler . . ." Annie turned away to hide a grin. In the Interrogation Tent, Team No. 4 concentrated on the search, and its captain, a white-haired Chastain lawyer, bore down on Reginald Hoxton.

"Can you tell us how you earn your living, Mr. Hoxton?"

Sanford lolled back in his chair, a wolfish smile on his dark face. He wore a pale yellow shirt with a round white collar and pale blue slacks. It wasn't nineteen-thirtyish, but he was the epitome of a man from whom you wouldn't want to buy a used car. For the first time, Annie suspected the abrasive doctor of having a sense of humor.

"Investments," he replied airily.

"Investments in what, Mr. Hoxton?" the lawyer persisted.

"One business today, another one tomorrow."

"Perhaps your real business is taking advantage of women, Mr. Hoxton."

"Those, sir, are scurrilous words."

"Oh? Can you explain the testimony of Lady Alicia's maid? She tells us Lady Alicia owed you 3,400 pounds."

"Lies, all lies."

"Agnes tells us you have badgered her poor mistress for huge sums of money, claiming she owes them to you for losses at cards. Is this true, Mr. Hoxton?"

Smiling, Annie moved on and came up behind the circle of questioners around Agnes.

Her smile faded. Poor Lucy was obviously miserable. She sat unsmiling and rigid in her chair. Tonight she wore an attractive black-and-white silk dress and white gloves. Her face carried an unaccustomed splash of color on each cheek, and Annie knew she'd tried to use make-up to hide her pallor. Lucy listened attentively to her questioners, answering each question dutifully, but her gloved hands were clenched in her lap.

"Agnes, what exactly did you hear Mr. Nigel say to Miss Snooperton?"

Lucy glanced down at her prep cards. "It was shocking to me, sir, *that* I can tell you. Mr. Nigel was all upset. He kept saying he wanted to know how long she'd been seeing Lord Algernon on the sly. Miss Snooperton denied it had ever happened. Mr. Nigel said he wasn't going to marry anyone who would lie to him, but Miss Snooperton told him he'd given his word and she wore his ring and it would be a scandal if he broke it off. Mr. Nigel stormed away, but she called after him that she'd talk to him later, as they'd planned."

Team Captain No. 6 probed deeper. "Funny how you can see and hear so much about everyone but your mistress. Tell us now, when was the last time you saw the necklace in her possession?"

Lucy's distrait silence was perfect. Finally, she responded sharply, "I know that necklace like my own hand. I saw it that very morning. But you can't fault me for having eyes and ears, and Mr. Nigel's not telling all he knows."

A high, sharp voice urged her teammates, "Oh, let's hurry. Let's get a search warrant against Nigel Davies."

Annie would know that voice anywhere. As the team members broke into a trot, heading for the Police Investigation Tent, she called out, "Mrs. Brawley."

Slowly, reluctantly, a slight figure with a fox-sharp face paused for an instant.

Annie reached out, gripped a bony elbow. "You were here last night."

Mrs. Brawley lifted her chin defiantly. "I have a ticket tonight, too."

"That isn't fair."

"There's not a thing in the rules that says you can't come every night, if you buy a ticket." Mrs. Brawley shook free of Annie's hand. "And I bought a ticket for every single night." She darted away.

Annie stared after her.

Obviously, it was cheating. By the time she'd been on four different teams, it would be a bloody miracle if she weren't the first to figure the mystery out.

But Mrs. Brawley was right. There wasn't a single thing in the rules to prevent it.

It was not, Annie decided, a surprise that so many murders occurred, but so few.

She stalked after Mrs. Brawley and her team, and arrived in time to see the members receive their information from the search warrant on Nigel Davies.

They learned: Nigel Davies had been expected to marry his girlhood sweetheart, Susannah Greatheart, and friends had been surprised when his engagement to the worldly Miss Snooperton was announced. Nigel and Miss Snooperton had been observed quarreling, with Nigel threatening to break the engagement. The search of his room at the Manor revealed a note from Miss Greatheart, which threatened suicide if he did not return to her.

With happy clucks of anticipation, the team rumbled off en masse to return to the Suspect Interrogation tent and a session with Miss Greatheart.

Annie glanced at her watch. Nine-forty. Thank heavens, the madness would soon be over.

"Miss Laurance."

She knew that voice, too.

"Could I talk to you for a minute?"

It was politely phrased, but Bobby Frazier's tone brooked no disagreement. His face was shadowed by a tall, perfumed pittisporum shrub.

"Certainly."

He jerked his head toward the Benton House. "Let's walk over by the fence."

They found an oasis of quiet near the gate between the two houses.

In the yellowish glare of the overhead security light, he looked drawn and tired, tension lines bracketing his mouth.

"What did Gail tell you?"

Annie didn't like his peremptory tone.

"Why don't you ask her?"

Frazier swallowed jerkily. "Look, I've got to know. I've got to know what the hell is going on."

"Pick up a phone," she retorted. "Call her."

"I can't." He grabbed a bar of the fence. He should have looked inoffensive, a young man in khaki slacks and a yellow sports shirt with pencils poking out of the pocket, but he reminded Annie uncomfortably of a predator crouched to spring, every muscle taut, every nerve stretched to the highest pitch. Then, with evident effort, he smoothed out his tone. "Look, Miss Laurance, I just want to know what she told you. It's no state secret, right?"

"She told me about her talks with you the day Corinne was murdered."

His hand tightened convulsively on the bar. "You may have gotten the wrong impression."

She waited.

"Gail's a nice girl, but she's not interested in me—and I'm not interested in her."

"Oh?"

"Yeah. We're just friends. That's all."

"I guess you forgot to tell her."

He reached out, gripped her arm so tightly that Annie gasped softly. "What the hell do you mean?"

Because his tone frightened her, Annie responded fiercely. "Gail is a nice kid, Mr. Frazier. She doesn't know any better than to tell the truth, and she's telling everybody—and I'll bet that includes Chief Wells—that you didn't give a damn about her not having any money and you intended to go on seeing one another."

"Oh, shit." His fingers unloosed her, and he banged through the gate and was gone.

Annie stared after the yellow shirt until it was swallowed by the darkness. What did that mean? Nothing good for Gail. Was this a less than graceful effort by Bobby Frazier to remove himself from suspicion?

Annie sighed, turned to return to the fray, and froze. Was there a rustle in the bushes behind her? Swinging around, heart thudding, she peered into the shadows. Yes, there was movement and a dark splotch of cloth. Suddenly, she shivered. The bushes lay quiescent now. But she had glimpsed a wizened face and malevolent eyes.

Hadn't she?

With a feeling of horror, she plunged up the path toward the tents.

17

ANNIE WATCHED IN DISMAY as Max poured their coffee. "Can't you see? It's *yellow*. It's not even brown."

"We could walk down the street to the Harbor Lights. I understand they have wonderful Belgian waffles and excellent coffee."

Annie glowered down into her coffee cup. "She'd find out, then we'd never get another word out of her."

"I'm not sure she knows anything." Max's tone was reasonable.

"She *has* to. She's too nosy not to know something useful. Shh-h. Here she comes."

Idell Gordon swept into the patio, smiling in satisfaction at the crowded tables. She stopped beside Annie and Max.

"Good morning. And how are our detectives this morning?" she asked archly.

After a restless night on a lumpy mattress, a two A.M.

search for a three-inch cockroach, and a rapid approach of a crise de nerfs because of severe caffeine withdrawal, an honest reply quivered on the tip of Annie's tongue. However, she forced a grim smile and remained tactfully silent.

Max, annoyingly, rose gallantly to his feet. "Will you join us for some breakfast, Mrs. Gordon?"

"Oh, my dear boy, I've been up since dawn. A proprietor's work is never done, you know." She waved him back to his seat. Her protuberant, questing eyes dropped to the newspaper, the Wednesday edition of the *Chastain Courier*, with its screaming headlines about the investigation into Corinne's murder. "Did you notice who wrote the story?"

She didn't have to say which article.

They nodded. It was bylined to Bobby Frazier.

"What would Corinne think, if she knew?"

Considering the question rhetorical, they waited.

This morning, Idell had ill-advisedly chosen to wear a faded pink shirt and tight white polyester slacks. Neither were flattering. She stood by their table and stared down at the newspaper, her eyes shiny. "Did you see where Leighton is offering a $5,000 reward for information leading to the arrest of the killer?" She looked at them sharply. "Are you going to try for the reward?"

Max shook his head. "No. We hadn't even thought about it."

"Are you?" Annie asked.

Idell stepped back a pace, a hand at her wrinkled throat. "Oh, no, no. Of course not. How would I do that? Well, enjoy your breakfast. I must check the kitchen now," and she scuttled away.

"She has something on her mind," Annie observed,

tartly, "but it will be a cold day in hell before she tells us."

"Do you really think so?" He yawned and picked up the paper.

Annie sighed and took another sip of what purported to be coffee. "Anything new in the story?"

"A few things. Let's see, Mrs. Webster was last seen by the cook, starting down the path from the kitchen steps. That was about five o'clock. Nobody admits seeing her after that time."

Annie fished the spiral notebook out of her skirt pocket and flipped to a fresh page.

5:00—*C.W. leaves Prichard House.*

5:30—*Annie discovers body.*

She checked back at some earlier notations.

4:25—*Annie at gazebo, Gail and Bobby arrive and quarrel.*

4:30—*Bobby follows Gail, tells her to find out what happened to C.W.'s check.*

4:35—*Gail to Prichard House, calls back, quarrels with C.W.*

4:50—*Gail leaves in search of Bobby, finds him, tells him C.W. intends to block her inheritance. Gail returns to house, Bobby where?*

5:00—*C.W. leaves house. Why?*

She studied her times. "Where was Corinne going?"

"Since I don't specialize in seances, I can't tell you."

"Max, be serious. This is important. Why did Corinne leave the house? Where was she going?"

"Maybe she was ready for the start of the evening's festivities."

"It wasn't time. The gates were to open at six. So where was she hotfooting it at five?"

He put his hands behind his head and stared up at the three stories of balconies, which slanted suspiciously toward the patio. "One good earthquake and I'll bet this place collapses." At her impatient wiggle, he held up a broad hand. "I *am* pondering. Why did Corinne leave the house? Oh, offhand I can imagine at least six reasons. She wanted to come and harass you a little more. She was going to check on the arrival of the caterer. She decided it was an opportune moment to commune with nature. She had a secret lover, and they planned a rendezvous behind a yew hedge. She was on her way to Roscoe Merrill's office to deal him a little grief, or ditto Dr. Sanford. That's six, isn't it?"

"Five o'clock," she muttered. "She must have had something specific in mind. It wasn't time for the gala to start, and she'd already been on my case several times. No, this is important. We've got to find out *why* she left the house."

Chloe was small, dark, and weary. "No'm, Miss Corinne she didn't say nothin'."

Sunlight sparkled in the immaculate kitchen of Prichard House. The copper cookware above the chopping block glistened. The smell of apple pie and roasting meat hung in the air, but there was no corresponding holiday mood. Chloe was preparing food for the family after the funeral that afternoon.

She looked at them with teary eyes. "She was upset, and walking mighty swift."

"Do you think she was on her way to meet someone?"

Chloe kneaded her hands against her crisp white apron. "I don't know. She'd had too much upset. Miss Gail's a foolish girl, running after that upstart young man. She ought to have listened to Miss Corinne. And they'd fought something awful, and Miss Gail burst out of the house. Then the phone done ring."

Annie leaned forward. "Was it for Mrs. Webster?"

The little woman nodded lugubriously. "Yes'm. She said, sharp like, that her mind was made up, that's all there was to it. Then I went to the pantry. In a minute or so, that was when she left."

Max frowned. "Where was Mr. Webster while all this was going on?"

"In my study."

Leighton Webster stood in the doorway to the kitchen, his heavy face cold and unfriendly. There was no genial charm in his manner today. His powerful hands were bunched into fists at his side.

Max was always willing to try. He smiled goodhumoredly at Webster. "We're trying to discover your wife's destination when she left the house. Did you happen to hear any of her conversation on the phone?"

"I was not in the habit of eavesdropping on my wife. Furthermore, I believe the police are in a better position to ask questions such as these." His eyes flickered over them dismissively. "I understand Gail's asked you to investigate, which I consider absurd—and offensive."

"Why do you object to our trying to discover the murderer?" Annie demanded.

Leighton rubbed a hand across his cheek, then sighed heavily. "I don't know what happened." Truculence gave way to uncertainty. "I can't believe anyone would hurt Corinne intentionally, and certainly not anyone she knew. It had to be a stranger, one of those dreadful things that can happen." He looked at them in mute appeal. "Don't you agree?"

"It could be," Max said gently.

"You're going around, talking to people. Ask them if they saw any strangers."

"It wasn't a stranger."

Leighton and Max both stared at Annie.

"How could it have been?" She lifted her hands in a query. "Think about it. Corinne turned her back on the person who struck her. It *had* to be someone she knew —and didn't fear."

"I don't believe it. I'll never believe it." Leighton's voice was rough with anger.

"Why not? She'd made everybody in town mad— and how about you? After I read that letter at the Society, didn't she ask you whether you were involved with another woman?"

Annie was aware in the shocked silence that followed of Max's incredulous glance and of Leighton's sudden immobility.

She'd prodded a raw wound. There was no righteous anger of the innocent.

He made no answer at all, but looked past them, as if they weren't there, misery and heartbreak in his eyes. Then, without a word, he turned and stumbled blindly from the room.

Annie and Max were silent as they headed down the back steps of Prichard House. They started down the path toward the pond.

"Poor bastard."

"I know. I'm sorry," she said defensively.

"That's all right. God knows he should be at the top of Wells's list."

"Except Wells can't see past the fact that he's mayor." Annie scuffed through a covering of pine needles.

"Do you suppose he did it?"

Reaching up, she grabbed a crinkly handful of Spanish moss. "His insistence on the mysterious stranger makes me wonder."

They came up on the gazebo. Beyond it the pond lay placid and blackish-green without a breath of breeze to stir the reeds. Their footsteps echoed in the morning air as they climbed the steps. They sat down on the wooden benches, and Annie stared glumly at the place where Corinne's body had lain.

"It makes a hell of a lot of difference whether somebody got mad at her and serendipitously picked up the club and swung, or whether somebody lured her down here with murder in mind."

"Why?" Max asked.

"A difference in the kind of person. Take Leighton Webster for example. I can't imagine him plotting a murder in advance. He's too much of a gentleman. But if he got mad, and there was a weapon handy—"

"Why would he be quarreling with her at the pond? They had that enormous house to quarrel in."

Annie shot him an appraising glance. "I think you're sorry for him. Maybe Leighton had just asked her for a divorce, and she'd said no deal, he couldn't have one. Chloe may have been mistaken about the phone; maybe Corinne was talking to Leighton. She was mad, so she stalked out to take a walk. He went after her, found her at the pond, they continued fighting, and whammo."

"Maybe," Max said doubtfully, scuffing the dust with his shoe tip. "That would be unpremeditated, but I think the murder was planned to the last detail. Somebody knew that mallet would be here, called Corinne, and talked her into a meeting. That's how I see it."

She tapped her fingers impatiently on the arm of the bench. "What we need is some clever analysis of our suspects. Kate Fansler *always* figures out how everybody's mind works."

"I'm agreeable, whoever Ms. Fansler may be. What do you suggest?"

"Some tête à têtes."

Edith Ferrier reluctantly invited them inside and led the way to a side piazza. Cheerful red and black cushions made the white wicker furniture comfortable. A partially completed yellow afghan lay atop a wicker coffee table.

She gestured for them to sit on a divan and took her place opposite in a straight chair. She looked at them unsmiling, her heavily mascaraed jade green eyes wary. "I don't know why you want to talk to me." Her chin gave an infinitesimal backward jerk.

Here, you couldn't hear the tourists. Bees droned in the honeysuckle that nuzzled the verandah balustrade. Swallowtail butterflies flitted near a blossoming dogwood with white flowers as brilliant as a snowy peak. The manicured garden, though much smaller than those of the show houses, was April perfection, but the tension on the porch was thick enough to cut.

"We're talking to everyone who had a motive to kill Corinne." Annie knew it was the equivalent of a flung gauntlet, but why not?

Again, that nervous tic, but Edith kept her awkwardly rouged face impassive. "That doesn't include me."

Annie continued on the attack. "You were the clubwoman mentioned in the letter."

"No one can prove that." Her fingers nervously worked the pleats in her navy silk skirt.

"It's obvious. And you admitted on Monday, when Corinne was deviling you, that she'd kept you from being president of the Society."

Edith picked up the afghan and began to crochet, her eyes intent on the flashing hook.

"I am busy with a number of organizations. Certainly, I can find plenty of opportunities to fill my time, and there are many in Chastain who appreciate my efforts."

Before Annie could speak again, Max knocked his knee against hers and smiled winningly at Edith. "Actually, I've been looking forward to our chance to visit with you."

The crochet hook eased to a stop.

"Since Annie and I are strangers, we have to depend upon others for information about Chastain and the people who knew Corinne. As a mainstay in the city's power structure, it seems to me that you are an invaluable resource with your contacts, and, even more importantly, that you are singularly well qualified because of your extensive volunteer work to be able to look past the obvious and give us real insight into personalities."

Annie would have gagged except for the magical effect of this honeyed flow upon Edith. She was settling back into her chair, the afghan draped loosely over her lap, and a faint flush of pleasure stained her powdered cheeks. "I've dealt with all kinds of people over the years, Mr. Darling, and, let me tell you, I can see through a false face pretty quick."

Max beamed at her. "I knew you were the right person to talk to."

Annie might as well have been invisible. She stifled a malicious urge to give a piercing whistle.

Max's voice was as smooth as chocolate mousse. "Tell us about the Board members. What are they really like? And who do you think wrote the letter?"

Edith's face sharpened, like a hawk preparing to

dive. "You're right, of course." Her voice was more animated than Annie had ever heard it. "It must have been done by a Board member. And I think I know which one."

She paused and received the attention she sought. "I think Gail wrote it."

"Gail!" Annie's voice rose. Max nudged her again, harder.

"You can only push any living creature so far. Corinne was killing that girl, crushing the life out of her." Edith's voice vibrated with emotion.

"Would Gail know all of the things in the letter?" Max asked.

Edith moved her hands impatiently, jangling her silver charm bracelet. "Of course, she would. She lived in that house. And everyone in town knows how Corinne and John Sanford were wrangling over the hospital funds, and about Tim's paintings and Sybil." She paused, and a frown drew her carefully lined brows down. "I don't know about Roscoe, though. I had heard a few whispers, something about some young woman lawyer in Atlanta. I suppose if I'd heard, Gail could have heard." She tossed her head and her red-gold hair rippled. "It's like Gail, though. A weak person pushed to attack and doing it secretly."

"So you don't think John or Roscoe were likely to have written the letter?" Max persisted.

Edith didn't dismiss them outright. "Oh, I don't think so. It's too calm and studied for John. As for Roscoe—actually, Roscoe is a very complex man. You rarely know what Roscoe is thinking; he keeps his own counsel. He seems so dry, such a stick, but I don't think he really is. He's absolutely crazy about Jessica. That's why I thought that story about a girl in Atlanta might be false—but he did seem upset when you read the letter. I was watching him, and his face went absolutely livid for a minute. So I can't imagine that he would have written it."

"Unless that was a particularly clever double bluff," Max suggested.

"What would that achieve?" Edith asked reasonably. "No, I can see where John and Roscoe would have the necessary knowledge, but they both seem unlikely."

"How about Lucy? She's an old Chastainian," Max observed.

Edith nodded. "Oh, yes, she is. And I've heard, too, that Corinne ruined her romance with Cameron. But that was a long time ago. Isn't it a little late to try for revenge? So far as I know, they were on the best of terms. In fact, I guess Lucy was about Corinne's only friend."

"How about Sybil?" Annie ignored Max's involuntary wriggle and concentrated on Edith.

"Sybil." Edith dropped the name like a pound of butter in boiling chocolate. "Ah yes. Sybil."

For the first time in their acquaintance, Annie saw a glint of humor in those huge green eyes.

"I'd like to think it was Sybil. Everyone believes Sybil capable of anything outrageous, but frankly it would take too much time and be much too subtle for her." Her mouth curved in a sardonic smile, admiration mixed with disgust. "If you dumped Sybil in the middle of the Sahara, there would be a half dozen sheikhs there within the day. There's something about her—"

Max opened his mouth, intercepted Annie's glare, and wisely remained silent.

"She sends out signals," Annie said dryly.

Max opted for a diversion. He ticked them off on his

fingers. "So, John's too abrupt, Roscoe's too careful, Lucy's too unlikely, Sybil's too—impetuous. You think it's Gail."

"I'm afraid so."

But Annie was shaking her head. "You're both wrong. It's obvious as it can be. Miss Dora wrote that letter."

To her surprise, Edith was adamant. "Oh no, she wouldn't do that. No, you have to understand Miss Dora. She's devoted heart and soul to Chastain, to its history, its traditions. Nothing matters as much to her as Family. She wouldn't do anything to harm the Society."

"Just strangers she sees as a threat," Annie muttered. "Like me."

Annie wasn't enchanted about their next interview, but she realized it was necessary.

It didn't improve her humor to see one of Miss Dora's placards posted on the main entry gate.

"The present structure, built in 1833, is the third home at this site. It is Chastain's oldest surviving Greek Revival home. (The Prichard House on Ephraim Street was built in 1834.) The first home at this location was built by Chastain's founder, Reginald Cantey Chastain, and the property remains in the Chastain family to the present day. The younger son of an English settler in the Barbadoes, Chastain established the settlement which bears his name in June of 1730. Of an energetic and adventurous nature, he came to the province of Carolina at the age of 23 years and, within five years, amassed a fortune to compare with those of the factors in Charleston. He was a well-built man, standing almost six foot tall with curly chestnut hair and eyes of the palest green. He was married to Anna Margaret Hasty on January 9, 1736, and they had five sons, Thomas, Nathaniel, William, Percival, and Harold."

Reginald was probably a rapacious swashbuckler. Sybil no doubt came by her appetites honestly. Heredity, Annie decided, was an awesome force. She glanced up at Max, who was striding eagerly toward the marble steps, his dark blue eyes gleaming with anticipation. Perhaps she should give some thought to Mendelian truths before September.

Max poked the doorbell, then bent down to whisper. "Look, honey, why don't you let me handle this one?"

"Are you suggesting that I lack tact?"

"Mmmm," he said, displaying his own exceptional perceptiveness, "let's just say, I think this one needs a man's touch."

"Ooh-la-la," she hissed as the door opened.

Annie immediately felt like a pile of sunbleached bones. Today Sybil wore red. Flaming red. A red that rivaled that of the San Francisco fire. She was riveting in a linen dress that most women would categorize as skimpy even while recognizing a Bill Blass original and lusting in their hearts. Whether for the dress or a little of Sybil's panache, it would be hard to say. Who else but Sybil, at her age and voluptuous state, could look magnificent in a dress that ended three inches above the knee? When she turned to lead the way down the hall, navigating on four-inch red leather heels, the curving hem rose high in the back, revealing more leg than a rack of lamb. She managed to overshadow even the spectacular length of hallway with three intricately patterned oriental rugs and a spectacular four-tiered crystal chandelier.

Sybil led the way to the library. The Pompeian red walls certainly provided a dramatic backdrop for her raven black hair, Annie thought cynically. She dropped into a Queen Anne wing chair with embossed creamy satin upholstery and waved them negligently toward a Chinese rosewood couch with scrolled back and arms. As they sat, Sybil deftly fitted an extra-long menthol-tipped cigarette into an ivory holder, lit it, and blew a cloud of minty smoke. She gestured at a heap of brightly colored brochures and magazines spread across the mahogany Sheraton drum table.

"I've had the most marvelous day." Her throaty voice was as mellifluous as the warble of feasting doves. "Trying to decide just how the exhibition folder should look." At their blank silence, she crossed one silk-clad leg over a knee, and jounced her foot impatiently, exposing a well-endowed thigh. "Timmy's New York exhibition, of course." Her crimson lips curved in open amusement. "What's wrong, sweeties? Do I seem to lack a funeral air?" She shrugged, and Annie sourly noticed that the dress also provided ample view of fulsome breasts. "Don't worry, I'll be at the funeral. But I don't believe in crocodile tears. And, certainly, it does solve a problem for us."

"Have you expressed this sentiment to Chief Wells?" Annie inquired.

She tapped the cigarette in a silver ashtray. "Oh, he won't bother me," she said carelessly. Her eyes, as black as licorice, swept Annie, but with as little interest as an electronic eye in an elevator. "I was talking to Leighton. He told me Wells is after you. Or that reporter."

"Hasn't Wells even talked to you?" Annie demanded, feeling her cheeks heat. "Doesn't he know how you and Corinne were feuding about Tim's paintings?"

"I don't know." Her indifference was monumental.

"Now, let me ask you, don't you think two paintings per page at the most?" She reached out and picked up a brochure. "Here's a good one from a recent sale at Sotheby's. What do you think of this format?"

Annie would have exploded, except for the viselike grip Max wisely planted on her wrist. She swallowed angrily, and glared at him. He'd pay for this—later.

"Sybil, I know you don't think it's too important," Max said smoothly. "But we're trying to account for everyone's whereabouts at the time of the murder. Can you tell us what you were doing?"

Those pit-black eyes moved to Max, lingered on his face, moved slowly down his body.

"What you were doing," he repeated stoically.

"Oh sure." She smiled, and this one was X-rated. "Sure. I was making Timmy feel better." She put the cigarette holder in her mouth. "We were upstairs in my room. For a long time."

Annie was still seething as they fought their way up the marble steps to the double, fourteen-foot-tall bronze doors that marked the entrance to the Prichard Museum. It was slow going because everyone else was herding down the steps. When an elbow cuffed her in the ribs, Annie snarled, "Hey, watch where you're going!" "Honey," a soft voice soothed, "you're goin' the wrong *way*. There won't be another magic show for twenty minutes." But, finally, a bit battered, they reached the doors, and Max pulled one open. They stepped into a magnificent rotunda, and Annie was delighted to see only a sprinkling of tourists. She was, all things considered, getting tired of tourists, no matter how many t-shirts they bought from the Death on Demand display.

Sunlight sparkled through the stained-glass dome, illuminating the glass cases that sat around the perimeter of the circular room. Annie paused by the first one, which contained a silver-plated reproduction of a silver trivet created in 1763 by a London artisan. Other cases held reproductions of authentic colonial pieces, including candlesticks, doorknobs, wall sconces, and bookends. A neatly printed card in the corner of each case announced: *Replicas created by Tim Bond, artist-in-residence, Prichard Museum, Chastain, S.C.*

A brisk young woman greeted them eagerly. "I see you are interested in our reproductions." Perhaps they were a welcome change from the magic devotees. "Prichard Museum is famous for the quality and quantity of its reproductions, and, in the bookstore, we have a catalog which lists all of our offerings. If you would like to tour the Museum, tickets are two dollars each. The Prichard Museum was built in 1843 as a meeting place for the Chastain Thursday Night Club. As you can see, it is built on three levels, and the supporting columns are Doric on this floor, Ionic on the next, and Corinthian on the third. The ballroom is on the second floor and is still used today for the winter balls."

"We would love to see the Museum," Annie said, "but today we've come to see Tim Bond. If you can direct us to his office . . ."

"Oh, certainly. This way." She led them through the bookstore in an ornate sideroom to a back hallway. "Tim's office is in the basement. Now, these stairs are dreadful. Watch your step as you go down. The offices are to your right." She opened the door, and the faraway bang of a hammer echoed up the stairwell.

Annie led the way and was glad of the advice. The steps pitched so steeply that she had to cling to the metal banister for balance. A light dangled from a cord at the landing. Unshaded bulbs hung in various parts of the basement, providing brilliant circles of light that emphasized the dark reaches between them. The rhythmic thud of the hammer masked the sound of their footsteps on the cement floor. They passed a door labeled Darkroom and a second one with Curator stenciled on it. A third door, a dingy yellow, bore a placard with the warning POISON. Tables and workbenches paralleled the corridor. At the far end of the basement, Tim Bond stood beside a cluttered workbench, driving nails into the ends of a crate. The light here was very bright, a circle of yellow against the blackness of the cellar's recesses.

"Hello, there," Max called out.

For an instant, those narrow shoulders stiffened, then he turned and faced them, hammer in hand. The harsh light bleached the color from his gaunt face. In silence, he watched them approach. He wore a paint-spattered shirt and frayed cut-offs. His sea-green eyes had a wild look, like a horse ready to bolt. He shifted from one big foot to the other.

"What do you want?"

"We just wanted to visit with you a little," Max said soothingly. "What are you working on?"

Tim sniffed around the question as if expecting a trap, then answered sullenly. "I'm crating my paintings, getting them ready to go to New York."

Annie twisted to look at the canvases lined up in a neat row. "That's pretty important to you, isn't it?"

"Any reason why it shouldn't be?"

"Was it important enough for you to kill Corinne?" Annie asked abruptly.

His Adam's apple jerked in his throat. "Hell, no." But his voice was shrill.

"You were mad at her. She wasn't going to let you go

to New York. She was sending your paintings on a tour."

Tim licked his lips. "It would've been all right. Sybil was going to make her give me my stuff."

"How could she do that?" Max asked.

His eyes slid away, focused on the white pine board. "I dunno." He lifted the hammer, slammed the nail in solidly.

Annie raised her voice. "Where were you when Corinne was killed?"

He stood very still, hunched over the crate, then, with a look of great cunning, said, "How should I know? I don't even know when she was killed."

"Don't you read the paper?" Max asked.

The big head swung toward him. "Why should I? I don't care."

So much, Annie thought, for rapport between patroness and artist.

"Where were you between 5 and 5:30?" she asked briskly.

"Oh. Here and there," he said vaguely. "I don't pay much attention to time. I don't even own a watch."

A telephone jangled behind him. He reached out a big hand to pick up the receiver. "Yeah." His pale eyes flickered from Max to Annie, then his face reddened, until his skin was scarlet to the roots of his soft, curly hair. "Oh, yeah. They're here. Okay."

He hung up, then glared at them defiantly. "I was with Sybil. I was with Sybil the whole time."

Annie pulled the booth door shut, which immediately made it airless and hot, but there was too much noise from the parade proceeding up Federal to the accompaniment of a rousing "Stars and Stripes Forever" to leave it cracked. While she waited for Gail to come to the phone, she entertained herself by admiring Max's sun-touched profile through the smudged window.

"Hello?"

"Hi, Gail. This is Annie. I'm sorry to bother you, but there's something we really need to know."

The tiny sigh on the other end said more clearly than words that Gail was disappointed in the caller. Hadn't she talked to Bobby yet?

"What can I do for you?"

"Who is Leighton involved with?"

Now the silence tingled with dismay.

"I know," Annie continued quickly. "You don't want to say. I understand that. But we have to talk to everyone concerned—and believe me, it's up to me and Max. Chief Wells isn't talking to *anybody* but me and Bobby."

"Oh, God." Silence again, then a hoarse, unhappy whisper, "Peggy Taylor. She teaches at Chastain High."

18

THE SWIMMER KICKED a steady four beats per stroke, and her elbows came high as her hands knifed cleanly into the water. At each end of the pool, she made swift, nicely executed flip turns.

Annie waited patiently beside the diving board. The water glinted satiny green beneath the overhead lights, and the heavy smell of chlorine hung in the still, moist air. The high school secretary had directed her to the pool. "Miss Taylor works out at noon every day, but she won't be finished yet."

The swimmer neared the deep end, but instead of flipping, she surfaced and clung to the rim. Shaking her hair back, she glanced around the deserted pool, then up at Annie. "Are you waiting for me?"

"Yes. I'd like to talk to you for a minute, Ms. Taylor."

She pulled herself up and out of the pool, without

apparent effort. She had a swimmer's body, lean, firm, and shapely.

A woman more different from Corinne Webster would be hard to imagine.

Peggy Taylor moved with the unselfconscious grace of a superbly conditioned athlete. Her Lycra racing suit revealed high breasts, a narrow waist, slim hips. She pulled off her goggles, looked curiously at Annie, then held out a firm hand. "Peggy Taylor."

Annie shook her hand. "Annie Laurance."

"What can I do for you?"

"You know Leighton Webster."

Peggy's face closed, became carefully blank. "Yes."

"You know, of course, that his wife was murdered."

"Why have you come to see me? I didn't know Mrs. Webster." Her voice was even and colorless.

"But people say you knew him very well indeed."

"People be damned." She stared at Annie, her tanned face set and stiff.

"Do you think he could kill his wife?"

"No." Her voice was harsh; the denial was explosive. But her gray-blue eyes were full of fear. She slapped a hand against the webbing on the board. "That's absurd. Leighton isn't that kind of man. He's gentle and kind and honorable."

"Have you spoken to him since Monday?"

"No." She looked away from Annie, stared down at the water lapping against the lane ropes.

"When did you last talk to him?"

She didn't want to answer that question. Her reluctance quivered between them. Finally, grudgingly, she said, "A week or so ago. I don't know exactly."

"Had you quarreled?"

"Oh, go to hell," Peggy cried. She grabbed up her towel and stalked away.

"Where were you Monday afternoon?" Annie called after her.

The slim figure paused. For a moment, Annie was certain she would not answer, but then Peggy Taylor looked back. "In a bloody faculty meeting that ran late." Then she headed swiftly toward the girls' locker room.

Annie stopped at a pay phone in the main hall of Chastain High and dialed the Prichard House again.

It took a minute, but Leighton Webster came on the line.

"Mr. Webster, I just talked to Peggy."

There was a sharply indrawn breath. "Miss Laurance, I find that an unwarranted intrusion in my life."

"I have just one question. What happened the last time you saw her?"

"She didn't tell you? No, I don't suppose she would. Actually, Miss Laurance, it might interest you to know that she told me of her future plans. She has joined the Peace Corps. Peggy's leaving Chastain when school ends next month."

Even the cheery smell of pipe smoke and the club comfort of the richly padded brown leather armchair couldn't offset Roscoe Merrill's icy reception.

"Mr. Darling, I don't appreciate your telling my secretary you wished to see me about a murder. That kind of loose description can give rise to heated imaginings."

"I assumed your secretary was discreet."

A dull flush rose to Merrill's cheeks. "She is, of

course. Nonetheless . . . Well, you're here. What do you want?"

"Where were you at five o'clock Monday?"

"Here."

"With a client?"

"I'm not too sure of the time. Perhaps. But I may have been working on a will."

"Don't you keep time slips?"

Wariness flickered in Merrill's hooded eyes. "Of course. I could check them."

"Why don't you?"

"I will—for the properly constituted authority."

Obviously, Max didn't qualify, and, equally obvious, Merrill had no intention of being helpful.

"Anything else, Mr. Darling?"

Max decided Annie's rhinocerous approach sometimes had its good points. He stretched out comfortably in the enfolding softness of the leather chair. "Just one thing. Does your wife know you're involved with another woman?"

"That isn't true!"

There was a ring of sincerity in the pronouncement that brought Max up short.

Merrill sat like a bronze Buddha behind his desk.

"Then why was Corinne threatening to tell her that you were?"

Merrill began to roll a pen in his fingers, his eyes seemingly intent on the leisurely revolution.

Max pressed ahead. "You can't deny you were the lawyer mentioned in that letter."

The pen moved faster.

"The letter made it clear Corinne intended to tell the lawyer's wife."

Merrill's chair creaked as he leaned back and stared up at the beamed ceiling. "For the sake of argument—

and I wish to make it clear that this constitutes no admission of any kind—but just for the sake of argument, let's talk for a moment about the lawyer mentioned in that letter. You will remember the letter indicated Corinne felt the lawyer's wife had a right to know of an incident?"

Max nodded.

"Corinne believed one act of unfaithfulness should be reported to his wife, no matter how happy the marriage in question. Now, this lawyer—" he paused and the muscles worked in his jaws—"has a marriage everyone envies—and rightly so." He gave Max a considering glance. "I would imagine it is the kind of marriage you hope someday to have with Miss Laurance."

Max felt a tightness in his chest. That dry, unemotional voice and, beneath it, a passionate caring.

Merrill threw down the pen and looked past Max at the painting of the wood ibis. "That kind of marriage is made up of many things. It's made up of love and passion and friendship and laughter—and trust. That lawyer's wife has always trusted him implicitly, and rightly so." Merrill rubbed the side of his face. "Now, let's talk for a moment about that lawyer. He's middle-aged, and he's always been faithful to his wife. He's involved in a lawsuit in Atlanta. There's a young woman lawyer, a rather lusty, hungry young woman lawyer, representing a co-defendant in the case. They work together very closely for several months, and he's quite aware that she is available. He isn't interested." Now he paused and took a deep breath. "Unfortunately, he's human. The night the case is won, they return to the hotel, he has too much to drink—and the young woman lawyer—"

Max waited.

Merrill's mouth turned down in a humorless smile. "Of course, it is an uncanny fact of life that you always see someone you know when it is least convenient. In this case, Corinne was staying at the same hotel." He picked up the pen again, balanced it in his palm. "The lawyer was unfaithful to his wife. On any serious level, it is meaningless, which his wife would both understand and appreciate. On another level, the knowledge of this incident would destroy that absolute trust." His hand closed convulsively around the pen. "It would not destroy a marriage, Mr. Darling, but it would blemish what has been perfection." Merrill cleared his throat. "As you must appreciate, keeping this incident secret is important to this lawyer. Yet, I think you would agree that preventing his wife from learning of this stupidity would scarcely warrant murder."

Annie caught up with Max as he was turning into the yellow stucco building where Dr. John Sanford had offices on the third floor.

On the way upstairs, she told him about Peggy and Leighton. "Don't you see? She must have given him an ultimatum. Get a divorce, or she would leave town."

As they reached the third floor landing, Max observed reasonably, "This is the 1980s. Why not just get the divorce?"

"Maybe he's too honorable."

"Is it more honorable to bash in your wife's head?" He opened the office door.

Even empty, the rectangular waiting room had a cramped appearance. Cheap plastic straight chairs were wedged around three walls, and tattered copies of *Sports Illustrated*, *Guideposts*, *Reader's Digest*, and *Mc-Call's* were stacked on a chrome-edged coffee table. A rustle of papers beyond the untenanted counter indicated someone was present.

Max punched the bell on the formica-topped counter.

A sweet-faced nurse with thick glasses poked her carefully-coiffed head out of an adjoining room. "Sorry. Doctor doesn't hold office hours on Wednesday afternoons."

Max leaned on the counter. "He's here, isn't he? They told me at the hospital I could catch him here."

"Yes, but he doesn't hold—"

"Tell him Max Darling and Annie Laurance want to talk to him about Corinne Webster's murder."

She raised an eyebrow, then withdrew into the adjoining room. In a moment, she returned and gestured for them to come through the swinging door.

Sanford was in his office, which overlooked the cobblestoned alley.

"No Wednesday afternoon golf, Doctor?" Max asked.

Sanford ignored the pleasantry, and looked at them with cold, brooding eyes. He looked capable, confident, and controlled. If he had a bedside manner, he kept it under wraps.

"I'm busy," he said brusquely. "What do you want?"

Annie pointed at the window behind him, which framed a portion of the McIlwain House and the Prichard grounds. "Did you happen to look out that way Monday afternoon?"

He shrugged his thin shoulders impatiently. "I've got better things to do than stand at my window."

Max took it up. "What were you doing at five on Monday?"

Sanford beat a silent tattoo on his desktop with his

right hand. "Finishing up patient folders for the afternoon."

"In here? By yourself?"

"Right."

"Can anybody vouch for that?"

His chilly eyes moved toward Annie. "I was here
when Leighton called."

"That was at five-thirty." Max didn't amplify, but
the implication was clear enough.

For the first time, a smile touched that swarthy, intense face. "Plenty of time to meet Corinne, bang her
over the head, and get back here. Is that what you
mean?" His laughter was a cynical bark. "Actually, I'd
liked to have strangled her a hundred times, but they
don't include justified homicide in the Hippocratic
oath."

"Why did you want to strangle her?" Max asked,
with the politeness a dozen governesses had instilled
in him.

"Did you ever deal with Corinne?" Disgust
weighted Sanford's voice. "God, that woman. The
brains of a flea, and the tenacity of a leech. And selfish!
All she thought about was the Prichard name, the
Prichard House, the Prichard Museum, and, God forbid, the Prichard Hospital. She figured it was some
kind of personal fiefdom just because her precious
great-grandfather founded it. Do you know what she
wanted to spend money for?" He slammed his hand
on his desk, and papers slewed. "A restoration of the
lobby to its original state in 1872. Jesus. And when I
wanted to increase the hours for outpatient consulta-
tions . . ." His eyes glittered. "Stupid, bloody bitch."

"If you felt that way about restorations, why are you
on the Board of the Historical Preservation Society?"

He looked at Annie as though he ranked her intellect

on a level with Corinne's. "This is a small town. A damn small town in the South." His voice capitalized it. "It's a pain in the ass, but you have to play the game to get along with people. And the game in Chastain is historical preservation."

"Why come here? You could have set up a practice somewhere else, couldn't you?"

For a moment, the anger and irritation left his face, replaced by eagerness. "Oh no, I couldn't go anywhere else. This is one of the best places in the world to study parasitic diseases. I came here to work with Byron Fisher." He looked at them expectantly, but when the famous name didn't impress them, his face wrinkled in disgust. "Why, we've got research underway here that isn't duplicated anywhere." His eyes alight with excitement, he drew sketches, cited tables, described his laboratory.

"Was this part of your work at the hospital?"

Once again, his face reformed into an angry glower. "Certainly. It was understood when I came."

"Was Corinne in favor of this use of the facilities?"

"What do you think?" His snort was contemptuous. "But I would've gotten my way."

"Was she trying to block your plans?"

Sanford leaned back, placed his supple hands flat on the chair arms. "Oh, yeah. But I have a way of winning." Then his mouth twisted in a sardonic smile. "Without resorting to murder."

Max fastidiously averted his eyes from Annie's chili dog and root beer. They'd made two stops for lunch. One at the hot dog stand for her order, the second at a seafood restaurant for his shrimp and crab salad and Bud Light. There wasn't a spare foot of space along the bluff, so they finally ate standing up at the corner of Lookout Point, then dashed across Ephraim to the Inn. There was just time to change for the funeral.

Every seat was taken at St. Michael's. Annie realized anew how important a figure Corinne had been in Chastain. The family sat in the first pew on the lesson side of the aisle, looking rigidly ahead. Gail sat between Lucy and Miss Dora. The priest made no mention of murder as he intoned the stately funeral service from the Book of Common Prayer, but Annie sensed a peculiar undercurrent in the sanctuary. Instead of the usual quiet reverence that underscores an Episcopal service, she felt an unmistakable air of tension, a mixture of grief, fear, and pernicious curiosity. As they rose for the recessional, and the pallbearers walked up the aisle beside the casket covered by the silk funeral pall, sidelong glances followed its progress, then turned toward the family. Was it her imagination or was there almost a tiny pool of space around each person who had been associated with Corinne?

After the final prayer, Leighton took Gail's elbow as they left the pew. Lucy and Miss Dora came after them. Lucy pressed a gloved hand to her mouth. Miss Dora stumped up the aisle, her wrinkled face as dark and unreadable as mahogany.

Annie spotted Roscoe, his eyes downcast, his balding head bent. Jessica held his arm tightly. Edith Ferrier stared straight ahead, her face solemn. Tim Bond yanked at his collar, making his tie hang in disarray. Sybil strode forward as if she couldn't leave the church soon enough.

Out in the bright afternoon sunlight, the mourners— or those who had attended the funeral—began to drift toward the bright striped tent that marked the open grave. Corinne, of course, would be laid to rest in the graveyard, which held dead kinsmen back to Morris and Elizabeth Prichard, who died of yellow fever in 1766. A gap opened in the crowd for the family to pass through. Once again, Annie pondered the kind and quality of the sidelong glances directed at Leighton Webster.

Edith stopped beside Annie and Max. "My God, doesn't Lucy look awful."

Lucy's thin face was gray with faint splotches of make-up high on her jutting cheekbones and a thin red line of lipstick on her mouth. Her cheeks were sunken; her navy blue silk dress hung on her. She carried a prayer book in gloved hands that trembled. Her eyes followed the casket, but every step seemed an effort.

"I can't believe she's taking it so hard."

"They were friends for a long time, weren't they" Max asked.

Edith fell into step with them. "Oh, sure. They grew up together. But if that old story's true, she ought to clap her hands at Corinne's demise. I'll tell you, if somebody'd ruined the love of my life, I wouldn't count her as a friend."

That old story. Annie glanced across the crowded churchyard and caught another glimpse of Lucy, who did indeed look dreadful. Then she glanced at Edith, whose dark brows were drawn in a tight frown. No, Lucy and Edith weren't cut from the same cloth. Unlike Lucy, Edith would be a good hater.

"Oh, Lord." Now Edith's tone was sympathetic.

Peggy Taylor would be a standout in any crowd because of the aura of health and vigor that she carried with her. She was especially noticeable today, waiting in the shade of a weeping willow near a mossy gravestone, just beyond the path. When Leighton Webster, walking heavily, came even with her, he paused for an instant. He lifted his hand. There was an open hunger in his eyes.

She stared at him, her eyes aching with questions.

Then it was over, the moment gone, as he moved on, walking toward the gravesite, ignoring the crowd's murmurs.

Peggy Taylor looked after him. Her face crumpled. She held a handkerchief to her mouth and turned and walked swiftly away.

"She's afraid he's guilty. Poor devil."

Annie wondered who Edith was calling a poor devil. Leighton—or Peggy?

"And look there."

Annie looked past Max. Bobby Frazier stood at the edge of the crowd, his eyes on Gail's slender figure. And what did his gaze hold? It was hard to know, but she felt certain she saw a jumble of emotions and an agony of indecision. He took a step forward, as if to walk to Gail. Gail looked up, saw him, and her face brightened.

He took one step toward her, then swung around, head down, and walked away.

"WASN'T IT A LOVELY funeral?" Idell's froglike eyes glistened with pleasure. She still wore her funeral dress, a shiny black polyester. She leaned on the Inn counter, obviously eager to talk.

Lovely? How lovely is it to watch lives disintegrating from the pressures of public and private suspicion?

"Everyone came," Idell prattled on. "Corinne would have been pleased."

Certainly Idell was. She radiated good humor, and something more. Excitement? Anticipation?

How much did Idell know about her recently deceased neighbor and those who hated her? Swallowing her distaste, Annie leaned on the counter, too. "Mrs. Gordon, I'd *love* to have your opinion on this case. You know these people *so* well. You must have a great deal of insight into who Corinne's enemies really were."

The landlady bridled with pleasure. "I know a lot

about people, that I can tell you. Why, you'd be surprised what you learn running an inn. Why, people can be just dreadful!"

Annie lowered her voice. "Now, just between us, what do you think about Mayor Webster?"

"Oh, poor Leighton. She led that man around like he had a ring through his nose. I thought it served her right when he took up with that Miss Taylor. Met her out on his walks."

"Do you think he would have asked for a divorce?"

For an instant, genuine sympathy gleamed in those shiny brown eyes. "I would have hoped so, but Leighton always was such a gentleman. Even the way things are today, everybody getting divorced, I don't believe he could have brought himself to do it. Poor Leighton."

Was he too much of a gentleman to murder his wife?

"But Leighton didn't do it. I'm sure of it."

There was such a ring of confidence in her voice, Annie looked at her in surprise.

Idell's gaze fell away in confusion, and she began to rearrange the drooping daffodils in the tarnished holder next to the telephone. "These flowers. Must see to them. It's better to have fresh every day."

Feeling that her prey was slipping away, Annie plunged ahead. "And you knew Corinne as well as anyone."

Idell was suddenly less absorbed in the flowers.

"Oh, yes, of course. Known her forever!"

"How did she seem the last time you spoke to her?"

"She was *impossible*. No wonder she got murdered." Idell yanked viciously at a dead bloom. "Always trying to cause trouble. She said the Board was going to have to bring me into court if I didn't shore up the fence between the Inn and the Society Building. Claimed it was unsightly for visitors. Well, why couldn't the Society help? I need every penny I can get to keep the Inn going, with utilities going up every year and people using air conditioners even in April. I told her I couldn't do it, and I didn't have the money to go to court. Oh, she was a mean person."

"I guess it did make it hard, having the common boundary with the Society."

Idell looked at her gratefully. "Well, you run a business. You can understand. And the Inn is all I have." There was a note of fear in her voice, the spectre of old age and no money and all her assets gone. But there wasn't the least bit of concern about her quarrel with Corinne. Obviously, Idell didn't see herself as a potential suspect. So scratch that dark horse.

A sudden thought struck Annie. "You're right next door to the Society. Did you happen to look out that way—" She paused and thought. "It was one of three nights in the middle of March that we think the letter was typed next door. The nights of March 19th, 20th, and 21st. I don't suppose you saw anyone going in or coming out of the building after hours?"

Idell's eyes slid away from Annie. Then she shook her head vigorously. "No. But I remember the middle of March." She touched her jaw. "Oh, I had an awful toothache."

Annie stood in the middle of the room, holding the large cylinder of cardboard that contained the five Death on Demand mystery prints, and checked to see if she'd forgotten anything. Max had already taken down the stacks of mimeographed sheets with the Mystery Night information, the autopsy report, the suspects' original statements to police, and the clue box. She was walking toward the door when the phone rang.

"Hello."

"Miss Laurance."

Chief Wells's voice reminded her of gravel being dumped from a truck. Annie gripped the receiver tightly and knew her voice was strained when she answered. "Yes, Chief?"

"Got a tip on the murder."

She waited.

"Got a waiter here from a restaurant over on Broward's Rock. Says he thinks he's got a description of the killer. Cute blonde about twenty-three or so, gray eyes, good figure."

"Oh, now wait a minute—"

The heavy voice rumbled over her protest like a steamroller squashing rocks. "Know what he overheard? Girl said she'd decided to bash the lady with a croquet mallet."

"I was talking about the Mystery Nights plot," she said furiously.

"So you admit that's what you said?"

Annie phrased it very carefully indeed. "On the occasion in question, I was describing to Mr. Darling the means by which the mythical murderer in the mythical Sticky Wicket murder intended to attack a *mythical* victim."

He wheezed loudly. "So you say."

"So I say."

"You'll be at the Prichard House tonight?"

"I'm not fleeing to Timbuktu, if that's what you're asking."

There was a long pause, and she thought she detected the juicy mastication of a tobacco wad. She wondered if there were a Mrs. Wells.

"Smart ass talk won't get you far, young lady."

"I understand you haven't even bothered to talk to Sybil Giacomo and Tim Bond."

His voice scraped like flint on a fire rock. "I can manage my own investigation, young lady. And I'll tell you this much, if I can prove either you or that reporter had a handkerchief on Monday, I'll arrest you."

"A handkerchief?"

"Yeah. Think about it, Miss Laurance."

Annie thought about it as she introduced the suspects for Wednesday's Mystery Night. She thought about it all evening, between frantic moments of the Mystery Night. Why a handkerchief? As a matter of fact, she never carried one. Which would distress her maternal grandmother, who expected a lady always to possess a dainty, lace-edged hankie. But hankies went out with garters and girdles. Who, today, carried a handkerchief? Apparently not Bobby Fraizer, either. If the killer carried a handkerchief, that narrowed the circle indeed. At one point, she whispered her query to Ingrid, who with a true librarian's skill could be expected to find the answer to any question. She came back in less than half an hour with this news: Leighton, John Sanford, and Roscoe, as might be expected, always carried handkerchiefs in their left hip pockets. Tim Bond, also as might be expected, owned not a single handkerchief, although he occasionally wore a ragged red bandana. Gail didn't carry handkerchiefs, but sometimes Edith, Lucy, and Sybil did. Miss Dora, of course, was always equipped with one.

Her head spun.

A hand tugged at her arm. "Miss Laurance, there's a discrepancy."

It was hard to say whether Mrs. Brawley was delighted or offended. Her nose wriggled with eagerness.

"What's wrong?"

"Last night Lord Algernon said that he gave Miss Snooperton the ticket to Venice on the Orient Express *before* they played croquet. Tonight, he said he gave her the ticket *after* they played croquet." She waited eagerly.

"Very good," Annie praised. "We'd better take care of this at once."

Mrs. Brawley padded happily alongside Annie to the Suspect Interrogation Tent. Annie patted her on the shoulder, then stepped up to Max and whispered in his ear.

He grinned and said firmly, "I gave the ticket to Miss Snooperton before we played croquet."

Annie and Mrs. Brawley exchanged satisfied smiles. Annie moved slowly around the tent. She paused behind Lucy, who still wore her navy dress and white gloves. She looked bone weary, but perhaps all of this at least took her mind off of the murder for awhile.

Sanford continued to play his role with panache.

Mrs. Brawley's team (No. 7 tonight) clustered around him. This time, Annie noted with amusement, Mrs. Brawley was Team Captain, and savoring every moment of it. She leaned forward, finger waggling, a picture of ruthless inquisitorial determination.

"Mr. Hoxton, have you ever before been a guest at a country home where a jewel theft has occurred?"

Sanford stroked his chin. "Ah, my dear lady, perhaps. It's so hard to remember when one is so often a guest."

"You can remember," she snapped.

"I do believe there was one instance. At Lord

Healy's home, Castle-On-The-Thames. I think I recall the disappearance of a diamond brooch."

Mrs. Brawley stalked nearer. "Was that theft ever solved?"

"I don't believe so, dear lady."

"Did you then enjoy a spurt in your income, Mr. Hoxton?"

He registered shock. "That is an unwarranted assumption."

Mrs. Brawley raised a hand. "It is time to demand a search warrant of Reginald Hoxton's room and its contents."

Her group stormed triumphantly after her and received this information: In the pocket of Hoxton's trousers worn that afternoon, the police laboratory (with emphasis on the second syllable) discovered a fragment of gold, apparently from a jewelry setting, and a trace of putty.

Smiling, Annie moved on to Edith, playing Miss Susannah Greatheart.

An eager questioner demanded, "Isn't it true that Miss Snooperton had stolen Nigel Davies from you, and you quarreled with her shortly before her murder?"

Edith dabbed at her eyes with a crumpled linen handkerchief. "Oh no, I never quarrel with anyone, and I felt certain Nigel would come to his senses when he discovered that Miss Snooperton was involved with Lord Algernon."

"And how did you know this?"

"Why, dear Lord Algernon felt I would be sympathetic to his problems. He was trying his best to be rid of Miss Snooperton. He thought her a dreadfully fast young woman, who had tried to ensnare him with her wiles. I do find Lord Algernon to be such a gentleman."

After a hasty consultation with his team, Team Captain No. 3 brayed, "We demand a search warrant against Miss Greatheart."

The warrant revealed: A ruby necklace stuffed in among Miss Greatheart's lingerie, and a bloodied croquet mallet thrust deep in her wardrobe. Upon investigation the necklace was declared a replica of the missing Red Maiden, and the mallet was identified as the murder weapon.

Taxed with these facts, Miss Greatheart broke down, declaring she had been framed. "Someone must hate me very much."

Team No. 3 stampeded to surround Lord Algernon. The intensity of their questions delighted Max, who responded with élan.

"I had broken off my involvement with Miss Snooperton. Fact of the matter, gave her a ticket to Venice this morning, then wrote her a note I couldn't meet her at the arbor after tea."

"Was it your note that was found in her pocket?"

"Must have been."

"You say you were finished with Miss Snooperton. Was she finished with you?"

"Felt like Nigel had taken me off the hook there, getting himself engaged to her. Damn disgusting the way he was treating Miss Greatheart. Tried to cheer her up."

"Isn't it more, Lord Algernon, that you were exhibiting your longtime weakness for members of the opposite sex other than your wife?"

"Oh, that's a rum suggestion. Besides, Alicia's a sport."

He finally admitted, though he downplayed its significance, that he'd had a few angry words with Miss Snooperton at the rose arbor, but he insisted that he left her alive with the clear understanding their affair was ended, whether or not she accepted the ticket to Venice.

Team Captain No. 8 demanded a search warrant against Lord Algernon, and these facts were unearthed: A packet of angry letters from Miss Snooperton threatening to reveal their affair to Lady Alicia unless he made a substantial settlement upon her. One letter stated: *Cough up or sweet Lady Alicia will learn about our weekend in Nice.*

From there Team Captain No. 8, a mild-mannered professor of medieval poetry at Chastain Community College, bounded across the grass to attack Lady Alicia.

Jessica Merrill, stately this evening in an ankle-length pink-and-white dimity dress, faced the barrage of questions with haughty disdain.

"Was I aware of an involvement between Algernon and Miss Snooperton? Why, of course not. That is truly absurd. And, of course, even it it were true, I would merely pity the poor boy to have become entangled with such an unattractive and predatory woman."

"Didn't you earlier say Miss Snooperton was a dear girl?"

"Oh, did I? Perhaps. I've no real opinion in the matter."

"How much money did you owe Reginald Hoxton, my lady?"

"Merely a small debt between friends."

"But how could you hope to pay it off? You have no money of your own, have you?"

"There was no pressing need to resolve a trifle between friends over a card game."

"But Miss Greatheart says she heard him threaten to tell Lord Algernon if you didn't pay up?"

"She must have misunderstood. Such an insipid young woman."

Jessica Merrill refused to buckle beneath the spate of questions. Lord Algernon had harummphed and said Lady Alicia was a sport about his extra-marital activities. How would Jessica Merrill feel about her husband's involvement with a predatory lady lawyer?

Every so often, to the enormous disappointment of the besieging detectives, one or another of the English Manor suspects would hang a Back Soon sign in their chair and slip away for a few minutes of rest or refreshment.

When Jessica took her break, Annie followed her out to the main sidewalk. As she hurried to catch up, she overheard a middle-aged woman returning to the detection area tell her friend, "This has just been the most fun I've had since I was seven and my mother gave me *The Clue In the Album*. Doesn't the investigation remind you of the house party at Lady Billington-Smith's in Georgette Heyer's *The Unfinished Clue*?" Her companion nodded energetically. "Oh Hetty, I know just what you mean. I keep remembering Chayning Court in Gladys Mitchell's *Speedy Death*." Buoyed by her eavesdropping, Annie spurted ahead and called out, "Jessica," as her quarry turned into the inn.

"Oh, hello, Annie. Decided I needed a drink. God, it must be exhausting to actually be a suspect in a murder investigation."

Annie settled for an enigmatic, "I suppose so," rather than a query about Roscoe's emotional temperature.

They settled in a corner of the coffee bar, which offered a very limited drink list, coffee, house wine, white and red but provenance unspecified, and a bottled wine cooler. They both opted for the last.

"One more night," Jessica sighed.

"It's good of you to keep up, considering the circumstances."

Jessica poured the cooler slowly over the ice, then picked up her glass. She looked very self-possessed, her dark hair curling softly away from her face, her large, attractive eyes meticulously outlined in eye shadow. She smiled at Annie. "It's been difficult, of course. Corinne has been our friend for many years. I know she would have wanted the garden nights to continue, and, of course, as a member of the Board, Roscoe certainly feels a responsibility to see that the Society's efforts aren't damaged."

"Did you like Corinne?"

Those large eyes returned Annie's gaze steadily. "That is a remarkably tactless question at the present time."

"Being one of two primary suspects in a murder investigation has put tactfulness pretty low on my priority list."

Jessica sipped at her cooler. "Roscoe doesn't think anyone will be arrested. Apparently, there is no direct physical evidence linking any one person to the crime scene, and he says it's very difficult to sustain an arrest or obtain a conviction without clear-cut evidence or a confession." She smoothed her softly waving black hair back from an unlined forehead. "It will probably be one of those famous unsolved mysteries."

"That's pretty lousy for everybody. Me included." And especially, Annie thought, for Gail and Bobby, and Leighton and Peggy. "And I'm not at all sure Wells won't jump on Frazier or me, just to quiet the newspapers." Annie thumped her glass onto the cocktail table.

"Dammit, Wells won't even *talk* to people who could have done it. Like Sybil and Tim." Then she glared defiantly at Jessica. "Or Miss Dora."

To her surprise, Jessica was neither shocked nor outraged. Instead, her eyes narrowed thoughtfully. "Miss Dora."

Annie tried to interpret Jessica's Madonna-like face, so smooth, calm—and masklike.

"It's funny you should think of Miss Dora. She's such a fixture around Chastain that no one even sees her, despite those outlandish clothes and her hats." Jessica smiled, but her brown eyes were serious and intent. "Miss Dora has spent her life trying to preserve Chastain's history. That is all that matters to her, that and family. She opposed almost every innovation Corinne proposed for the Society. Miss Dora hates these garden weeks. She thinks Chastain should belong to its own and never to outlanders." Jessica toyed with her lapis lazuli necklace. "But, of course, it's absurd to imagine her creeping up behind Corinne and striking her down."

Annie almost corrected Jessica. No one had crept up behind Corinne. Corinne had turned to walk away. But it didn't really matter.

Jessica took a last swallow, smiled. "Well, I suppose we'd better get back—or the detective teams will track me down here."

As they rustled in their purses for money, Annie asked quickly, "Had you talked to Corinne recently?"

Jessica's hand momentarily froze, then she lifted out her billfold. "Yes. Last week." Her voice was placid.

Annie added her portion to the tray. "What about?"

"Nothing special. She called me to ask if we should add a new line of reproductions at the Museum. I'm

rather an authority on colonial glassware. She wanted
my opinion.''

It was so smooth, so easily delivered, and, Annie felt
certain, absolutely false. Especially when she looked
into those eyes, now curiously defiant.

"You and Roscoe have a wonderful marriage."

Jessica didn't challenge the non sequitur. She merely
nodded as she pushed back her chair.

Annie rose. "I don't suppose the same could be said
of Corinne and Leighton."

"I wouldn't know."

"Rumor has it that Leighton was involved with a
young woman."

Jessica forced a smile. "That happens, doesn't it,
when men reach a certain age. It usually isn't of any
importance."

And with that, Annie realized that Jessica Merrill
knew full well about Roscoe's lapse, and, if the matter
were ever raised, would dismiss it as unimportant. The
corollary being, of course, that if it didn't matter to her,
it certainly couldn't provide a motive of any kind for
Roscoe to silence Corinne.

But had Roscoe known—in time—how his wife felt?

The detective teams swarmed into the Suspect Investigation Tent full of last-minute questions.

"Miss Laurance, did the lab report say that footprint
by the body belonged to Nigel Davies?"

"Yes."

"How about that broken lock on the tool shed? Did it
have any fingerprints?"

"No. It was wiped off."

Fingerprints. Wiped off. Why did Chief Wells want
her or Bobby to have a handkerchief?

A high squeal of sheer excitement erupted from Mrs. Brawley when her team received a search warrant to Reginald Hoxton's car. In the boot was found one of the croquet balls. It had been tampered with, and secreted within it was a handful of red rubies.

She was marking times on the last envelopes, when Bobby poked his head in at the main opening. He looked around, glared, and left.

Max plumped the final box down next to the wall. "Next time you plan a Mystery Night, I'll hire a pack horse."

"Next time I plan a Mystery Night, you can buy me a one-way ticket to El Paso. It would be more fun."

He sighed and draped himself against the poster of the rice bed. "How about a drink?"

She shook her head wearily.

"Rain check? I'm bushed."

He didn't even protest.

She didn't blame him. The room was stuffy and airless and about as comfortable as a wadi in the Sahara. Damn Idell. You couldn't leave the room for five minutes without her slipping in to turn off the air conditioner. Crossing to the window, Annie punched the button. After a shuddering cough, it slowly ground to life. She glanced out, admiring the patterns of shadow the moonlight splashed across the grounds and the Society Building next door.

The Society Building. If only stones could talk. Who had typed that letter after hours? If they only knew that. . . .

A S ANNIE LIFTED the brush to stroke her hair, a shriek from downstairs knifed through the thin wooden door. She stared at her early morning reflection in the mirror, her eyes startled, her mouth parted in surprise. A second scream resounded, louder still and with a growing undercurrent of hysteria.

Something was very amiss within the stuffy confines of Swamp Fox Inn. Max burst through their connecting door, and Annie grabbed her shorts.

He looked tremendously relieved, then his eyes widened with pleasure.

She stepped into the shorts and pulled on a t-shirt. They moved toward the door. Max opened it, and they scrambled through at the same time.

On the balcony, the sounds of distress were louder still, and the words bubbling between sobs brought them both pounding down the stairs.

"Dead . . . horrid . . . sticky and wet . . . oh my God, dead . . ."

The assistant manager shook the shoulders of the gray-haired maid. "Shut up! You're going to wake everybody up. Dammit, Frieda, you're not making any sense. Shut up! Who's dead?"

"Idell. She's laying in there . . ."

The assistant manager and Annie and Max turned at once, abandoning the sobbing Frieda. They halted abruptly in the open office doorway. Idell Gordon sprawled stiffly on the love seat behind a small glass-topped coffee table. A decanter sat on a Chinese lacquer tray. She still wore her black polyester funeral dress, and it pulled at the seams against her ungainly pose. Staring eyes were fixed on the ceiling. Her face was pinkish, and her mouth agape, the lips strained back in a twisted smile.

The young man made a noise deep in his throat and backed up, crushing Annie's foot. She yelped; he jumped, glared at them, and yanked the door shut. "I've got to call the doctor."

"And the police," Max added quietly.

A woman in the knot of guests clustered behind them began to whimper.

"Everybody go to your rooms, please. We'll be talking with you as soon as possible. If you have important business, Sergeant Harkey will take your name. Back to your rooms please, ladies and gentlemen, we have an unexplained death here, and it will take time for everyone to be seen. Back to your rooms, please."

Annie leaned disconsolately against the window, an elbow on the hiccuping air conditioner.

"God, it's my fault. It's my *fault.*"

"How old was she?"

"I don't know. Fifty-five. Sixty? She'd be older if—"

"A grown woman. If she knew who the murderer was, she knew who to tell. Chief Wells. That she didn't tell him is no fault of yours. Besides, it doesn't sound all that clear-cut to me that she knew."

"She's dead."

"Okay. Good proof. But nothing she said to you yesterday was that obvious."

"I guess you're right. But she was excited—and positive Leighton wasn't the killer. She *must* have seen someone slipping out of the Society late at night." Annie whirled around, paced to the door. "Wells *has* to listen to me now."

A vein pulsed in Wells's bulging forehead. The wad of tobacco in his cheek was motionless.

"She was excited! And she asked if we were interested in the reward. Chief, I'm sure she saw the letter writer."

His big hands balled into fists. "I got a murder here. Another one. And it's the kind of murder smart people try. So I don't give a damn about that stupid letter. I want to know how many times you came back to the Inn last night?"

Wells had ordered Annie to stay in her room, but Max made forays in and out, and he picked up quite a bit of information from other guests. Idell had been quite cheerful the last night of her life, visiting animatedly with various guests. She hadn't changed from the dress she wore to the funeral. She ate dinner in her apartment on the east side of the second floor, and was on duty at the desk during the early evening, giving way to the night clerk at nine P.M. When found Thursday morning, she was dressed as she had been the night before. She was in her office, which was to the left behind the counter area. A door from the office opened out into the Inn grounds. That door was open. The office light was on. On the floor, where it had fallen from her hand as she fell back in a seizure, was a single sherry glass. The sherry remaining in the glass had spattered on the wooden floor. The glass with its dried residue had been sent to the laboratory for examination, as had the crystal top of the sherry decanter. The sherry too, had been sent to the laboratory. Beneath her body, crushed against the faded damask rose upholstery, was the Wednesday afternoon issue of the *Chastain Courier*. Red pencil circled Bobby Frazier's byline to the lead story, and red pencil underlined the sentence reading: *The bereaved widower is offering a $5,000 reward for information leading to the arrest and conviction of Mrs. Webster's murderer.*

After the last policeman finally left, Max and Annie slipped out the back door.

Annie glanced back over her shoulder. "Do you suppose Wells will arrest me if he finds out I've left my room?"

Max wasn't worried. "No. You just hacked him, bringing up the letter again."

They took the alley to the McIlwain grounds. Annie stiffened at the back gate, pointing to the placard jammed into the grayish dirt.

"Although this is now known as Whitsett's Alley, after the proprietor of a print shop which stood here in the early 1800s, this is the site of the earliest Chastain racecourse, which was laid out in January of 1735. Races began in February and nearby planters entered the pride of their stables. Prizes included silver cups, bowls, or salvers. Race week culminated annually in the Jockey Ball, which opened with a stately minuet but included vigorous country dancing. Supper might have included baked turkeys, terrapin stews, iced cakes, partridge, quail, and goose, Madeira and Port wines, and punch."

Annie glanced wildly around. "That old woman is everywhere, but you never see her. It's giving me the creeps!"

The gate screeched like a cat with a stepped-on tail, and Annie jumped a foot.

"Gothic heroine," he murmured.

"Don't be obnoxious," she retorted.

They found Lucy at the side of the house, pruning a wisteria vine. She wore a floppy pink gardening hat, a denim skirt, and tailored cotton blouse. At the sound of their footsteps, she looked up, took a deep breath and visibly gathered strength.

"I suppose it's true." But she didn't need their confirmation. "I don't understand it, though. Corinne and Idell had nothing in common. Oh, they knew each other, of course. We all know each other. We've lived here so long, and we are neighbors. But why would anyone kill both Corinne and Idell? I don't suppose Idell had a heart attack?" She looked at them hopefully. "Could it be that?"

"They aren't sure yet what killed her," Max said, "but I heard the cops talking about poison. That's what they're looking for."

"It doesn't make any kind of sense. Not Idell."

"Actually, it does make sense." Annie described

Idell's interest in the reward, and the idea that she may have seen the writer of the plot letter.

Lucy's face looked as though it had been chiseled out of pond ice.

"Louisa Binning insists the letter must have been written after hours," Max explained.

"And that means the typist had a key to the Society building."

Lucy drew her breath in sharply. "That's dreadful." If her face had looked worn before, now it appeared absolutely stricken. "Oh, my God. Someone with a key." Then she shook her head. Her voice was high. "Chief Wells doesn't believe the letter matters."

Annie looked at her gravely. "Don't you see how wrong that is? Lucy, please. You know these people. You know everyone who could have gotten into that building. Won't you help us? Won't you tell us what you really think?"

For an instant, Annie felt that it trembled in the balance, because Lucy understood.

Who could better judge the motives and passions of her longtime friends and neighbors? Lucy knew them all:

Leighton, the charming, handsome, not-so-grieved widower.

Gail, the emotional, love-struck, frightened niece.

Bobby, the abrasive, tough, self-serving reporter.

Roscoe, the self-contained but passionate lawyer.

John, the ambitious, determined, aloof doctor.

Sybil, the lusty, willful, spoiled sybarite.

Tim, the gifted, immature, self-centered artist.

Edith, the nervous, sensitive, hardworking clubwoman.

Miss Dora, the eccentric, unpredictable, waspish old woman.

Annie held her breath. Lucy could help them. She felt so sure of it. If only she would—

Lucy tucked the shears under her arm, slipped off her gardening gloves. Then she clasped her hands together to hide their trembling. Tears glistened in her eyes as she shook her head. "No." Her voice was as faint as the whistle of wind in a cavern. "No!"

Max ordered veal marsala. Annie debated between corned beef on rye and a chili hamburger and picked the latter.

"There has been some mild concern of late about cholesterol," he said converstionally.

"I think I'll have chocolate fudge pie for dessert."

"How about adding a dollop of whipped cream?"

"Good idea."

He sighed. "You are almost Victorian in your pigginess."

"If I could go back in time, for culinary pleasures, it would be difficult to pick between a Christmas dinner in Victorian England and a wedding feast in ancient Rome."

"Does this mean you are going to develop a matronly figure in your old age?"

"Gee, I don't know. Stick around and find out."

"And have a lot of fun along the way."

"I'll shake on that," and she stuck out a hand. She pumped his hand hard for an instant, then paused and the pleasure seeped out of her face, replaced by worry and discouragement. "Dammit, Lucy knows who wrote that letter. Don't you think? Why else would she always get in such a swivet when we ask her about it?"

Max put down his fork, looking about as stricken as Lucy had.

She mumbled past a mouthful of chili hamburger. "What's wrong?"

"God, do you suppose Gail wrote it?"

Annie stopped chewing to stare at him. "What makes you think that?"

"Lucy's crazy about Gail—and she's looked like hell ever since Corinne got bumped off."

She put her burger down on the plate. "That makes just enough sense to be true." She squinted in concentration. "No, no, wait a minute. That doesn't jibe, because Gail's panicked about Bobby."

"Is she?" Max said coolly.

"Sure she is. She ran to us to see if we could help. She's acted like a heroine tied to the rails every time Bobby is mentioned."

"Look at it this way," Max suggested. "If she's a double murderess, that lavender blue persona of hers has to be more than a little contrived. There may be a hell of a lot more to her than just a pretty face."

Annie looked at him admiringly. "Beneath that Jack Armstrong exterior lurks a Stephen King imagination. I'm impressed."

He smiled modestly.

They ate in silence for a moment, then, as Annie swallowed her last fat-laden bite, she said purposefully, "Okay, we've got first-class analytical brains. Right?"

"Of course."

"So let's think. Why was the letter written?"

"One, to embarrass Corinne," Max suggested. "Or, two, to warn her. You know, something on the order of those street corner signs: repent while you have time."

"Or, three," Annie offered, "it might have been designed to stir up trouble between Corinne and the not-so-well-disguised suspects in the Moneypot plot so that the water would be well-muddied when Corinne was murdered. Or, four, to implicate me."

Max pounced on the last two. "But they would presuppose that murder was intended when the letter was first written."

Annie sighed heavily. "Maybe we don't have first-class brains."

The waiter removed their plates, and Max ordered two beers.

Annie reached for the dessert menu, murmuring, "Fudge pie."

"Nobody would mix beer and fudge pie." But his tone wasn't altogether certain.

Annie reluctantly put down the dessert menu. "Actually, I'm full. Another time."

Max returned to the letter. "If we knew the real reason it was written, it would be a hell of a lot easier to pick out the writer."

She propped her chin on her hand. "Sure. Reason one is motivated by anger. Reason two is more ambivalent. The writer is mad but willing to give her another chance. But reasons three and four—"

He nodded. "Yeah. The die is cast."

Max pulled an envelope from his pocket and listed their suspects.

Annie nodded at the first name. "Okay. Let's take Leighton. He married Corinne and lost the career he wanted. No kids. Not much to care about in his life, so he started to go to seed. Drank too much. But always a gentleman. Then he meets this attractive young woman, who cares about him as a person, not as the financial underpinning of a big house."

"If he wrote it, it would have to be Reason Three."

"Because he wasn't really mad at Corinne, was he? He was disillusioned, and maybe a little bitter. But not mad. And he wouldn't expect that letter to change her, certainly not in any way that could benefit him. Her pride would never allow her to agree to a divorce. So his only motive to write the letter would be to provide a handful of suspects in her murder."

"Which it should have accomplished—except the police chief suffers from xenophobia." Max put a checkmark by Leighton's name.

"Is Leighton that kind of man?" Annie wondered doubtfully. "Devious and crafty? He seems so above-board, so likable—"

"Such a gentleman," Max parroted sarcastically.

"Well, he is!"

"Yeah. But he's a man, too. And he'd fallen in love. What was it worth to him?"

"I don't know." She looked at Max for a moment. What was his love worth to her? Everything. Anything. Yes, maybe she had to reconsider Leighton's motives.

"As for Gail, I hate to say it, but I sure can see her writing the letter."

Annie nodded reluctantly. Gail was weak, but she had the cunning and stubbornness of the weak. She would fight for what mattered to her, with any weapon she could find. "She could have written it to strike back at her aunt."

"Or she could have figured that a letter like that would go a long way to spread the wealth in a murder investigation."

"That's too Machiavellian for her," Annie objected.

"How about Bobby? He could have gotten Gail's key to the Society."

Annie shook her head vehemently.

"Sure he could have," Max insisted.

"Oh, I know that. But he wouldn't have written that letter. He's too direct. Too masculine."

Max's brows drew down in a dark frown. "I seem to notice a pattern to your objections. Apparently, good-looking men are exempted from suspicion."

"Don't be silly. I can't help it if Leighton and Bobby are attractive."

"How about Sanford?"

"He isn't attractive, but that's not the reason I can see him doing the letter. Actually, he's a natural. He acted furious when I read the letter, but that could be a cover." She remembered his angry face in his office, and his cold laughter. *I could have strangled her.* She shivered. "He's kind of scary."

"How about Roscoe?"

"No way. He's much too *careful* to do something like that. I mean, he is a lawyer. He'd figure out the letter could be traced to the Society. He'd think it was a crazy idea."

"Something no lawyer would dream of doing. Right?"

"Oh." She considered it. "He might have done it because he'd figure nobody would expect him to do it. That would be doubly clever."

"He's a very clever fellow."

"How about Jessica?" she asked.

"Jessica would act out of pure anger, if she knew how Corinne were upsetting Roscoe."

"The same would go for Edith. And believe me, Edith would have loved to sandbag Corinne. As would have Sybil." Her mouth twisted dryly. "But I doubt if Sybil can write her name. And the same goes for Tim."

"Oh, I think you underestimate Sybil," Max began.

Annie almost rose to the bait, until she saw the mischievous pleasure in his dark blue eyes. She folded her lips firmly shut.

Max made a star by the last name. "Of course, Lucy's

an excellent suspect. She has keys and lives right next door to the Prichard House."

"She certainly could have managed it," Annie agreed, "but what happens when we try on the motives? Did she have any reason to be angry with Corinne? All we've picked up is an old story about Gail's father. Seems a little weak to me." She finished her beer, thought briefly about fudge pie, and turned her hands up in defeat. "I still think it's Miss Dora. Or maybe it's like *Murder On The Orient Express*. The Board members all got together at three in the morning and wrote the damned thing together."

Every time Annie saw one of the people on their list that evening during the final Mystery Night program, she wondered: Did you write the letter? Kill Corinne? And Idell?

The Mystery Night crowd was sparse. Only fifty-seven showed up, although the evening had been a sell-out like all the others. Both detectives and Mystery Night suspects showed a marked lack of enthusiasm and a tendency to look over their collective shoulders, except, of course, for the indefatigable Mrs. Brawley, who cornered Annie in the Suspect Interrogation Tent.

"Was the footprint at The Scene of the Crime traced to Nigel Davies?"

Annie looked at her blankly, her mind still juggling the names and faces of the Board members. "Footprint. Oh yes, it matches the shoes he was wearing after tea."

Mrs. Brawley's fox-sharp nose twitched. "After tea. Then he *lied* in his statement." With a whoop, she turned and lunged across the room to the Investigation table. "A search warrant against Nigel Davies. At once!"

The warrant revealed: A note from Susannah Greatheart to Matilda Snooperton, angrily demanding that she release Nigel from a loveless engagement.

Information in hand, Mrs. Brawley scooted across the tent to Roscoe Merrill.

"Your footprint places you at The Scene of the Crime!"

Roscoe went through his lines accurately but without verve, his mind clearly elsewhere.

"I dispute your assumption."

"It is admitted," Mrs. Brawley pressed, "that you wore these shoes *after* tea. Therefore, your presence at the site where Miss Snooperton died cannot be denied. Further, in your room, the search revealed a letter from Miss Greatheart to Miss Snooperton. How could it have come into your possession if you did not take it from Miss Snooperton, dead or alive?"

Roscoe skirted the attack. "I did not take it from Miss Snooperton. I found it in the area where she was killed. It must have dropped from her hand. But I did not see her to speak to."

A careful, lawyerlike response. Annie would have smiled, if murder were a topic for smiles. At this moment, it was not.

At nine o'clock, she looked up to see Chief Wells standing near the main entrance to the Suspect Interrogation Tent. He motioned for her to join him.

"Last night, did you leave here between nine and ten?"

"Is that when you think Idell was killed?"

"Just answer my question."

She fought down the impulse to back away from his bulky, dominating figure.

"I went down to the Inn once. Most everybody took at least one break during that time," and she waved her hand at the suspects, all of whom were watching avidly. She talked too quickly, trying to crack through the glower that seemed a permanent part of his face. "I was with Jessica Merrill. She can tell you. We walked down there and back together."

"You could've gone back."

"Anyone could have," she retorted angrily.

He stumped off then, moving heavily to each Mystery Night suspect. Was he asking about their movements—or hers?

Lucy frowned in concentration and looked as if she were conscientiously struggling to remember. There were dark shadows under her eyes. The bright patch of lipstick on her mouth and the round circles of rouge on her cheeks had aged her decades. She had tried to dress for her role, a silk dress with a gold-and-red flowered pattern and crisp short white gloves. The overall effect was garish.

Roscoe's face was as bland as that of a poker player with a big pot, but the wariness in his shrewd eyes made it clear he was answering carefully. He looked comfortable and assured in his dinner jacket, a man of means, innocent of anything more damning than a regretted romantic interlude.

Jessica smiled and replied briskly. Only the quick slant of her glance toward Annie revealed uneasiness. She wore a silk dress with interlocking shafts of crimson, purple, and cobalt blue, which emphasized her slim grace.

Max glanced once toward Annie, then shook his head sharply and spoke persuasively.

Dr. Sanford smiled lazily. He didn't seem discomfited by Wells's questions. He was his customary arrogant, confident self.

Edith's huge green eyes flicked nervously from the

chief to Annie and back again. She smoothed back a vagrant red-gold curl and answered in monosyllables.

Any one of them could have stepped into Idell's office from the Inn grounds and accepted an offer of sherry. She looked up at Prichard House. The bottom floors were dark, but light streamed from both front and back on the second floor. More than likely, Leighton and Gail were at home and had been at home last evening. Either of them could have walked through the shadows of Swamp Fox Inn and a final visit with Idell. And Bobby Frazier had come by the tent, looking for Gail. As for Sybil and Tim, it would have been simple enough to reach Idell. And Miss Dora was omnipresent.

Whose face had been the last seen by Idell Gordon?

21

ANNIE PUT DOWN her coffee cup with a click and craned her head to peer through the pillars supporting the patio to the garden outside the Inn. Popping up, she told Max, "I'll be right back."

Bobby Frazier bent in a half-crouch, photographing the door to Idell's office. When he lowered the camera, Annie approached.

"Won't you join us for some coffee?"

He looked tired this morning, and he'd nicked his chin shaving. He had the air of a man struggling with an inner crisis, his brown eyes abstracted, his mouth drawn in a grim line. Now, he stared at her, his face neither friendly nor hostile. Then he shrugged. "Yeah. I'll have a cup."

She led him back to their table. He and Max shook hands, exchanging curt greetings.

As he pulled out a chair and it scraped noisily

against the flagstones, Frazier looked around the empty patio. "Got it to yourselves this morning." He dropped his camera bag beside the chair.

"They checked out in droves yesterday," Annie explained, then added, as she sipped the pale yellow coffee, "Wish we could have. But tonight's the last night." And how much fun would the Denouement Ball be, under the circumstances?

She tried for a light tone. "How do you like being tied with me as Wells's favorite suspect?"

"Oh, yeah." He wasn't interested.

Annie looked at him sharply. That was funny. He'd tried every way he knew to make it look as though he had no interest in Gail, and, ergo, had no motive. So why did he shrug away Wells's suspicions as unimportant?

But Bobby seemed preoccupied with his own thoughts. He picked a pencil from his shirt pocket and tapped it in an uneven rhythm on the table, but, obviously, he wasn't even aware of his action. "Have you heard about the autopsy report?" he asked abruptly. But he didn't wait for an answer, and his voice was grim as he summed it up for them.

Idell Gordon had a meat pie, orange sherbet, and coffee for dinner, eating alone in her apartment on the second floor. Analysis of the foodstuffs was negative, but the laboratory report found a heavy concentration of cyanide of potassium in the dried wine residue in the sherry glass and in her stomach. Idell Gordon had died of acute cyanide poisoning. Her fingerprints alone were on the wine glass. The remaining sherry in the decanter contained cyanide of potassium. The crystal top of the decanter yielded smudged prints identified as those of Idell Gordon.

"Cyanide." Annie had just picked up her coffee cup. She put it down again. "Oh, my God."

"Yeah." The pencil beat a frenzied tattoo. "They figure she invited somebody to have a glass of sherry while she put the bite on them. She must've decided she could get more than the $5,000 from Leighton."

"Oh, hell yes," Max exclaimed. "That makes all kinds of sense. Idell went after the murderer and threatened to tell Wells unless she were paid off."

"Money's all she ever talked about," Annie agreed. "Money and what a tough time she was having meeting her expenses." She pictured that fat face, the spriggy orange hair and protuberant, greedy brown eyes. "Blackmail." Only this time, Idell's reach had far exceeded her grasp. "She must have contacted the murderer, made an appointment for Wednesday night."

"But the murderer brought cyanide, not money," Max concluded grimly.

Bobby jammed the pencil so hard against the tabletop that it snapped, then he stared down at it in surprise. "Stupid bitch. And I should have known. I should have taken Wells by the scruff of his goddamned neck and insisted he talk to her."

"Why? You had no reason to guess she was onto the murderer."

"She called me Wednesday, asking about the reward, how it was going to be handled, what a person would have to do to get it. I rattled it off, then I came down on her, asked what she knew. She backed off, said she was just curious, one of her guests had asked her. I thought that was phony, but I was busy, had a deadline, so I said oh sure, give us a call anytime. But I should have kept after her."

"You didn't go to meet her?"

There was an instant of stiff silence. Bobby stared at Annie. "No." He spoke carefully and distinctly. "I did not meet her."

"I didn't mean—" She flushed and started over. "I saw you at the Mystery Night, and since it's just next door . . ."

"I was looking for Gail."

Max poured fresh coffee for all of them. "Did you find her?"

"Yes. We had a nice talk." He sounded like a high school principal describing a Kiwanis luncheon, but the muscles in his jaw were rigid.

Annie squashed a desire to tell him to come off it. She realized more and more that she lacked the finesse needed to inveigle answers from sullen, angry, or frightened people. If only she had the suavity of John Appleby or the unassuming, quiet manner of Father Bredder.

Max, however, excelled in finesse. He propped his elbows on the table and smiled with the blandness of Lord Peter Wimsey. "Is Gail doing okay? What did she have to say?"

"Oh, she thanked me for the stories in the *Courier*, said they were well done. I thanked her. You know, we became acquainted when I did a series on the programs and outreach of the Prichard Museum. She's a very knowledgeable curator, and she's done an outstanding job with limited resources."

Oh, my God, Annie thought. Next he'd list her degrees and publications. She'd had enough.

"When did you fall in love with her?"

His head jerked up; he glared at Annie. "You've got it all wrong. We're friends, that's all."

"Then why did you tell her it didn't matter whether

she had any money, that you were going to keep on seeing her no matter what her aunt did?"

"As friends," he reiterated stubbornly. "That's all."

Understanding exploded in her mind, like Fourth of July fireworks. "So Gail didn't have any reason to kill her aunt. Is that what you're saying?"

"Right. It's absurd to even think so. It's laughable, a gentle girl like Gail." But he wasn't laughing, and Annie knew that a frightful scene lurked in the dark corridors of his mind: Gail and Corinne, a quarrel, a burst of white-hot anger, Corinne face-down on the path, Gail standing there, a mallet in her hand.

Behind the tough newsman facade, fear for Gail ate at him. He tried to hide behind bluster. "Any idea Wells has about Gail, it's crap. That's all. Just crap."

As much to distract him as anything else, she said, "I guess they're sure about the autopsy report?"

Frazier looked at her blankly.

"Was it really cyanide that killed Idell?"

If possible, Frazier looked even grimmer. "Yeah. Cyanide of potassium."

"That ought to clear Gail. How could she possibly have access to cyanide of potassium?"

Bobby looked like a man who had opened a door and walked into hell. He didn't seem to be aware of their presence for a long, agonizing moment. Finally, he said dully, "That's a good point." He managed a travesty of a smile. "Of course, nobody with any brains would even consider Gail."

Except Bobby, obviously.

He drank some coffee, put down the empty cup. "Well, I'd better get back to the newsroom." He jerked his head toward the grounds. "Now that I've got a picture of the Death Door." He gave a mirthless laugh. "If you see Gail—Never mind. See you later."

As he strode away, Max sighed. "Poor devil."

"He thinks she did it."

"Yeah."

Annie looked at Max, unaccustomedly somber across the table. He looked tanned and fit, his thick blond hair cut short, his dark blue eyes alert and thoughtful. All as usual, except for the furrow of worry on his brow.

"Dammit," he said, "maybe you should go back to Broward's Rock."

This was so unexpected that she stared at him, momentarily speechless. "Why?"

"Cyanide is nothing to fool with. How do we know the murderer won't sprinkle it everywhere?"

She poked the half-eaten spongy croissant. "It might add a little flavor to this."

"For God's sake, Annie, be serious."

This was such a turnabout that she couldn't repress a grin.

In a moment, he broke into a reluctant smile. "Okay. I know. You *are* serious. Your virtue and your defect."

"I don't know who wrote that damned letter. Or who pinched some cyanide. Or who murdered Corinne and Idell. I'm perfectly safe."

That diverted him. He jammed a hand through his hair. "That's what we need to work on. Where could Gail get cyanide?"

"Bobby obviously has a very clear idea where she might have obtained the poison." And she concluded thoughtfully, "If he knows where Gail could have found cyanide of potassium, that means he knows how to get it, too."

.   .   .

Gail led the way up the magnificent staircase. It rose for three stories, the banisters carved at top and bottom, the railing a gleaming mahogany, the ornate fretwork glistening white. Her room was on the top floor, a bedroom and sitting room that overlooked the front gardens. A group of garden club women snapped pictures of the sweeping azaleas, with occasional furtive snaps aimed at the cane that hid the pond where Corinne died. The sitting room was papered with a mid-eighteenth century Chinese wallpaper with orange-tiled pagodas and tan mud-brick walls. Annie and Max sat on a Chippendale loveseat. It had delicate Chinese fretwork and was upholstered in tan and cream satin. Annie looked for reflections of Gail in the lovely, almost period-perfect room. An open copy of the April *Vogue* lay face down on the woven wicker coffee table. A modern black rocker with a Clemson crest sat beside the fireplace. A collection of miniature pottery dogs decorated half the Adam mantel. Portrait photographs sat at each end, one of Corinne, and the other of a man Annie felt certain must be Cameron, Gail's father. It was the same strikingly handsome face, auburn hair, sky-blue eyes, but there was an air of resignation in his face and perhaps a touch of weakness in his mouth. A chairside booktable held an extensive collection of art books, along with three booklets from the Prichard Museum. The top one pictured a magnificent silver punchbowl. The cover blurb advertised historic reproductions.

Gail stood in the center of the sitting room, her feet wide apart as if braced against a storm. She wore a print dress in khaki and peony, jungle flowers bright against the tan background. The vivid colors of the dress underscored the waxen shade of her face and the dark smudges beneath her eyes.

"I can't believe it. Why would anyone kill Idell?"

Max spread his arm behind Annie on the sofa top. "The police think she tried to blackmail the letter writer. She'd talked to Bobby Frazier about the award being offered by Leighton. She definitely had money in mind."

Gail's hands curled into tight balls. "She called Bobby?"

"Yes. But when he pressed her about what she knew, she backed off, claimed she was asking for a guest."

She looked at them doubtfully. "That's not likely, is it?"

"No." Annie put it bluntly. "What's likely is that she thought she could get more money somewhere else. Instead, she got cyanide in her sherry."

"Cyanide? Is that what killed her?" Gail sounded interested, but not threatened.

Annie had it down pat by now. "Cyanide of potassium."

Horror dawned slowly on Gail's face. If Bobby Frazier could have seen it, Annie thought, surely he would have realized her innocence.

Then a slimy thought wriggled in the recesses of Annie's mind. If Gail were a double murderer, once out of anger, the second time from fear, she would have given thought to the moment when cyanide of potassium would first be mentioned to her.

"Cyanide of potassium." She whirled away, walked to the window.

"Do you know where anyone could find it?"

Gail was silent for so long that Annie thought she didn't intend to answer. Finally, she turned and faced them, her arms folded tightly at her waist. "It doesn't mean anything. It's used for lots of things."

"At the Museum," Max suggested.

Her blue eyes troubled, she turned to him. "Yes." She almost managed to sound conversational. "I believe there is some at the Museum. Tim uses it in electroplating." At their silence, she continued, "You know, in making historical reproductions of things like candlesticks and punch bowls and tankards. We have an extensive line of reproductions that we make and sell through the Museum to raise money."

Annie darted a look at Max. He was so busy suffering for Gail that he didn't say a word. Annie didn't believe in festering sores. A lanced boil heals.

"How did Bobby know about it?"

She swallowed jerkily. "It was last fall, when he did a series of articles on the Museum and its programs. He did a special Sunday feature on Tim and all of his talents, as a painter and engraver—and in electroplating." She rubbed her temple as if it ached. "Tim is truly an outstandingly talented person. I believe it was that article that caught the attention of the New York gallery." A touch of color seeped back into her face. "You see, everyone read about it. I heard so many comments, and we received a spurt of letters from people eager to know all about our line of reproductions."

"Did the article include the information about the use of cyanide of potassium in electroplating?"

"I don't suppose in so many words," she admitted reluctantly. "But anyone who knows anything at all about the process would know. So anyone who read that article would realize we had cyanide of potassium at the Museum. That's obvious."

It was a good deal more obvious that at least three of the people who were intimately associated with Corinne Webster knew about the cyanide of potassium: Gail Prichard, Bobby Frazier, and Tim Bond.

But she was cheering with every word. "So, of

course, it doesn't mean a thing that Bobby wrote those articles. Anyone could have known." Then her eyes darkened with pain. "Besides, Bobby didn't have a motive. When I talked to you the other day, I gave you the wrong impression about Bobby and me. We're just friends. Nothing more than that."

"Oh, for God's sake!" Annie exploded. "Don't be such a fool."

She flushed. "I don't know what you mean."

"I mean any idiot—including Chief Wells—can see that Bobby's besotted with you. I don't mean he killed your aunt, but you can't be dumb enough to believe he doesn't care about you."

"He told me it didn't mean anything." Tears brimmed in her eyes. "He said—"

"Of course, he did. The boy's trying to protect you. He's doing his damnedest to keep Chief Wells from even looking your way. You'd have to be blind not to see it."

Gail's strained face reflected a series of emotions— shock, uncertainty, then burgeoning hope.

As the Porsche lunged away from the curb, Max shook his head chidingly.

"Well," Annie said defensively, "I hate stupidity."

"Sometimes, it's better for things not to be quite so clear-cut."

"Do you think he's fooling Wells?"

"No. But he was fooling Gail."

"So what's good about that?"

"It kept her from worrying about him, didn't it?"

. . .

They arrived at the Museum right on the heels of Chief Wells.

He disposed of his chewing tobacco in a silver spittoon, then turned his watery blue eyes on them.

"Aren't you people out of town yet?"

"I didn't know I was free to go. Besides, we have the ball completing the mystery event tonight."

"I know where to find you if I want you," he growled. "What're you here for?"

Max jerked his head toward the basement stairs. "We heard about the cyanide, too."

"Yeah, the cyanide." His eyes lingered on Annie for a long moment. "Since you're so curious, you can come on downstairs, little lady."

Said the spider to the fly, Annie thought. But they followed him down the steeply pitched stairs to the basement. The hollow echo of hammering led them to Tim, still crating his paintings. He looked at the Chief, and beyond him at Annie and Max, with no enthusiasm. "Look, I've told you everything I did on Monday, and I don't see why I have to go through it again. And I don't know anything about the old lady at the Inn." Sweat trickled down his face and stained his paint-spattered work shirt. His chestnut curls lay limply on his shoulders.

Wells ignored his objections. "Where's the poison?"

Tim led the way to the end of the corridor and a warped yellow door. The poster on it warned POISON. Tim unlocked the door and a heavy, sour smell of chemicals wafted out. He turned on the light. The trays and vats needed for electroplating were neatly arranged on a table against the back wall. A shelf to the right of the table held a number of bottles.

Wells found what he sought on the third shelf from

the bottom, a large green stoppered bottled labeled CY-
ANIDE OF POTASSIUM.

"Jesus Christ, there's enough poison in that to kill
every living soul in Chastain!" His heavy head swiveled toward the door. "That goddamn lock's a joke."

Bond looked at him in disgust. "We don't feed it to
anybody, Chief."

"It killed Idell Gordon," the Chief rasped.

If Tim Bond were acting, he exhibited considerable
talent. His eyes went blank with shock, his bony jaw
dropped. He took a step back, then said, "Hey, what
the hell. Somebody's trying to frame me." His paint-
stained hands clenched convulsively. "Listen, I don't
know what the hell's going on, but nobody's going to
lay this on me."

But Annie abruptly realized the Chief wasn't watching Tim. Instead, those probing, hostile eyes were
pinned on her.

"Tell me something, little lady."

She tensed.

"Sybil told me you and your feller came down here
and badgered Tim the other day. That's right enough,
isn't it?"

"Is it badgering to ask a man who has a damn good
motive where he was when the murder was committed?"

But Wells was intent upon his own train of thought.
"Now, when you came down here, you couldn't help
but see this here yellow door with a POISON sign.
Now, could you?"

22

ANNIE DUMPED THE envelopes out on her bed, then stared at them in dismay. How could there be so many? She looked at her watch. Almost four o'clock. Where had the day gone? But she knew. It had fled as they fought their way through the clogged streets (Friday featured a Fried Chicken Cook-Off, a China Painting Exhibition, and the finals in the Chastain Speedboat Classic), seeking more information about Idell Gordon, cyanide of potassium, and the whereabouts of all the suspects between 9 and 10 P.M. Wednesday evening. She'd had two more acerbic runins with Chief Wells and made another abortive visit to Miss Dora's shuttered home. Now she had only a few hours before the Denouement Ball began—and she'd damned well better have a denouement in hand, or she would be attacked by a band of enraged mystery buffs. And the prizes for the five best costumes—she rummaged frantically in the bottom of the clue box, then heaved a sigh of relief. There they were, five certificates, ranging in value from $5 to $25, good toward any purchase at Death on Demand. So, all she had to do was figure out which team, if any, had named the murderer of the Sticky Wicket Mystery. If more than one had come up with the right answer, then it would come down to which team turned its answer in first. The mystery winners and costume winners were to be announced at the stroke of midnight.

She stacked the envelopes by day and felt the beginnings of panic. Could she possibly read and digest all these answers in time? It had all seemed so reasonable when she and Max planned it. But they hadn't counted on two real murders.

Max tapped on the door and poked his head in. "Let's go down to the *Courier* and see what we can pick up."

She flapped her hands distractedly. "Tonight. I haven't checked the entries. No time. Go ahead."

He leaned against the doorjamb and chuckled.

She turned on him with slitted eyes. "Can't you see?" She pointed at the four untidy stacks of envelopes. "I've got to read all of those."

"Oh hell, just throw them up in the air and pick a winner."

She glared at him, horrified. "Do you honestly think Mrs. Brawley wouldn't catch me?"

"I guess you're right. But relax, love, you're a speed reader." Kissing her lightly on the cheek, he departed.

It didn't take as long as she expected. For one thing, only two or three teams each evening came up with the right name. Of those, a Monday night team, No. 2, had the right answer for the right reasons, and the time on the envelope was 8–04–36. When she read the name of the team captain, she didn't know whether to laugh or to cry. There was a winner from last night, ringing in at 8–04–37. The Team Captain was—she stared at the list of team members for a long time, then took her pen and carefully altered the time to 8–04–36.

How about that. A tie.

At six-fifteen, she changed into her costume for the Denouement Ball. Max, too, was dressed for his part when he knocked on her door. They grinned at each other.

"That the twain never met was a grave error on the part of the Stratemeyer Syndicate," she said.

He was a marvelously handsome and clean-cut Joe Hardy as he nodded in agreement. "Right on, Nancy. But it might have hacked Ned Nickerson."

They slipped away to Confederate House for an early dinner. As they climbed gray wooden steps to the refurbished barn that overlooked the river, Annie clutched his argyle sweatered arm and pointed to the placard.

"Before the occupation of the area by Federal troops in 1863, work began here on earthwork fortifications. The last remnants of Ft. McReady were washed away in the hurricane of 1893."

Annie peered into a thicket of southern red cedars. "That woman is haunting me."

"I'd say she's the least of your worries."

They settled at a wooden planked table on a gray porch, and Max unloaded the latest.

"Bobby said Wells had his men print practically every square inch of Idell's office, and he's having the lab check any latent prints against yours, his, Gail's, and Tim's. If he finds a match—"

"There I never was. So maybe he'll finally give up on me." She studied the fake parchment menu. Should she go for Daufuskie crabs or duck, oyster and sausage gumbo? "How about the others?"

"They all claim they've never set foot in Idell's office."

Then Max dampened even her appetite.

"One grim note. Apparently, a hell of a lot of cyanide of potassium is missing from that bottle."

What a difference a day made. Whether it was simply the number of hours that had elapsed since Idell's murder or whether the Mystery Night participants were willing to risk all to discover the identity of the Sticky Wicket murderer, the night's turnout was excellent and the mood upbeat. The variety of dress for the ball amazed her. She spotted two Inspector Maigrets, four Hercule Poirots, a sharp-visaged Dick Tracy, and a prim Miss Silver complete with knitting needles, fluffy pink wool, and a brooch on her bosom.

Annie wandered among the tents, eavesdropping.

"Asey Mayo" confided to "Inspector Roderick Alleyn," "This is more fun than *The Mystery of Edwin Drood.*"

"Oh, that *was* fun," "Miss Pinkerton" replied. "But my all time stage favorite is *Arsenic and Old Lace.* It's always funny."

In the distance, sheet lightning flickered. They'd been so fortunate with the weather all week. April, of course, was a spring month, and heavy storms rare. Gentle rains were not. She crossed her fingers. If they could just make it to shortly after midnight, it could rain as much as it pleased. She felt uneasy, and was uncertain whether to attribute it to the ominous weather or to the evening.

The mystery enthusiasts were having a wonderful

time. The Sticky Wicket cast members were not. They had all dutifully come and mingled with the guests, but their generally stiff and distrait appearances singled them out. Although they knew Wells's suspicions were targeted on Annie and Bobby, they were like horses sensing a coyote's presence. Wells had talked to all of them, once or more. They all knew he had charted their movements to the Inn on Wednesday night. It put an edge to their voices and wariness in their eyes.

Rumors abounded.

Edith insisted to Annie that she'd heard Leighton had been arrested.

Roscoe said that was all wrong, a warrant was being charged out against Bobby.

Max disappeared for awhile and returned with the news that the lights were still burning in the forensic lab at the police station.

Even Sybil and Tim showed up, and Tim said loudly that he didn't know what the hell was going on, but Bobby Frazier'd gone into detail with him about the chemicals he used in electroplating.

It was just short of midnight when Annie looked down from the speaker's stand at a black-clad figure leaning on a silverheaded cane, staring with a death's-head face at the Sticky Wicket suspects as they gathered for the finale. Annie's hand closed on her sheaf of papers. Miss Dora! She took a step toward the stairs, then St. Michael's bell tolled midnight. As lightning blazed in the east, the old woman turned and melded into the deep shadows beneath a live oak tree. Annie hesitated, then faced the audience. Her heart was pounding. The band played a drum tattoo. "Ladies and gentlemen, this is the moment you've all been waiting for."

A vigorous burst of handclapping and cheers was almost lost in the roll of thunder.

"And I believe we just may make it under the wire before the storm breaks. But it is my pleasure first," Annie cried, "to announce the winners of the costume contest."

Max was leading a pleased and excited line of participants to the stage.

"Our fifth place winner is—" She waved her hand and glanced at the card in her hand. "Mrs. Harrison Frankfurt of Savannah, who came tonight as the inimitable Miss Maude Silver, complete with a shawl and brooch."

Mrs. Frankfurt came on stage.

"Our fourth place winner is Mr. Michael Forbes of Charleston, who you will undoubtedly recognize as the greatest sleuth of all time, Sherlock Holmes."

Forbes was tall enough and lean enough to look the part of the master detective in his deerstalker hat and Inverness cape. He waved his Meerschaum pipe and bowed to the cheering crowd.

"Our third place winner is Jeremiah Winston of Hilton Head Island. Let's give him a hand for his portrayal of Sam Spade." Winston slouched on stage in a loose tweed overcoat. A hand-rolled cigarette dangled from his lip.

"Our second place winner is Mr. Bill Brown of Atlanta." A little man with a truly egg-shaped head bounded up the steps. He wore spats, a European-cut suit of the 1920s, and he twirled a sleek drooping mustache with pride. "Ladies and gentlemen, I give you Monsieur Hercule Poirot.

"And, finally, our first place winner, America's favorite detective, Miss Marigold Rembrandt, as portrayed by her creator, America's most popular mystery writer, Emma Clyde."

Cheers, stomping feet, and thunderous applause erupted.

Annie passed out the Death on Demand certificates, shook everybody's hand, allowed Emma to kiss her on both cheeks, and turned back to the mike.

The costume winners filed down, and the Mystery Night suspects mounted the platform.

Annie saw Bobby Frazier standing in front of the platform, notebook in hand. His face was somber, and he needed a shave, which made him look almost unsavory.

"Before we reveal the perpetrator of our Sticky Wicket murder, I want to introduce our suspects to you in their own right, so that you may thank them for the splendid efforts they've made this week to provide you with a challenging mystery and a pleasant evening.

"Lord Algernon has been played by my good friend and coconspirator, Max Darling.

"Lady Alicia is Mrs. Jessica Merrill, who has worked very hard for the Historical Preservation Society of Chastain.

"Roscoe Merrill, a member of the Society Board and a Chastain lawyer, has played the role of Nigel Davies.

"I'm sure many of you recognized Edith Ferrier, another active clubwoman in Chastain, as Susannah Greatheart.

"And Dr. Robert Sanford has served most capably as the dastardly Reginald Hoxton.

"Finally, Miss Lucy Haines, a very active member of the Society, is Agnes, Lady Alicia's maid.

"A round of applause for our players, please."

Gail stood on the side of the platform opposite Bobby. She was clapping for the suspects, but her eyes were on Bobby. Annie wondered if the damned fools had talked honestly to each other yet.

"Now, for the real story behind the Sticky Wicket Mystery." She paused dramatically, but her eyes skimmed the crowd for Miss Dora.

"These are the clues which should have led you to the correct solution:

"The broken piece of gold link from a necklace which was found in Reginald Hoxton's trouser pocket.

"The telltale mound of wood shavings on the workbench in the toolshed.

"The smudge of putty in Reginald Hoxton's pants pocket.

"The discovery of real rubies secreted in a croquet ball.

"The imitation necklace discovered in Susannah Greatheart's lingerie.

"The attempts of Lady Alicia's maid to scatter suspicion among the guests.

"Lord Algernon's partiality for a pretty face, other than that of his wife.

"What happened at the Gemtree Court on this fateful Saturday? We have a group of guests with some rather dark secrets. Reginald Hoxton is known about London as a man who plays cards too well and too often. Lady Alicia owes him 3,400 pounds, and he is pressing her for payment.

"Miss Matilda Snooperton is a rather unattractive lady, with a penchant for blackmail and illicit liaisons. She has managed to snare a rather unworldly University don, Nigel Davies, but at the same time she is carrying on an affair with Lord Algernon, who has wearied of it. He tells her Saturday that they are through and the best he will do is give her a ticket to Venice.

"Miss Susannah Greatheart is enamored of Nigel Davies and very bitter over his involvement with the insidious Miss Snooperton. She is quite pretty and rather naive and doesn't realize that Lord Algernon has taken a fancy to her.

"Agnes, the maid, is fiercely loyal to her mistress and quite eager to pass on to the police any information she has that would compromise the other guests.

"Lady Alicia professes to have no interest in Miss Snooperton, terms her a dear girl, but she is quite snide about Susannah Greatheart.

"So who did the dastardly deed?"

"Hoxton," a voice rumbled.

"Susannah Greatheart! She's a thief."

"Daves, that's the ticket!"

The Mystery Night participants exploded in chatter. It took Annie a couple of minutes to quiet them down.

"Here is what actually happened. Saturday morning Miss Snooperton sees Lady Alicia in a clandestine meeting at the gazebo with Mr. Hoxton. Lady Alicia gives him her ruby necklace, which is famous throughout England. Miss Snooperton threatens to tell Lord Algernon unless Lady Alicia pays her a substantial sum. Of course, our gambling Lady Alicia is strapped, or she wouldn't have agreed to give the necklace to Hoxton in the first place. She tells Miss Snooperton to meet her at the arbor after tea. They meet, Lady Alicia snatches up a croquet mallet, and that is the end of Miss Snooperton's career in extortion. Lady Alicia's motive, of course, is twofold. Lord Algernon mustn't learn that the necklace has gone to Hoxton, and she is furious over Algernon's involvement with Miss Snooperton. To pay off Hoxton without discovery, she had recently had a copy made of the necklace. However, now she knows there will be a murder investigation. She decides to confuse the issue by pretending that her necklace has been stolen, in hopes the murder will be linked to the robbery. In the excitement after she announces the robbery, she takes Hoxton aside and tells him that she returned to her room, found her copy gone, and had no choice but to reveal it had been stolen.

"Hoxton, of course, is thrown into a panic. Of all the weekends for someone to rob Lady Alicia! He must hide the real necklace before he is accused of stealing it. However, he is resourceful. Under the guise of searching for the missing Miss Snooperton, he dashes down to his car, gets the car tool, uses it to prize open the lock to the toolshed, drills a hole in one of the croquet balls, and takes the rubies, which he has ripped from their settings, and hides them in the ball, which he closes up with putty. He paints over the spot and hides the ball in the boot of his car.

"Lady Alicia, meanwhile, hides the fake necklace and the murder weapon in Miss Greatheart's room, because she is jealous of Lord Algernon's attraction to her.

"The detectives who correctly identified Lady Alicia as the murderer did so because they realized that only Lady Alicia or Lord Algernon could have arranged for the creation of the fake necklace. Of the two, who needed money? Lady Alicia. The detectives realized, too, that Lady Alicia's maid would know her mistress had removed the necklace for a period of time. They also observed Agnes's frantic efforts to direct suspicion away from her mistress. The successful detectives considered and discarded the idea of two crimes (a fake robbery and an unrelated murder) occurring independently on the same day and concluded the perpetrator was indeed Lady Alicia."

The garden exploded with noise. Annie knew there would be some diehards who would protest, but her strategy was to sweep them right along.

"I know you are all excited to learn who our successful detectives are. I am delighted to tell you that we have a Monday night team as a winner."

Cheers and moans.

"Team No. 2 from Monday night, will you please file up on stage. Look who our mystery captain is! Come right on up here, Marigold Rembrandt—or should I say Emma Clyde?"

Another familiar face, heavy with disappointment, stood near the platform.

"But that's not all." Annie had to shout to be heard. "We have another winning team, which tied for the honor, turning in its solution at the same time last night. Team No. 6!"

Annie would never regret that changed time.

Mrs. Brawley charged up the steps, caught Annie's hands and raised them high, like a prize fighter in triumph.

"Our second winning team is captained by one of Broward's Rock champion mystery readers, Mrs. Henrietta Brawley."

The band began to play, the winning mystery participants cheered, and the crowd yelled, whistled, and stomped.

Annie grinned. She looked at the cheering mass of spectators, then her face stiffened.

Chief Wells was shouldering through the crowd toward the platform, and there was no mistaking the grim jut of his jaw.

23

THE CROWD THICKENED at the base of the platform as mystery buffs moved toward the steps, eager to congratulate the winners. Annie lost sight of the Chief for a moment, then saw him bulling his way through a clot of contentious losers. The druggist from Broward's Rock was shaking his head in disgust. Wells stepped around him and reached out to clap Bobby Frazier on the shoulder, and she heard snatches of his low-voiced command, ". . . arresting you . . . murders of Corinne Webster and Idell Gordon. I wish to inform you of your rights . . ."

Those near enough to hear stood still to listen, but most of the Mystery Night participants continued to press noisily toward the platform. Lightning flickered on the horizon.

From her vantage point, Annie saw Bobby's head

jerk back, but he made no move to escape Wells's grasp. His eyes searched the crowd. She looked, too.

Gail stood at the other end of the platform, caught up in a milling stream of people. She stood on tiptoe, her eyes wide, her face stricken. She struggled to push her way past the crowd, and she began to scream.

"No, he didn't do it. He didn't!"

Bobby started toward her, but Wells yanked his arm. Bobby gave one last despairing look, then walked with Wells to the circular drive where a police car waited.

Stymied by the surging crowd, Gail turned and ran toward the platform steps. She stumbled up them in her haste and darted to Annie. As she yanked the microphone away, her voice, high and strident, boomed across the night. "I killed my aunt! I killed Corinne Webster and Idell Gordon. I did it!"

Lucy huddled on a chair beside Gail's bed, clinging to the girl's hand. The convulsive sobs were beginning to ease.

John Sanford closed his bag and motioned for Annie to come out into the hall.

He rubbed a hand against the stubble on his chin. He looked tired and thin and irritated. "The girl's about to snap. That shot will take hold pretty soon. For Christ's sake, what got into her? What a damn fool thing to do! I've known that kid since she was born. She couldn't kill a cat. Frazier probably did it. A guy like him would never pass up a chance to marry millions." He took a deep breath. "Look, I've got surgery in the morning. I need to get home, get some sleep, but I want you to take this." He opened his bag and lifted out a couple of tablet samples of Valium. "See that Lucy takes these and goes to bed. She's about ready to collapse."

After he left, she eased open the door and stepped back inside Gail's room. The girl's breathing had slowed. Despite her efforts to stay awake, her eyelids kept flickering shut.

Annie walked across the room and stood beside Lucy, who never even looked up, her gaze locked on Gail's pale face. Sanford was right. Lucy needed help, too. She hunched in the chair like an aged crow in bright garb, her red and gold silk dress a shocking contrast to her grieving face.

Annie gently touched her shoulder.

Lucy slowly looked up, her eyes full of distress. "This is so hideous, so dreadful. To see Gail scream and cry . . ." Tears slipped down her cheeks, staining the silk of her dress, falling as gently and steadily as the spring rain against the windows.

"Shh now. She's asleep. It will be better tomorrow."

Lucy lifted the flaccid hand, held it to her cheek. "She loves him terribly. Oh, God. What are we going to do?"

Annie felt incredibly weary. The delicate Dresden clock on the bedside table chimed twice. Two A.M.

"We can't do anything more tonight. Max is seeing about a lawyer for him, but I'm afraid it pretty well tore it when he confessed, too, after Gail did. Wells got it down. And that seems to me pretty much all they'll need since they found a pencil with his fingerprints on it in Idell's office."

"A pencil?"

"Wells thinks it fell out of his shirt pocket. He always carried a couple of extra pencils there."

Lucy lifted her chin. "He could have gone by Idell's office that night just to talk to her, to see what she knew, then decided to keep quiet when she was found dead."

"He says he went by to talk to her about the reward
—and what she thought she knew. That's when he
says he dumped cyanide in the sherry, too."

It was almost three by the time Annie got Lucy settled
at her house, though she refused the Valium. Returning
to the Inn through the steady rain, Annie felt like she'd
been flattened by a bulldozer. Max wasn't in his room.
Was he still at the jail, or was he trying to explain to a
bewildered lawyer the ins and outs of a complicated
case: Two dead women, two confessed murderers, one
in jail, one ignored.

She sat down in the lumpy chair next to the window.
The shutters hadn't been closed for the night. The tan-
colored Society building looked insubstantial in the
rain. That was where it all started. No, not really. It had
begun years ago, when Corinne Prichard Webster began her imperious course through life. That was the
beginning, Corinne's arrogance, Corinne's absolute determination to control. But the end of her life had been
determined in that quiet building. And the end of Idell
Gordon's life had been determined the night she
looked out her window and saw someone she knew
leaving the Society late at night.

Who had she seen?

Annie jolted upright.

Not Bobby, for God's sake.

Idell was a born gossip. Her mouth never stopped
clacking. She talked whether she had anything to say
or not. The appearance of Bobby Frazier coming out of
the Society Building late at night would have been startling. She certainly would have mentioned it to someone. That meant—Annie pressed her fingers hard
against her temples. She was tired, so damn tired, but

she knew she was close to a revelation. It meant the person Idell saw that night was someone she knew whose late night appearance at the Society was surprising but not shocking.

A Board member.

She jumped up, began to pace, then gradually her eagerness flagged. Okay, a Board member. They'd been there before: Lucy, Sanford, Gail, Roscoe, Edith, Sybil, Miss Dora. Even the appearance of Leighton would not have surprised Idell. He could have been running an errand for Corinne.

So all she'd done, in her own mind at least, was clear Bobby. And probably Tim.

Damn, damn, damn. It was impossible, a mess. They'd never get it right. And she was too tired to take another step or think another thought. Suddenly, she had an overpowering desire to lie down and sink fathoms deep into sleep. The bed was covered with Mystery Night materials, dumped without any attempt at order as Max hurried to get to the police station and Annie to the Prichard House. Wearily, she began to move the boxes. At least the Sticky Wicket murder was history now. Too bad the clues to Corinne's murder couldn't be tabulated as neatly. Physical clues like snapping red flags. But, actually, actions pointed toward the murderer, too, because murder arose from actions: Lord Algernon's repeated involvement with other women, his wife's jealousy, her avid dependence upon gambling, her desperate efforts to extricate herself from debt, all leading up to the final moment when she struck down her tormentor. And the obvious and pathetic attempts of her loyal maid to—

Annie stood in the middle of the room, clutching a poster container.

Actions.

Images flooded Annie's mind, Corinne's imperious will to rule, the abiding anger resulting from love denied, the conspiratorial eagerness of Idell Gordon to talk, talk, talk, the location of the pond, the telltale placard describing the superstitions of the Low Country, Miss Dora's desperate assertion of Annie's guilt, the croquet mallet with her own fingerprints, a few smudged, Idell's certainty that more money could be had for silence, her offer of sherry to her murderer.

And Annie knew with certainty who had murdered Corinne Webster and Idell Gordon.

She walked back to the chair, dropped into it, and absently put the poster container atop the air conditioner. She knew, and she took no pleasure in knowing.

But Bobby was in jail, and Bobby could be convicted of murder. Would a jury understand his confession, understand it was a last, desperate, foolish attempt to protect the girl he loved?

Only one thing could save Bobby Frazier.

She jumped up, began to pace. Once, she reached out and touched the phone, ready to call Chief Wells.

But he would never believe her.

She continued to pace.

One action she could take. It would be a gamble. It could have no effect, or it could result in another death.

She didn't want to do it. It was a fateful step. But, finally, she reached out and picked up the telephone and dialed.

It was answered after one ring.

"Yes."

"You killed Corinne. And Idell."

Silence. Annie could hear her own heart hammering.

"How did you know?"

As Annie spoke, her own voice was equally weary.

She listed her reasons, then said, "You know, only one thing will save Bobby Frazier—your confession."

There was no answer. Perhaps the lightest of sighs, then the connection was broken.

Annie wedged a straight chair beneath the doorknob. She moved the rest of the materials from the bed and turned off the light. She lay down, but her eyes didn't close for a long, long time as she watched the tiny line of light that seeped beneath the door. It was almost an hour later that she heard Max come into his room. She wanted very much to call to him, but this decision had been hers and hers alone. She would carry it by herself. She listened to the falling rain.

Max carried the last of the boxes into Death on Demand, then he turned and faced Annie.

"What's going on?"

"What do you mean?"

"Love, I've known you when you were up and when you were down. I've made love to you in the moonlight, danced with you until dawn, witnessed table piggery unbounded, admired your intellect, your serve, and your verve—and I've never known you to say less than three thousand words a minute since the day we met. So something is screwy as hell this morning. I know we haven't had breakfast, and we drove our cars separately back to the ferry, but you haven't said anything but uh-hun and hmm since we got back to the store. You haven't even commented on the strategy the Atlanta lawyer has in mind for Bobby Frazier. So what gives?"

The bell rang as the front door of Death on Demand opened.

She looked past Max up the central aisle of the store.

Bobby Frazier, his eyes red-rimmed, his jaws covered with the stubble of beard, walked toward them.

Tears brimmed in her eyes. "The case is over," she said, and she reached out to grab Max's hand.

"Over? How can it be over?"

But she was watching Bobby.

He held out his hand, palm up. A cream-colored envelope bore Annie's name in a sloping, feminine script.

"I had to lean like hell on Wells to get it for you. But she wrote this to you, and I knew you should get it." His mouth twisted down. "Sometimes it's handy to be a reporter—when you're not in jail. I even threatened him with false arrest. But he had her other note, her confession." He swallowed jerkily. "She's dead. She had some more of the cyanide."

"Dead. Who's dead?" Max demanded.

They spoke at once, Bobby's voice somber, Annie's tear-choked.

"Lucy Haines."

24

L UCY HAINES!" MAX'S voice rose in astonishment. "How did you know? How did you ever guess?"

"Because of the way people acted." She managed a lopsided smile. "You know how your mother tells you actions speak louder than words? By God, they do. They really do. Just think for a moment:

"Who was crazy about Gail, and saw her chance for love and happiness being destroyed by the same person who had destroyed her own years ago?

"Who was distraught with unhappiness after Corinne was murdered?

"Who implied she'd broken off with Cameron, but *everyone* else remembered it the other way—and collective memory is what you call history.

"Who was a part of Chastain, by birth, by breeding, by social position? Who would Miss Dora protect?

"Who lived next door to the pond and could waylay Corinne there after calling for a meeting?

"Who knew all about the Mystery Nights and the croquet mallet?

"Who always wore gloves when dressed—but didn't have gloves on when arriving at the murder scene? Who helped me get Corinne out of the pond and thereby accounted for her muddied clothes?

"Who would Idell offer sherry to?" A tear slipped down Annie's cheek. Automatically, Max handed her his handkerchief, which she took gratefully. "So I phoned Lucy and told her I knew."

Max gripped her shoulders. "Why didn't you tell me? My God, what a stupid chance to take. What if she'd come after you?"

"I didn't think she would. She was so tired, tired of it all. And Gail meant more to her than anything, even her own safety. I didn't think she would come." Her voice was grave. "But I put a chair underneath the doorknob."

"And waited for dawn." Bobby looked at her admiringly.

"I hated doing it."

"You should have called me." For once there was no life and humor in Max's voice, just puzzlement and pain. She knew it was important for him to understand. She reached out, held his hands. "I knew I could. Believe me, I know I can always call you. But sometimes you have to do things on your own. I had to do this."

He pulled her into his arms, held her tightly for a moment. "All right," he said gruffly, into her hair. "All right." Then, jamming his hand through his thick blond hair, he herded them toward a table. "I don't know about you, Bobby, but Annie and I haven't had any breakfast coffee."

The reporter hesitated, but Annie took his hand. "Sanford said Gail would sleep 'til afternoon."

They sat at the table nearest the back wall. Max made wonderfully hot and strong Kona coffee, and Bobby told them what he knew.

"She called Wells this morning. Told him to come over, she had information about the murders, that the front door would be unlocked. She left two sealed letters. In the one to the chief, she said she killed Corinne and Idell. That was all."

Annie looked down at her letter. The penmanship looped gracefully, *Miss Annie Laurance*, in the center of the pale lavender envelope. Taking a deep breath, she picked it up, opened it.

Dear Annie,

I wanted you to know that I decided before you phoned that my only recourse was to inform Harry Wells of the truth. Please do not feel that you precipitated my death. That would grieve me, just as I am grieved over the course of events this past week.

I know this must sound odd to you and self-serving, but I am grieved and remorseful. I did not intend to follow this path.

[There was a splotch of ink, a word scratched out.]

But in this last watch of my night, I must be absolutely honest. I don't know exactly what was in my heart. When I wrote the letter, and Idell did see me leave the Society building late that night of March 19, I am afraid I was pleased with myself. I was going to make Corinne suffer. But did I then intend to take her life? I would like to think not. To be truthful, I don't know.

I hated Corinne. She lied to Cameron, convinced him I was interested in him for his wealth, and he went away and met and married someone else. Yes, I hated Corinne for that.

And I hated the way she treated those around her, poor Leighton and Edith who tried so hard and talented Tim. Everyone who came within her orbit was drawn close and destroyed.

But, most of all, I hated what she was doing to Gail. Gail is so like her father, trusting and open and generous. I wouldn't have chosen Bobby Frazier for her, but then, that's where Corinne and I differed. I loved Gail, and I would not try to choose for her.

You were right in what you said. It should have occurred to everyone that I lived closest to the pond. I was on my way early to help out with the gala, and I came upon Gail and Bobby quarreling. I could see Corinne's hand, see her succeeding again, as she had succeeded against me. I went back to the house. I was so angry, I paced up and down, up and down. Finally, I called Corinne and argued with her. She was furious. She told me it was none of my concern and that her decision was irrevocable. I didn't know that Gail and Bobby had talked again, and they were going to continue to see each other, no matter what Corinne did. I don't know if I would have acted differently if I had known. But I didn't know, and I asked Corinne to meet me at the pond.

Perhaps that reveals the truth of the matter, for why did I choose the pond? I could have gone to Prichard House; she could have come here. But in my mind I knew that the Mystery Night clues would be in place—and the croquet mallet.

We met, and we quarreled, and she turned to leave, imperious as always. I snatched up the mallet and struck her down.

When it was done, I threw the mallet into the water, then I leaned over Corinne. She was still breathing. It was dreadful and I hate remembering it, but I pulled her into the water —and left her to drown. My gloves, and you were clever to see that I must have been wearing them, were wet. I pulled them off and wadded them up and threw them into the center of the pond. My shoes and dress were wet, too, but I waited by the gate, knowing someone would soon find her and I could dash into the pond. Of course, I heard your screams when you found Corinne, and I came.

As for Idell, she called and said she was going to try for Leighton's reward, unless I could do better than the $5,000. She suggested $10,000. I told her I would bring some money during the Mystery Night program. That afternoon, I went to the Museum. The back door is never locked during working hours, and I slipped down the stairs to the basement. I've been on the Museum Board for years, and I knew all about the electroplating—and the cyanide of potassium. I took some with me in a plastic medicine vial. During the Mystery Night, I walked up to the Inn and went to the office

door. Idell and I visited. She wasn't worried.
After all, the desk clerk would hear if she called
out. We each had a glass of sherry. I told her I
thought it was excellent and shouldn't we have
another to celebrate our agreement. I was
wearing gloves. I got up and stood between her
and the decanter and emptied the vial into it,
then poured each of us a fresh glass, and
watched while she drank hers. It was very
quick. I felt sick then. I emptied my second
glass into the decanter, then took the glass with
me, wrapped up in a paper from her desk. That
night, after the mystery program was over, I
threw it into the pond.

The clock has just struck five. I've listened to
that clock all my life and the deep bell has
always meant '*All is well.*' Now it is tolling the
end. Please try to explain to Gail that I never
meant for her to be hurt, and forgive me for the
unhappiness I have caused.

                                      Lucy Haines

The phone rang. With a searching glance at Annie's
face, Max reached out and answered.

"Death on Demand." Then his voice relaxed. "Oh
sure, Barbie, I'll be down in a little while. Anything
new?"

Bobby finished his coffee, and pushed back his chair.

Max whooped on the phone. "Great. Yeah. Bring it
down. Right now. No, no, don't open it."

Annie and Bobby looked at him curiously.

Max looked enormously pleased.

Bobby pushed his chair up to the table, then turned

to study the watercolors. "I didn't really get a chance to see these during the Mystery Nights."

The front door bell sang, and Barbie came cheerfully down the aisle. "Hi, Annie. Hi, Max. Glad to see you guys back. Been having fun?" She peered at them more closely. "Gee, you look beat." Turning to Max, she thrust a small parcel into his hands. "Here's the package from London."

"Thanks, Barbie. I'll be down in a little while."

She smiled and left.

He took Annie by the arm and steered her up the central aisle to the diagonal shelving that held all the Agatha Christies.

He held out the parcel. "A little something for you."

Max did love a dramatic production. It was probably a first edition of one of her favorites, *Cat Among the Pigeons* or *The Hollow.*

She found some scissors at the main desk and carefully slit open the package. Reaching inside, she felt her first twinge of puzzlement. Not a book. Odd, that felt like a frame—

She pulled it out and lifted it to look. There was clear glass on both sides. Sandwiched between the plates of glass was a single sheet of extremely thin paper, the aerogram used in England during World War II. The writing was small, to conserve space.

7 May 1943
Highgate

My dearest Max,

I am involved in such an absurd project, and I don't quite know how it came about. Stephen Glanville is to blame. He's bullied me into setting a detective story in Ancient Egypt! I re-

sisted at first, but now I am quite into it
and . . .

The letter continued with a reference to the shortage
of eggs and news of friends in the theater, a discussion
of Iago's character, and how Rosalind, expecting her
first child, was feeling.

Annie read it through in a rush, looked up at Max,
eyes wide, read it again, then flung herself into his
arms.

"Max, Max, Max! Where ever did you get it? How
did you possibly find a letter from Agatha Christie to
her husband during the War? Oh, my God, she was
writing *Death Comes As The End*. How did you do it?"

He smiled cherubically. "I just called around,
nudged some people. You like it?"

"Like it? Like it!" She held the framed letter to the
light, trying to decide where it would fit best on the
shelf. Then she turned to him, "Max, you're wonderful."

He nodded complacently.

"What can I ever do—" She stopped short, looked at
him in growing understanding.

He knew when to attack. "Actually, you know, I've
been thinking about September."

She nodded in complete understanding.

"And I think you're right about a wedding here on
Broward's Rock."

She was speechless.

"Of course," he held up an admonishing finger, "I
thought up an innovation or two."

"Oh?"

"Yes, a lovely, simple wedding at St. Mary's-By-The-
Sea, then I'd like to plan the rest of it." He smiled his
best, most Maxish smile. "It's the latest thing." His

voice was at its smoothest, most persuasive. "You know, you've read all about it in the *New York Times*, the three-day wedding. We'll invite everybody, at my expense, of course, to the Island. We'll have a bachelor's golf game on Friday, and you can plan a tennis tournament for the bridesmaids, and a dinner that night at the club, then the wedding Saturday morning, and perhaps a regatta in the afternoon. On Sunday, we can—"

She looked at the precious framed letter and then at Max. Was she a pigheaded, stiffnecked, class-conscious spoilsport? Perhaps it was time to fish or cut bait. If she married Max, she married his millions. After all, marriage was for better or worse.

She was turning to step into his arms, when Bobby called out, "Hey, Annie!"

She gave Max a just-a-minute look and turned toward the coffee area. "Yes?"

"How much are these paintings? Gee, I'd love to buy them. I collect hard-boileds."

"Do you know them all?"

"Sure." He pointed to the paintings in order. "The first picture is Sam Spade in *The Maltese Falcon*, the second is Philip Marlowe in *The Big Sleep*, the third is Lew Archer in *The Moving Target*, the fourth is Travis McGee in *The Dreadful Lemon Sky*, and the last one's Spenser in *The Godwulf Manuscript*." He grinned. "Do you suppose we'll ever find out Spenser's first name?"

ABOUT THE AUTHOR

An accomplished master of mystery, Carolyn
G. Hart is the author of eighteen Death on
Demand mysteries. Her books have won
multiple Agatha, Anthony, and Macavity
awards. She is also the creator of the highly
praised Henrie O series.

One of the founders of Sisters in Crime,
Carolyn G. Hart lives in Oklahoma City,
Oklahoma.

Visit her website at www. carolynhart.com.